LAYING OF HANDS

By the Author

McCall

London

Innis Harbor

The First Kiss

Wild Wales

Laying of Hands

Return to McCall

Windswept

Undercurrent

Visit us at www.boldstrokesbooks.com

LAYING OF HANDS

by
Patricia Evans

2025

LAYING OF HANDS
© 2025 By Patricia Evans. All Rights Reserved.

ISBN 13: 978-1-63679-782-3

This Trade Paperback Original Is Published By
Bold Strokes Books, Inc.
P.O. Box 249
Valley Falls, NY 12185

First Edition: January 2025

THIS IS A WORK OF FICTION. NAMES, CHARACTERS, PLACES, AND INCIDENTS ARE THE PRODUCT OF THE AUTHOR'S IMAGINATION OR ARE USED FICTITIOUSLY. ANY RESEMBLANCE TO ACTUAL PERSONS, LIVING OR DEAD, BUSINESS ESTABLISHMENTS, EVENTS, OR LOCALES IS ENTIRELY COINCIDENTAL.

THIS BOOK, OR PARTS THEREOF, MAY NOT BE REPRODUCED IN ANY FORM WITHOUT PERMISSION.

Credits
Editor: Stacia Seaman
Production Design: Stacia Seaman
Cover Design by Tammy Seidick

LAYING OF HANDS

Chapter One

Adel Rosse wedged her luggage into the cramped glass vestibule in the Lockwood Planned Parenthood in upstate New York, her laptop bag slipping from her shoulder to dangle from the crook of her arm as she pressed the entry buzzer. For the third time.

"Yes?"

Adel glanced around for the camera she knew would be aimed at her and suppressed the desire to roll her eyes. "I'm Adel Rosse?" She slid the bag to the floor and shook out the cramp in her arm. "The Portuguese interpreter your office requested?"

The line crackled with static as Adel waited for the door to buzz open. Two minutes later, she was still waiting.

"I'm getting confirmation on that now." The receptionist's voice was replaced by a long stretch of static until it reemerged abruptly. "What's all that you have with you?"

Adel glanced down at the luggage scattered at her feet that she'd schlepped from LaGuardia Airport in Queens to Lockwood, New York, via a cramped flight and a questionable taxi.

"My luggage. I was at the airport when I got the message." Adel took a breath, shifting the weight of her suitcase off her ankle to lean against the wall, pulling her cell out of her pocket and scrolling through her recent calls. "I spoke to Hannah Myers?"

A long silence echoed around the tiny vestibule, followed by a sharp buzzer and the door clicking open. Adel reached down for the handle of her suitcase and jumped as the speaker crackled to life again.

"Leave that where it is until we clear it, please."

Adel straightened and pushed the door open with a sigh, stepping into a predictably beige waiting area as the receptionist rounded the corner of the desk snapping on a pair of latex gloves. She passed without a word, and Adel watched through the security glass window as she unzipped her overstuffed rolling bag. Piles of hastily packed clothing tumbled onto the floor in every direction, making the vestibule look instantly more like a frat house than a medical office.

Adel walked up to the desk just as a petite woman with a blond ponytail and a white medical jacket two sizes too big rounded the corner with a handful of files. She had dark blue eyes with blond lashes so long they brushed her cheeks as she glanced down at the computer, then back to Adel.

"Sorry. Have you been helped?" She scanned the waiting area as she spoke, which was empty except for one young woman wearing a long skirt and jean jacket in the far corner of the room. "There's actually supposed to be someone here at the desk, but I'm happy to help you."

Adel smiled, her eyes lingering on the pale dusting of honey-colored freckles across the woman's nose. "I'm actually looking for Hannah Myers? I'm Adel Rosse."

"Oh, thank God." The woman offered her hand to Adel with a genuine look of relief. "You're the translator?"

"Well, interpreter, but yes. I am." Adel paused. "And you are…?"

"Sorry!" A quick smile flashed across her face. "I'm Dr. Myers. I'm the one you spoke to on the phone a few hours ago. Just call me Hannah."

She walked out from behind the reception desk and opened the door for Adel. "Thank you so much for coming. We do usually have access to a local Portuguese interpreter, but she's in Maine for the weekend."

Adel walked through the door with a long backward glance at the entry door.

"When the receptionist gets through unpacking my bags out there, what are the chances she'll bring them in and stick them behind the desk?"

"Oh, God." Hannah peered around the door through the window. "Is she really doing that?"

"Yep." Adel smiled. "And it may have turned out to be a bigger job than she thought it was going to be."

Hannah rolled her eyes and motioned Adel down the hall.

"Jesus. Amber missed her calling as a Secret Service agent. My office is the second door on the left." She lowered her voice to a whisper. "Give me a second while I put one of our medical assistants on supervision duty."

Adel smiled and took a seat in Hannah's office. Framed diplomas from Yale Medical School and Wellesley College in mahogany frames lined the wall, the perfect backdrop to the empty Sonic wrappers on her desk. The room smelled faintly of lemon furniture polish and expensive perfume.

"Thank you for waiting. I'm so sorry about that." Hannah shut the door behind her and sank into the leather chair behind her desk as a deep sigh lofted a delicate strand of hair from her forehead. "We had a bomb scare last week and our staff is on high alert. I'm just used to it, I guess."

She reached under her desk and pulled out a cold bottle of water, handing it over to Adel.

"Thank you so much for coming, Adel. We have a client coming in that's a personal friend of one of our staff. I called for an interpreter when I heard she was hesitant to come in. English isn't her first language, and I hear you're the best."

"I'm happy to help." Adel shrugged off her jacket and draped it across her lap. "Is she new to the States, or just from a Portuguese family here in the upstate?"

"I actually have no idea. The only thing I know from Amy is that she's scared out of her mind, so I'm guessing this isn't just a routine visit."

"Well, I'm happy to drop by." Adel smiled. "I'm on assignment with *Vanity Fair* magazine but actually not supposed to be at the location until tonight, so I was at loose ends anyway."

"So you're going to be in town for a while?" Hannah walked over to the sink in the corner of the room and washed her hands, drying them with a paper towel as she turned around. "Where are you on assignment? I can't imagine anything happening in Lockwood that's exciting enough to warrant a visit from *Vanity Fair*."

"It's the camp on the edge of town, apparently. I haven't actually seen it yet."

The receptionist knocked lightly on the office door and stuck her head in. "Your four o'clock just got here. She's in exam room one."

"Great. How is she?"

"Honestly?" She paused, lofting an eyebrow. "Looks like she's about to bolt."

The receptionist closed the door quietly behind her as she left, and Hannah looked at Adel. "Looks like it's showtime. You ready?"

❖

After Adel had signed the routine visiting volunteer papers at the desk, she washed her hands and pulled her shoulder-length dark hair back in a ponytail with the elastic she always kept around her wrist. She'd been volunteering as an interpreter at Planned Parenthood since college, so at forty-one this wasn't her first rodeo, but the energy in the hall was strangely tense. She smoothed her hands over her travel-creased oxford shirt and followed the same receptionist down the hall to the last door on the left, where she handed Adel a clipboard and headed back to the front desk.

Adel opened the door slowly to find a teenage girl with dark, waist-length hair perched on the last inch of the exam table. She visibly flinched as Adel stepped in. Adel greeted her in Portuguese, and a look of relief flashed across her face like sudden sunlight.

"I'm Adel," she said as she put the clipboard on the counter and turned back to the girl. "What's your name?"

"Maribel." Her voice instantly disappeared into the silence of the room.

"Okay, Maribel." Adel spoke softly and watched as Maribel fingered the tiny gold crucifix at her throat. "I'm not your doctor—she'll be here in just a few minutes. I'm here to make sure you understand what's happening, and make sure you get to ask her any questions you need to ask, okay?"

Maribel nodded. She started to say something, then stopped short and jerked her attention to the door as they heard footsteps in the hall. Her shoulders relaxed slowly as the footsteps continued past the door and clicked down the hall.

"It looked like you were about to say something," Adel said gently. "It's okay to ask me anything. Nothing you say will ever leave this room."

Maribel bit her lip, taking a long moment to take the words in. "You won't tell anyone?"

"Absolutely not. Whatever you say is between you and your doctor. I'm here to make sure you get the best care you can, but I'm bound by the same confidentiality rules as she is."

"It's a woman?" Maribel hesitated. "The doctor?"

Adel nodded, noting the long breath Maribel let out slowly. Adel picked up the clipboard and asked the first few questions on the forms, with Adel translating from Maribel's Portuguese to written English.

"And what is the reason for your visit today, Maribel?"

Maribel twisted the hem of the thin exam gown with her fingers, her hair falling forward into her face, followed by tears that disappeared into the fabric of her gown. Adel wanted to pull her into her arms, make her feel safe, tell her that no one would ever hurt her again…but they both knew no one could promise her that. So they sat in the silence until Maribel steeled herself and slowly squared her shoulders.

"Do I have to tell?"

Adel thought for a moment. She'd never been asked that question, but she'd been with Planned Parenthood long enough to know that a woman's emotional and physical welfare was paramount, so she took a guess.

"No. You don't have to tell. But anything you tell me or your doctor is confidential, so if you feel like you can share what happened, your doctor may be able to know better what care you might need."

Maribel's fingers were curled into a fist, her fingers white with tension.

"I didn't want to." Another tear dropped from her cheek as if the first had left the door open for the rest. "I said no so many times."

Adel slowed her breath, aware from experience that even that sound could startle a traumatized client. "You didn't want what, Maribel?"

"I didn't want to do the sex." The next words tumbled out as if she needed to clear them from her body. "But he said it was my fault. That I wanted it."

Adel caught her eye, and Maribel reached for her hand. It was small and cold.

"Maribel, you don't have to have a reason to say no to sex. Just that one word is always enough, no matter what anyone says."

Maribel nodded, squeezing Adel's hand as a soft knock on the door was followed by Hannah's voice.

After waiting for a nod from Maribel, Adel told her they were ready.

Hannah came in and smiled warmly at Adel but gave her space, sitting on the rolling doctor's stool by the counter. Adel introduced Dr. Myers, and Maribel nodded, looking unsure whether to breathe or bolt. Surprisingly, she chose neither.

"Maribel," Adel said softly in Portuguese. "Is it okay with you for me to share what you just told me with your doctor?"

Maribel nodded, and Hannah listened carefully to what Adel said, concern flashing across her face. She thought for a second when Adel was finished, then asked a few more details about what had happened. Maribel haltingly recounted the recent experience of being held against her will in the back of the restaurant where she worked by the owner, who had forced himself on her for hours until she managed to escape when the workers started coming in the next day.

Hannah looked at Adel. "Can you get a rough idea of the level of violence we're talking about here, so I know a bit more before I start?"

A few more harrowing details from Maribel led to the next question.

"And is she on any form of birth control?"

Adel relayed the question, which was answered by a silent shake of the head.

"And was this her first sexual experience?"

Adel spoke softly in a reassuring voice, which was followed by a nod from Maribel.

"Okay." Hannah smiled at Maribel. "So let's take a look, if that's okay with her?"

After Adel translated, Maribel responded with another nod and allowed Hannah to guide her feet into the stirrups. Silent tears slipped down her sides of her face and dampened the dark, glossy hair at her temples as Hannah gently started the exam, explaining everything she did before it happened through Adel. Maribel said that the attack had happened about three weeks prior, so Hannah said she'd do a pregnancy test with the urine sample that they'd already collected.

"Let her know the STI checks will take a bit of time. We'll follow up with the results and recommend treatment if needed, but the pregnancy test will be back in just a few minutes."

Hannah told Adel they were done as she scooted backward on her stool and snapped off her latex gloves, dropping them in the trash. She smiled reassuringly at Maribel as she guided her feet out of the stirrups and had her sit up, then handed her a blanket from a warmer by the cabinets. Maribel pulled the blanket up to her chin and spoke softly to Adel.

Adel listened, then looked at the doctor. "She wants to know if anyone will be able to tell that she's had sex? Her family are conservative Catholics and she thinks no one will marry her if they find out."

Hannah stood, speaking directly to Maribel as if she could understand without translation, holding her eyes with a soft understanding that slowly melted the fear from Maribel's face. Maribel took a deep breath and closed her eyes as Adel told her what the doctor had said.

"Maribel," Adel said softly. "Dr. Myers said to never forget that this was not your choice and it was not your fault. She wants you to know there's a difference between having sex and being sexually assaulted against your will. You didn't choose to share yourself with someone else that day, you were assaulted. Those are two different things."

Maribel's face softened, and she met Adel's eyes. "So, it doesn't count?"

Adel smiled. "No," she said. "It doesn't count."

Maribel nodded, her eyes shut tight against the tears, as Hannah squeezed her hand softly and left them alone in the room.

❖

An hour later, after Maribel had walked through the front doors and disappeared into the busy stream of rush-hour traffic, Adel finally gathered her bags from behind the front desk.

"Sorry about your suitcases." The receptionist, in faded Disney scrubs, glanced up at Adel as she squirted a white pile of gardenia lotion into her palm. "It's my responsibility to keep things safe around here."

Adel thanked her and hid a smile as she wedged her rolling bag out from behind the front desk and into the waiting area as the door buzzed open in front of her. She'd started to regret packing so much stuff, but her editor had been worryingly vague about how long she'd actually have to be on location for this assignment. It had been originally assigned to a senior reporter who had prepped for it for months, but he'd had a sudden heart attack the week before and was unable to fly. Which worked out well for her. A story like this was a huge opportunity that could land her name on the cover if she nailed it, and that was the holy grail of anyone in the magazine industry, especially in Manhattan.

The late afternoon sun was intense, even for early June, and hovered above the street in a dense gold haze that instantly enveloped her as she stepped outside the doors. Adel parked her suitcases on the sidewalk and opened her Uber app before she realized the address was buried in the bottom of her laptop bag. She let it slip from her shoulder to the crook of her elbow as a taxi whizzed by, searching the bottom of the bag with her fingertips until she found the crumpled notepad she'd scribbled it into. The wind picked up and ruffled the pages as she flipped to the last page and typed the address into the app with one hand.

She glanced up to pull her luggage closer to the side of the building, and something at the end of the building caught her eye. Long, dark blond hair blowing past the edge of the brick building, only to fall and rise again with the next gust like an ocean wave breaking on the shore. The traffic waned just enough for Adel to hear muffled crying from the same direction, and she sighed as she clicked off her phone without finalizing her ride.

She leaned against the wall of the building, rubbing her temples and looking longingly at the specials board at the diner across the street. The short flight she thought she was signing up for had been delayed that morning, so she'd spent the first part of the day in the airport, and the second she'd walked off the plane she'd picked up the call from a volunteer coordinator for Planned Parenthood. She quickly accepted and headed for the taxi rank outside the airport, the vague possibility of lunch forgotten in the rush.

Adel spoke fluent Spanish and Portuguese, but it was the fact that it was a call for a Portuguese interpreter that ended up being the deciding factor in accepting the call. Her own family was Portuguese, from Mystic, Connecticut, and she'd seen firsthand how difficult it was for the poorer community with limited English to get adequate health care, especially in the recent political climate surrounding immigration. All in all, it had been a much longer day than she'd planned, and all she wanted to do now was to get to where she was going, order a massive pizza, and watch trash TV. Crime documentaries, preferably, but after the day she'd had, she could even zone out to one of those car-crash *Real Housewives of Orange County* reruns.

She glanced down the side of the building again. The hair had stopped blowing around the corner, but she still heard sobbing. Enough to know that it was a woman.

Fuck.

Adel hiked her bag back up on her shoulder and scraped the wheels of her suitcases behind her over the cracks in the sidewalk as she approached the corner of the building. When she looked around it, a young woman sat sobbing against the side of the building, her knees pulled up to her face, the wind still picking up her hair and dropping it around her shoulders, her long skirt pooled like water around the white Keds on her feet.

❖

Grace felt the presence of someone else rounding the corner but decided not to look up and draw attention to herself, her entire body tensing as she silently willed them to just move on.

"Hey. Are you okay?"

The voice was surprisingly gentle, but Grace didn't respond, just nodded slightly, her forehead still pressed to her knees. There was a heavy pause. Grace held her breath.

"Are you sure?"

Lifting her head was the last thing she wanted to do, but when she finally did look up, she saw someone half leaning around the corner of the building.

The words were out of Grace's mouth before she thought to catch them. "What are you doing?"

The woman leaned back and sank down to Grace's eye level before she replied. Her skin was darker than Grace's by a few shades, she wore slim khakis and a black denim shirt, and her dark hair just skimmed her broad shoulders. Grace realized suddenly that she was staring, but it was suddenly impossible to look away from the kind crinkles at the edges of the woman's amber eyes.

"You know what? I think we may have met." The woman nodded toward the front of the building. "You were just in the clinic, right?"

Grace nodded, then swiped at her cheeks with her palm and pulled the length of her hair over one shoulder. Her stomach sank as she realized that the only thing that mattered was to put as much space as possible between herself and anyone who'd seen her in a Planned Parenthood.

"I appreciate you stopping." Grace squared her shoulders and took a deep breath. "But I can't talk to you." A red convertible passed them on the street, kicking up the leaves settled at the edge of the sidewalk. "I just need to forget that today ever happened."

"Okay." The woman nodded, her gaze intense, but strangely soft. "You don't have to talk about it."

An unusually loud grumble from her stomach interrupted at that moment, and they both looked at each other and smiled, then laughed when another rumble erupted, this one lingering for an insane amount of time.

"Well," the woman said. "Either I'm about to give birth to an alien, or I might die if I don't get some of whatever they're cooking over there."

They both glanced across the street to the small diner with a pink-and-white-striped awning and poster boards taped in the windows announcing the specials, faded and curling at the edges. The air held the faint scent of grilling meat, slowly melting into the haze of late afternoon heat.

The woman looked back at Grace and smiled. "So, what's your name?"

"Um..." Grace hesitated, everything inside her screaming at her not to answer that question. "Grace."

"Well, my name is Adel." Adel stood, extending her hand with a nod in the direction of the diner. "I'm new in town and it would be downright rude to make me eat alone, so I guess you're my dinner date."

"Date?" Grace looked up, startled. "I can't..."

Adel smiled, still holding out her hand. "I don't mean that literally. Although if you've somehow found me a decent patty melt, that's a definite possibility."

Grace hesitated again, then looked around before she reached up and let Adel pull her to her feet.

"Don't worry, I'm kidding." Adel flashed a wide smile with perfect deep dimples on each side. "Let's go eat."

Grace glanced nervously to both sides as they walked across the street and through the smudged double glass doors into the diner. A yellowed postcard taped to the cash register directed them to "Seat Yourselfs," so Grace followed Adel as she led them to a small booth in the corner by the windows.

A rip in the black Naugahyde booth audibly scraped the back of Adel's jeans as she sat down and handed Grace one of the menus tucked behind the glass sugar container. Grace glanced out the window as two women passed, at least until she remembered where she was, and dropped her eyes back to the table. When she finally looked up, she realized Adel had never taken a menu.

"Are you not eating?"

"Oh, I'm definitely eating." Adel smiled and nodded toward the front door. "I'm getting that patty melt on the specials board outside."

Grace took another look at the menu and tucked it back behind the sugar. "So, what's a patty melt?"

Adel clicked off her cell phone screen and laid it on the table. "Are you kidding me with this?"

The server, a round woman in acid-wash pleated jeans and a western shirt with pearl snaps down the front, stepped up to their table, her pen poised above her order pad. A worn brown nametag introduced her as Doris.

"Afternoon, girls. What can I get ya?"

The curls in her gray hair were perfectly round tubes stacked in neat rows across her head, as if she'd just slid the curlers out the side and varnished it into place with a slick of Final Net hairspray.

Grace hesitated, then asked for grilled cheese and a Coke, which she wasn't even sure she'd seen on the menu. Adel ordered the patty melt with extra sauce.

"Smart," Doris said, sticking the end of the pen in her mouth and tearing the order off the pad. "Those assholes wouldn't know how to sauce up a decent patty melt if it was the only thing they had to do all damn day."

Grace couldn't quite suppress a smile as Doris left to slam the order down in the kitchen window and ring the bell with equal force. "What's this sauce that everyone's so passionate about?"

"Wow. You really haven't had a patty melt, have you?" Adel shrugged off her jacket and rolled up the sleeve of her black denim shirt to her elbows. "Actually, I don't know the answer there. I'm not sure anyone really does."

"Well, what does it taste like?"

Grace watched as Adel's eyes settled onto hers, then moved slowly to her lips and lingered.

"Do I have something on my face?" Grace brushed her fingertip under her eye. "An eyelash?"

Adel looked quickly up to meet her eyes. "Sorry, no, I just lost my train of thought. It's been a long day, to say the least."

She glanced over Grace's shoulder toward the entrance as a cash register door slammed shut, followed by muffled voices as a group of diners made their way out the door and onto the sidewalk. "A patty melt is really just a hamburger patty in a sandwich. It's the sauce that makes it, but it's hard to describe. It tastes like mayo, ketchup…and relish, maybe?"

Grace smiled, pulling her fork and knife out of their white paper bag and laying them on the table. "So you're saying I'm not missing much?"

"Keep talking, newbie." Adel smiled. "You'll be begging to switch plates with me after one bite."

Grace looked out the window toward the clinic, her smile slowly fading. The silence settled between them for a long moment, until Doris brought their drinks and rolled her eyes at the bell that clanged at the order window the second they hit the table.

Grace unwrapped her straw and sank it into her glass. "You saw me in the clinic, didn't you?"

Adel nodded but didn't say anything else. Grace jumped when the bell clanged against the glass door as another couple strolled in, and she remembered Adel had been behind the counter in the waiting area. "Why were you there?"

"I'm a volunteer interpreter with Planned Parenthood." Adel pulled her staff card out of her wallet and held it up. "Usually I get called in on an as-needed basis in Manhattan, where I'm based, but my branch happened to see a request come through here in Lockwood and knew I'd be close to the area, so she put me in touch."

Grace nodded, tracing a scratch in the tabletop with her fingertip. "I was wondering why you disappeared down the hall without them calling your name."

Adel just nodded, and Grace felt her watching as she twisted an empty straw wrapper tightly around her finger.

"I left right after you got there."

The wrapper split and fell apart around her finger. Grace picked up the pieces and closed them into her fist.

"Why did you leave?" Adel lowered her head to catch her eye and smiled. "And yes, I realize it's none of my damn business."

Grace laughed suddenly, letting the pieces of wrapper flutter out of her hand to the table. Adel reached out and swept them aside, replacing them with her own unused straw. Grace looked up and smiled, peeling the wrapper carefully and setting it aside.

"Well, I almost didn't get to. The receptionist was unpacking like a stack of random suitcases in front of the doors, but I managed to squeeze past her."

She started to say something else but stopped herself, then twisted the soft plastic of the straw around the same finger. Adel was silent, listening as if Grace was still talking. She wasn't. But something about Adel made her want to.

"I shouldn't have been there in the first place, but it just seemed like my only shot, and if I didn't take it, I wouldn't get another one."

Doris appeared out of nowhere with their plates, settling them onto the cracked Formica tabletop with a clatter and disappearing again without a word.

"Why do you say that?" Adel pulled the patty melt plate over to her side. "Your only shot at what?"

"I shouldn't be talking about it. I need to just forget it." Grace sat back in the booth and met Adel's eyes for the first time since she'd brought it up. Tears crowded the words in her throat, and she looked up to the ceiling as she spoke. "I don't know why I can't just be normal."

Adel paused, then dipped a French fry into the ramekin of sauce beside her sandwich and offered it to Grace, who ate it, then quickly took another fry off her own plate and dipped it into Adel's sauce. It was a while before she spoke again, her sandwich forgotten in front of her.

"I'm engaged." She pressed the aluminum edge of the table with her thumb, watching it slowly fade to white. "I just found out."

Grace watched as Adel glanced at her bare ring finger and picked up half her sandwich. "I'd say congratulations, but you don't look too excited about that." Adel paused, patty melt suspended in midair. "What do you mean you 'just found out'?"

"I am. Excited, I mean." Grace stared out the window as a crowded group of cyclists sped by, then disappeared around the corner of the building. "Or I will be. That's what everyone says, anyway."

Adel nodded in the direction of Grace's plate. "Based on the look on your face, I'm guessing that grilled cheese might end up being more exciting than your wedding."

Grace picked it up and took a bite. The golden brown, buttery bread offered a satisfying crunch as it gave way to the center melt. She smiled and savored the bite, eyes closed, then took a long sip of her Coke.

"Well," she said, examining it leisurely at eye level before taking another bite. "That certainly raises the bar."

"Damn, girl." Adel shook her head and picked her sandwich back up. "You look like you appreciate good food."

"Always."

Adel smiled and sat back in the booth. "Well, you don't know me, and you'll probably never see me again…" She paused. "So you might as well tell me what's got you so freaked out you ran out of the clinic."

Grace dipped another fry in the sauce that Adel had pushed to the center of the table. She was quiet for more than a minute, then looked up and met her eyes.

"What do you think it is?" She paused again. The fact that she'd secretly tried to get birth control she knew was forbidden suddenly seemed like a surreal, faded dream. "I mean, the reason I left?"

Adel smiled, leaning back and stretching her arm out onto the back of her booth. "Well, it's entirely possible you found me so attractive you knew you needed to leave before you jumped over the front desk and kissed me."

Grace stopped, her sandwich frozen in her hand halfway between her mouth and her plate.

"What?" she said softly as a slow flush crept up her neck. She laid down her grilled cheese and gripped the edge of the table with both hands, her jaw suddenly tense. The chilling sensation of being suddenly naked, as if everyone in the diner was staring, washed over her like water laced with shards of ice. "Why would you say that to me?"

"I'm kidding." Adel sat back up quickly and held Grace's eyes, her voice suddenly soft. "I was just joking, I promise."

Grace looked around the dining room, then picked up her jean jacket with shaking fingers. "Thank you for what you did, Adel, but I have to go."

The reality of what she'd just done hit her like a bullet from behind, taking the memory of breath with it. She stopped, her eyes closed tightly against the panic squeezing her heart from every direction. Just by allowing herself to be seen at Planned Parenthood, she'd just given this stranger the power to derail her entire life. Or, if that information reached the right people, end it.

She struggled with a tangle of bills in her jacket pocket, but Adel shook her head.

"Don't worry about that." Adel met her eyes for just a moment before Grace looked away. "I'm just sorry I upset you."

Grace slid out of the booth like it was on fire, pivoting sideways to avoid running into a group of giggling teenage girls on their way into the diner. She glanced up at Adel again before she slipped out the glass front door, where the wind picked up her hair and spun it around her shoulders like a makeshift curtain as she ran down the sidewalk to the corner and disappeared.

Chapter Two

*G*reat, Adel thought, sinking back into the seat and glancing at her watch. *Fuck the undercover gig. Clearly I should write an article on how to make beautiful women disappear in fifteen minutes or less.*

Doris passed her table and plunked down a paper bill with a torn edge. She nodded toward the window. "What happened to her?"

"I spooked her, I guess."

"Well, I can't imagine it took much." Doris clicked her pen shut and slid it back into her shirt pocket. "That one was wound tight."

Adel smiled. "You noticed?"

"Next time…" She paused, her nails clicking against the edge of the table. "Treat her like a colt that just bolted past you out the corral."

Adel leaned back in the booth and waited; she had a feeling there was more.

"You have to make a colt come to you. If they're spooked, you can chase 'em all damn day and get nowhere."

Doris looked out the window again, unsnapped the pearl snaps on the cuff of her shirt, and rolled it up her arm as she walked away.

By the time Adel got a cab and managed to wedge her suitcases in the trunk, the light was fading fast. She leaned her head against the cool surface of the window as the driver followed an endless winding road into the mountains. A vast, navy-blue lake appeared not long after they'd left Lockwood, the last of the sunlight sparkling faintly on the surface, then melted into a slick of onyx as they continued to climb and night fell silently around them. Manhattan seemed like a distant memory as the last sliver of the sun sank behind the Adirondacks, leaving only a few fading streaks of copper and sienna sunset to warm the sky.

Adel leaned her head back on the seat and stared out the window at the blur of fir trees that lined the edges of the road. What happened with Grace bothered her. For one, she didn't usually go to diners with girls she'd just met on the street, and for another, she was good with women. Very good. So to have one bolt meant there was something hidden going on, something underneath, and she wanted to know what it was.

Not that she should be thinking about Grace at all. The night before she left she'd cooked dinner for Katya, her girlfriend of nine years, which was never an easy feat. Katya grew up in a privileged home in Manhattan and had a high-profile job as the assistant district attorney in Queens, so it was fair to say she was familiar with the city's best restaurants and took her side job as a food snob seriously. But Adel's butter chicken with basmati rice and fresh cilantro was the only time Katya allowed herself to stray from the diet she clung to like the last breath of fresh air in the city. She was a size zero and stayed that way with a membership to the most elite health club in Manhattan and professional training sessions at the crack of dawn in the city. She'd been late that night, two hours past the time she said she'd be home, and Adel listened from the kitchen as she took off her heels, dropped her bag on the entry table, and walked around the corner, rubbing the back of her neck.

"Oh, God, that smells amazing," she said, leaning against the kitchen island. "Tell me you have some wine chilling somewhere."

"There's Riesling in the fridge," Adel said over her shoulder, stirring the sauce that was coming to a slow simmer, the rich scent of smooth curry and sautéed onions rising with the steam. "Do you want me to pour you a glass?"

"I can get it." Katya reached for the white wineglasses in the rack above the kitchen island. "How was your day?"

"Well, my editor at the magazine dropped something major in my lap this afternoon." Adel poured the sauce carefully into a wide, shallow serving bowl, garnished it with torn herbs, and nodded toward the stack of plates and cutlery on the counter. "You remember Ed Goldberg, right?" She handed Katya a stack of yellow linen napkins. "You met him at the Christmas party last year?"

Adel brought a steaming copper dish piled high with basmati rice to the table with the butter chicken and sauce, then poured herself a glass of wine while Katya finished setting the table.

"Babe, this looks incredible." Katya spooned rice onto her plate and handed it to Adel, who ladled the still bubbling sauce over the rice, the steam rising and fragrant with the earthy scent of garam masala spice and rich, slow-simmered cream. "Okay, so tell me." Katya inhaled deeply and looked lovingly at her plate as she picked up her fork. "What happened today with your editor? I got your message that you had big news. His name is Ed, right?"

"Yeah, and do you remember Frank Taylor?" Adel paused, her fork in midair. "The guy I work with who had a heart attack last weekend? I think you met him at that fundraiser in Queens last year."

Katya nodded and took a long sip of her wine, crystal drops of condensation glossing the tips of her fingers as she set her glass back down on the table.

"Well, no one knew this, but he was supposed to leave tomorrow for a major undercover assignment in Lockwood, up in the lake region."

"Upstate?"

"Yeah, in the Adirondack Mountains."

Katya refilled her glass nearly to the rim and handed over the empty bottle as Adel got up to replace it.

"Anyway." Adel cut the foil from a new bottle of chilled wine and twisted the corkscrew. "I guess they've put a good year of research into this project, and if we can pull it off it could be a bombshell, so it didn't make sense to just drop it."

"So they're sending *you*?" Katya's phone pinged beside her plate. She picked it up, fingers flying over the surface as she replied. "How long will you be gone?"

"That's the thing. I have to stay there until I get the story, and depending on how hard that is to get without tipping anyone off, I'll be up there for at least two months, maybe three. The subject matter is controversial, so if I can pull it off it could fast-track my career, but at the very least, it will be a cover piece with my name beside it on the October issue."

Katya continued to text, then finally put her phone down and drank half her glass of wine before she looked up at Adel. "Why you?"

Adel looked down at her plate and let out a slow breath while her girlfriend turned again to her phone. They'd been together over nine years, and for most of that time, Adel had been focused on helping Katya achieve her dream of becoming the assistant DA of Queens.

Over the same span of time, Katya seemed to forget what Adel even did for a living.

"Because I've earned it."

As Adel walked through the sliding glass doors of the airport the next morning, she realized as she watched the disappearing taillights of her girlfriend's BMW that Katya didn't even know where she was staying. She hadn't asked.

Adel was still lost in thought when the driver took a sharp right off the main road and drove under a tall, split log arch shaped like a steeple, lit from ground level with gold floodlights. *Valley of Rubies* was carved across the top, and a long asphalt drive continued past it, stretching like a wide black snake into a grove of dense pine trees. A full moon, heavy and vivid, rose like a suspended sculpture behind it and illuminated the silver fog hovering in the air.

When the trees finally thinned, a three-story Adirondack-style lodge came into view, filled with warm amber light that spilled from the windows onto the long circular drive below. The lake to the left of the lodge shimmered in the moonlight, the docks stretched out like wings over the water, and just past that, a string of small clapboard cabins lined the shore.

The driver pulled up to the entrance and helped her with her bags. Adel stood at the front of the lodge watching the hazy red glow of his taillights until they were swallowed up by the dark pine grove. There was no hint of movement inside. Adel stepped back as she scanned the bay windows, then glanced at her wrist. *Jesus, it can't be that late.* She pushed her sleeve up her arm. *Do they roll up the sidewalks around here at sunset?*

Her heart sank when she saw her bare wrist and realized she'd left her Piaget watch, the one passed down from her grandfather in Portugal to her father, and most recently to her when her father had passed, on the sink at Planned Parenthood when she'd washed her hands.

"Fuck."

Just as she said the word aloud, she felt the deep swish of the immense wooden door opening behind her and spun around. A tall woman with a tight chestnut bun on the top of her head, more storm-cloud-gray than brown, stood in the open doorway, her mouth replaced by a thin, pressed pale line.

"Can I help you?"

"Yes, um..." Adel dug in her bag, trying desperately to locate the airport napkin she'd scribbled with the name of her contact person at Valley of Rubies. She finally felt it graze her fingertips and pulled it out, smoothing the crumpled layers with her fingers. "I'm looking for Hazel Whittier?"

The woman looked her up and down with no change of expression. The silence stretched longer than Adel knew what to do with, so she tried again.

"I'm Adel Rosse. I'm the replacement instructor you're expecting for the creative writing course?"

There was a long pause, then the woman stepped back wordlessly and opened the door just wide enough for her to step through.

"Should I bring my luggage into the lobby, or...?"

Adel's voice trailed off as the heavy wooden door clicked firmly shut behind her.

"Of course not, that will be taken to your cabin for you. Just follow me."

Adel waited until the woman strode in front of her and led her down a hall to roll her eyes. Clearly, she either literally owned the world or she was the gatekeeper to whoever actually did.

It turned out she was neither. After she'd led Adel into her office and closed the door behind them, she settled into a chair on the other side of the desk and continued her cool assessment of Adel.

"I'm Hazel Whittier," she said finally, as if that revelation routinely led to a response of shock and awe. "I'm the director here at Valley of Rubies."

Adel ran a hand over the sides of her simple ponytail, ignoring the buzz of her cell phone in her back pocket.

"It's actually been quite a long day." She glanced over the woman's head at a painting of Jesus propped up on the bookcase behind her. He was bathed in sunlight in the picture, but time had curled the edges of the paper behind the frame, and a drift of dust and dead bugs had gathered at the corners of the glass. "If you don't mind telling me where I'll be staying, I'll get those bags out of your way out there and settle in."

She realized as soon as she'd said it that the woman had told her that her bags would be delivered to her room. Wherever that was.

"I like to get to know new instructors a bit before we trust them with our girls." She looked Adel up and down, clearly unimpressed, but kept those details to herself. "I understand you are our replacement for Frank Taylor?"

"Yes, ma'am." Adel layered confidence into her voice and met Whittier's gaze. "We used to work together in Manhattan. He called from the hospital and asked me to take over the creative writing class he was scheduled to teach here."

Ms. Whittier held her eyes, the tips of her fingers tapping the armrest of her chair as if that was a response. Adel just waited until finally she spoke again.

"I was sorry to hear about his heart attack. We don't usually allow male instructors at Valley of Rubies—the only males here are the chaperones, we refer to them as the Brethren—but his sister is associated with one of our congregations in the Midwest."

Another long pause stretched like a wet spiderweb in the air between them.

"He assured me that your background was similar. That you're familiar with Sanctity Covenant principles?"

Adel nodded. Which was the only safe response since she didn't have a clue what this woman was talking about. To say she'd been briefed on this assignment on the fly was the understatement of the year. She'd literally heard most of it on the way out of her editor's office door the previous day, although he'd promised to email her with more in-depth details as soon as possible. She'd memorized the basic tenets of the Sanctity Covenant movement on the plane, which were startlingly cultish to say the least, but she was going to have to bluff her way through the rest until she had a moment to do better research.

"Yes, ma'am, and it's a privilege to be here."

Hazel's eyes sank to her black jeans and Doc Martens. "And I trust that you will be more appropriately dressed for your classes tomorrow?"

Adel nodded, wondering suddenly if there was any possibility the lodge had a bar. "Absolutely. I brought professional clothing, I'm just dressed for travel today."

"Specifically, our young ladies dress to magnify modesty and humility here, and although it's not required that you wear skirts and dresses as they do, I'll expect that your attire be in accordance with our principles and the guidelines set forth by the Prophet." She paused, her lips stretched to a thin, tense line. "Which I'm sure you're familiar with."

Adel nodded as she took a hurried mental inventory of the clothing she'd packed in a flurry the night before. Clearly tomboy staples like her black leather jacket and Docs were on the cut list; the rest she could probably work with.

"And will your husband be joining us for visits?"

"I'm not married," Adel said, crossing her legs and meeting Ms. Whittier's eyes. "It's just me, I'm afraid."

"That's just as well." Whittier touched the collar of the shirt that was buttoned beyond her neck and jotted something down on a notepad. She tore it off and handed it over the desk to Adel as she continued. "As you know, the only men here at the retreat center are the Prophet and appointed male chaperones, so it goes without saying that any additional visitors would not be appropriate."

"I understand," Adel said, turning the note over in her hand and scanning it as Whittier picked up the phone. *Proverbs 19:9.* "Believe me, that won't be a problem."

Adel folded the note into her jeans pocket as Whittier plunked a hardback book on the edge of the desk and nodded toward it.

"I'm sure that coming from a Covenant background, you don't need a reminder of our principles, but in case you have a question at some point, I'll allow you to borrow the manual of our Prophet's directives."

Adel reached out and took the book, tucking it into her book bag she still had slung over her shoulder. Whittier dialed a single-digit code and spoke too softly into the receiver for Adel to hear.

"If you don't mind my asking," Adel said, partly because Whittier had finished with the phone and was now coolly regarding her from the other side of the desk, "what is the age range of girls who will be taking my class? Just roughly?"

"Because this retreat center is designed to help educate and prepare our young ladies for marriage, you'll find most of your students will be in the range of seventeen to twenty years of age." Whittier pulled a glossy red folder out of her desk and handed it to Adel. "You'll find your daily schedule outlined here, along with mealtimes, etc. You'll also find the key to the vehicle you've been assigned while you're here, which is in the numbered lot just past the stables. Every staff member has access to a vehicle, although access is shared. This will allow you to go into Lockwood to do library research, grocery shop if you'd like, or get any necessary supplies you need for your classes." She paused, looking again at Adel's choice of outfit. "You'll be teaching in the morning and assisting with physical education in the afternoons. I was assured you would be ideal for that placement."

"Well, I was a college athlete, so I'm sure I can be of some assistance—"

A soft knock at the door interrupted her, and Whittier stood as Adel gathered the folder and book she'd been given, then turned toward the door when she heard Whittier speak.

"Adel, this is Grace Waters, our program director here at Valley of Rubies. She'll be showing you to your cabin."

She met Grace's eyes slowly, who was standing, pale and motionless, in the doorway.

"And Grace, this is Adel Rosse. She'll be leading our creative writing class as well as assisting you in the afternoons with physical education."

Somehow, Adel managed to keep her face neutral as she stepped into the empty hall with Grace and shut the door softly behind her.

❖

Grace led the way without a word until they were out of the range of the lodge spotlights and almost to the edge of the lake where she turned onto a pine straw footpath that lined the shore. It was illuminated only by small amber lights along the edge, and even those were half hidden by thick, tangled ivy. Invisible birds stirred in the trees as they walked, and the dark lake water beside them held the reflection of the pale moon hanging heavy over the ridge of the mountains.

Grace stayed slightly ahead on the path, the wind running its fingers through her hair just enough to sift the clean scent of Grace's soap into the chilled night air. Adel's own breath and the faint lap of the lake water against the wet sand shore were the only sounds. She started to just ask Grace why she'd run out of the diner but remembered what Doris had said about the colt just in time to bite back her words.

The lake shimmered to their left, and to the right were small, silvered cedar cabins facing the water. Lamplight glowed behind white muslin curtains, each crinkled at the edges as if they'd all been crumpled into the same fist.

"This is it. That's your key in the door." Grace slowed at the last cabin in the row. "You're in cabin twelve. I had someone deliver your bags already, so they should be there waiting for you."

Adel reached out and touched her arm as Grace turned to walk away.

"Grace."

Grace flinched, then froze, her eyes shut tight for a moment before she turned to meet Adel's gaze for the first time since they were in Whittier's office.

"What?"

"I need you to know that I won't tell anyone where you were today." Adel's voice was low and soft. "No one will ever know unless you decide to tell them."

Grace's eyes glinted suddenly with fire or tears, Adel couldn't tell which.

"Yes, you will." She looked at Adel's hand, still on her arm, until Adel let it drop slowly to her side. "No one keeps a secret like that."

Grace's dread was palpable in the air between them.

"You don't know me, Grace."

Grace closed her eyes and turned toward the lake. A tear dropped from her lashes to the top of her cheek, and Adel looked away until she'd swiped it away with the tips of her fingers and turned back.

"Did you know I was from here?"

"No." Adel softened her gaze and held Grace's eyes. "But I do now, so I get how important this is. No one will ever find out from me. You have my word."

Grace hesitated, then turned to leave, pulling her jacket tight around her as she walked back down the path.

❖

Adel let herself into her cabin and dropped her bag onto the bed, reaching back to rub the back of her neck as she took in the main room. It was simple but clean, with light wood floors, a seating area to the left, and a small kitchenette beyond that. The love seat looked like it had been stolen from a dentist's waiting room, with flat, faded needlepoint pillows at each end and a folded striped wool blanket draped across the back.

Adel reached down to pick up the only book on the coffee table, hardbound and covered in worn navy cloth with gold lettering.

Guidelines for the Godly Wife

Adel dropped it like it was on fire, and it clattered back down onto the coffee table as if shocked to be rejected. She turned to find another book on the desk, but that turned out to be just a Bible, accompanied by a glass pitcher of pale pink roses with sepia edges. An antique glass lamp that glowed the apricot color of dawn warmed the scarred plank surface of the desk.

Her bags were sitting by a door at the back of the room, which opened into a tiny bathroom with an oval mercury mirror and chipped claw-foot tub smack-dab in the center.

Great, Adel thought, unzipping the closest suitcase and pulling out a white ribbed tank top and blue oxford pajama bottoms. *No bar within walking distance and no shower. This just keeps getting better and better.*

After she'd taken a quick bath and settled into bed with her laptop and a smashed Snickers bar from the bottom of her bag, she clicked open a new email from her editor. Not for the first time, she gave Ed a silent thanks for pushing through the tech requisition for a laptop with a built-in secure hotspot. For all his faults, he at least carried the old-school reverence for journalistic integrity and the need for private communications. The pale blue light from the screen that washed across her face was the only light in the room.

> *Hi Adel,*
>
> *First of all, let me say thank you for taking on this assignment at the last minute. I know because of the rush we didn't have time to cover all of the details, but that said, you're there to bring back an unbiased report, so perhaps that's for the best.*
>
> *As you know, Valley of Rubies is a retreat exclusively for young Sanctity Covenant women, and its sole purpose is to prepare them for marriage. The more I've learned about the Covenant movement, the more having a woman undercover as opposed to a man makes sense. I won't go into detail here, but I'm concerned about some possible sexual abuse taking place there—or at the very least, multiple underage marriages. I'm looking forward to hearing your first impressions when we speak next week.*
>
> *Frank, the reporter who originally held this assignment, has ties to the religion, just enough to have been able to recommend you as a replacement. From what he said, he told the retreat director you were familiar with the Covenant, but not much more than that, so the rest of the backstory*

you'll have to invent on the fly, according to what you think may keep you under the radar. As for timing, we are looking to have this wrapped up at the latest by September first. If all goes the way I expect it to, I'm planning to use it for the October cover, with your byline front and center.

I look forward to speaking to you next week. Dig deep and stay safe.

Best,
Ed Goldberg
Editor in Chief, Vanity Fair Magazine

Adel set her glasses on the nightstand, then closed her laptop, listening to the faint lap of the lake water outside her open window. She'd intentionally looked into Grace's eyes and promised to keep her secret, then watched the words fall flat onto the ground between them as Grace turned and walked away. She'd stood on the path where she was and watched Grace's shoulders slope toward the ground as if gravity had suddenly doubled. She knew what that meant.

Adel would keep Grace's secret, just like she'd kept a thousand others, but it was clear that Grace had no idea what it felt like to not be betrayed.

As she reached to switch off the lamp, she picked up the note that Whittier had handed her in her office. She typed the Bible verse into her phone and scoffed at the result. "A false witness shall not be unpunished, and he that speaketh lies shall perish."

She balled up the paper and tossed it toward the trash.

Chapter Three

It wasn't the familiar songs of the Adirondack blue warblers or the gentle lap of lake water that woke Adel in the morning. It was a foghorn. Possibly one specially designed by evil geologists to speed up the movement of a tectonic shift, but the sheer vibration from it literally shook the glasses on the kitchen shelves.

Adel yanked the quilt over her head as a slew of curse words drowned in the second round of blasts from the supersonic horn, now with a new addition of multiple cabin doors slamming shut down the row from hers. She reached one hand down from under the quilt into her laptop bag, pulled out the folder Whittier had given her the night before with the schedule, and fumbled around the nightstand for her glasses.

Morning worship, 7:00 a.m. Campfire Bowl.
Breakfast, 7:30 a.m. Lodge.

A few minutes later, just as she was stepping out of the tub, the phone rang. It was Nico, the oldest of her four younger brothers. He called her exactly once a year, about a month before the big family weekend they had every summer at their mother's house in Mystic. He was already talking before she got the phone to her ear.

"Listen, Delly, I know you're trying to think of some reason why you can't come, but you try that every year and I'm not buying it this year either."

Adel sighed. The irony of the fact she actually had a valid excuse this year yet couldn't tell him wasn't lost on her. "Look, Nico, this year is different—"

"Why, because you're still with that rich girl with the stick up her ass who thinks she's too good for us?"

Adel opened her mouth to answer, but Nico cut her off. She put the phone on speaker and laid it on the bed long enough to pull on some black boy shorts and a sports bra.

"And I'm telling you, she's an idiot. Anyone who won't eat Ma's cooking is an idiot."

Adel covered her mouth to stifle a sudden urge to laugh. Nico was six foot four, covered in tattoos, and the owner of the most successful construction company in Mystic. He'd inexplicably talked like a mobster since he'd tossed out his first word at three years old, so everyone assumed he was a tough guy. Adel knew he secretly knitted baby cardigans for his kids when he was stressed and made a lemon butter pound cake to die for. And he adored their mother.

"Nic, calm down. She was just on a diet."

"Dell." Nico took a dramatic breath and let it out slowly. "If you shoved a nugget of coal up her ass, it would take exactly three seconds to turn into a diamond. It takes an average New Yorker like a month. That's all I'm sayin'." Adel listened to her brother roll his eyes for good measure. "Speaking of that, what's it been for you, now, nine years? You wising up yet?"

In fairness, Katya had spent exactly one holiday with her family where she'd refused to drink their table wine at dinner and turned up her nose at Nico's butter pound cake, instantly pissing off everyone but their mother, who still made a point to send her a handwritten invitation to Mystic every Christmas.

"Actually, Nico, you've got a point there."

Nico started to go on and stopped short. "Wait, what?"

"I know it's been a while since I've been home. I'm actually teaching a creative writing course at a camp upstate, but I'll make it this time. I promise. Just text me the date, okay?"

The line was silent for a few seconds, and when he spoke again, his voice was soft, as if the words were a secret. "I'll tell Ma. We all miss ya, ya jerk."

"Hey, Nico?"

"Yeah?"

"Any chance I can get that lavender-honey layer cake you did last time I was home?"

"I don't know…" Nico cleared his throat, and Adel heard him glance over his shoulder. "You gonna tell people I made it if they ask?"

"Not a chance." Adel smiled. "I know the drill."

"You got it, then. I have the kids growing lavender this year, so we'll make it together."

❖

It was after seven thirty before she took a wild guess at what to wear to class and headed for the lodge. In the end, she'd gone with white jeans, a white linen tee, and a navy blazer. Her camel Bed|Stü boots, unlaced at the sides, would have to do, since clearly wearing her Docs would start a religious uprising of epic proportions based on Whittier's prolonged look of disdain the previous evening.

The lodge looked even more imposing in the sunlight as she approached, and a small group of girls, a sea of flowing pastel skirts and glossy hair, turned together to look as she walked through the doors toward the scent of breakfast. It didn't take her long to find it, just to the left of the main lobby area of the lodge. Countless rows of tables with attached benches were lined up along both sides of the dining area, with the bustling kitchen at the far end. Adel walked toward the first glimpse of actual food and took a tray, handing it to the first girl behind the glass sneeze guard, who took it, dumped a ladle of scrambled eggs in the center, and handed it back with no change of expression.

"What else do you want?" Candy-pink gum appeared between her front teeth for just a second before she started chewing again and arched an eyebrow.

"You might want to take her up on that before she gives up on you." Adel turned to the woman beside her. "Rumor has it she has a short attention span."

"Shut up, Bethany." Gum Girl's voice was teasing. "Or I'm not giving you any stripples."

Bethany just winked and held her tray out for eggs. She was the only woman Adel had seen wearing pants, tight Wrangler jeans to be exact, with boots and a T-shirt streaked with red dust. Her hair was the color of sunlight, in a ponytail and pulled through the back of her IHOP baseball cap.

"What's a stripple?"

Both girls looked at her for a long moment before Bethany smiled and nodded at Adel's tray. "Load us up, Nora. And don't be stingy."

What looked like a cartoon replica of bacon landed on her tray from an impressive height, and Adel moved down the line, serving herself from a bowl of fruit salad and plucking up one of the last two pieces of toast on a crumb-scattered platter at the end of the row. Adel looked behind her and out into the dining room before she turned to Bethany again.

"Hey, do you happen to know where the coffee is?"

"Ha!" Bethany laughed, nearly spraying Adel with the orange juice she'd just lifted to her mouth on the way out to the dining room. "Dude. Don't tease me."

If the Wranglers hadn't clued Adel in already, being called *dude* certainly tipped her off that this girl was way more likely to be hired staff than one of the instructors. Thank God.

Bethany nodded toward one of the empty tables and they slid in, plastic trays clattering onto the tabletop in front of them. Adel grabbed the salt and shook it onto her eggs before she even had the first bite. From what she'd seen on the serving line, chances were slim they'd been seasoned.

"So, seriously." Adel replaced the salt shaker and grabbed the pepper as she turned to scan the area behind her. "Where's the coffee?"

"Well, you're clearly new." Bethany smirked, folding a piece of the cartoon bacon into her mouth. "Coffee. That's cute."

"Shit," Adel said, the truth settling around her like a cold fog. "There's no coffee, is there? That's why I couldn't find a coffee maker in the cabin."

"No, ma'am." Bethany arched an eyebrow and downed the rest of her orange juice in a single gulp, then turned the cup upside down on her plate. "No meat, no caffeine, no alcohol, and no fucking swearing."

"Well, that leaves me with absolutely nothing to do with my day." Adel shook her head and smiled. "So, what do you do here?"

"I'm in charge of the horses and stables at the top of the hill. I'm there at five a.m. every morning." She dropped her voice to a dramatic whisper. "And if you drop by tomorrow before breakfast, I'll show you my coffee maker."

"I might be in love with you." Adel flashed her a smile, taking a cautious bite of her stripple and setting it gingerly back down on her tray.

Bethany winked, her deep blue eyes flecked with bronze. "You wouldn't be the first."

❖

After breakfast Adel ran her hand through her hair and headed up one of the dual staircases, one on each side of the entry area, that led to the second-floor classrooms. According to her instructions, her classroom was the last door on the right. As she walked through the hall, the last of the girls were filing into the rooms, all wearing ankle-length skirts with long-sleeved shirts, mostly in denim and nondescript florals, buttoned to their necks. Their hairstyles, long and pulled back at the crown, were nearly identical as well, which made Adel feel like she was walking through the set of *Stepford Wives, Student Edition.*

She took a deep breath and pushed the door to her classroom open, where twelve girls were gossiping and laughing, their desks pulled into a semicircle that faced the front. The window in the back of the room was open, the breeze silently ruffling the sunflower-dotted curtain. Framed pictures of male biblical characters were the only decoration on the walls, but they were painted a sunny yellow, and the wide hardwood planks were finished with a warm maple glaze. The overall feel was less stark than she'd expected.

A wide teacher's desk with scarred edges sat in front of the chalkboard, and as she laid her bag on top of it with a *thunk*, every head in the room swiveled toward the front. Sudden silence hung heavy in the room, illuminated by golden sunlight streaming in from the windows.

"Hi, girls. I'm Adel Rosse." Adel watched as their collective gaze swept her from head to toe. "I'll be teaching your creative writing class this summer."

The only girl leaning back in her chair tilted her head, coolly checking Adel out for a second time. "Does Whittier know that?"

Muffled laughs rippled from one end of the semicircle to the other.

"She does. In fact..." Adel stepped to the front of her desk and leaned back on her hands. "I borrowed this outfit from her."

The girls looked at each other for a long few seconds before they figured out it was a joke and laughed hesitantly, the tension in the air strangely lifting and multiplying at the same time.

"Kidding," Adel said, a genuine smile flashing across her face. "I'm kidding. But let's just keep that little joke to ourselves."

She had grabbed an armful of black-and-white composition books and a box of envelopes from the supply closet on her way upstairs, which she now stacked at one end of the semicircle, taking one off the top for herself and nodding for the girls to start passing them down the row.

"Okay." Adel grabbed a pen from the top of the desk. "Take one of these journals and write your name clearly on the front." She paused. "Write it like it matters, because it does."

A blond girl whose gaze hadn't budged from Adel since she walked in rolled her eyes and whispered to the girl next to her, but the rest of them reached for the ballpoint pens in small blue mason jars on the table. Adel waited for the last student, a heavyset girl with thick glasses, to finish writing her name before she went on.

"From now until the end of summer, the journal you're holding in your hands is yours alone. With the exception of myself, no one is allowed to read someone else's book, and if you find one unattended, it needs to be returned to me without being opened." She paused. "Are we clear?"

The girls looked at each other, not Adel, but turned their attention back to her when she brought out the box of envelopes.

"I'm also going to pass around envelopes that each of you will staple to the back cover for memos or whatever else you want to put in there. Those are also not to be opened by anyone but the owner of the journal."

This time the girls nodded in tentative unison and waited for her to go on.

"What you write in your journal will be between only you and me." Adel picked up her own journal, folded one of the pages in half toward the spine, and held it up. "With one exception."

Hesitant glances ricocheted around the room. Adel cleared her throat and waited until every eye was back on her.

"If you write something here that you'd rather keep private, just fold the page over and I won't read it unless you tell me I can."

The heavyset girl raised her hand slowly, and Adel nodded in her direction.

"But what if..." She paused and looked around at the other girls. "How do we know you won't read it?"

"Well." Adel smiled. "I guess we're just going to have to trust each other."

She picked up an empty chair in the corner and placed it at the open end of the semicircle, then sat down with her journal and took a good look at the students. Some of them looked much younger than she'd expected. Whittier had said their ages ranged between seventeen and twenty. Clearly that was a lie, but in fairness she was also used to Manhattan girls, who tended to look twenty the second they turned twelve.

A mousy girl in a plain pink dress raised her hand and snapped Adel back to the present.

"Um," she said, not quite meeting Adel's eyes. "I think the teachers are supposed to sit behind their desks."

"Yeah?" Adel turned to the first page of her journal and clicked open her pen. "But this is our class." She paused. "I think we should get to do things our way, don't you?"

Not a single girl nodded.

❖

Grace pulled her cabin door shut behind her and folded the last of the sandwich she'd thrown together for lunch into her mouth, dropping both her keys and a wayward tomato slice in the process. She tossed the tomato into the lake and started walking toward the rowing docks, trying to suppress the memory of Whittier's news that she'd be working with Adel. When the door to her office had swung open and she'd recognized her, every drop of blood in her body rushed to her head, and suddenly she couldn't hear anything above her own heartbeat pounding like ocean waves crashing onto a cold, rocky shore.

Grace leaned down to pick up her sandals and dug her toes into the soft sand, letting the water flow over her feet. She paused to shake her hair out of its bun and felt it graze her waist through the thin fabric of her skirt. The sun warmed her face when she tilted it toward the sky, and everything seemed exactly the same as it had the day before. But it wasn't the same. After she'd walked Adel to her cabin last night, she waited until Adel's lights went out, then crept to her own cabin and sank slowly down onto the couch in the dark. Everything had changed in the span of a single day, and even in the silent darkness of her cabin, it was too much to take in.

The reality was that this was her fault, and she knew it. Being told she was engaged was a sharp, sudden shock because she'd let herself think for years that she'd escaped. That the rosy dream of marriage most Covenant girls lived for wasn't inevitable. That all she had to do to avoid that fate was keep the same secret she'd guarded since the summer she'd turned thirteen.

Her parents had called camp the previous morning and she'd taken it on the phone in Whittier's office. Her mother's voice was just a single step above disdain, although that was somehow preferable to the impenetrable silence of the last few years, and she'd heard her father talking in the background.

"Grace." Her mother drew in a slow breath and paused too long before she spoke again. "The Lord has seen fit to provide you with an opportunity for marriage, and your father has accepted on your behalf."

The desk scraped her back as she slid to the floor in the office, hand trembling around the handset. Static buzzed on the line, and the next voice she heard was her father's as he took the phone and cleared his throat.

"Grace, I was doing some work in the attic yesterday..."

She held her breath as she listened to his voice trail off in disgust. She was alone in Whittier's office, but she still felt the rough scrape of the noose tightening around her neck. His voice bottomed out into the deep timbre of hate, and Grace squeezed her eyes shut tight as if that could stop his words from sinking into her heart.

"We told the pastor about your deception, and he has offered an opportunity of marriage with a member of our congregation, which you know you don't deserve." His voice shook and the next words resonated like thunder. "May God forgive you for how you've disgraced this family."

Grace listened to him shove the phone back into her mother's hand. Her voice was cold and flat as she told her about the wooden box they'd found, the one that held the hollowed-out Bible with the tampons inside, kept hidden in the attic. Grace had known, somehow, that day that she'd turned from child to currency in the blink of an eye, that everything depended on keeping her period a secret.

Her mother had become increasingly concerned with each passing year and had taken her to doctor after doctor, each of whom seemed puzzled and eventually concluded there wasn't an obvious problem or diagnosis. Then, when she was seventeen, her father shook her awake in the middle of the night and drove to the Prophet's home without a single word. She was lashed to his bed for three straight days while they recited scripture over her and cast out demons from her body. The scent of the olive oil they'd anointed her with made her retch—she could still feel it trickling into her eyes and down the sides of her face—and the thick scars circling her wrists from straining against the ropes had never faded. At the end, she couldn't stand even one more second of hot, musty breath as they chanted over her, and she felt herself sinking into the bed, damp with sweat, as it swallowed her up. She prayed aloud to die and refused the water they'd finally forced down her throat after days of manic thirst and captivity. Everything started to go dark at the edges, and that's where her memory stopped.

Her father had given up after that. The shame of even acknowledging her presence was too much, and she'd wordlessly become the permanent unpaid caretaker for her younger brothers and sisters. They'd allowed her to spend her summers as staff at the Valley of Rubies, which they saw as a glimmer of redemption through service to the church. She was effectively barren—useless to them, and useless to God. Everyone knew they only let her go because they couldn't stand to look at her.

Grace reached the docks finally, memories shaking her hands as she unlocked the boathouse. Tears dripped from her chin, but she wiped them away and twisted her hair into a knot on the top of her head. She had a job to do, at least for a few more weeks, and the last thing she needed was the girls to see her crying. She allowed herself to close her eyes for a last second and listened to the gentle lap of the lake against the wet sand outside the door of the boathouse.

At least she'd gotten to believe she'd escaped for a few years. That was something.

❖

After lunch, Adel headed back to her cabin to change for the afternoon. According to the info packet Whittier had given her the night before, the physical education classes met at the docks at the north end of the camp. She slipped into her navy Speedo bikini and threw a white T-shirt and some khaki shorts over that.

Something tells me this outfit is going to stand out, she thought as she stepped out into the sunshine, slid her aviators onto her face, and locked the cabin door behind her. *But I'm fresh out of prairie dresses, so I guess it's going to have to do.*

According to the camp map in her packet, the North Shore was past the staff cabins and something called the Campfire Bowl. Hers was the last cabin in the row, so from there she followed the shoreline north, stopping when she got to the water to slip off her shoes. Half a lifetime in Manhattan had erased memories of the sensual warmth of sand under the sun and the swirling chill of the lake water around her ankles as she walked along the shore. Sunlight sparkled on the surface of the still, blue water and mirrored the reflection of the evergreens that seemed to follow her. The sun warmed her skin as she slowed her pace, listening to the far-off sound of laughter filtering through the trees.

In the city, she was always rushing, dodging traffic and bodies on the sidewalk, breathing in clouds of exhaust and the mingled scents from a thousand restaurants stacked like Legos and crowded into downtown Manhattan. She'd gotten used to strangers crushed against her on the subway, taxi horns blaring at every corner, even the constant shouts from the vendors that had blurred together after a few years, stealing her memory of silence.

It was hard to remember anything before Manhattan, or maybe she was just afraid that if she let herself think about it, she'd miss the home in Connecticut she hadn't been to once in the last three years. After a disastrous visit when they'd first started dating, Katya had declared she loathed Adel's hometown of Mystic, so they'd spent most of their holidays after that skiing with Katya's friends in Aspen.

Mystic was tiny, just over four thousand residents, and almost everyone worked in hospitality or the fishing and boating industry. Adel was the only girl in a sprawling Portuguese family with four brothers, so no one even noticed she was a tomboy. In fact, they barely even noticed she was a girl, which was fine by her. She'd also been the first person in her family to go to college and graduate. With the exception of two of her brothers, Nico and Marco, the rest of her family still worked on the docks, even her mother, who'd sold shrimp and lobster at the seaside market for as long as Adel could remember. Even now the scent of seawater in the air or rain-dampened wool reminded her of helping her mom sort through that day's catch in the predawn cold when she was a kid. The shoulders of her wool sweaters were always coated in a fine silvery mist from the constant fog rolling in off the water.

When she looked down the shore, the sounds of teenage girls and a long stretch of faded dock in the distance told her she'd arrived. A small boathouse, painted like a sun-bleached patchwork quilt, sat a few yards back from the edge of the water, wooden paddles stacked against the side in every direction. Scuffed canoes on racks lined the shore on the other side of the boathouse, and a catamaran with pristine, bleached white sails was docked farther down in its own slip, the wind clanging the ropes and pulls against the metal poles that stretched up into the sun.

Adel shaded her eyes as she got closer to the dock. From the looks of it, they'd be sculling. Two eight-seater rowboats were pulled up to the long side of the docks, and there were already a few girls sitting around it soaking up the afternoon warmth, faces tilted toward the sun. Grace stepped out of the boathouse just as Adel reached the end of the dock. Adel slowed and watched the sun light up the layers of blond hair piled in a loose bun on top of her head, although as she leaned over to grab an armful of life jackets in the doorway it fell in every direction around her face. She dropped the jackets and swept her hair out of her face, tucking it behind her ears as Adel reached the boathouse.

Adel snapped a hair band off her wrist and held it out to Grace. Grace hesitated, then took it and pulled her hair into a quick ponytail, smoothing back the wisps that escaped with the flat of her hand. She didn't say a word, just looked past her to the docks where some of the girls were now lying back on the dock in the sunshine, feet propped up on the side of the boat.

She looked back at Adel finally, her eyes skimming the taut lines of her arms before she looked away. "Do you row?"

"Yeah. I coached our varsity crew at Syracuse." Adel shot a dubious glance toward the dock. "Can *they* row?"

Grace looked for a second like she was going to laugh, then shifted her face back into neutral just in time.

"The short answer is no. They're all homeschooled, so camp is usually their first time doing anything athletic at all. The Prophet doesn't approve of sports for women, so I'm surprised we even get to do this, actually. I had to teach myself years ago."

Adel shook her head as she leaned over to scoop up an armful of life jackets and loop them onto her arm, and Grace picked up the rest as they stepped out of the boathouse into the sand and started walking toward the dock. She caught the girls' attention and waved them in before she turned back to Adel and dropped her voice.

"So, unless we can teach them some basic techniques, enough to actually get them interested in rowing, it's going to be a long summer."

Adel let the jackets slide off her arm into a pile where the dock met the sand and reached out for the jackets Grace was still carrying. "What have you done so far?"

"Camp has only been in session for two weeks, so I've swim tested them, taught them basic terms and commands, and we've been out there exactly once to get a feel for their individual skill levels." Grace shook her head, her eyes fluttering closed for a long second. "Which was an undeniable disaster."

Adel nodded, silently watching the girls ignore another attempt from Grace to wave them down to the end of the dock. "So, do they need to go get changed, or are you planning on doing some more land instruction first?"

"What do you mean?" Grace rolled up the sleeves of her white linen shirt and buttoned them at the elbow with tabs. "Like change their clothes?"

Adel glanced up as she started unbuckling the first of the life jackets. "Yeah. What did you think I meant?"

Grace handed her the armful of jackets at her feet and smiled, squinting into the sunlight. "You're serious, aren't you?"

Adel nodded, unbuckling the rest of the jackets, ordering them by size, and laying them out on the dock. "Yeah. Am I missing something here?"

"Those dresses are what the girls wear for physical education. It's what they wear for everything, actually."

Adel took a long look down the dock. Nothing but long sleeves and skirts in varying lengths, from mid-calf to ankle.

"You've got to be kidding me with this." Grace met her gaze long enough for Adel to realize she wasn't. "Those skirts could wind around their legs in the water and drown them. They can't go in like that."

"Now you see why the swim tests were a disaster." Adel paused and lowered her voice, turning her face slightly away from the few girls who were paying attention. "But, to be fair, they actually don't have a choice. This is my eighth year on staff at the waterfront, and it's taken me this long to get Whittier to even *consider* letting them swim in knee-length shorts, but she's still dragging her feet on an actual decision, so for now we're stuck with this."

Grace turned and called to the girls to gather at the end of the dock. A few looked up at the sound of her voice before they turned their faces back to the sun, but not one moved in her direction.

"And unfortunately," Grace glanced down at her watch, "when I finally took them out yesterday, half of them flat-out refused to wear their life jackets."

Adel nodded, then put two fingers to her lips and whistled at a deafening pitch. Every head whipped around in shocked unison.

She stopped only when every head was turned and arched an eyebrow in Grace's direction. "Do you want to take them out again today?"

Grace looked too startled to reply for a second, then looked out at the water. "That was the plan. Good luck with that."

Adel looked back to the girls and raised her voice to coach volume. "I need everyone down here at the end of the dock. Now."

She saw Grace look up in shock out of the corner of her eye, then fixed her attention back on the girls who appeared frozen in place on the dock.

"*Move* it."

Finally, the shock of being whistled at seemed to propel all of them into motion at the same time. Within a minute, they were all standing at the end of the dock next to the line of jackets, and the smallest girl in the back was kicking them lightly with the toe of her sneaker.

"Girls, this is Adel Rosse," Grace said with a nod at Adel. "She'll be assisting me with the physical education classes this summer. Rowing, canoeing, and sailing."

For the first time, the girls were silent and focused. Every wary eye was on Adel.

"Right." Adel took a second to wrap her head around the fact that her rowers looked like they'd just jumped off the back of a covered wagon. "I need everyone to grab a life jacket and put it on. It needs to be buckled and snug before we get on the water."

A couple of the girls in the back made a halfhearted attempt to sort through them, but most just stood where they were.

"Um…" A taller girl spoke as she looked at her watch. She was beautiful, in a forgettable way, with light blond hair and eyes the color of Indiana cornflowers. "There's no way I'm putting one of those on. Besides, Grace didn't make us do it yesterday, and no one drowned." She paused, nodding at Grace. "In fact, she's right there. Ask her yourself."

Adel held her eyes for a few silent seconds. "I recognize you from my creative writing class. What's your name?"

The girl shot a smirk at the girls behind her and turned her attention back to the front.

"Um…" She paused to look Adel up and down. "Ruth Blankenship."

"First of all, Ruth, your instructor's name is Ms. Waters, not Grace." Adel paused and nodded toward the boat. "And unless you'd rather spend the next two hours doing an endurance run up the nearest mountain with me, I suggest you pick up a life jacket."

"Clearly you're new." Ruth locked her eyes on Adel. Her voice was the only sound in the suddenly still air. "You can't make me do that."

"I assure you, Miss Blankenship," Adel slowly laced her fingers behind her neck and held Ruth's gaze with a strength that shimmered in the space between them, "I can. And I will."

The shocked silence continued until Ruth narrowed her eyes and leaned over to grab the closest vest. Grace and Adel stood on the deck and watched as she walked slowly back up the dock with the rest of the girls, dragging it behind her by the buckles.

❖

Two hours later, the boats were tethered back to the dock and the last girl had dropped her dripping vest at the boathouse and trudged back up the hill toward the bunkhouses. Adel picked up the last few life jackets and shook the water off at the door, then leaned in to hand them to Grace, who hung them on the rows of pegs lining the inside wall.

Grace rubbed her temples with her fingertips for a moment, then pulled the tie out of her hair, handing it back to Adel as she draped the length of her hair over one shoulder. It fell to her waist in wild waves as if still being blown by the wind; darker at the roots, but the rest of it still held the sunlight of the last few summers, fading it into pale gold toward the ends.

Adel took the hair tie, slipping it back onto her wrist as she watched Grace unroll her sleeves to her wrists and button them.

"So." Adel picked up the broom that was leaning against the door frame. "You're an instructor, right?"

Grace nodded, slicking vanilla ChapStick across her lips and dropping it back into her skirt pocket as she met Adel's eyes.

"So, can you wear what you want, or do you have to dress like they do?"

Grace shook her head and picked up her shoes. She stepped out onto the sand and looked back at Adel, shading her eyes from the sun.

"It doesn't matter what I want."

Adel leaned against the door frame and watched her walk away, shoes dangling from her fingers, until she disappeared into endless pines shifting in the breeze around her.

Chapter Four

The next morning was Saturday, and Adel rolled away from the blade of sharp sunlight edging into the room between the curtain and the windowsill. Her phone rang just as she closed her eyes again, buzzing and insistent on the nightstand. She knocked it over as she reached for it, then scooped it off the ground when she saw who it was and pressed it to her ear, eyes still squeezed shut.

"Hello?"

"Adel, why are you still asleep? It's past eight in the morning."

Adel lowered the phone and pressed it over her heartbeat as she stared at the gray drift of dead bugs in the overhead light fixture. Her attention drifted from a distance as Katya told her about an early morning spin class, then a breakfast meeting she'd had with the Bronx DA.

"So?"

Adel lifted the phone back to her ear when she heard Katya pause for a breath, realizing too late she'd missed the question.

"What do you think?"

Adel squeezed her eyes shut against the headache looming behind them.

"Think about what?" She swung her legs over the side of the bed and rolled her neck to loosen the muscles.

"Oh, sorry. I guess you're not even awake yet." Adel heard the click and sizzle of Katya's straightening iron in the background. "I thought they'd have you up and going to church already or something."

"Yeah, well, I wouldn't be surprised if that's in my immediate future."

Adel picked up the schedule and scanned it, noting that she had exactly twenty minutes to get her ass in gear and get to the lodge if she was going to make breakfast.

"Listen," Katya continued. "Just think about it. He's right, it would look better. I know you wanted this years ago, but it just makes sense now. I think we should do it."

The line beeped, then went silent for a second before Katya came back on.

"I gotta go. But we'll talk about this later, right?"

"Yeah."

Adel ran her fingers through her hair, slowly put the phone back down on the nightstand, and clicked the screen to black.

She did know one thing. There was no way in hell she was going to marry someone who hadn't touched her in over four years.

❖

Adel threw on some jeans and a light hoodie, pulled her hair into a ponytail, and locked the cabin door behind her as she headed toward the lodge on the off chance she might catch breakfast. She barely managed to squeeze into the front door; the vestibule was packed with ornate white flower arrangements, candelabras taller than her, and countless delivery and catering personnel. She stepped aside to avoid a workman carrying a faux marble statue of Jesus with his arms wide open. Once she'd gotten past them, she saw Bethany edging out the cafeteria door with two brown lunch bags in each hand.

"Hey, city girl," she said, blowing a stray wisp of hair out of her eyes. "You're not headed in there, are you?"

"Yeah, I thought I'd catch the tail end of breakfast." Adel turned to glance behind her, dropping her voice to a whisper. "What's all this, by the way? Is Elton John getting married again or something?"

Bethany snorted, then looked behind her into the cafeteria, muttering under her breath. "Look, if I were you, I wouldn't go in there. They'll recruit you to help with this shit in two seconds flat. Breakfast is over, they're just giving out sack lunches at this point anyway."

"Damn." Adel looked at the double sacks in each of Bethany's hands. "So does that mean you're going to share?"

Bethany paused, considering her options. "Maybe, but if there are brownies in here, I get first dibs."

"Deal."

Bethany nodded for Adel to follow and led her back through the entryway of the lodge, almost colliding with a massive wreath of pale yellow roses being carried by a delivery guy significantly shorter than the wreath itself. Once they'd made it out the door, Bethany walked over to a dented golf cart parked on the circle drive and dropped the sack breakfasts on the back seat. She slid behind the wheel and pulled her ball cap down over her eyes in one smooth motion. "You care if I drive?"

"Whatever." Out of the corner of her eye, Adel caught a glimpse of Whittier at the door. "Let's just get the hell out of here before someone hits me with a bouquet."

"My thoughts exactly, dude," Bethany fired up the engine and started backing up before Adel's ass had even hit the seat. "I'll explain on the way."

Bethany yanked the gearshift into reverse and they backed down the circle drive until a narrow path opened up to the right that wound up the steep wooded hill behind the lodge. The lake shimmered navy gold through the trees, and distant ski boats revved, skimming across the mirrored surface. Faint laughter from the camp below rose as the sound of the engines faded, merged with the heavy, constant splash of boat wakes crashing onto the rocky North Shore.

The engine lagged and chugged with the incline of the hill, but after a few minutes the path suddenly opened up into a clearing. A large red barn sat to the right, with outdoor corrals on the opposite side ringed with hay bales and lush, green grazing fields beyond.

"This must be your neck of the woods."

Bethany skidded to a stop outside the barn and climbed out, taking off her cap and hanging it on the nearest fencepost.

"Yes, ma'am. The only door in the entire camp that Whittier never darkens."

"Now, that's some useful information. Why is that?" Adel grabbed the paper bags from the back seat and followed Bethany into the barn, where she swung open a door marked *Staff Only*. "Is she scared of horses?"

She turned to a light pine picnic table in the narrow room, which was surrounded by ropes, harnesses, and an assortment of worn saddles hanging haphazardly from bent square nails on every wall. Adel followed the familiar scent of sun-soaked summer prairie up to see that the tack room was open to a loft above, where bales of golden hay were stacked at perfect angles to the rafters. She breathed in the clean, mingled scents of dry hay and leather, warmed by the steam rising from the mug of coffee Bethany handed her as she turned and they sat down at the table.

"Well, I can't say for sure that this is the reason, but my first year here, I led a staff trail ride, and her horse got a little frisky on the way back." She smiled, then looked up at Adel. "To make a long story short…" She paused as she dumped a spoonful of sugar into her coffee from the bowl on the table. "Well, let's just say I had to retire her saddle after that ride."

Adel laughed so hard she almost snorted coffee out her nose as Bethany upended all four lunch sacks, creating a mountain of wrapped sandwiches, loose oatmeal-raisin cookies, and bagged carrot and celery sticks.

"Well, damn." Bethany stacked two of the crumbly cookies together and bit into both at once. "Not that I don't love cookies in general, but I swear I smelled brownies baking in the back this morning."

"Hang on." Adel sifted through and uncovered a parchment-paper-wrapped square, half hidden by the pile of sandwiches. "It has *XO* written on it, so unless I suddenly got lucky, I'm pretty sure that one was meant for you."

"God." Bethany tore the wrapper off and looked lovingly at the brownie, the top dotted with tiny peanut butter chips. "I think I might be in love with Nora."

Adel smiled, wadding up the discarded wrapper. "Looks like the feeling might be mutual."

"Nah, I'm kidding." Bethany arched an eyebrow and popped a wide piece of brownie into her mouth. "We're just hanging out. For the moment, anyway." She winked. "I like the way she looks bent over the hay bales in the loft."

"Yeah, well. That's how it happens." Adel carefully unwrapped one of the sandwiches and held it up to the light, tilting her head to the side. "Then before you know it you've got an endless mortgage and a nonexistent sex life."

"Ah, *fuck* no." Bethany shook her head. "I'm thirty-two. I know myself well enough to know I've gotta have women. Plural."

"Yeah, good luck with that." Adel looked dubiously at the sandwich, then held it up again. "What the hell is this?"

Bethany leaned in to look, then took it out of Adel's hand and bit into it, her face thoughtful.

"I think…that's Wham Salad. It's like ham salad: chopped-up

celery, diced pickles, mayo, and Wham." She took another bite and gave the other half back to Adel. "I love that stuff. They haven't made it for ages."

Adel arched an eyebrow. "Like, 'Wake Me Up Before You Go-Go' Wham?" She set it carefully back down on the wrapper, tilting her head to the side to look closer. "You've got to be shitting me."

"Oh yeah, the food at this place is all kinds of crazy. Everything is vegetarian, so there are some really interesting variations of fake meat like veggie corndogs, soy scallops, you name it." She folded the last of her half into her mouth. "You'd be surprised, though. It actually grows on you after a while."

Bethany nodded at the sandwich. Adel picked it up and took a bite, then pulled another of the wrapped sandwiches to her side of the table.

"Not as bad as I thought for something named after an eighties pop band."

"Right? I actually like some of this stuff now. Only took a couple of years."

"So you're full-time staff, right?" Adel got up and retrieved the coffee pot, warming up both their cups before she set it back on the shelf. "You're here year-round?"

"Yeah, the camp operates all year, and aside from the summer session, it's mostly for Covenant group retreats. Family Camp happens for a couple months in early fall, too, where individual families rent a cabin and it basically just becomes a resort for them. They kinda have to do it that way since most of the men have multiple wives and, like, a thousand kids."

"So, how many full-time staff are there?"

"Not many, and most of those live in town and just come here to work during the day. There are only a handful of us that actually live here. They don't like hiring people outside the church, but sometimes they have to. Like you and me, I guess."

"You live in the staff cabins down by the lake too?"

"Yep. I'm hardly ever there, though." Bethany unwrapped her next sandwich, balling up the plastic wrap and tossing it into the trash barrel across the room. "You're on the end, right? I'm two doors down. The program director, Grace, is between us."

Adel nodded, noting that bit of information as she gathered up her wrappers and tossed them in the direction of the barrel. She missed.

"PCW camp happens every summer, though. They bring in male chaperones for the girls, and everyone refers to them as the Brethren. I don't even know why they're here, they basically just stand around and ogle the girls. It's creepy if you ask me."

"What does PCW stand for?"

"Brace yourself," Bethany said with a wink, drawing out a pause for effect. "Principles of Christian Womanhood."

Adel thought back to the book that was on her coffee table when she arrived at the camp, which suddenly made a lot more sense.

"Basically, it's a summer-long camp for girls only, and the sole purpose is to train them to be good wives, or to get them to be better wives if they're already married and somehow managed to hang on to a personality."

"Hold up." Adel almost choked on her sandwich as she set it down on the table. "Some of these girls are married?"

"If the married ones aren't living up to the standard, they get shipped out here too. They are supposed to only be here as staff to do custodial and grounds jobs, and you'll see them around—they have the camp logo on their shirts—but I *know* some of the actual campers are already married. It's supposed to be a secret, like their ages, but you'd be surprised how much they talk when we're out on trail rides." Bethany rolled her eyes and paused. "It's like they've morphed into that that huge painting in the Fellowship Hall. Still creeps me out every time I have to go in there."

"I don't think I've been there yet." Adel looked up as a wren fluttered to a stop on one of the hay bales above and looked down at them, twitching her wings.

"Yeah, well, you're not missing much. It's like the main worship hall, I guess, but something about that place is fucked up."

Adel's heart started to race, but she consciously relaxed her face into casual concern. "What do you mean?"

Bethany was silent for a second, smoothing the palm of her hand over a long scrape on the corner of the tabletop. "You know how churches are usually open in the day? For prayer or whatever?"

"Let me guess." Adel nodded. "This one's locked up like Fort Knox?"

"Yeah. Like you have to have a golden key to go in or something. There aren't even any windows on the main level to let in light, and there's a whole basement level that no one has ever even seen." Bethany swirled the last of her coffee thoughtfully in the bottom of her cup. "I left my phone there last year, and when I checked, the door was open for once, so I went in. I was looking between the pews when one of the

Brethren walked up behind me, and not two seconds later, another one blocked the other end of the pew. They were both just fucking staring at me, so I hopped over the back of the pew and left."

"Damn, that's some *Dukes of Hazzard*-level shit." Adel balled up her latest sandwich wrapper and studied Bethany's face. "I can tell from your face it still bothers you."

"Yeah, but it's not like they did anything to me. I can't even tell you why except for the fact that they're all just controlling assholes."

Adel shook her head and popped the last of her sandwich into her mouth. "Yeah, well, blind and deaf people can see that."

"It's where they're having the event tonight, though, so steer clear until tomorrow. But when you do see it, look on the back wall as you come in."

"For the painting? What is it?"

"Just some biblical scene with three huge words painted across the top. *Modesty*, *Submission*, and *Denial of Self*."

Adel got up and refilled her cup, looking back over her shoulder at Bethany. "So, basically, your life's motto?"

"Oh yeah. I'm all about denial of self." Bethany winked and folded the rest of a cookie into her mouth, but her smile faded slowly as she took a sip of her coffee, sweeping the crumbs and a stray raisin off the top of the table with the flat of her hand.

"I guess the thing that has always freaked me out is that the campers are so young." She paused. "I love this job, but every year about this time I think about quitting."

"Jesus Christ." Adel paused, letting the information sink into her memory as she made the mental switch into reporter mode. Now she was getting the good stuff. "I'm almost afraid to ask how old they are when they get married off…"

Her voice trailed off and Bethany looked down, smoothing down the same sharp sliver of wood on the tabletop with her thumb.

"They make it a real point to keep quiet about how old they are." She paused and looked up to meet Adel's eyes. "But they're not old enough, let's put it that way."

"What happens after that?"

"They have babies. A lot of babies." Bethany shook her head and Adel watched her choose her words carefully. "They have like one every year or something. Most Covenant families have over twelve kids. Way over."

"What if she doesn't want to have kids?"

"Well, that's gonna be hard to avoid since the main tenet of the Covenant religion advocates 'letting God dictate the size of your family.'"

"So, no birth control?" The memory of Grace sitting outside the clinic flashed through Adel's mind, and with what she'd said later, that she'd just gotten engaged, it now made a lot more sense. "And let me guess…If you admit you might want less than a hundred kids, word gets out pretty quick that you're a starting forward for Satan's team."

"Good guess." Bethany dumped her bag of carrots on the table and picked out the celery, setting it aside. "In fact, any hint that you have a damn mind of your own lands you on the Most Wanted list. And not in a good way."

"So I'm guessing gay as fuck isn't an option?"

Bethany looked up and tucked a stray lock of hair behind her ear. "It's not so bad for us if they find out, we'd just get fired, but there were a couple of girls that got caught in bed together a few years back. Rumor was that the chaperones decided to get together and teach them a lesson."

"What the hell does that mean?" Adel felt the answer she already knew hanging wordless in the air between them. "Did anyone report it?"

"To who?" Bethany spat out the words and watched them scatter across the table. "The police? They'd just come here and get nothing. Everyone knows better than to tell the truth. If they did, they'd be painting a target on their backs."

"Jesus Christ." Adel watched Bethany pile up the carrots and wrap them in a bandana for the horses. "That's fucked up."

"Girl," Bethany shook her head, arching an eyebrow as she tossed the bandana-wrapped carrots to the end of the table where they landed with a *thunk*, "you have no idea."

❖

Adel went into town later that day for some essentials and narrowly avoided ending up with only booze, coffee, and chocolate Moon Pies. The cafeteria food wasn't terrible, but it was always safer to have a stocked kitchen, and if she was going to be there for more than a few days, she knew she'd start to miss cooking. After she'd slid her grocery bags into the camp truck, she stopped by Planned Parenthood to pick up the watch she'd left on the sink the day she'd arrived. She stopped at the door and pressed the buzzer.

"State your name, please?"

Fabulous, Adel thought, reminding herself that Amber, the Disney-scrub-wearing militant, was watching her from the front desk on the security monitor.

"Adel Rosse. I was here a few days ago and left my watch. I'm just here to pick it up."

There was a long pause, then the door buzzed like a jet in a vestibule and Adel pushed the door open.

The same receptionist, Amber, leaned over the front desk as she walked in, looking her up and down. "No suitcase this time?"

"Nah." Adel winked. "You've already been through everything I brought."

"Yeah, well, I stand by that decision." She arched her eyebrow and motioned her back behind the front desk. "You look like trouble."

Adel stepped through the door and squirted a pump of hand sanitizer into her palm from the dispenser on the edge of the counter as she headed down the hall in the direction of Hannah's office.

"You'll be shocked to hear this," Adel said, looking back over her shoulder with a smile, "but you're not the first to tell me that."

When she finally remembered which door was which, she knocked lightly, opening it slightly when she heard Hannah's muffled voice on the other side.

Hannah was at her desk, both hands firmly wrapped around a Sonic triple cheeseburger. She waved Adel in, then took a massive bite as a ketchup-covered dill chip plopped down onto the lapel of her white lab coat and slid to her lap.

"Crap, I knew that was going to happen." Hannah swiped at the stain with a paper napkin, somehow managing to smear the ketchup onto her shirt. "Why is it that I can sail through med school in like five minutes, but I can't eat a burger without wearing half of it like a hungover frat boy?"

"It's not all bad. The ketchup brings out the blue in your eyes." Adel smiled, tilting her head to get a better look. "Or maybe that was the pickle."

"There's a pickle?" Hannah's eyes dropped to her lap and she sighed. "Of course there's a pickle." She plucked it off her trousers with the napkin and balled it up, sinking it dead center in the trash can across the room.

"Damn," Adel said. "You can save lives and sink a three-pointer. I'm impressed."

"All in a day's work." Hannah winked and sat back in her chair. "What can I do for you, Adel?"

"I think I may have left my watch on the sink when I was here the other day?"

Hannah pulled her desk drawer open and handed it over the desk. "I was wondering who left this. I knew it wasn't Amber, she's always worn a Minnie Mouse watch."

"Seriously?" Adel looked up as she turned her wrist over and fastened the clasp. "She's like thirty-five."

"Yep. And there's a Goofy bobblehead duct-taped onto the dash of her VW Bug outside."

Adel thought for a second and smiled. "What does the license plate say?"

"*MM-4Eva.*"

Adel shook her head. "Of course it does."

"Hey," Hannah said, opening the leather-bound datebook on her desk. "What are you doing for dinner this Friday night?"

Adel paused, trying to picture the schedule Whittier had given her. "Nothing I know of."

"I'm having a few friends over to the house." She looked up. "Nothing fancy, just a casual dinner, if you'd like to come."

Hannah raised the burger to take another bite and managed to get it back to the wrapper laid out on her desk just before a mayo-streaked tomato slice made its escape.

"That sounds great, actually." A vivid memory of the Wham sandwich flashed across her mind. "The place I'm at is vegetarian. It's not necessarily bad, but I might be having some withdrawal issues."

"I don't blame you. God help whoever tries to come between me and my food. Especially a juicy burger like this beauty." Hannah shook her Sonic cup to get the last bit before she put it back in the bag and crumpled the top over it. "Oh yeah, you're on assignment, aren't you?"

"I am." She paused. "I'm at Valley of Rubies, but I'm undercover, so keep that one under your hat."

"Oh, that's right." Hannah paused, then smiled, reaching for the sticky pad on her desk. "Which means this just got way more interesting." She pulled the note off the pad, handing it to Adel. "That's my address and personal phone number. Anytime around six is great."

❖

That night, Adel climbed into bed with a chocolate Moon Pie and took her black Moleskine notebook out of the nightstand. She'd kept a journal since she learned to write, and the closet in her childhood bedroom in Mystic was still crammed with scuffed spiral notebooks, the yellowing pages almost stiff with ballpoint ink, some randomly folded over by half and stapled to keep her deepest secrets private. It was the highest degree of security she could think of at the time, and it had worked as an effective deterrent against the prying eyes of her brothers—not that they really cared much about her innermost thoughts and middle school dramas.

She leaned back on the pillows and opened to the first page, printing *Valley of Rubies* across the top. The snowy expanse of the blank paper was soon dusted with Moon Pie crumbs as she recorded her experience at Planned Parenthood and first impressions of the camp.

> *This place is like a religious version of the Stepford Wives. They dress in endless nondescript shades of pastel, and so far, the same can be said of their personalities. The only exception has been Ruth Blankenship, one of the girls in my rowing class. That one has got a mouth on her and an attitude the size of a yacht, but it was almost refreshing to see one of the girls think for themselves. Finally.*

She crumpled the wrapper of the Moon Pie and tossed it at the bathroom trash through the door. Missed again.

> *The creative writing class looked at me like I'd suggested they streak naked through campus when I told them they could write whatever they wanted in their journals, and that it would be private. The rebel from rowing class clearly didn't believe me, and the other girls weren't buying it either. How is this such a foreign concept to them?*

Someone walked past the window of her cabin, each step a rhythmic crunch into the gravel path, but the sound quickly faded, replaced by the almost familiar lap of lake water. Adel peeked out the window just in time to see it was two of the Brethren, who saw her the second she appeared in the window. It didn't make sense for them to be anywhere near the staff cabins, but lately they seemed to be everywhere. The creepiest thing to Adel was that she'd never seen one of them speak to anyone but each other; they just watched. Everything.

They disappeared down the shore and Adel shook her head, putting the Brethren out of her mind. Something about them wasn't right, though, and the way they stared at the girls was bothering her more and more. Adel popped the last of the Moon Pie into her mouth, pen hovering over the page until she remembered what she'd been thinking right before she got up to look out the window.

And I should probably figure out why I keep picturing Hannah, the Planned Parenthood doc, naked.

That can't be a good sign.

Chapter Five

Grace knocked softly on the door and held her breath, hoping Mrs. Whitter had forgotten she'd asked her to stop by that evening just before the start of the event. She told herself it was probably nothing; camp had only been in session for two weeks—what could she possibly have done already that warranted a visit to Whittier's office?

"Come in."

Grace forced herself to slowly let out the breath she was holding and opened the door, where Whittier was sitting behind her desk with her Bible, hands folded in front of her. Bookcases covered the wall behind her, mostly biblical reference collections punctuated by vintage group photos in dusty gold-painted frames. Her hair was pulled back in the same tight bun Grace remembered from her years as a camper, although it had thinned since then and turned a wiry gray at her hairline. Over the years, it had started to bother her that Whittier's hairstyle had never changed. She'd known her for over a decade and not a single hair had shifted.

"Good evening." Grace stepped into the room and turned to pull the door shut behind her. "You asked to see me?"

Whittier nodded for her to sit, then waited longer than she needed to before she spoke, until Grace looked down to smooth her skirt over her knees with damp palms.

"Tonight's event starts in just under an hour, so I'll be brief." Whittier glanced at her watch, then back to Grace. "I'm sure you have an idea why I asked you to my office today."

Grace searched her face for clues. She'd started at Valley of Rubies as a camper, then the summer she'd turned eighteen she accepted a staff position on the waterfront before transitioning to the position of program director four years ago. She loved her job, although she worked the summer session only, but in the last few years, she'd felt the energy between herself and Whittier start to shift, and not in the right direction. She cleared her throat and forced herself to smile.

"I'm sorry, I don't. But I've been so busy with the last-minute details today that I may have missed something."

Whittier smoothed the sleeves of her blouse and straightened the cuffs at her wrists before she answered, her eyes narrowing with the intensity of her gaze.

"Grace, tell me again what the purpose of this camp is?"

Grace forced herself not to look away as she felt the slow retreat of any hope that this might be a casual visit. Clearly it was not.

"I believe the summer session has always been an opportunity to educate and prepare young women for marriage."

"That's right." Whittier pulled a piece of paper out of the stack on her desk. "To become a helpmate to a man of God is our greatest privilege. But to be frank, I'm concerned that you seem to have lost sight of that goal."

"But I haven't—"

"I had an interesting conversation with your parents yesterday, Grace." Whittier picked up her glasses and slid them on to her face, holding the yellow paper with handwritten notes on it at arm's length. "They tell me they'd been asked for your hand in marriage. I don't remember you mentioning to anyone that you are engaged."

Grace sat as still as church dust hovering in a silent sanctuary. Actually, she'd not been asked, but that wasn't worth mentioning. Her father didn't care if she would be a good match for Edward Dooney, the oldest son of the pastor of their home church. He just wanted her out of his house so he could pretend she didn't exist.

Technically, there was nothing wrong with Edward beyond being bland looking; his skin and hair had always been the same forgettable shade of beige, and he somehow managed to look skinny and fleshy at the same time. He was in line to take over the church they'd grown up in when his father retired, but he was still unmarried at thirty-one. Most likely because he gave off an energy that made you want to pull your little sister close as he passed you in the hall.

Grace cleared her throat. "My parents have spoken to me about that, yes."

Whittier put the paper down and leaned toward her over the desk. "Grace, I'm concerned about you. From what your parents said, you're not on board with this marriage." She leaned back then and folded her hands again into the identical position they'd been in. "Do you even *want* to get married and fulfill God's chosen plan for your life?"

Grace paused before she answered, choosing each word carefully. "Someday, yes, I just think…"

Her voice trailed off as Whittier shook her head and looked down at the desk. Grace felt the air leave her lungs, and suddenly she felt too exhausted to breathe in again.

"Grace, as you know, tonight's event is the Purity Ball, and its purpose has always been to start preparing our young girls for their roles as wives." She locked her emotionless gray eyes on Grace and paused. "Marriage is a woman's greatest calling, and after talking to your parents, I'm starting to think you may not be the best influence for our girls here at Valley of Rubies. Especially not on a night like tonight." She looked hard into Grace's eyes. "I think it best that you not attend."

Grace sat back in the chair as if someone had shoved her in slow motion. "I've been working here for the last eight summers and have had nothing but positive feedback."

Whittier slowly picked up the Bible beside her and set it between them on the desk. "You're correct, Grace. You've never been reprimanded." She paused, turning the thin gold band on her finger. "But that doesn't mean your heart is truly right with our Lord or the teachings of our Prophet."

Grace heard the string quartet she'd hired for the event start to warm up in the lobby of the lodge, the halting discordance melting into molten harmony as they started "Come Now Fount of Every Blessing," her favorite hymn and the one she'd chosen for the first song of the evening. She noticed her dress was crumpled hard into her fists and she let them go slowly, raising her eyes slowly to Whittier. Grace opened her mouth to speak before she realized there were no words, so she walked through the silence and pulled the office door shut behind her, the hymns she'd chosen surrounding her like a makeshift shelter.

❖

Grace was walking down the North Shore when it hit her. The cold lake water pooled around her as she dropped to her knees, her shoulders heaving as her body tried to rid itself of Whittier's words. She'd felt this sea change gathering for the last few weeks, dark and humid around her, weighing down her shoulders and warning her not to lift her eyes from the safety of the ground.

Evening light was darkening around her, glossing the lake to reflect the green firs on the opposite shore. The water lapped around her thighs as she sat back on the underwater sand and looked up at the first stars moving past a smudge of gray-violet clouds. The silence of the empty camp seemed too calm, but she knew why—everyone was at the Fellowship Hall by now. The girls lined up outside, nervously adjusting their dresses and smoothing cherry ChapStick over their lips as they peered inside through the windows. That image was enough to send her toward the water again, and her shoulders heaved with the strength of her entire body to rid itself of the memories, but the events of her own Purity Ball, the summer she turned twelve, were part of her now. They had permeated her blood, her muscles, even the hair that fell around her face and floated in the water.

The nervous excitement at being called after the ball to a special meeting with the Prophet. Her damp palms smoothing the front of her dress and the acrid smell of mothballs as an elder led her down to the lower level of the Fellowship Hall. The white robe hanging on the back of the door and the smooth click as he shut and locked it behind him. The black night beyond the windows as a single lightbulb overhead hissed and flickered.

"Grace?"

No. Grace's breath caught in her throat and she froze as she realized who it was, her body tensed instantly to the density of stone. *Please, God, anyone but her.*

Grace felt Adel kneel silently beside her in the water, then the warmth of her palm soft and slow against her upper back. Grace swallowed the last wave of nausea and sat slowly back again, eyes still focused on the water, intensely aware of Adel's touch.

"What's wrong?"

Adel's voice was smooth, husky, surrounding her like water warmed through by sunlight. Grace felt herself relaxing into it against her will, the muscles across her shoulders softening and unfolding onto her bones.

"Are you sick?"

Grace shook her head, then covered her face with cold lake water hands, her eyes fluttering shut beneath them. She knew she had to say something now. But there was nothing. No words. There never had been.

"I can't."

She'd willed her voice to be firm, to somehow make Adel just stand up and walk away, but neither of those things happened.

"That's okay." Adel paused, then got up and stood in the shallow water beside her. "You don't have to say anything."

Grace's hands slipped from her face down to the water, and she saw that Adel was holding out her hand. She took it after a long few seconds and let Adel pull her to her feet. The sand clung to the hem of her skirt, dragging it around her ankles like shackles as they stepped out of the water and back onto the shore. Adel shrugged off her jacket and draped it around Grace's shoulders, then picked up the two paper grocery sacks tipped over onto the soft sand at the edge of the water.

"I'm sorry," Grace said, reaching out and taking one of them from her arms. "I made you drop these."

"Hey." Adel stopped walking and waited until Grace met her eyes. She paused so long that Grace wondered if she was going to say anything at all, and when she did speak, her eyes were soft and intense. "You didn't make me do anything."

As they turned and started walking toward the cabins, the last of the fiery sunset illuminated the sand under their feet just before the cool edge of the water slicked it away. Black-crowned night herons called to each other as they swooped in from the lake to land among the branches on the other side of the shore, disappearing into the falling darkness between them. Grace tilted her head back to listen to the hymn that had started to float across the tops of the trees, shifting the leaves as it moved through the air: "Lead Thou Me On."

"I thought you'd be at that event tonight." Adel shifted her sack to her other arm and reached out to pull the shoulder of the jacket tighter around Grace's shoulder. "Whatever it is must be a big deal—I had to park way past the stables to even wedge my car into a space."

"Yeah," Grace said, her fingers tracing the edges of the note in her pocket that contained her opening remarks for the ceremony. She silently crumpled it into a ball in her fist before she went on. "It is a big deal."

When they finally reached the row of staff cabins, every one of them was dark. Adel handed her bag to Grace to retrieve her keys from the pocket of her jacket.

Adel smiled, unlocking her door and reaching out to Grace for the groceries. "So I hear we're neighbors."

"Yeah." Grace smiled for the first time and glanced next door to her cabin. "I noticed."

Adel leaned into her cabin and switched on the light, then turned back to Grace. "You look pale. When's the last time you ate anything?"

"I'm fine."

"Yeah." Adel smiled, nodding for her to walk through the door first. "That's what I thought you'd say. Doesn't make it true."

Grace hesitated, looking back down the row of dark cabins.

"If you're worried that someone might see you in my cabin, those odds might tip in your favor if you actually step in it and shut the door."

Grace smiled despite herself and followed Adel in, locking the brass dead bolt behind her.

"Do you mind if I close these drapes?"

Adel glanced back from the kitchen area and shrugged. "Feel free. I forgot they were even there. By the time I go to bed, no one's walking past my cabin anyway."

Grace closed the drapes and looked around the simple cabin. It was much like her own, with one major exception: the open closet, where Adel's clothes were hanging under stacks of denim folded neatly on the shelf above the closet rod. She felt her heartbeat slow and fought the urge to walk toward them. These were actual clothes, not a row of pastel dresses; she wanted to touch them so badly she made herself look away. It had always been easier to just not think about normal clothes. If she pretended they didn't exist, she was less likely to covet them.

"What are you staring at?"

She snapped back to reality to realize Adel was holding out a glass for her and looking in the direction of the closet.

"Did you see a ghost?"

"Yeah." Grace took the glass, pulling her eyes away from the clothes and shaking the thought from her head before she remembered how odd that would look. "Something like that."

She took a breath, then followed Adel back into the kitchen, where a quart of strawberries were strewn across a cutting board. She watched as Adel cored them and tossed the wet, green stems in a small bowl to the side. She leaned against the counter and watched the translucent red juice stain the pine board in layers, the color intensifying in the scratches crisscrossed into the wood. Grace closed her eyes and drew in the sweet, grassy scent of the berries until she felt it start to blur the memory.

"There's always something going on in that mind." Adel's words jolted Grace out of her trance, and she realized she'd been standing there with her eyes closed. "What are you thinking?"

"Sorry." Grace faltered and thought for as long as she could without having to say something. "I guess I'm not used to doing things like…" She hesitated. "This. With you."

Adel shot her a smile over her shoulder and went back to slicing the strawberries. "You may have to elaborate on that for me."

Adel reached for the next strawberry and held it out for Grace to bite. Grace leaned back slightly, then smiled and held out her hand for Adel to drop it into.

"I can't elaborate." She bit into the cool strawberry, so ripe it melted in her mouth and glossed her lips with juice. "I don't know how to describe it in words."

"Okay. What if you just use three words?" Adel sliced the last berry and dumped them into a glass bowl, reaching in the grocery bag for a small, brown paper bag. "I do that sometimes when I'm writing but can't seem to wrap words around a thought. I just try to come up with three words that come close and start with that."

Adel took a sip from her glass, then paused and reached quickly over the counter toward Grace's glass. "Oh, God, this is Chardonnay. I should have remembered you don't drink."

Grace met her eyes for a moment, slid her fingers under the glass, and took it back.

"Well, all right then." Adel smiled, arching an eyebrow. "Have you ever had wine?"

Grace smiled back, still holding Adel's gaze. "I'm not telling."

"Well," Adel said, tipping a bit of the powdery contents of the bag onto the berries. A hand-printed brown paper label on the side said *Caster Sugar*. "That's almost certainly a no, so go easy."

Grace watched Adel mix the sliced strawberries and sugar gently until it melted into a simple syrup. "What are you making?"

"Balsamic strawberries." Adel added a few splashes of acrid, dark balsamic vinegar that burned Grace's nose when she leaned over to breathe it in. "Have you ever had them?"

"Um…vinegar on strawberries? No."

Adel glanced down and set the bowl aside.

"Hey, your clothes are still wet. You must be freezing. Do you want to go next door and change?" She pulled a frying pan out of the bottom cupboard and turned on the gas to a low flame. "This won't be ready for a few minutes."

Grace nodded and started toward the door, then paused, unsure. Adel looked up. "You can't risk being seen, can you?"

She froze as Adel went over to the closet and pulled down some clothes, stacking them into a neat pile on her palm and holding them out to Grace on the way back to the kitchen.

"I don't know if you'll be comfortable in these, but I'm fresh out of dresses." Adel flashed her a smile from the kitchen as she picked her bowl back up. "Those might help you get warmed up, though, and you can drape your dress over the radiator in the bathroom. By the time you're ready to go next door, it should be dry."

Grace reached out for them and headed for the bathroom, closing the door softly and turning the lock, her breath catching in her throat. Adel had given her a hoodie with NYU on it in capital letters and a pair of faded Levi's. She set them on the sink and took a step back, watching her reflection in the mirror as if she were someone else. It was surreal to be in this moment again. She'd seen herself in jeans only once before, the summer she'd turned twelve, and she'd not let herself think about it since. Grace's gaze settled on the locked door and she closed her eyes, stepping into the searing memory she had to walk through to get to the other side.

She'd been at home when it happened, stripping and remaking the beds upstairs. During the week she helped homeschool her twelve brothers and sisters in the morning, then she and the rest of the younger girls spent the afternoon doing housekeeping chores before dinner. She'd been leaving her brother Hirim's room, a laundry basket overflowing under her arm, when she saw them. She stopped and stared at Hirim's dresser, fingers tightening slowly around the cool metal doorknob. A rush of heat washed up her neck and across her face, her heartbeat pulsing at her temples. The bottom drawer had been left open, revealing stacks of his work jeans, all neatly pressed and folded.

Grace leaned on Adel's sink and tried to bring herself back to the present, but all she could feel was the rough scrape of the denim across her fingertips as she sank down on the floor beside the dresser. She'd pulled the top pair onto her lap, smoothing them with her palm. Hirim was a few years older than she was but around her size, and Grace had coveted her brother's jeans for as long as she could remember. She knew it was a sin for girls to wear pants, but as she traced the faded center crease with her fingertip, she also knew this might be her only chance to know how it felt to wear them.

She'd just zipped them up when her older sister Naomi walked past the room and stopped in her tracks, her mouth going slack with shock in slow motion. Grace watched her sister's reflection in the mirror and realized with a sudden trapped sickness that she'd forgotten to close the door. But it was too late; Naomi's eyes narrowed and she ran out the door, calling for their father before she'd even reached the bottom of the stairs. Grace was frozen, standing in the center of the room, the jeans partially hidden underneath her pastel yellow dress. She listened to her father's muffled footsteps as he came up the stairs and closed the door softly behind him. He was smiling as he slowly stripped his belt from his pants, the buckle clanking against itself as he wound the opposite end around his fist. She could still hear his voice as he asked her, almost tenderly, to remove both garments. She let the jeans drop to her ankles and stepped out of them, then pulled the dress over her head with shaking hands, watching it drop to a lifeless pastel pool onto the floor beside her.

Her father's face slowly twisted into rage and the beasts of Revelation flashed red and gold across her mind as he beat her with the buckle end of his belt. She remembered him calling her a harlot right before she lost consciousness, and thick crimson blood seeped through her dresses for days afterward, as if offering proof. He insisted she wear the same stained dresses for weeks to remind her of her sin, but the deep white scars that still crisscrossed the back of her thighs never let her forget.

Grace closed her eyes and listened to Adel scraping a spoon against the sides of a mixing bowl in the kitchen, acid burning and twisting in the pit of her stomach. When she finally opened her eyes, she unfolded the jeans with shaking hands and stepped into them, but they tangled in the length of her skirt. She held her breath, anger rising like a flash of sudden fire, then hooked her fingers under the neck of her dress and ripped it down the front of her body, relishing the sound of the cloth tearing, the cries of demons being ripped from her body and cast off into the darkness.

It was a moment before Grace remembered she was in Adel's bathroom and forced herself to take a breath, the dress now just a pile of wide torn strips around her bare feet. It looked strangely lifeless now, drained of power. She stepped on it as she buttoned the jeans low on her hips, then turned to look in the full-length mirror standing against the wall.

In most Covenant households, adult men were allowed to have full-length mirrors but women and girls were restricted to mirrors that stopped at the shoulders. The only one in her house was the one in Hirim's room, which her father used occasionally when he dressed for church. She'd asked why girls weren't allowed to look in it only once; her mother had looked at her as if she wished she could shove the words back into her mouth and whipstitch it shut. When she finally spoke, her voice was empty, sharp, and metallic around the edges.

Your body is not yours to look at. It is a sacred temple only for the eyes of God and your husband.

Grace shook the memory from her mind. It was odd looking at herself now in the mirror, like walking in on a stranger who'd assumed she was alone. Her hair had fallen out of her bun, and she reached up to pull out the hair tie from the last few strands, shaking it into loose waves around her shoulders. It had always been an odd combination of golden blond and the rich brown of wet earth, as if it belonged to two different people. Her skin was darker than the rest of her family by a shade, as dense and delicate as desert clay. The lean lines of her torso softened at the hips with a deep curve, which was even more noticeable when she unpinned the binding she wrapped tightly around her chest every morning, letting it drop to her feet. Her breath caught when she saw the pale gold birthmark in the center of her chest, reaching across to touch both breasts, like light had fallen across them and chosen to stay.

"Grace?"

She closed her eyes at the sound of Adel's voice and reached for the binding, winding it hurriedly back around her breasts as she answered back, her voice too loud and quick.

"I'm…I'll be out in just a minute."

"Take your time." Grace heard her pause, as if choosing her words. "I just wanted to make sure you were all right."

Grace heard her walk away and continued binding her chest, tighter, then tighter again, until she could barely breathe. She anchored the end with the pins she'd laid on the sink and pulled on the hoodie that Adel had given her, zipping it to her neck. She didn't look at the mirror again, just swiped her eyes with the cuff of the sweatshirt and walked out.

❖

A few minutes later Adel handed her the plates and nodded toward the coffee table, following her with their wineglasses and the bottle. Grace saw Adel smile out of the corner of her eye as she watched her lean into the rich, savory steam rising from the plate.

"What is this?"

"Well," Adel said, picking up the bottle and pouring wine the color of sunlight into her glass. Her hand hovered over Grace's glass until she looked up. "How are you feeling?"

Grace broke her gaze and looked down at her plate. She felt flushed and slightly dizzy, but lighter, somehow…and brave. She felt brave.

"Fine." She cleared her throat and looked back up at Adel, her gaze steady. "I feel fine."

Adel refilled her glass and sat down, handing her a fork and knife from the edge of the coffee table.

"So," Adel said, picking up her own utensils. "This is my favorite thing to cook in the summer. It's just some French crepes with ham and gruyère cheese." She paused, cutting into the thinnest pancake Grace had ever seen. "The green scattered on top is just some torn parsley and julienned scallions."

"I have no idea what you just said." Grace looked down at her plate. "Except for the parsley, I recognized that."

Adel smiled and pointed with her fork. "Don't worry. I figured you don't eat meat, so yours has chanterelle mushrooms instead of ham."

Grace sliced into the crepe and slid it onto her fork, winding the creamy melted cheese around the tines. It was salty, but only in a way that deepened the flavor of the cheese, and the mushrooms had been lightly sautéed in butter until they were tender and golden brown. There was a hint of smokiness, too, which Grace couldn't put her finger on.

"The mushrooms taste like…fire."

"I'm impressed you caught that." Adel laughed, her dark eyes sparkling in a way Adel hadn't noticed before. "And you're right. I actually held the chanterelles over the flame for just a few seconds before I put everything together."

Grace closed her eyes, savoring the last of another bite. When she opened them, Adel was looking over at her, with a smile that Grace couldn't quite decipher.

She reached over and stole a bite of crepe off Adel's plate. "Where did you learn to cook like this?"

"I spent a year in Paris in my early twenties." Adel looked up and winked in her direction. "It comes in handy when you're trying to convince beautiful women to have dinner with you."

Grace took a sip of her wine and tried to quell the flush she felt rising from her neck to her cheeks.

"Thank you for this. I guess I didn't realize I was so hungry." She speared another triangle of crepe and loaded it up with a melty drape of cheese. "And this seriously might be the best thing I've ever eaten."

Adel glanced over her shoulder, fork poised in the air. "So, what do you cook at home?"

Grace looked up as if someone had just burst into the room. "You mean when I'm not at camp? Like where I live?"

"Yeah." Adel speared a wafer-thin slice of ham and stacked it onto her crepe. "You're only here in the summer, right?"

Grace paused. "Well, I'm not married, so I still live at home with my parents. We make food that's easy to make in bulk, I guess. Haystacks more than anything."

Adel lofted an eyebrow as she folded another bite of crepe into her mouth.

"Um...it's like a taco salad, I guess. Covenant families are usually big—I have twelve brothers and sisters—so it's just something everyone grows up eating."

Grace paused and glanced over at Adel's plate. "What does that taste like?"

Adel took a sip of her wine and loaded her fork with another bite of the crepe. "You've never had ham, have you?"

Grace shook her head "I've never had any meat."

Adel held out the fork for Grace and she took it, gingerly putting the bite into her mouth and returning the fork to Adel.

"What do you think?"

"Oh, wow." Grace swallowed and drank the last of her wine. "That was intense. Not what I expected at all."

"Yeah, I thought you'd like it." Adel loaded up Grace's fork with a big bite and traded her for the empty one. "Next time I'm ordering you a patty melt whether you like it or not."

Grace took it and settled back into the couch, pulling her bare feet underneath her. She felt more relaxed than she could ever remember feeling, and suddenly brave enough to really look at Adel as she finished her food. Her skin was a dark amber, her eyes a rich, backlit brown that had shimmered with dark green and gold in the sunlight when they were out on the water the day before.

Adel looked over her shoulder as she loaded her fork with the last of her crepe. "What?"

Grace hesitated. She knew the right thing to do would be to thank Adel for dinner, walk next door to her cabin, and sink immediately to her knees. But that's not what she did.

"I have questions."

Adel laughed and leaned back into the sofa, wineglass balanced between her fingers. "Then we have that in common." She winked as she answered, her words slow and dense between them. "Hit me."

"Why did you say that in the diner?" She paused, her eyes focused at the wall behind Adel. "About me not being able to resist you?"

When Grace finally met her eyes, it was as if Adel was holding them, still and steady, to her own. It was a long few seconds before she answered.

"I guess because I was hoping it was true."

Grace looked down into her glass and bit her lip. There was nothing to say. Or there was nothing she should say.

Adel started to speak, then waited until Grace met her eyes. When she spoke, her voice was softer than her words. "And why did you run out?"

Grace tipped the rest of her wine into her mouth and set the glass on the table, her fingers sliding down the stem before she pulled the sleeves of Adel's hoodie over them and crossed her arms in front of her.

"I don't know."

Adel smiled, arching an eyebrow. "Isn't lying a sin?"

Grace laughed, the tense muscles in her shoulders slowly unfolding as she considered her words.

"I guess it is. You got me there."

"So," Adel said, pouring the last of the wine into Grace's glass and handing it to her. "Just say it. I live in Manhattan, I'm hard to shock."

Grace took a breath, time slowing as she listened to it fill her lungs. *It's not real if it's never said out loud. Everyone knows that.*

"Grace." Grace closed her eyes when she saw Adel lean forward as she spoke. "You're holding your breath. Breathe."

Grace closed her eyes tighter as the words tumbled out of her grasp and into the tide of her breath.

"It was you." She felt the warmth of a tear she didn't know was there slipping down her cheek. "This."

Adel reached forward and gently brushed the tear from Grace's cheek with her thumb. When she spoke, the words were a whisper. "We don't have to talk about it, Grace."

"I can't. I know I can't." Grace looked up, her eyes moving over the laugh lines at the corner of Adel's eyes, the ones formed from a million winks, the ones that made her look kind, like it was safe to tell her anything. But safe was an illusion, everyone knew that. "But you make me want to."

Adel took the wineglass out of her hand and pulled Grace into her arms. By the time she'd remembered to breathe again, she was asleep.

Chapter Six

The next few days flew by. The boats were out for maintenance and insurance inspection until Thursday, so Adel hadn't crossed paths with Grace until she walked up the North Shore to the docks on Friday afternoon. A crystal white crane poised on the end of the dock took off as she approached, stirring the still air on the empty beach.

Grace was inside the boathouse, hanging life jackets on wall hooks and checking them in on the clipboard in her hand. A small chrome fan whirred in the corner but didn't touch the heat hanging in shimmering sheets in the tiny, airless boathouse. Adel leaned against the door frame and watched as Grace pulled her waist-length hair up and wound it into a pile at the top of her head, fanning the damp slope of her neck with the clipboard. She was wearing a long-sleeved denim shirt and ankle-length skirt in nearly hundred-degree heat, and even from behind, Adel could tell her skin was flushed a deep, splotchy red.

She'd been leaning on the door frame of the boathouse for around a minute before Grace finally turned around. She jumped, startled, her hand covering her heart.

"I didn't know you were…" Grace's voice faltered, and she looked beyond Adel to see if anyone else was there. "How long have you been standing there?"

"Not long, I just wanted to get here to help before the girls made an appearance. We're taking them out again today, right?"

Adel's gaze dropped to the knot in the front hem of Grace's skirt that lifted it to mid-thigh.

"Oh, God, sorry. I don't normally do this, it's just been so hot in here all day."

Grace dropped the life jacket she was holding and tried to pry open the knot, but the material had obviously been wet when she'd tied it and seemed to be tightening by the second. Adel took a step forward to help, but Grace stepped back as she did, bumping one of the life jackets, which fell onto her shoulder and bounced to the ground.

"No." It was only one word, but it was as quick and desperate as if it were whispered in the dark. Grace looked up at Adel, then glanced down at her watch. "No. You can't."

Adel watched as she tried to loosen the soaked fabric, her fingers moving more quickly and less effectively with every passing second. Adel finally shook her head and pulled a folding chair in the corner over to Grace, the chair legs scraping across the wide plank floorboards. She sat on the chair, turning Grace swiftly toward her with one hand on her hip.

"Listen." Adel locked eyes with Grace and saw the panic that flashed like lightning across them. "You can let the girls see your skirt like this and think God knows what." They both glanced down at the skirt that revealed her legs to mid-thigh. "Or I can help you and we'll get this done. Those are your choices."

Grace looked at her watch again and bit her lip. It was a long few seconds before she nodded.

Adel dug her pocketknife out of the side pocket of her shorts and flipped up the flat wrench. She wedged it under the top layer of fabric and lifted it as she felt Grace's hand, as light as air, settle onto the back of her shoulder as she worked. Grace's fingers tensed as they started to hear the voices of the girls, getting closer as they walked down the beach. Adel worked steadily, the last of the material finally loosening and falling away as the voices sounded close enough to be rounding the corner. Adel stood quickly, shoved the chair away with her foot, and stepped away just as Ruth Blankenship rounded the corner of the open door and stopped in her tracks.

Grace turned casually toward the wall opposite the door and reached for a life jacket on the lower row. She tossed it over her shoulder to Ruth, who was still standing in the doorway.

She rolled her eyes. "Grace, you're not seriously going to make me wear this again, are you?"

A few more girls stopped behind Ruth, gossiping halted sharply by the tension in the air that sparked and crackled in the silence.

"Ruth, this is the last time I'm going to say this." Adel flicked her knife closed and dropped it slowly back in the side pocket of her shorts. "Your instructor's name is Ms. Waters."

Ruth put one hand on her hip and rolled her eyes at the girls behind her. "Oh, really? You were serious about that too?"

Adel locked eyes with Ruth and held her gaze until she looked away.

"Yes. And if you have trouble remembering it after today, we'll be going over it on that endurance hike I mentioned last time."

Ruth narrowed her eyes and held Adel's gaze for a few silent seconds before she tilted her head to the side and the sunlight glinted through her pale blue eyes. "You don't know who my father is, do you?"

Adel reached for the folding chair she'd been sitting in and snapped it shut.

"I can assure you, Ms. Blankenship." Adel's words slowed until they hung heavy and motionless in the air between them. "I don't *care* who your father is."

❖

Later that evening, Adel pulled up to a beautiful lake house the color of dusk, with pristine white shutters and pewter nautical lights. She double-checked the address Hannah had written down for her at Planned Parenthood, clicking the car locks as she walked up the circle drive. Lush emerald lawn stretched out in every direction, eventually sloping down behind the house to meet the glassy surface of the darkening lake beyond. The wake of a passing boat lapped gently against the shore, and the air smelled damp and fresh as if it had just been washed by the rain. Gaslights in forged iron lanterns lit the stone path to the front door, where a portly gold Labrador was stretched across the white boards of the porch. He lifted his head momentarily when Adel rubbed his belly, then burped loudly and fell instantly back to sleep as she stood to ring the doorbell.

Everything happened quickly after that. She heard running, then the door flying open and smacking the side of the house as Hannah darted past her, her blond hair flying around her face as she backed up to the edge of the porch. Adel pulled the front door closed and held her hand out to Hannah, who looked as if she was going to fall backward off the porch steps.

"Are you okay?" Adel pulled her gently forward and watched as Hannah looked twice at the door to be sure it was shut tight.

"I was pulling the bread out of the oven when I saw it so it's still there and it's probably burning by now but I can't go back in there and I—"

"Saw what?"

"The...thing." Hannah shivered and looked down at her feet. "I can't even say it."

Adel had to stop herself from smiling as Hannah shook her head so hard her hair swished around her face.

"Do you need me to get the bread out of the oven for you?"

"Oh, God, you can't!" Hannah walked to the door and touched the knob as if there might be a raging fire on the other side. "I mean, someone has to get it out, it's going to burn the house down, but I can't ask you to do that."

Adel shook her head and gave up trying not to smile. "So, what are we talking about here? A dragon?"

"Even worse. It's an opossum. In the mudroom off the kitchen." Another shiver. "With beady little red eyes and this gross scaly tail that..." Hannah covered her face with her hands and hopped from foot to foot, peering through her fingers at the door as if it might fly off its hinges at any moment. "I just can't..."

Her voice trailed off as Adel opened the door and walked in slowly, holding out her hand to keep Hannah behind her. As she rounded the corner of the hall, Hannah hissed to get her attention and jerked her finger toward the small, colorful room at the rear of the kitchen. Adel started toward the door and saw a shadow dart under the entry bench near the opposite door that led outside.

"What the hell was that?"

Hannah's words were more of a screech than a question. Adel picked Hannah up by her waist and sat her on the kitchen counter before she was even done talking. She held her there and nodded toward the mudroom.

"I'm going to nudge it out the other door, but in case that plan goes west and it runs this way"—she paused, looking back at her with a wink—"I don't want you to give it a heart attack."

"Yes, ma'am." Hannah ran her fingers through her hair and smiled, eyes locked with Adel's. "And I don't say that very often."

When Adel had seen her last, she was wearing a lab coat with no makeup; tonight she was in a pair of slim jeans, a white linen T-shirt with a deep V-neck to the center of her chest, and a smudge of black eyeliner around her light hazel eyes. Honey-colored freckles were scattered across her face like sudden sunlight, and Adel had to remind herself to step back, her hands sliding too slowly down Hannah's thighs.

"Actually," Adel said, glancing again at the mudroom where a tiny opossum was now visible underneath the bench by the door, "you don't know me this well yet, but you might want to keep that phrase handy for the future."

After telling Hannah to stay where she was, she walked back out the front door and around the house toward the double glass doors of the mudroom she'd seen on the other side. She carefully opened one of the doors and waited, and within a minute, a baby opossum appeared hesitantly at the threshold, then darted toward the tree line near the shore. A rustle in the brush she was headed for told Adel the mother was probably waiting, so she let herself back in and closed the door behind her.

Hannah was in the kitchen, in bare feet, a chopstick stuck through the bun at the nape of her neck. Adel watched as she pulled a golden loaf of bread from the red enamel Aga oven and slid it onto the maple butcher-block countertop, handing Adel a ramekin of melted herb butter and a small brush.

Adel flashed her a smile and started brushing the loaf with butter. "This looks amazing."

"I'm so glad it didn't burn. Although I think now I made way too much of everything, including this."

Hannah reached up to the wineglass rack above her head and took down two crystal glasses, then pulled a chilled bottle of Chilean white wine out of the refrigerator.

"There was supposed to be another couple coming, Anne Margaret and Marissa, but Marissa went into labor about an hour ago and they bailed."

Adel smiled. "The nerve."

"Right? Rude." Hannah poured a taste of the wine into a glass and handed it to Adel. "I mean, I offered to deliver it here after dinner, but they still opted for the hospital." She winked at Adel and poured a taste for herself into another glass. "So it will just be the three of us, I'm afraid. Kate should be here in a few minutes."

Adel recognized the wine, which was perfectly chilled and from one of her favorite regions in Chile. "Is this a Cachapoal Valley Chardonnay?"

Hannah flashed her a smile and filled her glass. "Yes, it is." She lifted her own glass and closed her eyes, tipping the wine almost to her lips and inhaling. "I'm assuming if you know what it is, you've had it before. What do you like about it?"

"Just that it's so unexpected. Dry, but a strange savory finish. I don't know how to describe it, I'm not even sure I like it, but my wine chiller at home is full of it."

"You don't have to know how to describe it to like it. In fact, that might actually be an advantage. An ex-girlfriend ordered this for me once at a restaurant in New York. She described it as 'big-boned and aggressive.'"

"I'm guessing she didn't last too long after that?"

Hannah smiled, slicing the end of the bread off and handing it to Adel. "Not even to the end of the night."

"So," Adel said, closing her eyes to savor the warm earthiness of the melted butter before she bit into the bread. "Is Kate your..."

"Girlfriend?" Hannah laughed, cutting another slice of bread for herself and glancing at the door. "Nah. I don't exactly do girlfriends. Or relationships. But we're..." Her voice trailed off as she searched for the right term.

Adel tipped her glass to her lips and met her eyes. "Fucking?"

Hannah laughed again, her fingertip tracing the trail of condensation on the Chardonnay bottle. "Well, I was going to say she's an ember, but yeah, I guess you could say that."

"What the hell is an ember?"

"Oh, wow...how did we get here already?" Hannah laughed and clinked her glass to Adel's. "I just...travel a lot."

"Yeah." Adel tipped her head to the side. "Nice try, but that still doesn't tell me what an ember is."

"Well, that's all the detail you get." Hannah cut another warm crust of bread from the loaf and stepped closer, brushing Adel's lip with her thumb as she put it in her mouth. "Until I decide to tell you more."

The front door opened down the hall just at that moment, and a few seconds later, a tall, very fit woman rounded the corner into the kitchen with long strides. Her hair was cut in a masculine style close to her neck, with a perfect hard part on the left side. She was wearing black suit pants that fit her perfectly, patent leather brogue lace-ups, and a sky-blue button-down shirt with the sleeves rolled up to the elbows. She also had a gold badge clipped to her belt.

"Hey, sorry I'm late." She put her briefcase down on one of

the kitchen stools and reached up for a wineglass, leaning in to kiss Hannah's cheek before she extended her hand to Adel. "I don't think we've met. I'm Kate Kilcullen."

"It's a pleasure. I'm Adel Rosse. Hannah and I met recently at Planned Parenthood."

"Ah, you're that Portuguese interpreter that saved the day."

Hannah pulled a small pottery dish of olives out of the fridge and set them on the counter between them. "She didn't tell me anything about the case, of course, just that it was a huge help having you there."

"I was happy to do it, although I'd actually just flown into Lockwood and came straight to the office hauling three stuffed suitcases."

Kate smiled and glanced back over her shoulder at Hannah. "And how did that go down with Amber at reception?"

Adel watched as Hannah lifted a pot of salted water onto the stove and turned up the flame. "I think it might have taken her a few hours to get her heart rate down after I got there."

"Let me guess. She unpacked them herself for a friendly little bomb check?"

"That about covers it, yeah. Outside on the entry steps, no less."

Kate smiled as she pulled out a stool for Adel and one for herself, reaching for the wine and topping up Adel's glass before she sat down. "The first time I came to see Hannah at work, she actually wanted me to leave my service weapon with her at the front desk."

Hannah looked at Kate over her shoulder and rolled her eyes, then went back to slicing what looked like pancetta on a scarred hickory plank.

"And no offense intended here, but the last thing that girl needs is a loaded Glock at her disposal."

"True story." Hannah slid the pancetta strips into a smoking hot cast iron pan. "She's great at what she does, but…damn."

Adel shook her head and smiled, imagining Amber squaring up against Kate, who had a good five inches on her. "What happened?"

"Well, she refused to open the door until I gave her everything else I had with me, so I just unloaded it all right on the counter in front of her."

Hannah turned around and winked at Adel.

"Which doesn't sound too exciting, but I had been at Kate's house the night before, going over a safe sex presentation I was giving at the high school later that week."

"And she left the demo items on my kitchen table." Kate took a sip of her wine and shook her head, clearly savoring the memory. "Which is why I dropped by the office, to return them."

"This just gets better and better." Adel shook her head and reached for her glass. "Why, what did you have? Tell me everything."

Hannah slid a pile of sliced parsnip and minced garlic into the pan from the cutting board. "A box of condoms, a dental dam, three packets of lube, and some black latex gloves."

Kate smiled. "In addition to my handcuffs, of course."

"Oh, shit." Adel laughed, reaching for another olive. "Did her head explode?"

"Oh yeah." Kate swirled the wine in her glass and laughed. "It was pretty entertaining. She pressed a button on the intercom and told Hannah that we had a 'situation' in the lobby and she needed to come to the front immediately."

"And she kept repeating the word 'immediately,' like every other second." Hannah stripped a handful of leaves off a potted thyme plant in the kitchen window and sprinkled them into the pan. "So of course I go running down the hall thinking some protester has gotten in and threatened her or something, but it was just Kate and a pile of sex stuff. She literally could not stop laughing the entire time she was in my office."

"I still laugh every time I think about it." Kate shot Hannah a smile. "And I make it a point to massively flirt with her every time I come in, of course."

"Well, yeah." Adel nodded and dropped her olive pit in the tiny dish beside the bowl. "That's just polite."

"Exactly my thought. She needs a little excitement in her life."

Hannah turned around and smiled. "Yeah, not much gets past her. Including any girl I'm seeing, apparently."

A few minutes later they all walked out to the hardwood deck that overlooked the lake. Kate brought another bottle of chilled Chardonnay to the table, which turned out to be an antique World War II factory sewing table, complete with random steel bolts and a scuffed machine base in the center. Hannah set a wide bowl of her creamy pasta on it, with the tender parsnip she'd sautéed in garlic then layered with savory pecorino cheese and crispy, smoky pancetta stirred in at the last second.

As they clinked their glasses in a toast, the sun was just sinking slowly out of sight over the water, as if it had been waiting for them to arrive, leaving a shimmering golden path on the still surface of the water. Fireflies wove an invisible pattern over the darkening velvet lawn, and the scent of cold lake water hovered in the air.

"I seriously can't get enough of this pasta, Hannah." Adel twirled her fork against the side of her bowl, loading it up with sauce and crispy bits of pancetta. "What herbs did you use in it? I can place the thyme, but there's something else."

"Summer savory. I grow it in that little pot under the window. I love it. I chuck handfuls of that and rosemary into everything in the autumn."

"So." Kate sprinkled a bit more of the shaved pecorino onto her pasta and nudged it back to the center of the table. "Hannah tells me you're on assignment here with *Vanity Fair*?"

Adel nodded. "That's true, but keep that under your hat. I'm doing an exposé piece so I'm actually here undercover, which sounds a lot more exciting than it really is."

"Where are you staying?"

Adel paused, unsure of how much she should say. The location itself hinted at what she was there to observe.

Hannah looked at them both and put down her fork. "Adel, let me interject here and say that the only thing I've told Kate is that you're a journalist." She then turned to Kate, with a nod to Adel. "And, Kate, I haven't told her anything about what you do for a living, although that sexy little badge on your hip probably gave it away." She topped up everyone's glasses and smiled. "And something tells me we're all going to need more wine for this."

Kate smiled, picked up her glass, and clinked it to Adel's. "*Now* this is getting interesting."

Adel took a long sip of the wine and locked eyes with Kate. "So what is it that you do exactly?"

"I'm a detective with the sex crimes division in Plymouth, the next town over from Lockwood." She held Adel's gaze. "And what is it you're here to uncover?"

"Possible sexual abuse of underage girls as young as twelve, or at the very least, illegal underage marriages."

Adel and Kate looked at each other over the table until Hannah sat back in her chair with her wine and smiled. "Yeah. I thought you two might have a few things in common."

❖

Later that night, Adel sat in bed with her computer on her lap, an empty page pulled up and waiting, the cursor blinking into the dark like a heartbeat. She and Kate had exchanged as much information as they could—which wasn't much—but promised to stay in touch with any developments on both sides.

She knew she should be thinking about her article. She should be writing down every sordid detail Kate had shared with her about Valley of Rubies. She should be doing anything but thinking about how close she came to kissing Hannah Myers.

She dragged her thoughts away from the memory of Hannah's mouth, the one she almost leaned into before Kate appeared. The voice mail indicator on her phone had been blinking for days with Katya's messages, all unopened, because it had started to dawn on her that it didn't matter if she actually listened to them or not. Her life was exactly the same without Katya as it had been with her.

Chapter Seven

The warm, dusty scent of sunlit hay enveloped Adel as soon as she stepped into the stables with the cold six-pack of Trailer Park IPA she'd picked up in town earlier that week. The late afternoon heat was settling into coolness like only mountain air can do in the depths of July, and dust hung silent in the wide sunbeams streaming through the open stable doors as she called for Bethany.

Bethany answered by tossing down a bale of hay from the loft that broke open at Adel's feet.

"Hey, girl." Adel held up the six-pack. "They're cold and free. Want one?"

"God, yes." Bethany tossed her pitchfork across the loft and motioned Adel up the stairs. "Get your ass up here."

Adel handed Bethany a beer as she got to the top of the rickety ladder and settled onto a hay bale, digging into her pocket for her knife.

"Don't worry about it, I've got it."

Bethany crossed her ankle over her knee and cracked open her beer with a bottle opener hidden in the arch of her boot. She handed it back to Adel and took another, popping off the top with a satisfying whoosh of foam that streamed instantly down the side of the bottle and over her hand.

"You weren't kidding about these being cold." Bethany pulled her hair into a quick ponytail and secured it with the elastic around her wrist. "And your timing is great. Anybody else today and I would have skewered them with that pitchfork."

Adel laughed, taking a long swig of her beer and looking over at Bethany. "That good, huh? What's going on?"

"I don't know, actually." Bethany picked up a long piece of bale twine on the bare plank floor and wound it around her fist. "But there's something not right about this fucking place sometimes, and I just can't put my finger on it."

"Well, you're not wrong there." Adel leaned back on the stack of hay bales behind her and leveled her gaze to Bethany's. "But what happened this time to make you think that?"

"Look, if I tell you, you have to promise me you won't tell anyone here about this, okay?"

Adel nodded, wondering if that was a promise she'd be able to keep. This assignment had seemed pretty straightforward when she'd accepted it, but now she was building unexpected friendships, and shades of gray had started to appear in the background.

"You got it." Adel got up to take a quick look down at the stables to make sure no one was lurking, then sank back into her seat. "Hit me."

"So last night I was in bed, right? Then Nora texted me that she'd left her cafeteria keys in the tack room earlier…"

Adel grinned. "And why would she have been in the tack room at night?"

"I'll let you figure that one out." Bethany grinned and downed the first half of her beer. "Anyway, she always opens up in the morning, so I told her I'd go get them for her and bring them to her cabin."

"She lives in our row of cabins? I didn't know that. I've never seen her down there."

"No, she lives in staff quarters. It's that row of log cabins on the right painted dark green as you come into the camp. They're set back into the trees, so they're easy to miss. The scrub staff work there, which is what they call basically anyone who doesn't teach classes, I guess. Most of them are Covenant girls there for discipline, although there are a handful of food service staff like Nora who are…"

"Civilians? Gotcha." Adel tossed Bethany another beer, which she caught with one hand while downing the rest of her first with the other. "I've seen them. They work in the cafeteria, grounds, that type of thing?"

"Yeah, they always wear the white long-sleeved shirts that button up the front with those ridiculous skirts. I do regular trail rides for the staff girls, even though they aren't technically supposed to participate in any of the camp activities, and they can't even wear pants for that."

"What the hell is up with everyone having to wear those skirts?" Adel rolled her eyes and shook her head. "I swear, I'm just waiting for someone to drown if a boat tips over in the middle of the lake. It's ridiculous."

"Yeah, well apparently it's the girl's responsibility to not to 'tempt men toward impure thoughts.' So it's all ankle-length skirts and long sleeves, all the damn time."

"You've got to be fucking kidding me with this." Adel shook her head and tried to get her mind around the reasoning behind it. "So if a man has 'impure thoughts' and chooses to sexually assault a girl, it's automatically her fault for tempting him to sin?"

Bethany tipped her bottle in Adel's direction. "And she's the one who ends up shamed for it, not him."

"Jesus Christ." Adel shrugged off the hoodie she was wearing and put it between her head and the hay behind her. "I don't even know what to say about that."

"Yeah, I love this job, but the more I know, the less I feel like I can stay here. It's a whole different level of fucked up than I even knew before I started hanging out with Nora this summer. I was just naive before, I guess."

A horse threw its head back and snorted in the stalls below, and Bethany stopped to drop some hay down from the loft, then sank back down into the bales, dust motes floating around her in every direction.

"All right, so what happened when you came to get Nora's keys?"

"Well, I'd seen where she threw them when we came in, so I walked in and grabbed the keys without turning on the light. But something just didn't feel right, so I hit the lights on the way out and looked around."

"Oh, man." Adel shook her head and kicked a clump of straw aside with her foot. "Why do I feel like I don't want to know what you're about to tell me?"

"You don't. It was one of the white shirt girls that work custodial or some shit. I recognized her face, I think she subs in sometimes in the cafeteria with Nora." Bethany paused, started to go on, then cleared her throat and stopped.

"Was she alone?"

"Yeah. She was by then." Bethany took her cap off and pulled the elastic out of her ponytail. Her hair fell around her shoulders in a thick swoosh, softening the angles of her face in a way Adel hadn't expected. "But she hadn't been alone very long. She was hiding in the tack room, and she was…a mess. I guess she'd seen it when we saddled up for the rides and thought she'd be alone here."

"A mess? Like how?"

"I don't even know what…it all meant. But I know when I see

something fucked up, and this was about a mile beyond that." She paused, shrugging off the dusty denim shirt she was wearing and letting it drop into a pile behind her, leaving just a white Seattle pride tee with the sleeves cut off. "She was just huddled there, under the table, with her knees pulled up under her chin. She was still wearing one of those long skirts, but all the buttons had been ripped off her shirt and she was holding it together in front of her with both hands."

"Jesus Christ." Adel ran her fingers through her hair and paused. "Did she look like she might have been attacked? Who the hell would do that here?"

"Dude." Bethany looked into the rafters long enough to blink away the tears Adel had already seen gathering in her eyes. "That girl's shirt had been ripped to shit. Even though she was holding it to her as best she could, it was barely staying together."

"Oh, my God." Adel locked eyes with Bethany. "What did you do?"

"I didn't have anything for her except what I was wearing, so I pulled my shirt off and gave it to her."

"Did she take it?"

"She didn't want to." Bethany slowly peeled the label from the bottle in her hand. "But she didn't have any other option."

Adel watched her crumple the damp paper label into her fist and toss it over the edge of the loft. "What else?"

"What do you mean?"

"I can tell there's something else."

Bethany shook her head and let out a long, slow breath. "She turned around to take off what was left of her shirt and pull mine on, and I took out my phone."

Adel held her breath. "You took a picture?"

"I know, I'm going to hell." Bethany rubbed her eyes hard with the tips of her fingers, then shook her head as if to clear it from the memory. "She trusted me, and I took a fucking picture." She drew a long breath and held it. "But I had to do it. Look."

Bethany pulled her phone from her back pocket and scrolled through it, finally pausing and glancing up at Adel before handing it to her. Just as Adel reached for it, Nora stepped through the stable doors downstairs and called for Bethany, who walked to the edge and leaned over, motioning for her to come upstairs.

Before she'd even thought about it, Adel had taken a picture of the image with her own phone and dropped it back into her pocket, holding Bethany's phone out as she turned back around. A few seconds later Nora got to the top of the ladder and froze, her eyes locked onto Adel.

"Babe, she knows." Bethany nodded in Adel's direction. "It's okay."

Nora's face didn't change expression, but she finally stepped off the ladder onto the loft and went to sit beside Bethany. She looked at Adel, unsmiling, until Adel arched an eyebrow.

"Listen, newbie," Nora said, her eyes narrowing. "If you tell anyone about us, I'll literally kill you." She paused with a pointed look at the pitchfork stuck into a bale of hay in the corner. "Like, myself."

"I can respect that." Adel leaned forward, her elbows settled on her knees. "But nothing in life is free, so it's gonna cost you."

Nora held her gaze as Bethany stifled a laugh, holding her hand up for another beer, which Adel plucked from the six-pack at her feet and tossed without taking her eyes from Nora's.

Nora leaned forward, mirroring Adel's stance. "I'm listening."

"I like that ham salad."

"Wham salad."

"Whatever." Adel smiled finally and saw Nora's expression relax just slightly as well when she felt Bethany's hand on her thigh. "I'm gonna need some of that delivered to my cabin. Weekly. If you can manage that, your secret's safe with me."

Nora finally flashed Adel a smile and sat back on the bale. Bethany winked at Adel and turned to Nora. "Besides, it looks like she's got a secret of her own going with Grace, so it looks like you're safe there."

"Wait." Adel tossed a bottle cap in her direction, narrowly missing her shoulder. "How did you know that?"

"Dude. I pay attention."

Bethany tossed the bottle cap back and turned to Nora. "So, you live in staff row...who's that redhead up there with the super pale skin, lots of freckles? She never comes on the trail rides."

"Audrey. She's the only real redhead this year, I think." Nora tipped her head to the side. "Why?"

"Have you seen her today?"

"Nope. Her cabin is the last one in the row, so I usually knock and we walk down to breakfast together, but she didn't answer this morning and I haven't seen her all day." Nora looked from one to the other, her eyes narrowing. "Something's up. What is it?"

Adel lightened her expression and tried to keep her tone casual. "Just...will you check on her tonight? Make sure she's okay?"

"Yeah, but you'd better not be messing with her. She's way too young to even be here. I don't care what Valley of Rubies says."

Bethany finished her beer and set the empty bottles beside the rest of them at her feet. "How old *is* she?"

Nora shook her head and brushed the hay dust off the side of her boot. "Trust me, you don't want to know."

"It can't be that bad, right?" Adel said slowly. "When I got here, Whittier told me all the campers were over seventeen, so that would make the staff all older than that by default, right?"

"That's what they told you?" Bethany stood, weaving her fingers behind her head and looking at the rafters. "That's total bullshit. There's not one camper here even close to that age. Most of them are between ten and thirteen."

Nora nodded, the light fading from her eyes as she pulled at a loose thread on the cuff of her jacket. "Audrey turned fifteen last September. I remember because it was the day before her wedding."

Chapter Eight

That night, Adel sat on her couch, turning Kate Kilcullen's card through her fingers like a forgotten pen. A single lamp on the desk was the only light in the room except for the soft indigo glow of the abandoned laptop in front of her. She ran a hand through her hair and sank back into the sofa cushions, squeezing her eyes shut against the thoughts like race cars careening around the track of her mind.

After she'd gotten back to her cabin from the stables, she'd opened an email from Ed Goldberg, her editor at *Vanity Fair*. He was fishing for advance details on the progress of the undercover work but was clear he was expecting a bombshell exposé that would garner international attention. A byline on a cover story like this, especially during an election year, could catapult her to the pinnacle of her field with a single assignment. The journalism industry in Manhattan was cutthroat, but if she managed to pull this off, it would open doors for the rest of her career.

When she'd started this assignment, she'd worried the scandal Goldberg was expecting would be nonexistent, but tonight, talking to Bethany and Nora, she'd felt overwhelmed by the scope of it. Clearly she'd only scratched the surface of what was happening at Valley of Rubies, and what was really happening started to slowly drift together in her mind as she'd listened to Bethany tell her about finding Audrey in the tack room. Little things that bothered her but were seemingly insignificant before had now started to become clear, like a picture slowly emerging from underwater. She walked over to her nightstand and grabbed her journal, writing before her pen hit the page.

>*Today, Nora let slip in conversation that the camp wasn't just to "prepare" girls for marriage, it's a "correctional*

facility" for willful new wives like Audrey, who are sent here to work as staff. The Brethren are in charge of them, which seems to be their only real role here at camp besides supervision.

For Adel, it wasn't just the Brethren's presence that was unsettling, it was the constant, collective gaze they swept the girls with, as if they were livestock at an auction. A gaze of ownership, achieved solely by virtue of being male. And the girls felt it—it was clear in the slope of their shoulders, the absence of connection to anyone, even in their voices. When the Brethren were around, the campers kept their voices low and their eyes lower. Adel had been at Planned Parenthood for twenty years. Long enough to know that something shifts when you're owned.

Adel laid the journal facedown on the coffee table and stepped out the door of her cabin, pulling it shut and locking it behind her. The air was warm, the same temperature as her skin, and the dusty silver light from the wash of stars overhead glowed like pewter dust above the endless black surface of the lake. The air was strangely still; even the wind through the trees had stopped, as if holding its breath and watching.

She walked the few steps to the door of Grace's cabin but hesitated as she raised her hand to knock. It was clear Grace couldn't tell her what was going on within the camp without risking her own safety, but Adel had a gut feeling that what was happening here was a slowly churning ocean beneath the surface, and it was starting to get personal.

She raised her hand again to knock just as Grace opened the door. She started to say something, looked to the right and left down the row of cabins, then back to Adel.

"What are you doing here?"

Adel hesitated.

Grace shook her head. "Wait. Someone might see us if we talk here. Just meet me at the boathouse in ten minutes, okay?"

Adel nodded and leaned back into her cabin as she passed it to grab a jacket for herself and another for Grace. The water lapped at the edge of her feet as she walked, and through the trees, columns of warm light spilled out onto the ground from the open windows of the Fellowship Hall. She still hadn't actually been inside the building, which seemed similar to the main lodge—no surprise, since it was mainly used for church services that were held there on the weekends.

Her orientation packet had emphasized it was "suggested" she attended as many services as possible, but so far all she could stomach was a glance into the open doors a few times on her way from class to the North Shore. Thankfully, no one seemed to notice her absence.

The inside seemed nondescript, heavy with the empty silence only churches have, although this one didn't have stained glass windows. Growing up in the seaside town of Mystic, Adel's large Portuguese family was always the first through the doors for Mass every weekend and she remembered the intricate stained glass panels that filtered the sunlight into the sanctuary as they walked up the steps. The colored light fell onto her skin as the sun moved through the panes, painting it with warm, translucent color, as if trying to pull her into the story.

Adel reached down and took off her leather flip-flops, relishing the cold swirl of the lake water around her ankles. The sand squished between her toes, softened by the water moving across it in the darkness. As she neared the North Shore, she saw a flashlight flicker on and then disappear in the boathouse. She looked around her as she walked, unnerved. The gravity of what she was learning had suddenly deepened her awareness of what someone might do to protect those secrets.

Adel slowed as she neared the boathouse, slowly pushing the door open into complete darkness, then stepped in and shut the door behind her. She felt the energy of another person and extended her hand slightly into the darkness, closing her eyes when her fingers brushed the fabric of Grace's blouse. She stilled, softening her hand against the center of Grace's chest, her breath rising and falling under the tips of Adel's fingers. Finally, she felt the warmth of Grace's hand over hers and heard a whisper so soft she wondered if she'd heard it at all.

"Let's get out of here." She paused, drawing in a shaky breath Adel felt swell under her palm. "The boat."

"I'll get it." Adel glanced out the window down the darkened beach as she spoke. "Stay here." She handed Grace the black hoodie she'd tucked under her arm. "I'll get it untied. Put this on and pull the hood over your head when you step out of the boathouse."

"But—"

"Grace." Adel paused and took a breath, brushing Grace's cheek with the tips of her fingers. "Just do it."

Adel slipped out the door and walked barefoot down the dock, the weathered boards smooth and soundless under her feet. She untied the boat quickly and looked up just as Grace was leaving the boathouse, almost invisible in the darkness with the hoodie zipped to her neck and pulled over the length of her blond hair. She walked quickly and silently to the boat, carrying her shoes, and slipped into the coxswain position at the rear, the same position she took when they taught together.

The water slipped silently around the oars they dipped in unison into the water, the strokes pulling them into the dark, moonless center of the lake. A swath of bats swooped over their heads from nowhere, and a single owl hooted from the grove of trees across the lake. They rowed in unison, even their breath perfectly together, until they reached an unoccupied island on the other side of the lake. It was lit only by the stars, too deep into the darkness to be visible to anyone watching from the main shore. Adel stepped onto a sandbar and dragged the boat to the shore, the grains grating underneath as the water slipped back into the lake without a sound.

Grace pushed back the hood of her jacket and shook out her hair, a flash of pale gold glinting into the pitch-black night. She stood there for just a moment, a slow smile forming underneath the hand she'd raised to her mouth.

"I can't believe I did that."

"I can't either, frankly." Adel smiled as she took off her jacket and spread it onto the sand beside her, motioning for Grace to sit. Grace hesitated and looked out over the black, glittering water with soft eyes, as if she were leaving something she'd never see again. Finally, she sat back into the sand that still held the warmth from the last of the evening sun. She scooped up a handful and watched it sift between her fingers before she turned to Adel.

"Why did you come to my cabin?"

Adel started to reply, then paused. She'd intended to tell Grace everything: who she was, why she was at Valley of Rubies, and the truth of what she thought might be going on behind the scenes. But as she'd started to speak, it occurred to her that she was assuming Grace would respond the way she would, the way most people would. But Grace wasn't most people. She was one of them. And if she went to Whittier, the entire undercover operation would be instantly shut down.

Adel paused, the silence stretching out between them like a silvery spiderweb at breaking point. The air was cooling at the speed of darkness and held the sharp scent of split pine. She took a deep breath of it and looked over at Grace, her face glazed by the scattered light of stars.

"Do you remember the first weekend I was here? There was an event that Saturday night?"

Grace nodded, still looking out over the water.

"What was that? It looked like a wedding or something."

Her eyes dropped before she looked over at Adel, and when she spoke, her voice was flat, as muted as if she were speaking from behind a wall.

"That was the Purity Ball." She pulled her toes back from the edge of the water and wrapped her arms around her knees. "It happens every summer."

Adel nodded, willing the sinking feeling she felt in the pit of her stomach not to show on her face. "What's it all about? It looked like a pretty big deal."

"It is. Girls look forward to it for years." She hugged her knees tighter and looked down. "They wear beautiful white dresses and take vows to remain completely pure until marriage. Their fathers also take a vow to safeguard their daughter's purity until she's given by him to her husband on her wedding day. It's a rite of passage, I guess."

"Let me get this straight." Adel paused, her voice low and controlled. "What you're saying is that this is a ceremony to announce that the fathers 'own' their daughters' virginity until the day they transfer that ownership to another man?"

"Yeah." Grace glanced up, meeting Adel's eyes. "I guess that's one way to put it."

"So the girls never get to make their own choices?" Adel shook her head, looking out over the water and then back to Grace. "What if she decides not to get married? Or if she thinks she might be gay?"

"Gay is not an option." Grace's voice started to fray at the edges. "For anyone."

She looked up after a moment to watch a golden lapwing skim the black surface of the water, then turned to Adel. "Why do you want to know all this?"

Adel lay back on the sand and put her arms behind her head. "I guess I just missed the whole thing because I'd just gotten here, so I've always wondered what the big deal was."

"Yeah." Grace wound her hair up into a bun. A single blond wave escaped and fell across her cheek, shifting slightly in the breeze. "Until a few years ago, a few girls from every ball were chosen to stay at camp after the ceremony. Supposedly it's an honor to be chosen, but they stopped doing it after…" Grace's voice trailed off and she looked up at the sky. "Something happened a couple of years ago." She lowered her eyes, trailing her fingers over the sand. "I was chosen after mine, but...I got lucky."

Adel followed her eyes and softened her voice. "So, what's up with the program director not attending the ball this year?"

Grace nodded, picking up a pebble and threw it into the water. It pierced the surface and the ripples unfolded on the water until they disappeared into the darkness.

"I didn't have that option."

"Why not?"

Grace shook her head and looked up again. This time, Adel could see the tears gathering in the corners of her eyes. "Apparently, because I'm twenty-six and still unmarried, I'm no longer a positive example for the girls."

"That makes no sense." Adel hesitated, choosing her words carefully. "But either way, aren't these girls way too young to be thinking about marriage? I mean, some of the girls in my class don't look anywhere close to the ages listed for them on the roster."

"That's because they're not." Grace laughed without smiling, her eyes fixed on the sheer wash of steam just starting to rise off the surface of the lake as the air cooled around it. "But it doesn't matter. We get married when the Prophet decides we get married." Her voice trailed off and she paused, her eyes following a silent white heron as it dipped dramatically toward the surface of the water, then disappeared smoothly into the distance. "I've just gotten lucky so far. Until a few weeks ago, anyway. I'm engaged now, not that it seems to make any difference to Whittier. She told me yesterday to go home this weekend and 'think about my walk with the Lord.'"

"She seems to have it in for anyone with a mind of their own around here."

Grace picked up a stick wedged between two rocks on the sand and peeled the bark off slowly, pausing to scrape every dark scrap from the pale, soft wood.

"A few years ago, there were rumors about two of the counselors that had..." Her voice trailed off and she looked over the water toward camp.

"More than a friendship?"

Grace's eyes didn't waver. "Yeah, or something that was heading in that direction. But it didn't matter. We didn't have the courage to fight back."

Adel watched her face, holding space between them for Grace to fill with the memories that had started to show on her face. Her forehead creased and she shook her head, her fingers white and tense around the bare stick in her hand.

"What happened?"

The stick broke suddenly into a jagged edge that pierced Grace's palm, and Adel watched the blood drain from her face and then from her hand, the drops beading up, slick and dark, until they sank silently into the sand.

Adel slowed her breathing and softened her voice, then reached for Grace's hand.

"No." The word was stark and staccato as it echoed off the water. "Don't touch me."

Adel slowly pulled her hand back and nodded, watching the blood drip down Grace's palm, willing it to slow and blacken. She wanted to strip her jacket off and wrap it around her hand, to pull Grace into her arms and tell her everything would be all right, to force her to believe it. Adel's body tensed against the urge to minimize, to smooth the splintering edges of that memory, to stop the dark red slick of trauma sliding off Grace's fingers and into the sand. But she knew that wasn't the way it worked, and it was enough that Grace was talking.

Grace closed her eyes and emptied all the air from her lungs. When she finally spoke, her eyes were shut tight, lashes dark and wet with tears.

"You must think I'm crazy."

When she answered, Adel's voice was as steady and constant as the lap of lake water on the shore.

"No." She paused, choosing every word slowly and deliberately, knowing they would be etched across that memory forever. "I don't think that at all." She paused as Grace's eyes fluttered open in the violet darkness. "I think you're having a really normal reaction to a fucked-up situation. Someday you'll surprise yourself with how much courage you already have."

Grace looked out over the water. "Do you really mean that?"

"Yeah. I do."

Adel also looked out at the water and forced herself to stop talking, to consciously hold that space for Grace. Over the past few weeks, as she'd read the girls' journal entries, she'd started to see patterns. Some of them, specifically the youngest girls, wrote dreamy entries about their future marriage and families, and some wrote of frustrations at home, which was predictable. But the ones who wrote stories instead of journal entries, the ones that wrote so hard the pen almost penetrated the paper, those were starting to paint a collective picture that was very, very real.

Grace looked up at the sky again, then and lay back into the sand next to Adel, her bloody hand over her heart.

"Grace, someday you'll do something that makes you realize how much courage you have, and to quote someone famous, with great courage comes...transformative power." Adel paused, her voice lightening to a teasing tone. "But if you wanted to get out of rowing that bad, you could have just asked me. Geez."

Adel looked over to her and waited until a smile lifted the corners of Grace's mouth, then she leaned up on one elbow. "I have an idea."

Grace's hair was pooled around her head, the wind picking up just a few strands and lightly draping them across her forehead. She shifted toward Adel and bit her lip, the clear, sky blue of her eyes pale and luminous even in the darkness. "Tell me."

"Every year, my family picks a weekend and we all stay at our summer house on the beach in Connecticut. I promised one of my brothers I'd go this year."

Grace smiled. "One of them? How many do you have?"

"I'm the oldest of five kids, so I have four younger brothers. Two of them still live at home, but the two oldest have moved out. One of them has three kids of his own now, so it's a full house when we all get together."

Grace pulled her hoodie around her and zipped it up, then leaned up on her elbow to face Adel. "That sounds beautiful." She traced the shape of the crescent moon into the sand between them and shook her head. "I want to see the ocean someday. I've wanted to since I was a kid, but—"

"Come with me."

Grace stopped, her eyes locked on Adel. "What do you mean?"

"Come with me this weekend. You haven't told your parents you're coming home, so they're not expecting you, and Whittier already expects you to be gone. Tomorrow's Friday, so you can come with me and leave early tomorrow morning. It's the perfect opportunity to get the hell out of here for a couple of days."

Grace shook her head again, before Adel had even stopped talking.

"I can't. I could never do something like that…just go to another state I've never been to? Besides, I don't even know your family."

"Well, let me see if I can sum it up." Adel paused for effect until she saw Grace smile out of the corner of her eye. "My mother is literally a saint, my brothers are obnoxious but I adore them, and there are wild kids that I'm not even sure I'm related to *constantly* darting around everywhere. That's about all there is to know, the rest you'd have to learn on the fly."

"What about your dad?"

"My dad died three years ago of cancer." Adel traced a star into the sand beside the crescent moon with the tip of her finger. "I haven't been home since."

Grace met her eyes then pulled her close, her voice warm against Adel's cheek as she let her go. "I'm so sorry."

Adel brushed a tear away with the heel of her hand, her eyes fixed on the emerging drawing in the sand. "Jesus, I don't know why I'm crying about it now. It was years ago."

"I do." Grace traced the outline of the cut on her palm with the tip of her finger. "People always tell you that time is the great healer, that it will get easier…" Her voice faded. "But people lie. It doesn't get easier. It just gets farther away."

Grace looked up at Adel with soft eyes and waited, her gaze returning to the drawing when Adel spoke.

"My brothers are all close to Mom, so they've stepped in and taken over everything she can't do, but still, I should have been home by now."

"Yeah, but it's not that easy. I know." The wind picked up suddenly and shifted the tops of the trees above them, but Adel didn't look up as Grace continued, her voice as soft as her gaze. "You're going now. That's all that counts."

Grace threw a stone into the water at their feet, then fell silent, her eyes focused on the amber lights of the lodge across the lake and their wavering reflection in the dark water below. "Thank you."

Adel turned to look at Grace. "For what?"

Adel's gaze shifted to Grace's mouth, then slowly returned but Grace never answered, just stood and held out her hand to pull her up. They slipped their boat back into the water, the oars disappearing as silent as thought into the dark, endless water.

❖

Once they'd docked the boat and walked through the woods back to the cabins, Adel held out her hand to let Grace know to stay behind her and out of the reach of the lights set on poles around the cabin path. Adel stepped up to each and silently unscrewed the bulbs as they walked, keeping Grace far enough behind her to ensure she wouldn't step into the light. After she'd gotten to her own cabin and unlocked the door, she motioned Grace in and locked it behind her. Grace leaned back against the door in the darkness, her fingertips light on Adel's shoulders as Adel fought the insane urge to kiss her. Instead, she leaned close, inhaling the warmth of her skin as Grace turned her face toward Adel, her lips brushing the delicate skin just under her ear.

Then she turned, locking eyes with Adel for just a moment before she stepped out and closed the door softly behind her. Adel raked her hand through her hair and fell backward on the bed, reaching for her journal on the nightstand.

It's time to tell Grace that I'm really here as a reporter. Past time.

Adel's fingers tightened around her pen.

But isn't it my job to gather information and expose secrets?
I can get more from Grace than I could ever uncover myself. But that makes me...worse than them.
Maybe I always was.

Chapter Nine

Adel left before sunrise the next morning, slipping a note under Grace's cabin door as she headed to the airport. Her eight o'clock flight to Mystic was inexplicably canceled, so by the time she got on the next available flight it was midafternoon. When she finally got to Connecticut, she picked up her black rental Jeep and tossed her bags in the back, connecting her phone to the music system with one hand as she drove toward town, the warm salt breeze sifting through her hair as the road disappeared behind her.

The sun shimmered low and gold over the ocean as she drove through the center of town, which looked exactly the same as the last time she'd seen it. Walker's bakery was just turning over the *Open* sign on the door as she passed, pink-and-white-striped awning fluttering in the breeze. No one had ever been able to figure out why the front windows always had mysterious flour streaks across them, but even those were still there. Her favorite open-air seafood market wedged into an alley off Main Street still had a line wrapped around the side of the nearest building as well, and one of the fishmongers flopped a wet fish into a hanging scale as she passed. Only the diner where she'd worked in high school seemed to have gotten a new coat of paint, but that was about it as far as progress.

Tourism and fishing were the main industries in Mystic, and almost everyone she knew had started working in one or the other the summer after high school. Despite being a destination for the New York elite "summer people," as everyone called them, the backbone of the town was Portuguese immigrant families, some first generation like Adel's family, but almost all were blue-collar workers whose families struggled when the rich white tourists left the coast in the fall and went back to their glittering cocktail parties in Manhattan.

Main Street ended quickly with a blur of whitewashed coastal vacation homes that lined the edge of town, accented by postcard-worthy identical American flags hung over freshly painted white porch rails. She drew the sea air into her lungs and held it as she drove toward the docks, smiling despite herself as the colorful houses of her neighborhood came into view. Vivid shades of aqua, orange, and pink paint lit up the houses lining the narrow streets, crowded with laughing children, most of whom were armed with water hoses and clearly knew how to use them. Fairy lights glittered in trees over mismatched, scattered chairs, and statues of the sacred Virgin Mary adorned almost every small, square front lawn. Adel slowed the Jeep almost to a stop and rolled down her windows to listen to a trio of men playing *guitarras portuguesas* on one of the porches, their worn felt fedoras leaned together, undulating with the music, fingers flying over steel guitar strings as rich traditional Portuguese fado music unfurled as a backdrop for the evening.

She realized suddenly as the ocean came into view that she'd missed the scent of wet salt and ocean foam always in the air, even the clanging sails of the fishing boats that ricocheted off the waves as they returned to the docks. Most of the boats had reached the dock slips with the day's catch by the time she passed them, and the cleaning and sorting stations were jostling with second-shift workers, mostly women, who cleaned and culled as the oysters and lobsters were unloaded from the ship decks. The stations were really just long wooden tables under a salt-rusted tin roof, surrounded by sorting buckets and the laughter of women, most of whom had worked together at the cold edge of the sea for decades.

When she was in school, she used to sit at the top of the stairs in her house and watch as her mom made lunches for her and her brothers before dawn. She laid them out on the dining table, always in the same even row, with their names written on the top of each folded-over paper bag. They rarely saw her in the morning; she'd worked the first shift for as long as Adel could remember. By dawn she was at the docks in her wool fisherman's sweaters tucked under a waxed canvas coat, fighting the driving wind and rain that whipped off the surface of the sea, laughing with her friends while they waited for the first catch to come in from the overnight boats.

She was sixty-three now. Adel's stomach twisted as she neared her home and she tried to piece together an explanation for why she hadn't been home since her dad died. She'd meant to, but she'd been the closest to her dad, and she knew she couldn't deal with the grief unless it was at a distance. Her heart pounded as she pulled onto her street and into the driveway of 311 Heron Way.

The three-story gray clapboard house looked as if time had tilted it—the porch railing had been painted bright tangerine since the last time she was home, and the brass door knocker had been replaced with a shinier model. The porch looked both lived-in and loved, home to both American and Portuguese flags, with a weathered navy-blue door and peeling trim. The lawn was small but well maintained thanks to her brothers, and as Adel slung her leather duffel bag over her shoulder, the smell of her favorite dessert bread, pão de Deus, drifted seductively from the direction of the house.

She stopped and closed her eyes when she reached the stairs, giving herself just a few more seconds to pull together the answers that didn't exist, then drew in a slow breath and turned to look over the calm surface of the ocean, streaked with the deepening, fiery hues of sunset. The wind lifted the edges of her hair and wrapped the scent of evening and salt water around her. The rush of sadness she'd expected had yet to appear, and the longer she looked at the sea, the more her apprehension melted into peace.

She heard the door open before she could turn around, then the sound of her bag dropping to her feet as she felt her mother's arms around her. Adel closed her eyes, breathing in the familiar, swirling scents of home, the sea, and life she'd tried to forget. When she finally stepped back to explain, her face was wet with tears and she watched the few words she managed to string together scatter and disappear with the wind.

"My baby." Her mother took Adel's face gently in her hands, her gaze soft and constant. "Don't apologize for taking the time you need to heal. I know you. You're my heart." Her familiar, faded accent warmed the air and smoothed the rough edges of Adel's memories. She smiled, wiping a tear from Adel's cheek with her thumb. "Welcome home."

Adel hugged her tight one more time, and then again, and finally dried her cheek with the back of her hand as she picked up her bag.

"Ma!" An impatient voice started in the kitchen and burst into the hall, followed by Carlos, her youngest brother. "How long till dinner? I'm dyin' here!"

He tilted his head to the side as Adel came up the stairs, taking her bag as he bumped her shoulder affectionately with his as they walked in.

"'Bout time you finally showed up." Carlos shot her a wink as they walked through the narrow entry hall to the stairs, school pictures lining every available space on the walls. "Although the least you could have done was bring me a date. I need a city girl. I've already gone through all Antonio's exes and shown them how it's really done. Didn't take long."

Adel's brother Antonio rounded the corner and loped down the stairs as they started up them, stealing Carlos's baseball cap from his head as he skipped the last three steps and turned around in the hall.

"Hey, Delly, long time no see." Antonio smiled warmly at his sister, then winked at Carlos, still holding Adel's bag and halfway up the steps. "Thanks for the cap, man. Your girlfriend likes it on me."

Carlos's eyes narrowed. "You better not be talking about Rosie, asshat, or I swear to God I'll—"

"He's winding you up, you idiot." Adel took her bag off his shoulders and nodded down the stairs. "But on second thought, this *is* Antonio we're talking about, so maybe you should make sure."

Carlos rolled his eyes and bounded down the stairs, shouting over his shoulder as he rounded the corner of the door. "Oh yeah, Ma set up your old room as a nursery, so we chucked all your stuff in the attic."

"She turned it into a what-?"

Adel's mother emerged from the other side of the swinging kitchen door just as he disappeared and reached up to hand Adel a thick slice of pão de Deus, delicate brioche baked around creamy coconut custard and flecked with the bright freshness of lemon zest. There was something different about her, something Adel couldn't quite put her finger on, but she was swiftly distracted as she reached out for the slice her mother was holding in a worn linen napkin.

"Oh, my God, Ma..." Adel bit into the bread, still warm from the oven, and closed her eyes as the rich rum-soaked custard literally melted in her mouth. "You have no idea how much I've missed this. No one in New York knows how to make this right!"

"That's because there are no real bakeries in New York." Her mom wiped her hands on her faded floral apron and sniffed, arching an eyebrow. "You can't just slap 'Portuguese' on the sign out front and expect people to think it's the real thing."

Adel laughed, and as her mother turned to go back into the kitchen, she looked over her shoulder at her daughter. "By the way, I put a bottle of Lourinha brandy by the bed in the attic. You might want to have a sip before you come down to dinner." She smiled. "Should be an interesting one."

By the time Adel opened her mouth to ask why, her mother had slipped back into the kitchen, her favorite Gipsy Kings album spinning at full volume on the other side of the door.

❖

After Adel had climbed the three stories to the attic, unpacked her bag, and found her bed amid all the boxes and old furniture, all she could do was collapse onto it and stare at the rafters. Someone had tried to make the space pretty, despite being shoved under the narrow wooden stairs leading up to the widow's walk in the corner of the attic. The bed was made up with clean linens and a fluffy pinstripe duvet, and a small antique milk bottle filled with bluebells and baby's breath brightened an antique whitewashed nightstand.

Sheer dust hung in the air between the unfinished rafters, and the sounds of family below suddenly seemed muffled and far away. Adel's muscles unfolded and sank slowly into the bed. Her fingertips found the phone tucked into the pocket of her jacket. She pulled it out and put it to her ear, her heart rate doubling with every ring.

"What the fuck, Adel?"

A long silence hung in the air with the fading amber sunlight streaming through the stained glass window at the apex of the roof. Adel put the phone beside her and hit the speaker.

"Katya, I'm sorry, I've had a lot going on here."

"*You* have a lot going on?" Katya spat out the words, then paused and took a measured breath. "I realize you're writing an article or whatever, but have you forgotten that the *elections* are coming up? We need to do this wedding thing before it gets too close and it looks like I'm just doing this for my image."

"Katya, tell me the truth." Adel paused, her fingers rubbing her forehead, trying to loosen the grip of the headache threatening to take hold. "Are you doing this for you?" Adel felt sudden tears burn the back of her eyes, and she fought to keep her voice steady. "Or for us? Do you even want this relationship?"

"Babe, you know I'm focused on my campaign right now."

Katya's voice softened, and Adel heard her run her hand through her hair. "I have to be focused on the election. I don't have a choice at the moment. Not if I want to win."

Adel closed her eyes, her heart turning to stone in the center of her chest. "You didn't answer my question."

Katya sighed in frustration, and Adel realized suddenly Katya *had* answered. She'd answered that question several times over the last few months, Adel just hadn't been listening. She hung up softly and closed her eyes, not bothering to wipe away the tears that slipped down her cheeks.

Adel was still lying on the bed when she heard Antonio fling open the door to the attic and bellow up the stairs that dinner was almost ready. She forced herself to get up and pull her hair into a quick ponytail, then change into her black skinny jeans, a crisp white tee, and a denim shirt. A slick of lip balm as she walked down the stairs and she was ready for whatever her mother meant by "interesting."

When she got to the bottom of the stairs and pushed open the door, it unexpectedly flung back in her face and she fell backward onto the stairs. Her brother Nico cautiously opened it again and offered his hand to pull her up.

"Damn, Delly. Sorry about that. Nina's pregnant again, and that door was between her and the bathroom."

Adel smiled and closed it behind her, reaching up to hug her brother as two of his daughters raced past on the way to the kitchen. Nico and his wife Nina already had two girls and a boy and, apparently, another on the way.

"No worries." Adel glanced down the hall toward the bathroom. "Does she need anything?"

"Yeah, she needs me to stop knocking her up." Nico grinned and dropped his voice. "Speaking of which, have you talked to Marco yet?"

Their brother Marco was a few years younger than Nico, but over the years they'd built the most successful construction company in town. Expensive vacation homes were always going up in Mystic, and everyone knew the Rosse brothers were the ones to go to if you wanted the job done right. As the years passed, money followed their success, and unlike Nico, who married his high school sweetheart and settled down early, Marco was known around town for his flashy single lifestyle and endless string of rich city girlfriends.

Adel looked up at her brother as she realized what he meant, and right on cue, the wail of a newborn baby cut through the silence. Adel's jaw dropped and she smacked him in the shoulder for emphasis.

"You've *got* to be shitting me with this."

"No, ma'am," Nico said, rolling up the sleeves of his shirt with a wink as he turned toward his girls speeding down the hall, this time followed closely by their younger brother. "And how many times do I have to say no running in the house? Go *upstairs*, ya heathens!"

Adel lowered her voice to a whisper and stepped out into the hall, looking toward the living room, where a baby was still screaming at an ever-increasing volume. "Who the hell is this girl, do we know her?"

"Um, no. Not before Marco got ahold of her, anyway." Nico shook his head, smiling over his shoulder as he started down the hall toward the bathroom to check on his wife. "Which didn't exactly surprise me. Let's just say she's not from this side of town."

Nico disappeared down the hall to check on Nina, and Adel walked into the kitchen just as her mother was trying to balance an enormous bubbling casserole and nudge the oven door closed with her foot at the same time.

"Ma, give that to me." Adel grabbed some oven mitts and held her hands out for the dish, then set it down on the nearest trivet and pulled the mitts off her hands. "Where is everybody? Why are you here getting dinner ready by yourself?"

"Because that's exactly how I want it." Her mother smiled, reaching for a glass from the top shelf of the cupboard. "You know as well as I do your brothers are useless. They'd just be under my feet in here."

Adel took the glass off the shelf and turned back around just in time to see a tall, elderly gentleman with a perfectly groomed wave of white hair come through the door in a rush.

"Maria, darling, what can I do to help?"

He stopped short when he saw her, and Adel looked at her mother, realizing suddenly what was different about her. She'd gotten a softer new hairstyle in place of the smooth bun Adel remembered, and had started wearing a bit of subtle makeup that took years off her face. She watched as her mother glanced at the gentleman and smiled, gesturing for him to come closer.

"Adel, I'd like you to meet my friend Sheldon."

Sheldon's face warmed instantly with a genuine smile as he shook Adel's hand while Maria reached for a slim dark bottle of port that she poured into a glass and held out for her daughter.

"Here, take this and go say hello to your new baby niece. They're in the living room."

Adel reached into the kitchen cabinet above the sink and found the Tylenol, shaking two into her hand. She downed them with the port, refilled her glass, and shook her head as she headed for the door.

"Keep that bottle handy, Ma. I'll be back."

She heard her mother through the kitchen door as it swung closed and rolled her eyes.

"No need, Sheldon will help me with dinner. You just go get acquainted."

Jesus Christ. She stopped short in the hall as the baby let out another ear-piercing wail. *Not one of my useless brothers thought to pick up the phone and give me a heads-up about this shitstorm?*

She leaned against the cool plaster wall, dropping her head back against the framed eight-by-ten portrait of her high school graduation. She was here, in Mystic, surrounded by more family than she knew what to do with, but all she could think about was the cool lap of lake water against the shore outside her cabin window, the scent of hay and silence in the sunlit stables...and Grace. She shook her head to clear it. After this weekend, she needed to shift her focus back to the article, get the fuck back to Manhattan, and get this girl out of her head.

Nico's heavy footsteps down the hall preceded the shove toward the living room she knew was coming. She attempted a swerve, but he was too quick for her and swiveled her back around in the right direction by the shoulder.

"Rip the Band-Aid off, sis. Let's go."

They rounded the corner of the living room together, and Nico introduced Adel to the woman sitting on the couch by Marco, which instantly set the baby off again. Marco got up and hugged his sister hard, then glanced back down with a look of pride Adel had never seen before.

"Adel, I want you to meet my wife, Amelia, and our daughter, Jasmine."

Adel smiled at Amelia and told her not to get up, which would have been impossible anyway. She had the baby against her shoulder by then and seemed trapped by the enormous baby bag between her feet and the coffee table. Nico wasted no time in asking Marco to look at something out in his truck and they sauntered out the door, leaving Amelia visibly uncomfortable. Adel made a mental note to smack Nico the second she caught him alone.

"Congratulations on the wedding, I just heard about it, actually." Adel set her glass on the coffee table and sat down on the couch. "So how did you and Marco meet?"

"Um…" She dug in the bag for a towel and put it between the baby and her shoulder. "He was doing some work for my parents in town and we just started hanging out, I guess."

Adel nodded. "Let me guess, you're not from Mystic?"

Amelia shook her head. She was expensively blond and sorority thin, with a perfect upturned nose and impossibly full lips that couldn't exist without the divine intervention of a plastic surgeon. Adel knew the answer to that question before she even asked. The fact that her playboy brother had settled down itself was shocking, but especially with a city girl who was clearly out of her element.

"So, when did you two get married?"

Jasmine hijacked the conversation with a hiccup and scared herself into another crying fit. Amelia shifted her to the other shoulder and looked out the window at her husband, who had mysteriously settled into a conversation with an open beer in his hand and a cooler at his feet.

"It was the week before the baby was born. It was just a courthouse thing. My parents didn't want to…" She hesitated, her voice faltering. "They didn't come. So it was just us and your mom."

Her eyes fell as she said the words and she looked away from Adel, who instantly softened and reached carefully for Jasmine. She knew how it felt to be judged for being from the wrong side of town with the wrong skin color; she couldn't imagine how it felt for Amelia to have her family ditch her on her wedding day because of it.

She held the baby up and smiled at her while she pretended not to notice Amelia using the towel on her shoulder to dab at her eyes. Jasmine stopped crying momentarily and peered down at Adel, then broke out into an unexpected smile, her eyes crinkling at the corners, her fat little baby cheeks still wet with tears.

"She likes you."

"Well, it's a miracle." Adel flashed her a smile and gave Jasmine a little bounce. "Nico's kids all hated me until they were about two, and I'm the godmother to every one of them."

"Well, she clearly doesn't feel like that." Amelia reached out and stroked Jasmine's curled fist. "But I don't think it's the same with me. I feel like a failure most of the time. All she ever does is cry." She shook her head and leaned back against the sofa. "She cried all night last night. I don't know what I'm doing wrong."

Adel leaned back with her and held Jasmine to her shoulder. "You're not doing anything wrong. Nina had the same problem with her first baby. I remember her telling me once she thought she was going crazy."

"That's exactly how I feel!" A sudden smile flashed across Amelia's face, then just as quickly faded. "I swear, I fell in love the second I saw her, but I don't even think she even likes me."

"How old is she, about six months?"

"Yeah, how did you know? She turned six months old last week."

Adel got up with Jasmine and walked over to the door frame that led to the hall, turning slightly so the couch was just out of Jasmine's line of sight.

"Tell me again how old she is?"

Amelia hesitated. "Six months?"

Adel turned slightly again. "One more time."

Amelia said it again and paused, confused.

"Did you see that?"

"See what?"

"She's looking for you." Adel turned back around and smiled. "She turned twice toward the sound of your voice when she couldn't see you."

"She did?" Amelia's voice cracked and she reached out for her daughter as Adel came back to the couch. "Sorry, I don't know why I'm so emotional. I guess..." Her voice trailed off and she kissed Jasmine softly on the cheek. "I just needed to hear that today."

Antonio and Marco stepped back into the hall, mid-conversation about the upcoming fantasy football draft, beers firmly in hand.

"Hey, Marco." Adel arched an eyebrow at her younger brother. "Amelia has Nina's number, right?"

"Hell, yeah."

Both he and Antonio heard their mother's voice in the hall and instantly necked the last of their beers with championship precision. Antonio grabbed both cans and headed back out to his truck while Maria announced loudly from the dining room that dinner was ready.

"I keep trying to get her to call Nina when she has questions, but she won't do it."

"I don't want to bother her." Amelia handed the baby to Marco and tucked the towel back into the baby bag. "I can imagine she's got enough on her plate."

"Are you kidding?" Nico said. "She's got three kids and another on the way. She's dying to talk to an actual adult."

Adel and Amelia got up from the couch to head to the dining room and Amelia laughed, tucking a lock of perfectly highlighted hair behind her ear. "Okay, I guess that's a good point."

"See? I'm telling ya, babe." Marco pulled her close and kissed her cheek. "She wants to help."

Adel nodded and winked at her brothers. "I'm not sure if this is good news or not considering these two, but you have a huge family now to help you, whether you want us or not."

"Yeah, but trust me, if I were you," Antonio said as he pulled out the chair for his sister and plopped down beside her, "I'd start running now and get a head start."

Adel started opening the bottles of wine her mother had already set out on the table, collecting the corks and dropping them into Antonio's lap over her shoulder. "Where are the kids?"

"Your mom put a picnic blanket over her bed and has them eating pizza in there." Nina fanned herself with her napkin and held her dark, glossy length of hair off her neck with her hand. "They're watching some Disney flick that's too complicated for your brothers to understand."

"Thank God," Nico said. "There's too many of our kids to count anymore. I love it when someone gets them all in the same room and it's not the room I'm in."

"Seriously," Antonio said, shaking out his napkin and tucking it into his shirt. "Where's Ma? I'm starvin' here."

Adel leaned back in her chair and peered down the hall toward the kitchen. "Dude, I'd go get her, but last time I was in there, I met her—"

"Boyfriend?" Nico pulled a piece of bread off one of the fresh loaves in the breadbasket wrapped in a red checkered cloth. Steam rose from the middle of the loaf as he pulled it apart, instantly scenting the air with creamy butter and fresh summer herbs. "We had to learn to say it, it's your turn now."

"Jesus." Adel poured an Oregon Pinot Noir into each glass, with the exception of Nina's, which already had ice water. "Thanks for the heads-up, by the way, dickhead."

"No prob." Nico winked at her as he finished his chunk of bread. "I just wish I could have been there."

"So." Adel sat down and ran her hand over her hair, picking up her wineglass and balancing it between her fingers. "What do you think of him...really?"

"I'll take this one, boys," Nina said, her hand sliding across her belly. "I'm guessing I have about two minutes before my next trip to the bathroom, so let's cut to the chase."

"This is why I love you, Nina." Adel winked at her and leaned forward on her elbows. "Hit me with the condensed version."

"He's a widower, owns his own real estate agency, he's richer than shit and adores your mother. He's been nothing but respectful to everyone and has the good sense to tread lightly around your brothers."

Adel nodded, trying to speak past the sudden lump in her throat. "Do you get a good feeling about him?"

"I do." Nina nodded, her eyes soft. "And you know I'd be the first one to tell you if I didn't."

Adel looked around at her brothers, who each nodded in their own way. It was surreal to see her mom with someone else, but even Adel had to admit she looked happy. And if anyone deserved that, it was her mother.

"Okay." She smoothed her hand down the back of her neck, kneading the concrete knots that spanned her shoulders. "That's good enough for me."

The doorbell rang just as her mother and Sheldon rounded the corner carrying a steaming beef pot roast and heaping bowls of potatoes and roast vegetables. Carlos got up to answer it as Adel and Nina took the dishes and set them out on the table.

He returned a few seconds later and plunked down in his seat, reaching for the mashed potatoes with a look of pure bliss. He looked up after a moment when he realized no one was speaking, his mouth stuffed full of potatoes.

"What?"

"Dude." Nico shot him a look and nodded toward the hall. "Who was at the door?"

"Oh yeah." Carlos took a sip of wine and nodded across the table. "Someone for Adel."

Adel pushed away from the table and headed for the door, delivering a sound thump on Carlos's head as she passed him.

Truth be told, it was good to get a few seconds alone. She was happy for her mom, but seeing another man with her at the dinner table was tougher than she was prepared for. At least sober, anyway.

She stopped just outside the dining room and took a deep breath, then opened her eyes and looked toward the door. Through the inset window she saw Grace, the wind blowing her hair around her shoulders like a snapshot from the first day they met.

Chapter Ten

"I can't believe you came." Adel pulled Grace into her arms and breathed in the familiar scent of her hair, like soap and faint tea rose, realizing suddenly she'd held her a second too long. "How did you get here?"

"Maybe I shouldn't have." Grace stepped back and looked nervously at the overnight bag at her feet. It was a moment before she spoke again. "It's just…" She twisted the small silver watch on her wrist. "I read the note you put under my door this morning, and you said if I changed my mind that I was still invited."

"Grace." Adel stepped closer and held her eyes until she smiled. "You have no idea how glad I am that you're here."

"Good." Grace smiled up at Adel and rubbed her hands together. "Because it's getting cold out here."

"Oh, my God, I'm worse than my idiot brother. I forgot to even invite you in." Adel laughed and opened the door again, noticing Grace's camp vehicle in the driveway as she picked up her bag. "You drove all the way here?"

Grace nodded, glancing back at the car with the Valley of Rubies logo on the door. "It was only four hours. Hopefully they'll assume I just drove the car to the airport."

They stepped into the hall and Adel set her bag just inside the living room door. She grimaced, glancing back at the dining room.

"I wish I had more time to prepare you for my family." She paused, her head spinning. "A good rule of thumb to start with is not to believe a word my brothers tell you."

Grace laughed as Adel led her into the dining room, where conversation that had been at full volume just a minute before stopped abruptly, sudden silence echoing in the room.

"Everyone, this is my friend Grace." Adel arched an eyebrow at her family in an attempt to quell the looks that ricocheted around the table. "Nico probably told you I'm teaching a writing course at a camp upstate this summer, and Grace works there as the program director."

Maria was the first to regain her manners and got up from the table with a warm smile. "I'm so happy to meet you, Grace." She gave her a quick hug on the way to the door. "I'm just going to go get another place setting while Antonio grabs you a chair."

Antonio rolled his eyes, pulled one of the extra dining chairs up to the table beside Adel's seat, and elbowed Carlos. "Shove over, loser."

Carlos scooted over to make room, still shoveling mashed potatoes into his mouth with impressive speed.

They settled into their seats as Adel introduced everyone, trying not to notice Carlos and Antonio checking Grace out. Her mother returned to the dining room with the extra place setting, and while she laid it out and chatted to Grace, Adel took out her phone and quickly sent a group text to her brothers.

Hands off Grace, and whatever you do, do NOT ask if we're together. I'll explain later.

By the time she'd slipped her phone back in her pocket, their phones pinged and all four took them out to read her text.

"So," Antonio said, the first to drop his phone back down his shirt pocket as he passed his plate to Nico, who had started carving the pot roast. "How long have you been dating my sister?"

Grace froze, but then Carlos laughed so hard he snorted, which was impossible not to laugh at. In just a few seconds, somehow her dumbass little brother had the entire table smiling and relaxed, including Grace. Even baby Jasmine was smiling and banging her little chubby fist on her high chair.

"So I haven't asked," Adel said, accepting her plate back from Nico, who had piled it high with pot roast. "Why are we here instead of the summer house? We always do this on the beach."

Nico shook his head. "Not since mice got into the main electrical panel in the summer house last week and chewed up all the damn wiring."

Maria nodded, feeding Jasmine a tiny bite of potato from her plate, which she promptly spit back out. "Sheldon had some electricians come out, but they said the damage was too extensive to fix in time for the weekend."

"Yeah, that's putting it lightly." Marco passed the bread to Amelia.

"I went and checked on it when Ma said the lights weren't coming on, and it looked like someone had been in there with a wood chipper. Even the door it was behind had little teeth marks in it."

"You're welcome to go out there tomorrow," Maria said. "But it would be a bit dark at night without any lights."

Nina poured wine into the wineglass she wasn't using and passed it across the table to Grace. "So, Grace, I know you're working at camp this summer, but where do you live the rest of the year?"

"My family lives in Arkansas." Grace glanced down at her plate and her smile had faded by the time she looked up. "But I look forward to camp all year. And it's been great having Adel to help the girls with the rowing class."

Carlos had slowed his pace with the potatoes and moved on to the roast, but paused to look down the table at Grace, fork in hand, dripping gravy onto the edge of his plate. "It's an all-girls camp? Because—"

Grace nodded as Adel gave Carlos a withering look. "Do *not* finish that sentence or I swear to God I'll dump that gravy boat on your head."

"What?" Carlos said with a quick wink across the table at his brothers, muttering under his breath. "I'm just saying. It's a target-rich environment."

"Hey, Grace."

It was Antonio's turn to get involved again, apparently. Adel was starting to feel like she was playing a rigged game of Whac-a-Mole at a twisted county fair.

"Did you know that Adel here used to have a mullet her freshman year? We've got pictures, I'll get them out after dinner."

Nico nodded and popped the last of his bread into his mouth. "Wasn't that the same year she had braces? I swear, those things were so big it was like they crammed three sets in there or something."

"Yep," Antonio chimed in around the bread he'd just wedged into his mouth. "More like box springs than braces. True story."

Adel sat back in her chair and sighed, trading her empty wineglass for her brother's full one and making a mental note to listen the next time her mother suggested a drink before dinner.

❖

By the end of the evening, Grace's cheeks ached from laughing—at least until Nico picked up her bag and headed toward the stairs, tossing casually over his shoulder that unless she wanted to sleep in a crib, she'd have to share with Adel in the attic.

The living room gradually emptied as Nina and Amelia went to put the kids to bed, then Carlos and Antonio left, saying something about a party and reeking of the same aftershave. The front door slammed shut and the boys revved up the truck outside. Suddenly, it was just her and Adel with the old house settling around them.

"Don't worry," Adel whispered, her dark eyes as soft as her voice in the empty room. "I'll show you where everything is, but then I'll come back down and sleep on the couch." She slid her hair out of its ponytail, and as her hair fell around her face, Grace's gaze dropped to Adel's mouth until she saw her smile.

She stood up from the couch, extending her hand to Grace. "Let's go, you've got to be exhausted from today."

Adel gave Grace a short tour of the house, then led her up to the third floor and showed her the bathroom and the door to the attic staircase.

"Oh, no." Grace paused, biting her lip.

"What?"

"I just remembered I didn't bring anything to sleep in, just clothes for tomorrow."

Adel smiled, raking her hand through her hair. "I think I can handle that. What do you usually sleep in?"

"A long-sleeved nightgown, I guess."

Adel laughed, shaking her head. "I mean, I can check with the guys, but I think it's pretty safe to say those are scarce around here." She paused, looking into Grace's eyes. "Let me put it this way. What do you wish you could sleep in?"

"You know what you gave me at your cabin?"

Adel nodded.

"Something like that."

"Done." Adel paused at the stairs, something intense in her eyes as if just her gaze pulled Grace closer. It hung in the air between them, and then in an instant, it was gone. Adel took a step back and ran her hand through her hair. "I'll just put them on the bed in the attic."

A few minutes later, Grace climbed the stairs to find a pair of flannel pajama pants and a white T-shirt neatly folded on the bed. She changed quickly, switching on the tiny stained glass lamp on the makeshift nightstand. The fairy lights twinkled into the darkness, but it wasn't enough to illuminate the boxes and old furniture that she'd seen as she walked in. Once she'd turned off the bare overhead bulb, the space felt as if she were in a play, waiting alone on a dusty stage for something to happen.

She heard Adel as she came up the stairs, although she knocked before she actually rounded the corner into the attic. She was in sweats and a hoodie, carrying two jackets over her arm.

"What are those for?"

Adel motioned for Grace to follow her through a narrow door in the corner of the attic, then into another short staircase, this one completely dark. The wind scraped loudly around the outside corners of the house, but the air within the staircase seemed dense, still, full of anticipation.

When Adel opened the door, the scent of ice and ocean rushed past her and the entire night sky unfolded like a bolt of navy silk. Cold salt wind sifted through Grace's hair, pressing the clothes tight against her from every direction. Adel took her hand and they stepped out onto a narrow balcony with a turned wood railing, the moon luminous and close above them, as if hanging there from a silver thread.

"What is…" Grace hesitated, standing on tiptoe to peer the more than three stories to the ground. "Where are we?"

Adel took the jacket out of her hands and held it open for Grace to slip into. "This is called a widow's walk."

The sea brushed Adel's face with undulating light as she turned to look out over the choppy silver surface of the sea. Angry clouds hovered low and dense over the water, and the scent of fresh rain hung in the air.

"A lot of old New England homes have them. Wives who'd lost husbands at sea spent long nights on these balconies, searching the ocean for a glimpse of their husband's ships." Adel leaned on the railing, the moon glossing the edge of her face. "The legend is that their ghosts returned after they died to walk the same planks, still searching for their lost loves."

"That…" Grace turned back toward the sea and gripped the railing, the wind whipping her hair back from her face. "Is the most romantic thing I've ever heard." She ran her fingers along the surface of the railing, the salt crystals from years of ocean mist rough under her fingertips.

"I know everyone wonders why I'm not married yet."

Adel stepped behind her, and Grace leaned back into the warmth of her body. "And why aren't you?" Adel's arms came around her and held her back from the wind sweeping in off the water.

"I guess I was waiting for someone that would…make me feel like that." She gazed out at the surface of the sea, then looked up at Adel, the clear blue of her eyes still like the summer sky in the darkness. "Someone I loved so much that if I lost him, I would still look for him forever."

Adel turned Grace around to face her, her eyes dark and intense.

"And have you ever come close?"

Grace shook her head, tucking a windswept lock of hair behind her ear.

Adel slid her hand behind Grace's neck, the warmth of her touch melting into Grace's skin, as light as air. Suddenly the only sound was their breath, warming the air between them as Adel looked into her eyes, stroking Grace's cheek lightly with her thumb. When she spoke, her voice was as soft as thought.

"Are you sure the person you're looking for is a *him*?"

Grace hesitated, then shook her head, closing her eyes against the burn of tears behind her eyelids.

"I can't…" She opened her eyes when she felt Adel wipe a tear from her cheek with her thumb. When the words finally came, the wind whipped them from her mouth as if it knew how dangerous they were on the outside. "That's not an option for me."

Adel looked over her head out to the sea, muscles flexing repeatedly in her jaw. She was silent for a long moment, then took Grace's face in both her hands, her eyes dark and intense.

"Grace, I know you don't believe this, but you deserve to be free to love who you love. Period."

She hesitated, then kissed Grace's forehead and pulled her into her arms, wrapping the sides of her own jacket around Grace, who relaxed into her warmth and closed her eyes the second before the first raindrop splashed onto the center of her head.

Adel looked up at the clouds the color of dark steel taking over the sky, already partially shadowing the moon. "Did you feel that?"

A booming clap of thunder answered her question, and she led Grace back into the dark staircase, heavy with the scent of dust and old varnish. The wind blew the door shut with a sharp crack and Adel locked it behind them, following Grace back down the staircase under the heavy raw beams of the attic roof. A jagged flash of lightning arced across the arched windows and illuminated the room as they stepped in, fairy lights twinkling into the darkness above it.

"I'll get you another comforter." Adel glanced through the windows and headed for the door. "With the storm, the temperature may drop lower than usual tonight."

Grace listened to her footsteps as she went downstairs, then looked into the shadowy mirror of an old armoire by the door. Her hair was windswept and her cheeks flushed, although not from the cold. She felt something building, something shifting inside her, as her life had soundlessly shattered into pieces around her feet and it was up to her to put it back together. She shrugged off Adel's jacket and hung it on the mirror, covering her reflection.

"Sometimes," Grace whispered into the darkness beyond the stage, "the whole point is to shatter the pieces so tiny they can't be put back together."

❖

She was still on the bed a few minutes later, her hair falling in loose waves to her waist when Adel bounded up the stairs, comforter slung over her shoulder and a bottle of water in her hand. She stopped short on the top step, then looked up at the rafters and raked her hand through her hair.

"What?"

"Nothing." Adel paused, then shook her head as she walked to the bed and laid the down comforter across the end. "I've just never seen your hair loose like that. You look…" She hesitated. "Beautiful. Too beautiful."

She walked slowly closer and set the bottle of water down on the nightstand. "You've never worn makeup, have you?"

"No." Grace touched her cheek with light fingertips. "They don't let us."

"I love it." Adel sat on the bed, her eyes dropping to Grace's lips. "It was one of the first things I noticed about you the day we met."

"What did you notice?"

"Everything." Adel paused. "Those eyes, the color of sunlit seawater. How delicate your fingers were when you were twisting that straw around them. Even the scent of the vanilla ChapStick you had on."

"How did you know that? It's the only kind I wear."

"It's not often I see someone that catches my eye." Adel smiled. "So when that happens, I tend to pay attention."

Grace held Adel's gaze for a long moment, waiting for her next words. But Adel just moved to the dresser, almost hidden among the night shadows of the attic, and picked up the dark bottle on the top.

"You know that wine you had in my cabin at camp?" Adel got up from the bed, filling a glass halfway and handing it to Grace as she walked back to the bed.

"This is Portuguese Lourinha brandy, my mother's favorite. She always leaves it up here for me." She smiled as Grace put it to her nose and made a face. "Brandy is distilled from wine, like what you had before, but it's much stronger, so just sip it."

Grace looked into the glass. "What does it taste like?"

Adel dipped her ring finger in the glass. She glossed Grace's lips slowly with the sweet amber brandy, stopping only when Grace's eyes closed.

"Taste it and see."

Grace ran her tongue over her bottom lip, opening her eyes to watch as Adel put her finger back in her own mouth.

"It tastes like…" She searched for the words. "Sugared fire."

Adel laughed and handed her the glass. "I grew up with this stuff, and I'm positive I've never heard it described like that."

She got up from the bed, corking the bottle slowly and setting it on the nightstand. "I'll come to get you for breakfast in the morning. Mom makes pancakes on Saturday."

Grace placed the glass on the nightstand by the bottle and watched Adel until she reached the staircase. This was the moment to make the choices she'd always made—to "keep sweet"—or she could be brave. And maybe for the first time, she realized that it was that simple.

"Adel?"

Adel stopped and leaned on the banister. "Yes?"

Grace pulled her knees up and wrapped her arms around them. Her voice was a husky whisper, almost lost in the shadows between them.

"Don't go."

Adel didn't move, didn't breathe, for so long that Grace wondered if she would. When she finally did, Adel's eyes didn't leave hers as she walked back toward the bed and slid her hand around the back of her neck.

"Are you sure?" Adel whispered the words, her eyes on Grace's mouth.

She nodded as Adel slid her thumb lightly across Grace's lower lip, then touched her only with the slow warmth of her breath. The intensity between them was dense, crackling like the sudden lightning that lit up the attic windows, then disappeared, leaving them slicked with rain and darkness. Grace shivered as Adel caught her lower lip lightly with her teeth before she kissed her, long and slow, then held her face gently and kissed down her neck. Thunder cracked the sky just above the roof as Grace breathed in the spicy scent of Adel's skin, her body responding hard when she felt Adel pull her ring finger slowly into the slick warmth of her mouth. Her breath caught and she closed her eyes, memorizing the feel of Adel's tongue circling her finger, lightly, teasing the tip before she let it go and placed Grace's hand in the center of her chest and covered it with her own.

Adel's next words were so intimate, so soft, that Grace wondered if she'd even heard them.

"How do you feel?"

Grace leaned back into the pillows and looked up at Adel. The honey amber of her eyes had darkened like the storm outside the glass. "I feel different. Brave."

"Grace." Adel shifted so she was above her, her hands on either side of her shoulders. Pale silver moonlight sifted through the settled panes of old glass in the attic windows and fell across Adel's face in a wavy, underwater pattern. "I haven't even begun to show you what brave feels like."

Adel lowered her body onto Grace's slowly, her tongue tracing the slope of her neck as Grace slipped her hands under Adel's T-shirt at the waist. She lifted one of Grace's knees up beside her, her hips sinking deeper against her as Grace arched her back, her breath deepening suddenly as Adel whispered just behind her ear.

"I need you to know something before this goes any further."

Grace opened her eyes slowly, as if in a delicious dream she was unwilling to wake from.

"I need to know you understand we can stop anytime, okay?" Adel paused, stroking Grace's cheek lightly with her thumb. "Just say no. You don't have to have a reason."

Grace nodded, her hand still on the warm, bare skin of Adel's back.

"But," Grace said, biting her lip as she chose her words, "what if I want…"

Adel smiled, capturing one of Grace's hands and pulling it to her mouth, kissing her palm slowly as she met her eyes. "What?"

"You." The word was a warm whisper against Adel's mouth. She bit Adel's lower lip lightly, letting it go only after she'd run her tongue along the edge of it. "This." She kissed her again, her breath soft against Adel's mouth as she pulled away. "Us."

She sat up then and slid her hands farther under Adel's T-shirt, lifting it slowly to her shoulders and off. The bare athletic lines of her body were sculpture—lean muscle rippled across her shoulders, and her arms were cut and defined. She trailed her fingertips down Adel's tight abs, following the definition to her waistband. Grace heard her let out a long, slow breath, then felt Adel's hand warm against her neck. When she looked up, Adel's eyes were dark and intense, the muscles in her jaw tense.

Grace followed the warm curve of Adel's breast with her fingertips, then brushed her thumb across the dark amber nipple she felt tighten under her touch. She paused and sat back, holding Adel's eyes as she lifted her own T-shirt, pulled it over her head, and bit her lip as she felt it slide off her fingers onto the bed beside them. Adel pulled Grace's body against hers, kissing her as if she'd been underwater and Grace was the cold salt air at the surface of the sea.

After a long moment, Adel pulled back slightly and pressed her forehead to Grace's. "I know how much courage that took. And it's none of my business why you bind your chest." She looked down at the beige sports bandage wound tight and flat around Grace's breasts. "But if you feel like telling me, I'd love to know."

Grace started to explain like it was no big deal, willing the words to smooth the sharp edges of being forced to alter the shape of her body for most of her life, but she faltered as Adel held her gaze. Instantly, Grace felt a hot rush of shame set her face on fire, but when Adel finally spoke again, her words were gentle, the softest whisper, as if she understood that everything in Grace's life was a secret.

"Grace." Adel gathered her into her arms as she pulled the duvet from the foot of the bed and wrapped it around them both. "I don't have a right to ask you about any of this, I know that. But if you choose to tell me, just know that you don't have to make any of this sound normal." She paused. "I know what they've done to you, and what they're doing now to the other girls, is fucked up." She kissed the top of Grace's head softly. "I already know."

Grace sat up to face her, tears shimmering in her eyes as Adel brought Grace's hand to her mouth and kissed it, then held it in both of hers as Grace started to speak.

"The night you got to camp, I knew you'd tell someone where you met me, especially when you started hanging out with Bethany." She tucked a stray lock of hair behind her ear. "So I waited. But you never did."

Adel nodded as another flash of lightning glazed the sky with momentary gold. She brought Grace's face to hers and kissed her, holding her eyes as she spoke. "I told you I wouldn't. It wasn't my secret to tell."

Grace waited for the thunder that shook the rafters, then settled back into Adel's arms, her head leaning back on her shoulder as she pulled the duvet back around them.

"The summer I turned eleven, I developed fast." Grace stared at the rain streaming down the attic windows as she spoke, every word quieter than the last. "And on my eleventh birthday, one of the Brethren from my church came to the house and talked to my father in the living room. I sat on the stairs the whole time he was there, trying to hear what they were talking about, but I couldn't make it out."

"You thought he was there about you?"

Grace nodded. She ran her fingertip slowly along the edge of the duvet, then crumpled it into her hand. "The night before in Bible study, that same elder had made a point to sit down the row from us in the pew and stare at me for the entire service, so I had a good idea it had something to do with me."

"He was staring at you?" There was an edge in Adel's voice and Grace felt her hand tense over hers. "Or your body?"

"I guess I didn't know the difference yet."

Grace sat up on the bed and brushed her fingertips instinctively over the pins at her side that held the bindings together. "But that night, my father came to my room and told me I'd been tempting men to sin with my body, and if I continued to do that and they gave in, it would be my fault. He said I was lucky the elder had been good enough to make him aware of the situation, as a courtesy."

Grace ran her hand through her hair and stared up at the rafters, her voice hoarse. "And then he dropped the binding on the bed and started to leave." She shook her head to rid herself of the memory. "I'll never forget the look on his face when I told him I didn't want to wear it. He told me my body belonged to him, and him only, until he released me to my husband. I've worn one every day and night since then."

Adel leaned up and turned Grace's face gently toward hers. "You know that's complete bullshit, right? Every person is responsible for their own actions. No one has the right to touch you without your consent, and no one..." She paused, her eyes never leaving Grace's face. "Ever *owns* another person."

"Maybe in your world." Grace shook her head, pausing before she went on. "But that's not how it works for us."

"Yeah, I'm starting to realize that." Adel took a slow breath, her eyes locked on Grace's. "And someone needs to change it."

Grace sat up and let the duvet slip off her shoulders as lightning flashed again outside the windows, painting her body with light, rivulets of rain reflected in shadow on her skin. She looked down as she started to unpin the binding, closing each brass safety pin as she pulled it out and handed it to Adel. When the last one was undone, Grace hesitated, her fingers pressed hard against the wide elastic strip, then slowly started to unwind it from her body. Thunder cracked against the rafters as the familiar deep red compression tracks appeared along her torso as she unwrapped the last layer. Grace held the last strip to her breasts with her forearm, then lifted her eyes to Adel's before she let it drop away from her body. She waited for Adel to look down, to stare, but she didn't. Adel's eyes never left hers.

"I was wrong." Adel leaned in to kiss Grace softly, whispering the words against her mouth. "You already know what it means to be brave."

Adel pulled her down into the bed, her body warm and close behind Grace, their fingers woven together over her heart. Suddenly Grace was exhausted, as if she'd swum a thousand miles to an island that had never existed.

"I just want to feel free." Grace's eyes fluttered shut as she spoke. "Just once. I'm afraid I'll die before I ever know what that feels like."

Adel turned off the lamp and pulled Grace deeper into her arms. She held her, strong and close, until Grace melted into the warmth of her body, imagining the deep click of the lights shutting down around them and the audience slowly fading away as she relaxed into the silent darkness of the empty stage.

Chapter Eleven

In the morning, Adel made herself slip out of bed before dawn and go downstairs. She pulled on a jacket she'd left in the passenger seat the night before as the seagulls started to appear and wove a pattern in the warming sky above her head. It hadn't taken her long to pack the Jeep, leave a note in the kitchen for her mother and sister-in-law, and load the two travel mugs waiting in the console.

She slammed the Jeep door shut and turned around to face the sparkling expanse of the sea just as the sun was rising, burning away the translucent haze over the calm blue surface of the water. She leaned against the hood, pulling her hair into a ponytail and through the back of a Boston Bruins cap. Herons called over the water as the morning wave of fishing boats glided out to sea, the deckhands clanging their iron deck bells as the sails lifted and caught the wind.

The air had a soft warmth to it that only happened for a few weeks in the summer, followed by the crisp bite of fall at the first hint of September. But this morning it was still here, hovering, light and silent, the opposite of the clash and chaos of downtown Manhattan that had become her life. Even in college, she knew she didn't want to stay in the city forever, but for Katya, the plans they'd made of moving to the countryside had faded into the blinking neon of Times Square years ago, just like everything else between them. For the past few months, she'd tried not to think about the fact they hadn't had sex for four years, but when it did creep into her mind now, the part that bothered her the most was that she wasn't even sure she cared anymore.

She pulled her phone out of her pocket and looked at the messages and missed calls. Nothing from Katya. Adel pressed the button to call her, and to her surprise, Katya picked up. Her voice was breathless, rushed. Adel looked at her watch—she'd caught her on the way to the subway.

"Hey."

Adel heard the clank of the ticket stiles in the background and pictured Katya, phone pressed against her ear, digging in her bag for her MetroCard.

"Look." Katya's words were rushed, half hidden by the sounds of the people streaming past her in the station. "I know you were upset last night and I was going to call you, but—"

"But you didn't." Adel closed her eyes and leaned against the cold metal of the Jeep door. "I need to know something, Kat."

"Adel, I can't talk right now, I'm getting on a train."

Adel watched as Antonio's truck turned into the driveway and pulled in beside the Jeep. Both doors opened and he and Carlos stepped out, laughing, still reeking of booze, cigarettes, and other people's girlfriends. She watched them drag themselves up the steps and disappear into the house.

"We're talking about this now." Adel didn't recognize her own voice. "We should have talked about it before I left. It's important."

"Jesus Christ." Katya sighed, the noise around her fading as she stepped out of the crowd. "Why are you bringing something up now? I have a stack of cases on my desk I can't see over, plus the press for the reelection, and I—"

Adel rubbed her temples with her fingertips and pressed the phone back to her ear.

"Are you fucking someone else?"

Sudden silence amplified the background sounds of the station, but all Adel heard was her own breath. She counted exactly three breaths before she spoke.

"Kat, if you can't answer me…then that *is* your answer."

Katya's voice had morphed into steel on flint by the time she finally replied. "Listen, I'm not going to address this now. Whenever you get done with your magazine thing, we'll sit down and talk about it, but I'm not doing this in the fucking subway."

"Who was it?" Adel looked out at the sea and wiped sudden hot tears from her eyes with the heel of her hand. "Was it more than once?"

"Jesus, Adel. I'm not answering that." Katya's voice faded as Adel listened to her step back into the fray of commuters. "You know we've had problems for a long time, and my life is a lot different than when we first got together." Adel listened to the whoosh of a train pulling into the subway platform. "I'll talk to you about this when you get home."

She heard the staccato click of her girlfriend's heels on the tunnel steps as she hurried down to the sliding doors as they opened.

"No. You won't." Adel turned and looked up at the widow's walk she'd stood on the night before, remembering the warmth of Grace's body in her arms. "This is over. I'll let you know when I'm headed home so you can have your stuff out of the apartment before I get there."

She clicked the button on the phone, then slammed the door shut on the last nine years of her life as she walked back up the driveway toward the house.

❖

"Wake up, sleepy girl."

Adel leaned into Grace and whispered the words into her shoulder. Grace turned over and shaded her eyes with her forearm as translucent beams of sunlight from the windows melted across her body, highlighting the mouthwatering curves of her breasts under the sheet.

"What time is it?" She squinted and raised her arm out of the covers to look at the watch she wasn't wearing. "Why is the sun up?"

"Morning." Adel smiled, nodding to the stack of clothes at the foot of the bed. "I'll tell you everything in the Jeep. Just get dressed and meet me downstairs."

"Are those jeans?" Grace perked up and looked instantly thrilled. She ran her hand through her hair, holding the sheet to her body. "But you don't have to let me wear your clothes. I brought some dresses."

"Trust me, you won't want to be wearing a dress where we're going." Adel got up and walked toward the stairs, glancing back over her shoulder as Grace reached for the stack of clothes. "Besides, I like how you look in my jeans."

She winked as she slipped down the stairs and headed back to the kitchen on the first floor, where her brothers were perched on the kitchen counters, folding the rest of the roast from the night before into endless slices of bread.

"What you doing up so early, Delly?"

Antonio blasted mustard toward the pile of meat on the slice of bread in his hands, then slapped on another slice on top and squeezed them together, blissfully unaware of the mustard dripping onto his lap.

"God, you two smell like someone mopped up a spilled keg with a bucket of Victoria's Secret body spray." She smiled, reaching for a pickle out of the open jar on the counter. "I'm taking Grace out to the beach house." She paused before she folded the pickle into her mouth and winked at her brothers. "I'd ask you if you want to go, but I don't want you two meatheads there."

Carlos rolled his eyes and glanced at Antonio. "Just tell me this means you ditched that skinny bitch you've been dating for the last twenty years?"

"Nine years." Adel lofted an eyebrow and smacked his arm. "And how many times do I have to tell you guys? You can't ever use that word when you're talking about women. *Any* of them."

"Oh, really?" Antonio cocked one eyebrow and swiped at a river of mustard sinking down his chin. "Well, Nico was too nice to tell you this, but that year you brought her to Christmas, Nina was pregnant. She asked him at dinner if he was worried Nina would stay fat after the baby was born."

Adel stopped mid-bite and stared. It was a long second before she shook her head and picked up a piece of roast beef, popping it into her mouth. "Are you fucking serious?"

Her brothers nodded.

Adel reached for a slice of cheese. "Jesus Christ. Why didn't he tell me?"

"Because he knew you liked her." Carlos dumped a few forkfuls of beef onto a piece of bread, topped it with cheddar and a dab of horseradish, and handed it to Adel. "And I guess you're his favorite sister or something. Don't get a big head about it."

"This girl doesn't look like that type, though." Antonio looked up the stairs and lowered his voice to a whisper. "And she's wicked gorgeous. I had no idea you could land someone that hot."

"Truthfully, me neither." Adel winked, nodding up at the stairs when she heard Grace start to come down. "And Jesus, I haven't 'landed' her, I'm just getting to know—"

"Yeah, but you're gonna, right?" Marco said, swigging the last of his brother's can of Coke. "Because if not, I got all the time in the—"

Adel picked up the ketchup and calmly squirted a lake of it onto her brother's lap before he could finish his sentence, two seconds before Grace rounded the corner of the stairs.

"Okay, I get it! Hands off." He punched her arm as he grabbed a mountain of paper towels from the counter. "Just offering. Geez, you'd think I'd at least get a thank-you or somethin'."

"Good morning." Grace smiled in their direction as she stood in the doorway, rolling up the sleeves of Adel's fleece, which hung a few inches past her fingertips. "I took a quick shower before I came down, I hope that's all right."

Her hair was pulled back into a smooth ponytail, and even indoors, it shone like a sunlit field of wheat. Adel's pale blue Levi's skimmed the curve of her hips in a disarmingly sensual way, and Adel shot Marco a look before he even thought to start staring.

"Is my sister's gargantuan fleece too big for you, Grace?" Antonio winked at Adel. "I probably have some better ones lying around."

"No." Grace shot him a genuine smile and finished the last cuff. "It's just the sleeves. I didn't realize how tall she was until the first time I put on one of her sweatshirts."

"I've got coffee for us in the car already." Adel stepped back to let Grace go first as they walked toward the door, then paused. "Hey, Ant, hand me that roll of paper towels on the counter?"

When her brother tossed her the roll, she whacked him upside the head with it, then set it back on the counter beside him.

"What the hell, Delly?" He picked it up and launched the roll at Carlos, who had instantly snorted laughter when he saw the roll hit his brother's head. "What'd I ever do to you?"

"Plenty, but that one was specifically for what you're gonna say about me when we walk out of here." She shot him an angelic smile over her shoulder as they headed for the front door.

❖

"So where are we going?"

Adel opened the Jeep door for Grace and walked around, sliding into her seat and handing Grace her travel mug from the console.

"I'm taking you to the beach house. Evidently, there's no electricity, but we don't need it for what we're doing."

"Oh, thank God." Grace took a second tentative sip from her mug and smiled. "This isn't really coffee, is it?"

"No, I figured you might not drink coffee, although Lord knows, why anyone in their right minds wouldn't want some hot Colombian bean in the morning is beyond me." Adel shot her a smile and shifted into reverse, pulling smoothly out of the driveway and turning down the street. "It's basically hot chocolate with heavy cream and cinnamon. It's my mom's favorite."

Grace smiled. "It's gorgeous."

She leaned over and kissed Adel on the cheek, then leaned back in her seat, the wind tossing her hair around her face. The ocean appeared on the right as they drove out of town, still sparkling in the morning sunlight, and the horizon was dotted with chunky white fishing boats, sails barely moving in the still air.

"I bet it was amazing having a house on the beach when you were growing up. I've dreamed about living in a lighthouse since I was a little girl."

Adel reached over and wove her fingers into Grace's, resting their hands lightly on Grace's thigh.

"We didn't have one then, actually. Nico started his construction business when I was in college, and they got pretty successful quickly. My dad helped them when he could, but he'd been a fisherman all his life, so he left them to it for the most part." Adel stroked the back of Grace's hand with her thumb, staring over the steering wheel at the pale blue horizon. "But I remember coming home from college for years wondering why my brothers still drove the same beat-up trucks, and Nico lived in a one-bedroom apartment in town until he met Nina and she put a stop to it."

"They don't exactly look like materialistic guys." Grace turned toward Adel in the seat. "Were they just investing it all back into the business?"

"Well, that's what we thought, and they were doing really well, working day and night. They even brought my mom in to help with some of the interior design work for the new construction, which she absolutely loved."

Adel drove carefully up a steep incline and the sky opened up around them as she crested the sharp curve at the top of the road, ocean waves crashing the jagged edge below them as if the earth had split and the other half had sunk back into the cobalt-blue, foamy sea.

Adel extended her arm out the window and let the wind flow through her fingers. "One of her favorites was for a client who didn't have many ideas about what he wanted, so Ma basically went nuts with the inside and decorated it in traditional Portuguese art, bright colors, this huge family kitchen with a bay window overlooking the shore, the whole nine yards. Nico said the client was crazy about it in the end, surprisingly."

Grace tucked a stray lock of hair behind her ear and smiled. "She must have loved that."

"She did, but then it was finished, the client took over, and she would never see it again. I know she missed it. She even had Marco sneak back over the night before the client saw it and bring her back an oil painting she'd said at the time reminded her of her childhood in Portugal. She told him to just get something else to replace it since the client hadn't seen it yet. Marco was not amused, but it's hung in our house ever since."

"It's the one over the fireplace in the living room? The beach scene with the colorful little huts along the water?"

Adel nodded and turned onto a smaller road that wound back down toward the shore. The Jeep windows were down, and the warm salt breeze had started to stir the scent of the sea into the air around them as they drove closer to the shore. Grace shifted her hand so that Adel's palm was on her thigh, fingers stroking the back of it as she looked out over the expanse of water, watching waves crest translucent green and fall into a thousand shades of blue before they slid onto shore in a rush of cold white foam.

Adel pulled a lip balm out of her pocket and smoothed it over her lips, and the fact that Grace seemed mesmerized by it was not lost on her.

"So." She pushed the balm back into her jeans pocket and focused on the road narrowing by the second. "About six months later, Nico and Marco called all of us with this endless list of everything we needed to bring, threw out some random address and date, and told us he would literally kill us if we said anything to our parents. I even flew home from college and spent all day with Nina cooking, even though neither one of us knew what it was for."

"I think I might know where you're going with this…"

Adel laughed, shifting into second as she maneuvered the Jeep through the suddenly narrow roads. "Well, you're smarter than any of us were, because we just showed up there, clueless, with more Portuguese party food than a fleet of Lisbon food trucks. Teams of people were already there setting up a stage for an acoustic band and this huge blazing bonfire on the beach. It seemed like everyone we knew was there already, and in our neighborhood, that's a lot."

"Let me guess…" Grace smiled. "They were on the beach just down from the house your mom had decorated?"

"Yeah." Adel shot her a smile and took a sip of her coffee. "Now you've got it."

She turned down a narrow street so close to the ocean that the waves breaking on the shore muffled her words, then took a sharp right and pulled into the driveway of an expansive white beach house, all three levels wrapped with glossy hardwood porches painted in the pale blue, stormy hue of ocean water. Bright green ivy climbed the sides to frame the second- and third-story windows, with brushed silver hardware that held back raw beachwood shutters.

Adel parked in front of an enclosed garage and watched as Grace took in the house.

"This is so…" Her eyes scanned the breadth of the house and the undulating sea beyond. "Wow."

Grace opened her door slowly, then climbed out and walked up the entry path made of snow-white concrete heavy with crushed oysters and creamy mother-of-pearl shells. She turned around suddenly right before she reached the steps, smiled, and bit her lip.

"Sorry, I know I'm being rude, but it's just so beautiful."

Adel laughed and waved her on, climbing out and shutting the door of the Jeep with a click of the lock. "No, feel free. I have to get some stuff out of the Jeep anyway."

She grabbed a duffel bag and cooler out of the back, watching as Grace climbed the steps and peered around the corner of the wraparound porch, standing with her fingers laced on top of her head, staring at the sea. Adel dropped the bags at the door, then stepped up behind her, hands on her shoulders. Grace looked back at Adel and covered her hands with her own.

"So what happened? That day everyone was at the beach house?"

"Well, it was a disorganized mess until the very last minute." A seagull landed on the porch railing a few feet away and tilted his head as if trying to determine whether they should be there, then took off just as suddenly. "I don't know if you've noticed, but Portuguese are not unlike Italians in that we tend to have big, loud, disorganized families. Which is great until you have to get them together for a plan."

"Yeah, I noticed." Grace smiled and leaned her head back against Adel's chest. "Your brothers are hilarious."

"Yeah, well." She smiled at the memory of squirting ketchup on her brother's best club jeans. "*They* think they are."

Adel led her off the porch and paused to take off her shoes. Grace followed, leaving them on the last step. They stepped down together into the soft, white sand, already warm from the sun, and walked down from the house toward the water.

Grace stopped to scoop up a handful of ivory sand and let it fall slowly from her fingers onto her bare feet.

"They finally had to let us in on the secret in a last-ditch attempt to get us to act right, but once he did, everyone pulled it together, and by the time my parents got there, the place looked amazing."

"So what happened then?"

"They walked in the front door and we heard them coming down the hall. We were all in the kitchen, but Ma walked straight over to the fireplace and looked at the painting above the mantel."

"But that painting she loved was at her house by then, right?"

"It was."

Adel waited as they reached the water's edge, and Grace bent down to put her hands into the water as it slid across the shore with the softest sandy hiss. She watched it gather around her ankles and picked up a tiny white shell, held it up to the sun, then tucked it into her pocket. The sun fell across her face as she looked out at the horizon and illuminated her eyes to the exact clear blue of the sky.

Finally, she looked back and smiled. "What did Marco pick out to replace it?"

"He'd taken my mother's favorite photo of all of us—we were on vacation at the beach in Portugal when we were kids—and had a local artist paint it onto canvas."

"Oh, my God. That's incredibly thoughtful." Grace shaded her eyes and looked up, cold water climbing higher and swirling around her ankles. "She must have loved it."

"She did." Adel smiled, leaning down to pick up a sand dollar and toss it gently back into the waves. "Until it dawned on her that it shouldn't be there, that it was still the client's home. I think my favorite memory is watching her look down to see the two brass keys Nico had laid on the top of the mantel."

"What did she say?"

Adel looked out over the sea, every detail washing over her at once as if it had happened yesterday.

"I don't remember, really. I just remember the look on my dad's face when he realized it was theirs. Ma had always wanted a beach house, and Dad used to rent one for her a week every summer on the coast. No one ever said it, but we all knew we'd never be able to afford to actually buy one."

"Wow. And then to have his sons do that for him..." Grace held Adel's eyes. "I can't imagine how that must have felt."

Adel looked down and watched the water as it slid back out to sea. "It was the only time I'd ever seen my dad cry. He just hugged my brothers and sobbed."

Grace leaned into her, arms slipping around Adel's waist as she squinted against the sun. "This the first time you've been back here since he died, isn't it?"

Adel nodded. She looked down into Grace's face and realized she'd been dreading this moment since her father died. But now the tears she felt on her cheeks were of remembrance, not sadness.

Grace smiled, reaching up on tiptoe to kiss Adel, then leaned back, her eyes soft. "Thank you for bringing me here. I'm honored."

Adel stroked Grace's cheek with her thumb, then leaned in to whisper into her ear. "Do you see that little boathouse behind you?"

Grace looked back over her shoulder and nodded.

"I'm going to get something from the porch." Adel took out her keys and slid a small silver one off the loop, pressing it into Grace's hand. "I'll meet you there."

Grace headed for the water, kicking at the surf as she walked, and Adel wiped her eyes as she grabbed her bag from the porch, stopping for a moment to peer into the windows. The glass panes were cool and smooth under her fingertips, and she realized as she leaned into them that she'd never told Katya the story of the beach house because Katya had actually never seen it. She'd always said she was too busy to come back to Mystic in the summer, and after a while, Adel stopped asking.

Adel had turned back toward the sea when her phone rang from her back pocket. She looked at it and put it to her ear.

"Bethany?"

"Hey, man. I know you're off camp this weekend, and I hate to bother you, but..."

"No problem." Adel glanced toward the boathouse and felt her stomach sink. "What's going on?"

The phone was silent for a long second.

"I don't know, but Whittier and her idiots have been in and out of Grace's cabin all morning. Nora was delivering some lunch to one of the staff who was sick, and she stayed to watch. She was out of sight,

I don't think they saw her, but it didn't look good." Bethany paused, and Adel listened to her draw in a long breath. "Something ain't right."

"What the fuck?" Adel kneaded the sudden tension balling up under her shoulders with the heel of her hand. "Why? Can they even do that?"

"They can do anything. Apparently, there's something in there they want." She paused. "Hey...did they tell her to leave this weekend?"

Adel nodded, her eyes on the boathouse until she realized she actually had to say something. "Yeah, and now that makes sense. She was supposed to go home, but she's in Connecticut. With me."

"I figured." Adel heard the faint sound of horse hooves clicking against rock and realized she'd taken out one of the trail horses to make sure she wasn't overheard. "Tell her if you think you should, but I just wanted you to know."

"Thanks, Bethany." Adel snapped back to reality and realized the risk her friend had taken to help her. "I'll call you when I get back tomorrow night. No one saw Nora there, did they?"

"Nah, but the kitchen supervisor sent her down there, so even if they did, it wouldn't have raised any eyebrows."

"Okay." Adel paused. "Lay low. I'll talk to you tomorrow."

She clicked the phone off and dropped it into the bag she swung over her shoulder. Whatever that was about, she had a feeling things were about to get a lot more complicated.

❖

When she got to the boathouse and swung open the wood frame door, Grace was running her hand over the handlebars of her brother's Jet Skis. When she realized Adel was there, she looked up and smiled, twisting her hair into a knot at the back of her head.

"These are Jet Skis, aren't they?"

Adel nodded, smiling as she dropped the bag and straddled the closest one. "Yeah, I didn't know if you've ever been on one, so I thought I'd bring you. Even if you have, there's nothing like riding ocean waves on one of these."

"No, Covenant rules don't allow women on the water in anything with an engine." Grace ran her fingertips over the white-and-navy glitter frame of the one closest to her, squeezing the handle gingerly as if she expected it to spring to life at any second. Adel dug into the bag she'd brought and handed her a folded stack of clothes with a wet suit underneath.

"Ready?"

"What? You mean we're taking these out there?" Grace's mouth dropped open as she looked at the wet suit in her hands. "Into the ocean?"

Adel laughed and pointed at the two-piece Speedo on the top of the stack. "Yeah, they handle much better outside the boathouse. You may want to change into that swimsuit before you get into the actual wet suit. I'm pretty sure what you're wearing isn't going to fit under there."

"No way. I can't do that." Grace touched the handlebars again, then handed back the wet suit. "I've never even ridden in a powerboat."

Adel didn't take it, just stepped up to her and kissed her, Grace's face soft and warm in her hands. "You can do it. And I'm going to be there the whole time."

A few minutes later, they'd changed and moved the Jet Skis to the water's edge, cold water lapping at their ankles. The wet suits had long sleeves but ended above the knee, and Adel tried not to look at the deep curve between Grace's hips and waist, then the softness of the breasts she'd been brave enough not to bind again. Not that she would have noticed if she had; Grace looked paler than Adel had ever seen her.

"Are you sure I can do this?" She anxiously brushed nonexistent sand from her hands. "What if I fall off?"

Adel smiled and handed her the key she'd attached to a black Velcro wrist strap. Grace looked so small in the shortie wet suit, her hair piled on top of her head, toes dug hard into the sand. Adel was used to seeing her in endless layers of clothing, but without all that on the outside, she looked almost delicate. Or maybe just stripped of her armor.

"If you fall off, the Jet Ski will sense that and shut off automatically. So if that happens, just get back on and take off again."

Grace looked out across the smooth surface of the sea. The sunlight had carved a golden path of light down the center that seemed to drop off at the far flat edge of the world. She raised her hand to her mouth, nibbling at the edge of her fingertip as she took a step back.

"Grace?" Adel stepped up to her, raised her chin with a fingertip, and met her eyes. "Remember what you said to me last night? Right before we went to sleep?"

She nodded, the first hint of a smile breaking through the dense wall of anxiety. "That I wanted to know what it felt like to be free?"

"Trust me." Adel smiled and stepped back, her eyes on the choppy blue horizon. "This is what it feels like."

Grace nodded, then listened intently as Adel quickly taught her the basics of how to drive, turn, and stop, and reminded her to keep her weight centered over the seat, especially if she stood up.

"Why would I stand up?"

Adel flashed her a smile and pushed the Jet Skis out into the water. "You'll see."

Adel pulled the skis side by side and made sure they were deep enough, showed Grace the easiest way to center her weight and climb on, then started it up for her. She was just about to fire up her own ski when Grace took off, slowly at first, then gaining speed and confidence as Adel scrambled to follow behind. The bun at the back of her neck slipped free and her hair blew back behind her like pale billowing silk, as if she were riding a mythical beast about to lift its wings to rise off the water and into the clouds.

Adel watched her ride for a few minutes, then let her have her space, and a few minutes later Grace haltingly stood, one foot on either side of the seat platform, ripping through the undulating shimmer of the gold path left by the sun. Adel still had her eyes on her as Grace gripped the handlebars tighter, finally standing to full height, only to be taken out almost immediately by a rogue wave she noticed too late to lean into.

Grace disappeared instantly into the deep blue water, and Adel opened the throttle as she sped toward the empty Jet Ski. It slowed and spun, slowly tracking in wide circles around the spot where she'd seen Grace go down.

Fuck. Adel bit her lip, tasting blood as she pulled up to Grace's Jet Ski, her eyes scanning the water for the blond slick of wet hair she wanted to see. *What if she doesn't come to the surface, what if...*

Before Adel even finished the thought, Grace appeared, her smile as wide as the horizon.

"Oh, my God!" Adel sat back on her seat and smiled, relief flooding her chest with such force it felt like it was going to burst. "You gave me a heart attack." She reached out for Grace's hand and pulled her back on her ski. "Get back up on that thing. I'm staying close to you this time."

Grace laughed as she settled back on the seat, and Adel reached over to pull her Jet Ski closer.

"So…" She faltered, then stopped. What had seemed like a great idea early that morning was suddenly daunting, but it was too late now; Grace had seen her tucking the small dry bag into the storage space of her ski before they headed out. "I brought you something."

"Is it in that dry bag I saw?"

Adel laughed, reaching behind her and clicking open the storage compartment to the rear of her seat. "Yeah. I was trying to be sneaky, but you don't miss much, so I didn't have a chance."

Grace took the dry bag when Adel handed it to her and unclipped the edges, rolling it up and open. She reached into it silently, slowly drawing out the length of binding she'd taken off last night in the attic. She paused, her hand still in the bag.

"Why did you bring this?"

Adel waited until Grace had it out of the bag, then watched as she pulled out the large stone she found under it. Soft waves lapped at the sides of the Jet Skis, and the sun was becoming more intense, drying the soft hairs around Grace's face and brushing them across her cheek.

Adel didn't answer, just waited until she saw understanding soften her face, then leaned over and handed her a black marker from the outside pocket of the bag.

Grace laid the binding on her thigh and wrote down the center of it in black block letters, then slowly wound it around the stone, tucking the last bit of the end underneath to secure it. Adel waited as she held it in her lap, holding space for Grace to experience this the way she needed to. The only words that mattered here anyway were written down the center of that binding, and when Adel saw them, she had to look out over the horizon and blink away the sudden sting of tears behind her eyes.

You never owned me.

She watched as Grace stood slowly as the wind picked up and whipped her hair around her face like a forgotten warrior standing in the sea. Her fingers were white and tense around the stone, and she faltered twice before she launched it suddenly into the choppy water. A gasp escaped her as it left her hand, as if she didn't know what to do without its weight to anchor her body to the earth.

When she finally sat down, Adel took her cold hands and warmed them in hers until she felt Grace relax, then kissed them and let them go. Grace dried her eyes with the heel of her hand, revved her engine, then took off suddenly like a rocket piercing the low-lying clouds in the distance.

This time Adel stayed close as Grace got the hang of riding the waves. She managed to flip a few more times, but she looked like a pro by the time Adel cut in close enough to wave her back to shore, pointing to the gas gauge on her own dashboard. Grace nodded reluctantly, then followed and helped Adel lift the skis back into the boathouse.

Adel ran her hand through her dark slick of wet hair and turned around to Grace after she'd secured the skis to the racks. "So, what did you think—"

Adel didn't get to finish her sentence because suddenly Grace was kissing her, softly at first, her hands light and warm against the back of her neck. Adel slid her hands around Grace's waist as Grace leaned in and kissed her deeper, every curve of her body slowly melting into Adel's. She kissed her until Adel picked her up and pressed her against the inside wall of the boathouse, wrapping Grace's legs around her waist. She bit Grace's lower lip and kissed her harder, only letting her back down when she knew if she didn't, she'd take her right there on the sand-scattered boathouse floor.

"Jesus." Adel gazed at Grace's flushed lips and her eyes that were heavy with desire, and forced herself to take a step back. "We don't have to do this. I don't want to make you feel—"

"Adel." Grace held her eyes and pulled close again. "I want to." She paused, appearing to search for the words. "You've never made me feel anything but safe."

Adel stepped up to her again and held Grace's face in her hands as she kissed her. Grace's body moved against Adel's again, and she had to stop herself from running her hands up the front of Grace's wet suit and sliding that zipper down to her waist.

"Although," Grace whispered suddenly against her lips, "I may starve and die a virgin before we get out of this boathouse."

Adel laughed and stepped outside with her clothes to change while Grace got out of her wet suit inside. She waited after she dressed, leaning against the sun-warmed planks of the boathouse, watching the pristine white gulls dip and glide over the water. Clouds had started to roll in, but the balmy sea air still unfolded the muscles onto her bones the way it had since she was a child. Her hair started to dry in the breeze, so she wound it into a knot at the base of her neck as the boathouse door opened and tucked the stray wisps behind her ears.

Once they'd gotten back up to the house, Adel handed Grace the soft cooler, then grabbed an armful of cut firewood from the porch. Grace unzipped the side of it and peeked under the ice.

"What's in here?" She lowered her face deeper into the bag. "I smell chocolate."

"None of your business, Miss Waters."

Adel smiled, led her down the stairs to the beach, and chose a sandy spot for their campfire. The waves slid up the shore just a few feet away, bringing with it the scent of washed rock and delicate salt-soaked seaweed. Adel arranged a pyramid of split logs on the soft, shifting sand and leaned down to hold her lighter under the frayed undersides of the wood.

"What about now?"

Adel looked up to see Grace with her hand poised over the cooler.

"What if I say no?" Adel sat back on her heels and tried to look stern, but Grace returned her gaze, eyes narrowing. The breeze sweeping across the shore blazed the wood into sudden flames, adding an appropriate dramatic touch to the moment.

"If you say no, I'm totally going to do it anyway."

Adel laughed and slid out the collapsible roasting sticks tucked into the side pocket of the cooler. "Actually, if you want to hand me those franks at the bottom, I'll get them started while you snoop."

Grace peered into the cooler, suddenly wary. "Franks?"

"I forgot you're a vegetarian." Adel turned the roasting sticks in the flames to warm them. "You're not exactly down with the lingo. The long, cylindrical thingies."

"Yeah, well." Grace handed over the package of hot dogs and shook the water off her hand. "No one ever asked me if I wanted to be a vegetarian, but that ham or whatever you made, with the mushrooms and cheese in your cabin?" Grace put her hand to her chest and closed her eyes with the memory. "Heaven. Just heaven. You had me right there."

Grace put her frank in the flames near the coals and Adel smiled, nudging the roasting stick up with her fingers. "Careful, these things will burn before you can yank them out of the fire."

"Well, it's a good thing you told me that, because this is yours. I'm practicing while you cook mine right."

"Ah, I see how it is." Adel smiled and shook her head. "Impressive."

She turned her hot dog slowly on the stick, watching it turn crispy and bubble at the edges.

"So." Grace glanced over quickly and turned her eyes back to the fire. A cooler breeze had blown in while they were talking, and the air hovered heavy and expectant as if waiting for the perfect moment to condense into rain. "You have a girlfriend, right?"

"And what would make you say that?"

"Maybe something someone said." Grace smiled. "Not that I was asking."

Adel turned to her, her eyes dropping to Grace's mouth. "This from the girl that's engaged?"

"Nope." Grace lofted an eyebrow and stared into the flames. "I called my parents before I left for the weekend and told them I wasn't getting married."

"Whoa, how did that go?"

Grace just shook her head and looked out over the water as her frank sagged perilously close to the flames.

"Well..." Adel paused, tipped the stick gently up with her finger, then waited until Grace met her eyes. "I'll see your dumped fiancé and raise you an ex-girlfriend."

"Ex?"

Adel smiled and pulled a bun out of the bag, nodding at the blackened hot dog touching the coals at the end of Grace's roasting stick. "Looks like mine is done."

Adel took the stick and slid the frank onto the bun, setting it on her lap while she did the same for Grace with the one she'd cooked perfectly. She reached for the condiments in the bottom of the cooler, passing them to Grace as she leaned back on the seating log behind them.

"I have a question," Adel said, the last word nearly lost as she caught a wayward dollop of relish making an escape out the bottom of her bun with the tip of her finger. "And the answer is absolutely none of my business, by the way."

"I'm nearly positive that's true, but that doesn't mean I'm not going to answer." Grace flashed her a smile and tipped her root beer bottle to her mouth. "Hit me."

Clouds shifted defiantly over the last slice of blue sky, and Adel pulled on the jacket she'd flopped onto the log before she started the fire. "Just now when we were in the boathouse, you said you were a virgin."

Grace nodded, balancing her hot dog between her knees as she braced her root beer in the sand beside her. "Yeah. Embarrassing, huh? I'm twenty-six, and being with you last night is the most I've done with anyone."

"But what about the girl—"

"At camp?" Grace shook her head, her words soft with the memory when she finally spoke. "We only kissed. Neither one of us knew what we were doing, and we were petrified of being caught. We didn't dare take any clothes off." A sudden wave slipped up the sand toward their feet, and Grace fell silent as it fell back into the sea. "How would we explain that if someone saw us?"

"So can they just walk into your cabin, night or day?"

"Of course." Grace paused and set down the last of her frank like she'd forgotten she'd been holding it. "They can do anything."

Adel took it and wrapped it up in the leftover foil. Grace stared into the flames, fingernails tense against the palm of her other hand, leaving scattered, thin white lines she never looked down at. "Something's bugging you." Adel bumped her shoulder softly against Grace's. "Tell me."

Grace looked up at the sky as invisible raindrops hissed into steam the instant they hit the fire, and she reached for the cooler as Adel extinguished the remaining flames. Lightning cracked through the sky above them, and the force of the rain had tripled by the time they skidded onto the porch, still barefoot, soft sand now grit under their feet. Adel dug her keys out of her back pocket and reached back to grab their bags, which she dropped on the porch before she followed Grace through the open door.

Once she'd dropped them inside and shut the door against the storm that was whipping the sea into a gray-green fury, she leaned into the wall and watched as Grace wandered through, exploring more by touch than sight, fingertips light and hesitant across the stained wood countertops as she walked slowly toward the open living area. The front wall of windows, reinforced for maritime weather, rose three stories above the stone floor and faced the churning sea. She touched the glass, then turned slowly and gazed up at the house that surrounded her in an open octagon shape. Suspended iron catwalks crisscrossed the two open stories above the main floor where Adel was still standing by the door, watching.

"I've never been in a house like this. It's beautiful, but…" She walked back toward Adel and leaned against the back of the couch. "I would be scared to death to walk across those skinny little bridges."

"The catwalks?" Grace glanced up again and tipped her head to the side. "Great. Now I've got to do it. That makes it sound like something in a movie."

Adel smiled and pulled Grace to her, smoothing a strand of damp hair from her cheek with her thumb. She held her for a moment before she spoke, drawing in the scent of sun-warmed sand and campfire that lingered on her skin. "You've got to be getting cold in here. I can show you where the bathroom is if you want to take a hot shower."

"No, I'm fine." Grace crossed her arms in front of her and rubbed her shoulders. "I didn't really get wet, and my clothes are dry. I think I may just need to warm up a bit. It feels like instant October here when the sun goes away."

Adel got her settled under a bright velvet throw in the main living area and stayed to build a roaring fire in the stone fireplace. As she climbed the stairs to the third floor, she looked down at Grace settling into the white denim couch, sinking slowly into the cushions under the crimson throw. Adel paused on the catwalk, her fingers warm against the cool metal railing, and watched Grace's eyelids flutter closed. She'd watched something unfold in Grace in the single day she'd been away from camp, like a tightly crumpled handful of paper tossed onto the glassy surface of a lake. Every sharp fold, every hidden crease, had been smoothed by the translucent slick of the water until nothing remained and it floated on the surface like a ghost behind a mirror.

The fact that she needed to tell Grace who she really was and what she was doing at camp was never far from her mind, but neither was the awareness that every passing day was making that more impossible. Manhattan seemed like a hazy memory from a past life, but she still had a job to do, and at that point, it was clear she'd need Grace to uncover what was really happening at Valley of Rubies.

Adel wound her hair into a bun and stepped under the hot water, closing her eyes as the enveloping warmth eased the knots across her shoulders. She watched the rivulets slick down her chest and over her abs, trying not to think about the glimpse of Grace's bare breasts she'd gotten the night before. Grace's frame was delicate, but her breasts were sensuous and full, with light pink nipples that looked like they'd melt like spun sugar under her tongue.

Adel shook her head to clear her mind and stepped out of the shower. *What the fuck is wrong with you, Rosse?*

Something had to give. She could write the article and skyrocket her career in the span of a day, or let herself fall in love with Grace.

Those two things couldn't coexist, and to help Adel get to the truth, Grace would have to betray everything she'd ever known. It was too much to ask, but Adel knew, deep down, that getting to that fiercely guarded truth about what was happening behind closed church doors might be impossible without her.

Adel pulled her clothes back on and raked a hand through her hair, then paused on the catwalk as she got to the stairs that led back down to the main level. Her father had bought her mother a piano the year before he died, and for the first time in years, someone was playing it. Someone with the kind of talent that washes over you like an unseen wave, leaving you breathless on the shore when your feet finally find the sand again.

She rounded the corner of the kitchen and leaned against the door frame, watching Grace play, her fingers light and sure, the music flowing from her fingers through her body, moving her as if she were underwater. Her hair fell over her shoulder as she leaned into the music, her eyes closed as her fingers flew over the keys.

Adel stood behind her until Grace noticed, the music stopping abruptly as she turned around on the bench. Adel held her eyes for a moment before she brushed her lips with hers, sinking into the instant chemistry that crackled between them. Adel kissed down her neck, then wrapped her arm around Grace's waist and pulled her to her feet, shoving the bench out of the way with her foot. Grace's hands slipped under Adel's shirt, pulling her closer as Adel pushed her back against the wall, her mouth hot, urgent, buried in the curve of her shoulder. Grace's breath caught when Adel grazed the delicate skin with her teeth, and when she finally spoke, her voice was husky and powerfully soft.

"Take me upstairs."

Adel stepped back slightly and held Grace's eyes. "Grace, we can wait—"

"Please." Grace's voice sank into a whisper as she took Adel's hand and slipped it under her shirt, closing her eyes as the warmth of Adel's fingers slid over her bare nipples. "I don't want to wait. I want this."

Adel found her breath enough to weave her fingers with Grace's and lead her up the stairs. Grace followed her gingerly across the catwalk to a bedroom painted the same dusky blue as the storm roiling beyond the bay windows. A lush four-poster bed with a crisp white duvet was at the center, framed by two seagrass lamps. The only sounds in the room were waves crashing onto the shore below and the staccato slick of rain hitting the glass when Adel slid her hands under Grace's fleece and pulled it off, dropping it on an overstuffed chair near the window. Her hands wrapped the warmth of Grace's waist and she whispered just behind her ear, more breath than words.

"The bed." Adel stopped to run her tongue slowly across the edge of Grace's ear. "I need you on that bed. Now."

Adel moved over Grace's body, spilled like molten gold onto the bed. She lifted the hem of her shirt and heard Grace take a sharp breath in as she traced the soft skin at the edge of her jeans with her tongue. Grace hesitated, then pulled her shirt over her head, her hands light and soft against the back of Adel's neck as Adel moved up her body.

Adel took in the full, sensual curves of her breasts, watching the pale pink nipples tighten as she ran her palm lightly over them, then laid her hand softly over Grace's heart.

"I want you to tell me if anything feels like too much, okay?" Adel's whisper was as intense as an unexpected touch. Grace nodded as Adel's thigh slid between hers and she moved over her. "You don't have to have a reason."

Grace looked up at her. "Why…" She hesitated, as if choosing the words one by one. "Did you say that to me last night?"

Adel shifted to lean on her elbow beside her. "Because no one, including me, has a right to touch you without your consent." She paused, her hand warm and soft against Grace's cheek. "So even if it's awkward, I need to know you want this. And especially if you don't. Just say stop and I'll stop no matter what's happening, okay?"

Grace nodded, then lifted Adel's hand and brought her middle finger to her lips, eyes locked on Adel's as she drew it slowly into the warmth of her mouth. Adel broke her gaze and struggled to stay in control as her body responded hard and fast, stealing her breath. She bit her lip finally as Grace let her finger go, then dipped her head to Grace's nipple and swirled her tongue achingly slowly around it. She heard Grace hold her breath, then let it go in a hoarse rush when Adel finally pulled the nipple deeper into her mouth, her tongue stroking with increasing intensity until she pulled away with a faint scrape of her teeth.

"Oh, my God." Grace's eyes were still closed, her voice raw. "I felt that…everywhere."

Adel smiled and teased her other nipple with the tip of her tongue before she sucked it gently, her tongue stroking the underside of it as she cradled her breasts in the warmth of her hands. She felt Grace arch as she leaned into body, still swirling the warmth of her tongue around Grace's tightening nipple. She moved down her body slowly, tasting every inch of skin until she paused at the button of her jeans.

"Can I—"

"Yes."

It was just one word, breathless and quick, as Adel unfastened every button down the front of her jeans, sliding them over the curves of her hips as she eased them off. She paused then, staring and speechless, at the sheer ivory lace panties that barely skimmed her hips and clung to every curve of her body in a delicate and disarmingly sexy way.

"Holy God." Adel leaned up to Grace again, kissing her as she brushed the lace with her fingertips. When she dipped lower, she sensed the heat and wetness that everything inside Adel wanted to sink into. "That was not at all what I was expecting. Those are sexy as fuck."

Grace smiled and lifted an eyebrow. "They're new. I decided on the drive to Mystic that I don't care what they think I should be wearing under my clothes. I have to have something that's mine."

Adel kissed her again, deep and slow, then got up just long enough to shed her clothes down to her black hipster underwear. She glanced outside, then rummaged through the cabinets in the bathroom until she came back to the room with an armful of mismatched candles.

"I forgot we didn't have electricity." She nodded toward the sky over the churning sea outside, already the color of velvet ash. "And either it's getting dark already or that storm is about to get worse, but either way, I have a feeling we're going to need these."

She retrieved the lighter out of her jeans and set the candles around the room, filling the space with a flickering amber warmth. Grace lifted the covers, her gaze braver now and heavy with desire. "Come back to bed."

Adel slipped in beside her, pulling the duvet around them. Grace drew her close, her fingertips skimming Adel's back as she spoke.

"I feel..." She stopped, her words falling away completely.

"Tell me," Adel whispered, her tongue following the words into the warmth of her ear.

"I just don't know..." Grace's words trailed off and she met Adel's eyes. "How to do this. I'm afraid I won't get it right."

Adel slipped her hand around the back of Grace's neck and kissed her, stroking her lip lightly with her thumb as she pulled away.

"There isn't a right way to do it." She kissed her again, fighting the urge to dip her fingers under those translucent panties and show her. "Especially with women."

Adel smiled, then pulled her close and whispered the question she already knew the answer to. "I know you haven't been with anyone else yet, but have you ever touched yourself?"

Grace nodded. "Yeah, since I was younger." She looked down as Adel brushed a stray lock of hair away from her face. "I mean, I know what feels good to me. I just always stop…"

"Before you have an orgasm?"

"I guess I just always feel guilty." Grace looked down and shook her head, hesitating before she spoke again. "Like I don't deserve it, or something, although I know that makes no sense."

"And how do you feel now?"

"I know I want to be here." Grace met her eyes, her gaze steady and sure. "And I know I want to be with you."

Adel paused for a long second, searching her face for any sign of hesitation before she hooked her thumb under the delicate lace of Grace's panties and eased them down her thighs. She pulled Grace's nipple into her mouth until she heard her breath catch, fingertips brushing the other into a tense pink bud. Windswept rain scraped the windows, blurring any trace of the outside world as she kissed down the slender planes of her body, bringing one of Grace's thighs up and settling it over her shoulder. Adel paused, drinking in the sight of her as melting wax sizzled in the darkness and the candlelight settled like shimmering gold mesh over her naked body.

"You're so beautiful," Adel murmured against the delicate skin of Grace's inner thigh. A trace of silky gold hair, like light falling against her skin, framed her dusky pink center as Adel touched her for the first time. She gently pressed Grace's thighs apart with her shoulders and listened intently to every breath as she slicked her thumb lightly over her clit, which responded instantly, tensing under her touch.

Grace whispered something as she wove her fingers into Adel's hair, but the words disappeared into the staccato rain pelting the windowpanes. Adel's mouth hovered low on the inside slope of Grace's hip, touching her first with only her breath, then she slid her hands under Grace's hips to span her waist from behind as she stroked her clit gently with her tongue. Grace was ready, the heat from her body melting into Adel's mouth as she worked her achingly slowly, her tongue slicking languidly over her clit. Silent lightning flashed across the glass, illuminating the room into a black-and-white movie set with amber candlelight as the only contrast, warming the space around Grace's naked body.

Grace tangled her fingers harder into Adel's hair, her inner thighs tensing against Adel's shoulders. Adel breathed her in, then drew her clit just slightly into her mouth, teasing it with the tip of her tongue, then with longer, deeper strokes. She dipped her head, tongue stroking Grace inside for just a moment before she returned to her clit. Grace's hips were restless, and Adel felt her fingertips move to the back of her neck. She brushed her thigh with her lips and then waited until Grace opened her eyes.

"I want to touch you inside." Adel slid her fingertips down, her own body responding hard to how intensely wet Grace was. "Is that okay?"

Grace nodded and shifted her hips closer. Adel watched her face as she gently slid her middle finger inside while working her clit with her other hand. She listened to every breath lengthen and deepen, then as her hips began to move, she watched Grace's face flush, a wash of deep rose sinking to her neck and across her breasts like silent watercolor brushstrokes.

Adel dipped her head to swirl her tongue across her clit again, and this time, Grace's breath turned to a soft moan as she gripped the sheet beside them. She arched her back against the rhythmic, insistent strokes of Adel's tongue as Adel slid a second finger inside and turned them, exploring until she knew what Grace needed. Adel kept her fingers gentle but her tongue intense, stroking Grace's clit with soft, steady pressure. Grace's entire body started to tense, her breath sharp, then silent, until Adel felt her fingertips against her shoulder and just one word.

"Wait."

Adel pulled the duvet around them and slid up Grace's body to lie behind her and pull her carefully back into her arms.

"Are you okay?" Adel whispered into her ear, smoothing damp strands of hair back from her face. "Tell me I didn't hurt you."

"No, it's not that." Grace paused as a little shiver ran through her body. "It's just that it's…" She faltered, searching for the word. "I don't know how to describe it, it's just…"

"Intense?"

"Yeah." Grace smiled and relaxed slowly into Grace's arms. "So much it's almost scary. Like I'm about to step off the edge of a cliff."

"It can feel like that." Adel brushed her fingertips up Grace's side and across the curve of her breast. Adel braced herself on one hand then moved above her, her hand between their bodies. She waited until Grace nodded before stroking her clit again softly, her words softer than breath against her lips. "But if you trust me, I'll catch you, I promise."

Grace nodded, her eyes fluttering closed, the tension in her body hesitantly unfolding onto the bed.

"Just breathe," Adel whispered against her mouth. "I've got the rest."

Grace was beyond wet, her clit tense under Adel's fingers as a fine mist of sweat started to shimmer on her chest. Adel slowed her hand, entering her again slowly with gentle fingers, the heel of her hand slick and light against Grace's clit.

She groaned as Adel started to move her own body and hand together, her face buried in Grace's neck, whispering as she stroked her inside and kept light, slick pressure over her clit. Grace gripped the back of Adel's neck, her forehead pressed against Adel's as they moved together. The heat between their bodies was intense, and Grace's wetness filled the palm of her hand like a sacred offering. Adel felt her start to get close, felt Grace's hips start to move with her, her back arch underneath her. She kept the same rhythm until Grace held her breath suddenly then cried out against Adel's neck, both hands tangled hard into Adel's hair as she shuddered into her first orgasm.

Adel waited until her body started to relax, then softened her hand and pulled Grace into her arms, smoothing damp strands of hair from her face. The rain had lightened finally, lazy drops sliding down the panes, but the sky was still dark, the same color as the churning sea below crashing onto the shore. She kissed Grace's forehead and pulled her closer.

"How do you feel?"

"I feel like…" Grace looked up at Adel and paused as a faint shiver moved through her at the memory. "I'll die if you don't do that to me again."

"Oh, I'll do it again." Adel smiled at Grace, pulling her closer and kissing her for a few long seconds, her hand moving from the deep curve of her waist to cup the lush curve of her ass. "Like, right now."

The phone she'd set on the bedside table started to buzz right at that moment, sending it inching toward the edge until Adel reached over Grace's naked body just in time to keep it from falling off.

She looked at the screen and sat up, pulling the covers slowly around her. It was Bethany.

Chapter Twelve

The next day, Adel dragged her suitcase off the luggage carousel and headed for the exit. It was past time to share what she knew—she should have done it before now—and the few texts she'd exchanged with Bethany as she'd boarded the plane made her wonder, with a searing rush of guilt, if it was already too late. The glass sliding doors shut with a whoosh behind her as she walked out of the terminal into the blazing sun hovering above the parking garage. When she got to the top level, the sun was sinking swiftly into the western sky and the air had chilled to crisp as she searched her pocket for her phone and dialed.

"Hello?"

"Hey, man." Adel slowed and took a breath. She had a sudden eerie feeling that everything in her life was about to change. "Sorry to bother you. This is Adel Rosse. Do you have a minute?"

"Yeah. I had a feeling I'd be talking to you again." The line went to static for a few seconds and then patched back together. "—this morning. In fact, I was going to—"

A revving engine firing in the background muted the next few words, and the wind on the top level of the parking structure threatened to whip away the rest. Adel tossed her suitcase in the back of the car, climbed in, and shut the door behind her, the sound of her breath suddenly deafening in the stale silence of the empty vehicle.

She took a breath and stared at the setting sun sinking past the concrete edge of the parking structure. "Do you have time to meet me for a drink somewhere we can talk?"

"Yeah, no problem." Adel heard the muffled slam of a car door, then sudden silence that mirrored hers. "I'll text you an address. Meet me there in an hour."

Adel clicked off the phone and dropped it into the console. Her other hand was locked and white around the steering wheel as she pulled the car into reverse.

❖

Exactly an hour later, Adel checked the address again on her phone, then pushed open the back door of a dive bar on what she could only assume was the wrong side of town. Her eyes adjusted slowly as she walked down a narrow hall adorned only with a scarred yellow mop bucket with gray standing water that blocked a door covered in graffiti. The cloying scent of commercial air freshener settled onto her skin as she headed for the bar, and the smell of stale beer and last night's cigarettes was actually an improvement as she rounded the corner toward the booths in the back.

Adel recognized her right away, sitting alone in the last booth, peeling the label from a Budweiser. Another bottle sat directly across from her, and she nodded at it as Adel slid into the Naugahyde booth.

"Thanks for meeting me." Adel scooped her hair into a messy ponytail as she glanced across the table.

"Yeah, no problem."

Kate Kilcullen took a long swig of her beer and raked a hand through her hair. Her detective shield glinted gold at her belt, and she was wearing a tailored navy shirt buttoned almost to the top and rolled up at the sleeves. She was impeccably dressed, but there were tired lines around her eyes as if she'd slept at her desk the night before.

"I thought we'd end up circling back around." She clinked her bottle to Adel's and glanced behind her. "So, what's up?"

Adel pulled up a picture on her phone, then pushed it toward Kate and waited. Kate picked it up slowly and stared, then shook her head as she zoomed in from two angles, pulling her glasses from her shirt pocket and locking eyes with Adel as she put them on.

"Where did you get this?"

"I don't know what I can tell you at this point." Adel let out a long breath as she met Kate's eyes over the table. "And what I can't."

"Adel." Kate paused and nodded at the waitress, who set another two beers on the scarred Formica countertop and walked away without a word. "Not telling me isn't an option right now."

Adel nodded, the gravity of what she was doing bearing down on her shoulders. "Yeah, I know."

Adel downed her beer and set the empty bottle at the end of the table, pulling the new one toward her.

"I'm not supposed to have it. And neither is the person who took it."

"And who was that?"

"A friend." Adel jumped as someone started the jukebox in the corner, then Def Leppard's "Hysteria" flooded in like a liquid wall between them and the rest of the dimly lit bar. "She's the horse wrangler at Valley of Rubies. She found this girl hiding in the tack room in the middle of the night and took the picture when she turned around. She showed it to me because she didn't know what else to do."

"And when was that?" Kate unbuttoned her shirt at the collar with long, quick fingers. Her eyes were kinder than her voice.

"A few days ago. The girl's name is Audrey, evidently. She's one of the staff members at camp."

Kate let out a long breath and put her hand back out for the phone. "What the fuck does all this writing mean? Is it code or some shit?"

"I don't know, but it means something."

Def Leppard jerked suddenly into Van Halen, and Kate held up two fingers with a glance at the bar. The same waitress dropped two shots of questionable whiskey by the table a few minutes later, pinched together with her thumb in one and forefinger in the other. She shook the booze off her hand as she walked back to the bar, slamming the stalled jukebox with the side of her fist as she passed it.

"Trying to get me drunk?"

"Nah." Kate clinked her shot glass to Adel's and downed it with no change of expression. "If I didn't think you could handle it, it wouldn't be in front of you."

Kate looked down again at the picture on the phone she'd set on the table between them. Audrey was standing with her back to the camera in the tack room, naked. Her back was covered with dark handwritten numbers that snaked down her arms, up her neck, and around her hips—all different, and all scrawled in scattered groups of four. Those were framed by bruises covering her arms in the unmistakable shape of handprints and ragged scratches across the tops of her shoulders and neck.

"What was she doing in that room?" Kate squinted and leaned closer. "Was she showing this chick—"

"Bethany."

"Okay, Bethany." Kate took a small notebook out of her shirt pocket and clicked open her pen. "Was she showing her what had happened?"

"Hell, no. She was naked and hiding under a table when Bethany found her. Bethany took her shirt off and gave it to her to cover up before she took her back up to her cabin." She glanced back down at the phone. "It looks like she took the picture when Audrey turned around to put the shirt on, I guess."

"And this Bethany chick." Kate looked up from her notebook. "Is there any way she'd be involved in this for some reason?"

"Fuck, no." Adel took a breath and leveled her voice, reminding herself that Kate had no idea who Bethany was. "She's the one who showed it to me in the first place, and she was upset about it. Really upset." She paused, remembering the tears she'd seen in Bethany's eyes that afternoon in the hayloft. "I haven't known her long, but I have the feeling it takes a lot to make that happen."

"All right. That's good enough for me." Kate's voice softened. She glanced up at Adel and leaned back in the booth, one arm extended across the back of it, the other rubbing at the deep lines in her forehead. "You know we gotta do something about this, right?"

"I know." Adel picked up the empty shot glass and put it back down on the table slowly. "But I have a job to do too."

"Dude. You're shitting me here." Kate slid the phone back over to Adel and shook her head, her jaw tense. "You're worried about your *article* right now?"

"Kate, I'm not thinking about myself here. I'm screwed no matter what. I'm saying that because this article has the potential of blowing up this entire shit show and exposing what they're doing behind closed doors. Believe me, this place only exists because none of these girls question anything these men do to them, not even to each other." She paused and downed the last of her beer. "The second that changes, that's when the Brethren, or whatever the hell they call themselves, start to lose their power."

"Yeah, I've heard. 'Don't betray the Brethren,'" Kate said, looking over her shoulder and leaning in, her voice dropping to the level of her elbows on the worn tabletop. "'Keep sweet. No matter what.'"

Adel thought back to the embroidered frame she'd seen on the wall in her cabin the first night. "How do you know about that? They say that shit to the girls all the time to keep them in line."

"Because we've been investigating this place for almost a year. We've got leads and speculation, lots of it, but what we really need is at least one credible complaining witness who's willing to testify so we can indict these bastards."

"And what if you can't get that?" Adel shook her head, picking at the tiny nails holding the aluminum trim to the table. "Because betraying the Brethren seems like it could get you killed."

"Then we've got fuck-all." Kate sighed and pushed her empty bottle toward the edge of the table. "Without that, there is no case."

❖

The next night, Kate and Adel sat across from Hannah in her dining room, who was still in her light green scrubs and completely distracted by the tower of a burger that Kate had brought over for her, with more slippery pickles and a mottled river of mayo and mustard threatening to drip over onto the wrinkled foil wrapper.

"Burger King this time, huh?" Adel nodded to the logo on her soda cup, blurred by dripping condensation. "I thought you were a Sonic girl?"

"What can I say?" Hannah raised the burger to her mouth and winked. "I have commitment issues."

"Yeah. That's putting it lightly." Kate smiled and arched an eyebrow, retrieving a paper towel from the kitchen counter and returning to the table to slide it in Hannah's direction. "God help you if you're a burger or her girlfriend. You never know where you stand with this one."

"That's actually never been proven." Hannah balled up the napkin and tossed it in Kate's direction, who caught it easily with one hand and lobbed it into the trash can in the corner. "Because I never have a girlfriend."

"All right, I hate to break up this tender moment of commitment phobia." Adel rolled her eyes and paused, tracing a deep scratch in the pine tabletop with her fingertip. "But I think we're waiting on nothing at this point. If she hasn't called by now, she probably won't. I can't say I'd be brave enough to take that risk if I was her." Adel looked across the table and arched an eyebrow at Kate. "By the way, I just gave her my number and Hannah's. No offense, but you sound a little rough around the edges."

"Probably smart." Kate pretended to be wounded at Hannah's laughter and winked at Adel. "Everyone keeps telling me I still have a few of those to sand down. I didn't exactly grow up in Hannah's neighborhood."

Hannah laughed around the bite of burger she had in her mouth before she turned to Adel. "I kept my phone with me all day, but no one called. I was hoping she had gotten in touch with you." Hannah checked her silent phone again and put it back down on the table. "So tell me about this girl. I was swamped at the clinic, so Kate couldn't tell me much today when she dropped by." Hannah popped a fry into her mouth and smacked Kate's hand as she tried to steal one for herself. "All I know is you think she might have been assaulted. What makes you think that? Did she tell someone?"

"Um, no. Not exactly."

Kate looked at Adel and waited until she nodded to bring up the picture on her phone and slide it over to Hannah. Hannah studied it for a moment, then slid it back to Kate.

"She's from the Valley of Rubies, isn't she?"

"How do you know that?" Kate clicked it off and slid the phone back into her pocket. "Do you recognize something?"

"Just those numbers." Hannah picked up her to-go cup and shook the ice to the bottom. "I came to work super early one day last year to try to get some paperwork done. It was still dark as I walked up and there was this girl just sitting on the steps." Hannah paused, her voice softening with the memory. "She never actually said it, but it was pretty obvious she'd been assaulted. Someone had written all over her like that, but these numbers were faint, like she'd been trying to scrub them off. I treated her and tried to get her to tell me what happened, but she never said a word, didn't even tell me her name. But I saw that camp logo on her shirt and wrote it down."

"I remember that report." Kate ran a hand through her hair and leaned back in her chair. "I didn't know you then, but you stated you thought she might be underage, and that's what got the whole investigation started. Is there any chance it's the same girl?"

"No. Not at all." Hannah sighed and pushed away the rest of her food. "I can't see her face in that picture, but that girl is a redhead, with pale skin and freckles. The girl I treated that morning was much shorter, with blond hair down to her waist."

Kate put her hand on Hannah's suddenly and leaned back in her chair, looking toward the window. "I think I just heard someone pull up outside. Are you expecting anyone?"

"Yeah, I left some files at the front desk and Amber is supposed to drop them by at some point."

"Well, whoever it is is driving a 1986 Jeep Comanche." Kate stood, pushing her chair back up to the table. "I'd know that rumble anywhere."

"Fuck *right* off." Hannah took an enormous bite of her burger and still managed to make her next few words sound like she was eating nothing at all. "How could you possibly know that?"

"Skills, baby."

"Yeah, well." Hannah wrapped up the rest of her burger and dropped it in the trash, hesitating like she'd just let the sapphire necklace from *Titanic* slip from her fingers and disappear into the Atlantic. "I'll give you that one. You do have some skills."

She started toward the door, then stopped when she got to the hall and looked back over her shoulder.

"You two have anything else to do besides watch my ass all night?"

Hannah rounded the corner to answer the door and Kate smiled, wiping a bit of leftover mustard off the table with a stray napkin. She crumpled it in her hand and sank it precisely in the center of the same trash can on the other side of the room. Again.

"Damn." Adel shook her head. "You do have some skills."

"Yeah, I don't think those are the ones she's talking about, not that they do me much good with the Ice Queen over there."

"How long have you two been together?"

"You mean *not* together?" Kate shook her head with a glance back at the hall. "About a year now. She just refuses to consider making things official. She's scared to death of letting herself fall in love again."

"Does she have a reason to be scared?"

Kate leaned back in her chair and linked her fingers behind her head. "Of me? No. But I met her when I handled a domestic violence case involving her and her partner at the time."

"Really?" Adel paused, glancing down the hallway and dropping her voice. "I can't see Hannah letting that happen to her."

"Domestic violence and rape happen to the strongest women in the world every damn day." Kate held Adel's eyes and leaned forward on the table. "No one chooses to be a victim of violent crime."

"You're right." The obvious truth of Kate's words washed over Adel in a hot, sudden rush. "I'm sorry. I'm an idiot."

"You're not an idiot." Kate's face softened unexpectedly, and she shook her head. "It's hard to understand something you might not have personal experience with. I get it."

Kate and Adel looked up suddenly when they heard footsteps in the hall, just in time to watch Hannah round the corner into the doorway. The girl beside her was small and pale, with freckles and wild, deep auburn hair that looked windblown even in the still, silent room.

Audrey.

Chapter Thirteen

Audrey pulled the long sleeves of her white blouse down over her hands as she stood beside Hannah. Her gaze was calm, but every muscle looked tightly wound, as if she were one second from bolting back down the hall behind her.

Hannah spoke first, softly, her voice tempered. Adel recognized it from the day they'd met at Planned Parenthood her first day in Lockwood.

"Audrey, I think you may recognize Adel from camp, and this is my friend Kate that I was just telling you about."

Audrey's gaze swept Adel slowly up and down. When she finally spoke, her voice was like a spiderweb shimmering at dawn—strong and fragile in the same breath.

"My little sister is in your creative writing class." Her gaze, slow and intense, settled onto Adel. "But Dr. Myers told me you're not really one of them. At the camp. Is that true?" She paused, her eyes narrowing. "And don't lie to me."

"Well." Kate leaned back in her chair, clearly trying not to smile. "I like this girl already."

Audrey turned to Kate and started to say something, then clocked the gold detective shield on Kate's hip and took a measured step back.

Hannah reached out to touch her arm, but Audrey flinched away.

"That one has a badge." Adel watched Kate hold Audrey's gaze gently while she unclipped the shield and laid it facedown on the table. "You didn't tell me that."

"Don't worry," Hannah said, with a wink in Kate's direction before she turned back to Audrey. "She doesn't know how to use it."

Adel tried to hide her laugh under a cough as Kate rolled her eyes, which dispelled the tension somewhat, but Audrey still kept her eyes firmly on Kate when they finally walked in to sit down.

"Are you hungry?" Hannah asked her, cracking open a Sprite from the fridge and turning back toward the table. "I always have lots of snacks in the pantry."

Audrey looked up, seeming to consider the question, her fingers still curled into a fist around the edges of her sleeves. "I don't know."

Hannah nodded like that made perfect sense and rummaged around in the pantry, emerging with an armful of Cheetos puffs, a sleeve of Oreos, and an opened box of Little Debbie snack cakes, and piled them all in the center of the table.

"Sorry." She smacked Kate's arm when she rolled her eyes and turned back to Audrey with a smile. "You'd think I'd eat healthier with the whole doctor thing, wouldn't you?"

Adel reached for a Little Debbie and watched Hannah work her magic putting Audrey at ease. She'd remembered from her conversation with Nora and Bethany in the hayloft that Audrey's staff cabin was the last in the row, so she'd stopped by earlier that afternoon with a note she slid under the door. It was short and to the point, mostly because she didn't know what to say, and she'd written Hannah's address at the bottom of the note under their phone numbers as an afterthought, just in case.

"So, Audrey," Hannah said, pushing the sleeve of Oreos in her direction. Audrey hesitated, then reached out for one and bit into it gingerly. "Tell me a little bit about what's going on."

"Look, I don't want to be here." Audrey laid the Oreo slowly down on the table, and it was a long time before she looked up again. "And I wouldn't be, but…I'm here for Chelsey."

Kate and Hannah looked at Adel, but she shook her head, so Hannah asked the obvious question.

Audrey pulled at a stray thread on the cuff of her blouse. "Chelsey is my older sister. And I need to…" Her voice cracked and she visibly steeled herself. She tilted her chin up as if she'd done it a thousand times and steadied her voice to continue. "I need to find out what happened to her. I've tried, but I'm just making everything worse."

"Okay." Kate had the good sense to soften her voice when she spoke. "Is Chelsey at the camp with you?"

Audrey shook her head. "The last time she was at camp was three years ago, when she was fourteen, for her Purity Ball." She paused, picked the Oreo back up, then set it down without eating it. She kept her eyes locked on it as she spoke. "She was a camper that year like everyone else, and should have finished out the summer there, but she came home the day after the ball and..." Audrey's voice cracked and she closed her eyes, steeling herself again before she continued. "She was just never the same."

The memory of seeing Grace on her knees in the water the night of the Purity Ball flashed through Adel's mind. "Did she ever tell you what happened?"

"No. In fact, she never spoke again. It was like she lost her mind or something. She just sat at home at her desk, staring at the wall."

Kate looked at Adel. They were thinking the same thing.

"She refused to leave her room for the next three months. She just sat there, either staring into space or scribbling in her notebooks so hard she ripped the paper when she got to the edge. She used these black permanent markers and just..." Her voice trailed off and she dug her fingernails into her palm as she took in a long breath. "I remember they were always frayed and flat at the end. She wore them down to the nub."

Tears welled up in Audrey's eyes but she refused to acknowledge them; they just spilled over her cheeks and landed on the table in silence. Nobody moved. When Hannah finally spoke, her voice almost a whisper.

"Did she ever get better?"

Audrey waited a long time before she answered.

"Only when she hung herself in the barn three months later. I found her there before church on a Sunday, and there was a black marker tied into the knot around her neck. I knew then that she'd done it to tell me something." She crossed her arms in front of her, each hand on the opposite shoulder. "I didn't understand it until a few days ago on the altar."

No one said a word. Adel watched as Kate reached out and covered Audrey's clenched hand with her own. "What do you need from us, Audrey?"

Audrey's shoulders crumpled. It was Kate who asked gently if it was okay to hug her, and surprisingly, Audrey sank into her arms, sobbing silently and struggling to breathe under the memory of her sister's trauma. They sat there together for a few long minutes until Audrey's breathing softened and she lifted her head. Hannah got up, retrieved some tissues from a box on the end table by the sofa, and handed them to Audrey as she sat back down. Moonlight shimmered across the lake just outside the windows, and it suddenly seemed like the middle of a long, exhausting night.

"I need to know what happened to my sister." Audrey looked at Hannah and Adel before turning back to Kate. "I need you to help me stop them. I tried to do it myself, but I can't. There's too many of them…and I'm nobody."

Kate took both of Audrey's hands in hers and held her eyes for a moment before she spoke.

"Audrey, you're not nobody. In fact, you might be the bravest girl I've ever met, and I've been doing this job a long time. You didn't know us at all, but you walked right in here and told three total strangers what happened to your sister because you want justice for Chelsey. We're going to do whatever it takes to make sure this doesn't happen to anyone else." She paused. "But we're going to need your help, and it's going to get tough. Can you do that?" Kate held Audrey's gaze for a long second before she went on. "For Chelsey?"

Audrey nodded, tears falling down her face again before she looked up finally and wiped her cheeks with the heel of her hand.

"I'll do anything."

Hannah wiped her own eyes and glanced down the hall. "The first thing we need to figure out is how to get you out of there so you're safe. I'd love for you to stay here with me, but you're a minor, right? They'll be looking for you."

Audrey shook her head. "If I can get a message to Nora to leave a note in my room, they won't question it if it just says I went home to my husband, and he'll think I'm still at camp."

"Your husband?" This from Hannah, who was struggling to keep her voice even at this point. "How old are you, Audrey?"

"I'm fifteen. I'll be sixteen in September."

Kate softened her voice when she spoke. "And I know in Covenant families sometimes men who are higher up in the ranks marry multiple wives. Is that right?"

Audrey nodded but didn't add any other details.

"Are you a first wife, or…"

Audrey nodded.

"How old is your husband?"

"He's thirty-four." She paused before she went on, gripping the edge of the table with her fingertips. Her eyes fluttered shut as she spoke. "No one else wanted to marry him, and now I know why."

"Okay." Kate rolled up the sleeves of her shirt as she spoke. "This is important. Do you remember if you signed anything before you got married? Like a legal document?"

"Yes. My parents had to sign it too. I remember them saying it meant we were really married."

Kate let out a long breath and rubbed her temples before she went on. "Adel, can you get someone to plant that note in her room tomorrow morning? Don't do it yourself, though, that would look suspicious, and at this point, that's all we need."

"Audrey, do you feel safe enough to stay here while we work on getting to the truth?" Kate glanced at Audrey and waited until she nodded.

"Okay." Hannah smiled, her shoulders relaxing a bit. "At least that's settled."

Audrey finally picked up the Oreo and put the rest of it in her mouth, keeping her eyes down as she chewed slowly. "And…I kind of stole Nora's truck to get here. She's the one who taught me to drive, so she won't be mad, but I need to get it back to her."

"Interesting." Kate shot a grin in Hannah's direction. "What kind of a truck?"

"A Jeep Comanche. She loves that thing. She rebuilt the engine herself last summer and taught me to drive it."

"Adel and I will get that back to camp for you tonight." Kate smiled. "You'll be safe here and we'll start figuring this out tomorrow. I'll even bring over some real food so you don't starve."

Hannah rolled her eyes, and the tiniest smile played around the corner of Audrey's mouth before she looked back down at the table.

"It's getting late, you've got to be exhausted. I'll call in and get a sub for tomorrow so I'll be here when you wake up." Hannah smiled as she got up from the table and handed Audrey the sleeve of Oreos. "Come on. I'll show you where everything is."

Audrey nodded and pushed her chair back under the table carefully as she followed Hannah into the long hall that led toward the back of the house.

"Wait." Kate looked up suddenly and leaned back in her chair. "Can I ask you something, Audrey?"

Audrey turned around and nodded.

"What does it mean at Valley of Rubies when you see numbers grouped together in sets of four? I stayed up most of last night trying to figure it out, but I couldn't find anything even similar. I got zilch."

Audrey walked back to the table slowly and lifted her blouse halfway to reveal identical groups of numbers, written in permanent black marker, the skin around them rubbed red raw. When she spoke her voice was empty, emotionless, as she pointed at each of the four numbers in a single group.

"Book, chapter, verse, and word."

She looked down at her body as if it didn't belong to her and let out a slow breath. When she spoke again her voice was a whisper, every word a secret.

"I can't get them off me, and it's making me feel like I'm going crazy. What if they never go away?" She raked across them suddenly with her nails, leaving angry red welts rising in their wake. "But I guess that's the point."

She turned then without looking up and walked back down to Hannah, who put her arm around her shoulder as they rounded the corner of the hall.

❖

"Jesus Christ."

Kate's voice was hoarse as she and Adel went out to the deck and leaned on the railing, drawing in the cool night air as if they'd just escaped the desert. Kate raked a hand through her hair, then walked over to a small table by the sliding glass doors. She returned with a box of menthol American Spirits and handed one to Adel, flicking a chrome lighter under the end of it.

"You didn't even ask me if I smoke." Adel looked up at the crescent moon hanging in the black night sky and exhaled the sheer gray smoke, watching it rise like a makeshift temple around them then dissipate into the darkness.

"Yeah, well." Kate closed her eyes as she inhaled, the tip of her cigarette blazing red and orange as the paper sizzled into ash. "Who doesn't smoke after something like that?"

Kate turned around to face the golden light in the house and leaned back on her elbows against the railing. "What are you telling your editor about this place?"

"Not much so far. He knows something's up with Valley of Rubies, which is why he wanted to do an exposé on it, but I don't think he's really expecting anything more salacious than polygamy yet."

"Yeah, I think we passed that point about fifty miles back." Kate flicked her ash over the balcony and turned back to Adel. "If you tell him something now, though, or write about this shit at all, it could tank the investigation, and we'd lose our chance to get these girls out of there."

The wind picked up the edges of Adel's hair and she tucked it behind her ear as she nodded. "I know."

"This was your big break, though, right?"

Adel arched an eyebrow and looked back as Hannah opened the sliding glass door behind them. "How did you know that?"

"My sister works for the *Chicago Tribune*, and she had an assignment like this dropped in her lap when she was in her twenties. No one was willing to put their name on it but my badass sister. It turned out she was right—it made her career."

Hannah stepped out onto the deck, shutting the slider behind her with one hand and zipping up her fleece with the other. She walked up and took the cigarette out of Kate's hand, drawing a long puff before she handed it back. She exhaled toward the moon and rubbed her forehead with the tips of her fingers for a moment before she looked up.

"Can someone tell me what the fuck a Purity Ball is? Because clearly, something really bad happened to Audrey's sister there. Just the name of that thing gives me the creeps."

"I don't know much about it." Adel zipped up her jacket against the wind picking up over the water. "But it's some sort of ceremony where girls as young as eight or nine promise to remain 'pure' until marriage, which is not even the weird part, believe it or not. According to a friend of mine at camp, it's this elaborate wedding-like event where the girls symbolically hand over their virginity to their father to 'safeguard' until the day he gives it to her husband at her wedding."

"So, essentially," Hannah turned to look at Adel as the meaning of what she'd said sank in, "they're sending the message that they never own their own sexuality or choices, and they're always the property of the men around them."

"Yeah." Adel finished her cigarette and dropped it in the ashtray Kate passed to her. "What could you possibly find creepy or inappropriate about that?"

Kate shook her head and looked up as a star fell across the sky, leaving a trail of silver dust across the inky darkness. "Well, I don't know what it is, but they're clearly hiding something. I've been working this case for a year, and that place is locked up tighter than Quantico. We need her."

"She's a minor, though." Hannah glanced over at Kate. "Can she get involved without law enforcement telling her parents?"

"Believe it or not, that's the only break we've gotten so far," Kate said, running her hand through her hair and leaning onto the railing. "She's under eighteen, but if her parents signed off for her to get married, which it sounds like they did, she's automatically considered an adult in the state of New York."

Hannah nodded. "Well, that's something, I guess."

Adel looked up at Hannah, who was rubbing her forehead and staring at the reflection of the moon as it rippled on the dark, glassy surface of the lake.

"Hey, did Audrey tell you who her other sister is? The one in my creative writing class?"

Hannah pulled her phone out of her pocket and scrolled down, a lock of blond hair tumbling out of her makeshift bun and falling over her face like light.

"Yeah, I asked her as I left and made a note. I figured you might want to know." She held up her phone to Adel. The name was stark black on the glowing white background of the phone.

Ruth Blankenship.

Adel hadn't known who to expect, but the blond, back-talking rebel from rowing class was certainly not at the top of the list.

Hannah clicked her phone off and dropped it back in the pocket of her scrubs. "And I'm guessing this isn't good news, but Audrey referred to their father as 'the Prophet.'"

Kate turned to Adel. Adel shook her head, then leaned back, her fingers gripping the railing and stared at the sky.

Hannah looked from one to the other. "What?"

Kate cleared her throat. "I think it's fair to say things just got a lot more complicated."

Chapter Fourteen

About an hour later, when Adel finally got back to camp, she walked into her cabin to find Grace asleep on her couch, curled up under a jacket that she'd left draped over the desk chair. She didn't stir when Adel shut the door quietly behind her and locked it.

"Grace." Adel reached out and smoothed her hair from her face, smiling at the sleep marks pressed into her cheek as she rolled over.

"Sorry." Grace sat up and pulled the length of her hair over her shoulder, blinking the sleep from her eyes. "I should have asked before I fell asleep here." She glanced toward the windows. "But Bethany was right, there's definitely been someone in my cabin. They didn't even try to hide it."

"No, I'm glad you're here." Adel set her keys down on the desk and went to the kitchen for wineglasses and a bottle of aged Barolo she'd picked up in town a few days before. Nothing like the world going to shit for inspiration to break out the good booze. "Did they take anything?"

"I'm sure they did." Grace rubbed her eyes and pulled the ponytail holder out of her hair, which dropped down over her shoulders to her waist. "I just don't know what yet. Or why."

Adel walked over and peeked into her nightstand to be sure her journal was still there. It was, and nothing else seemed to have been disturbed. That was the only thing she had that could really get her in trouble besides alcohol if they'd decided to rummage through her cabin at the same time. She ran her hand through her hair and headed back to the wine in the kitchen.

"Jesus." Adel pulled the cork out with a smooth pop and twisted it off the corkscrew as she watched Grace retrieve a package off the desk and hand it to her.

"What's that?"

Grace shrugged. "It came for you today. At least I think it did. It was in front of your door when I got back from the vespers service."

"Oh yeah." Adel smiled when she saw the return address and handed it back to her. "Actually, it's for you."

Grace turned it over in her hands. "Sometimes they do deliver to the wrong cabin, but it can't be for me, I didn't order anything."

Adel handed her a glass of wine and walked back over to the couch. "It's yours. I know because I ordered it."

"What?" Worry lines creased her forehead as she sat down with the package on her lap. "You just bought me something for no reason?" She tugged at the tape holding the box together, her gaze thoughtful. "Why would you do that?"

Adel took a sip of her wine, then swirled it in the glass, watching the deep berry color thin languidly into a lighter crimson. As it slowed, she set the glass in front of Grace and picked up the other glass.

"I did have a reason." She met Grace's eyes and held them for a moment, then continued. "When we were talking in the attic about the binding they forced you to wear, you said that you'd worn it every single day since your dad gave it to you."

"That's true." Grace dropped her gaze, smoothing her thumb over the packing tape on the top of the box. "Since I was eleven."

"Well, what you did this weekend took a lot of courage, and I can tell you're not about to go back to binding." Adel pulled a pocketknife out of her back pocket and opened it, handing it to Grace with a smile. "So you deserve this."

Grace took the knife, carefully slicing through the tape across the top. She pulled out a shiny black box tied with a pink velvet ribbon and set the shipping box on the floor, her eyes locked on the ribbon under her fingers as a reluctant smile spread across her face. She raised the lid to reveal three beautiful bra and underwear sets, one made of slinky black silk, one covered in delicate ivory lace, and the other the palest sheer aqua, the exact color of her eyes.

"I just guessed at your size." Adel set the box top on the coffee table and checked one of the tags. "But I've been gay since I hit the ground, so there might be an outside chance I got it right."

Grace ran her fingertips across the delicate fabrics like she was memorizing every detail, still and silent. When she finally looked up, her eyes were shimmering with tears. "I've never owned anything this beautiful. I can't believe you did this for me."

Adel slid closer and held her face in her hands. "Grace, you deserve so much more than this." She paused as she brought Grace's face closer to hers. "I know you've started to pick out some lingerie already, so these are just placeholders to get you started until you figure out more about what you like."

She kissed her then, tracing Grace's lower lip with her tongue as she brushed her cheek with her fingertips. Grace caught her hand and brought it to her mouth as she leaned back enough to look up at Adel.

"Can I stay with you tonight?"

"Are you scared?" Adel leaned back before she spoke, studying her face. "Because if you are—"

"No, it's not just about my cabin." Grace paused, biting her lower lip. She started to go on, but then stopped and searched Adel's eyes.

Adel kissed her again and nodded. "Okay." She took another sip of the wine and stood, shrugging off her jacket and laying it over the back of the desk chair. "I'm just going to take a quick bath, though. I'll be right back."

A few minutes later, Adel opened the bathroom door to find Grace already in bed, hair spilled out across the pillow. She turned toward Adel and smiled, reaching out to switch off the bedside lamp.

Adel checked the door again and turned out the rest of the lights, pausing by the window for just a moment before she turned back. The moonlight illuminated the white curtains, the muffled lap of dark lake water the only sound in the room, soft and constant. Adel pulled back the covers and got into bed, her hand sliding warm around the warm, bare skin of Grace's waist.

Grace held her eyes. "What do you think?"

Grace was wearing the pale blue silk bra, cut low enough that it barely covered her nipples, which highlighted her curves and pale, creamy skin. Adel closed her eyes and slid her hand over Grace's hip, the silk of the panties soft and warm under her fingertips.

"Grace, I don't want you to think—"

Grace put her finger on Adel's lips and smiled. "I don't. I'm in your bed because I want to be." She paused, trailing her finger over Adel's lower lip.

Adel groaned, pulling Grace over to sit across her hips. Her hair fell around her face and one bra strap slipped silently down her shoulder as she looked down at Adel with soft eyes, her voice suddenly hesitant. "I want you to teach me. To do what you did."

Adel wove her fingers into Grace's and rested them on her thighs.

"Just do what you feel." Her eyes dropped to Grace's mouth and she felt her body respond. "I'll guide you."

Grace leaned in slowly and kissed her, her breasts just brushing Adel's as she traced her nipples with hesitant fingertips, then her tongue, pulling Adel's nipple unexpectedly into the slick warmth of her mouth. Adel took a deep breath and gripped the headboard, mostly to keep herself from flipping Grace over and devouring her. Everything inside her wanted to sink down between those thighs and feel Grace's clit stiffen under her tongue, to watch as her body arched into the orgasm she didn't know was coming.

Grace held Adel's gaze as she reached back to unhook the bra, which hesitated before it fell from her shoulders, clinging to the curves of her body as if reluctant to reveal them. Adel slid both hands around her hips, drinking in the sight of her full, perfect breasts and soft pink nipples. The sheer panties were the only barrier between them as Adel grazed Grace's clit with her thumb through the fabric. Grace closed her eyes and bit her bottom lip, leaning into her touch. The silk was soaked through, the heat from her body intense across Adel's hips. It was all she could do to not slip her fingers underneath and watch Grace ride her hand with that hair falling all around her—

"Adel."

Adel snapped back to attention when she felt Grace lift her wrists to the top of the bed and lean into them.

"Don't move." Grace held her eyes, then kissed her, biting her lower lip as she pulled away. "Leave your hands right here."

Her sudden confidence made Adel instantly wet. "Yes, ma'am."

Grace held her gaze as she lowered a hand between their bodies. Her touch was light, thoughtful, and as her fingertips grazed Adel's clit her eyes fluttered closed and she held her breath. She rested her forehead on Adel's shoulder as she found a soft rhythm, exploring slowly, gently, dipping lower to slick her fingers and returning, memorizing by touch.

Adel's breath deepened and she buried her hands in Grace's hair. She hadn't been with anyone but Katya in over a decade, and their sex life, when they'd had one at least, was the equivalent to one of Katya's predawn workouts—just another means to an end, something else she could check off her to-do list. With Grace, she felt every secret breath, the lightest brush of her lashes against her cheek when they kissed, the intentional tenderness of every touch. She'd expected her to be nervous or hesitant, but everything about Grace felt like courage.

Grace's fingers were still gently stroking her clit, but she'd deepened her touch and lifted her head from Adel's shoulder, the blue of her eyes deepening to the color of a storm moving in from the sea. When she finally spoke, even her voice was dusky, the sound equivalent of the descent of violet evening into inky night.

"Can I?"

Her fingers sank lower but she waited for Adel to answer.

"Yes." Adel looked into her eyes as she whispered the words against her lips. "God, yes."

Grace entered her slowly with two fingers, her face still warm and soft against Adel's. She softened them when she was inside, stroking her as if it were their thousandth time together, breath deep and even against Adel's neck.

"Tell me." The words were a whispered secret against Adel's ear. "Tell me what you like."

Adel tried to speak, but her words got tangled in her breath. Grace sank down her body to sit between her thighs, her touch still deep, rhythmic, and surprisingly intense. Her other hand was low on Adel's abs, and Adel guided Grace's thumb over her clit until she found her rhythm and leaned in, breath warm against Adel's skin as she drew one hard nipple into her mouth, swirling it with her tongue.

"Fuck." It was only one word, but Adel barely got it out before it turned to a groan. Grace's hand was low on her abs as she worked her clit, and Adel pressed down on it gently with her own to teach her to meet the fingers inside with that hand, then reached up to grab the headboard again. Grace stroked her, slow and deep, her slick thumb still sliding over her clit. Every muscle in Adel's body tightened and she bit her lip, a fine mist of sweat glistening across her chest and shoulders. Grace looked up at Adel, her eyes heavy with desire. She was indescribably beautiful, her cheeks flushed, hair tossed around her shoulders as she worked Adel with delicate fingers.

"I need you closer," Adel whispered, her words warm in the space between them. "Stay inside, just lean into me with your hand under you."

Adel pulled her close, moving her hips against Grace's hand, her orgasm building as Grace started stroking her again, breath slow and heated against Adel's neck. Adel arched her back, holding Grace tight to her, their bodies moving together. She felt herself coming, felt their hearts beating together as she finally fell over the edge into an orgasm so intense she noticed only after it faded that most of the sheet was balled up in her fist.

Finally, Adel reached up to rake her hands through her hair, kissing the top of Grace's head as she shifted to lie in Adel's arms and trace the lean lines of her body with her fingertip.

"Come here." Adel pulled Grace over her body, her hands gentle, thumbs working her nipples as she glanced above her to the headboard. "You trust me?"

Grace sat up, her eyes on the headboard before they dropped back to Adel. She raised one eyebrow and waited. "That depends on what you're about to say."

"Should have seen that coming." Adel laughed, reaching around to her ass with both hands and pulling Grace up to kiss her. "That's my girl."

Grace leaned in, her breasts grazing Adel's chest as she kissed her. "So?"

Adel looked up at the headboard and lifted Grace's hands up to grip the top of it.

"You're about to teach me what you like." She smiled, her hands sliding warm up the outside of Grace's thighs. "Just keep your hands there and move over me."

Grace hesitated, then rose onto her knees and moved until her inner thighs were grazing the warmth of Adel's cheeks. Her eyes held Adel's with a steady, erotic gaze.

"Closer, baby," Adel whispered, her voice a slow burn in the darkness. "Just let me have you."

She wrapped her hands around Grace's hips, brought her down slowly, and went inside with her tongue, stroking deeply, then slicking her tongue up and around Grace's clit before she returned. She listened as Grace held her breath, then sank more deeply onto Adel as she moved her tongue to Grace's clit, stroking her as she wrapped her ass in her hands. She explored every silky inch with her tongue, noticing what made Grace shift closer or farther away, and listening to every breath as she started to slowly move with her.

"Oh, my God."

Grace's voice above her was hesitant, as if she'd forgotten the words and had to recall them one by one. She let the headboard go and ran her hands through her hair, piling it on the top of her head just to let it fall back down her arched back like water over a cliff.

Adel stayed on her clit as Grace started to work her hips above her, slicking her fingers before sliding one, then two, slowly inside her. Grace moved her hips to guide her to the right spot, and Adel wrapped her other hand around her thigh, by now tense and damp with sweat. She fucked Grace slowly, keeping her tongue swirling over her clit. After a few seconds, she heard Grace grab the headboard again, her thighs tensing around Adel's face.

"This..." Her voice trailed off and Adel felt her thigh shudder under her hand. "Just don't stop."

Grace leaned back hard against Adel's hand when she slowed and added a third finger, gently, noting the drop in Grace's breath, the sudden stillness that turned to her rocking her hips harder, her clit tense and responsive under Adel's tongue. She felt her start to come as she leaned back farther, fingertips barely clinging to the headboard, hips circling, her walls tightening around Adel's fingers. Adel's other hand was wrapped around Grace's thigh, and she used it to hold her steady as Grace rocked against her mouth, breath tangled into a moan. She felt the shudder of orgasm move through her body, then again, until Grace finally melted into Adel's arms. Adel wrapped her body around Grace's from behind, her hand soft and warm over her heart, memorizing the rhythm as it slowed to match her own.

Until Grace sat up on her elbow suddenly, looking down at Adel's hand.

"What?" Adel said, a tinge of sleep already coloring her words. "What's wrong?"

Grace's face suddenly paled and she looked over her shoulder at Adel. "Oh, no."

Adel leaned up as well and looked down, realizing quickly what was happening. Her hand was streaked with blood, which had then transferred to Grace when she'd pulled her against her body.

"I must have gotten my period." Grace's cheeks went from pale to flushed with embarrassment instantly. "I'm so sorry. I had no idea. I'm not even due for two weeks."

"Just stay there." Adel smiled. "I'll be right back."

Adel got up and washed her hands in the bathroom, then soaked a washcloth in warm water and wrung it out, handing it to Grace as she climbed back in bed.

"First of all," she tipped Grace's chin up with her finger gently, waiting for her to meet her gaze before she spoke, "getting your period is natural. We're women, and just in case you're worried, it doesn't faze me in the least."

"Yeah, but—"

"Secondly," Adel smiled, leaning back in the bed, "I actually don't think that's what's happening here."

Grace cleaned the streaks of blood across her breasts with the washcloth, then put it in Adel's outstretched hand and smiled despite herself as she watched her sink it into the laundry basket across the room.

Adel looked over and met her eyes. "Is this the first time, other than the time in Mystic, that you've had...something inside you?"

Grace started to speak, then paused, a smile spreading slowly across her face. "You mean..."

"Yeah." Adel wrapped her arms around her and pulled her over onto her body, kissing Grace's neck as she flipped her over underneath her. "I think you're just not a virgin anymore."

Grace looked away, and when she turned back, her eyes were filled with tears.

"Grace." Adel heard the tinge of panic in her own voice. "I'm so sorry, I wasn't trying to be flippant, I was just trying to reassure you."

Grace leaned up to kiss her, then lingered as the first tear slid down her cheek. "I know, silly. It's not that. I'm not sad, I'm just..."

Adel suddenly understood and smoothed Grace's hair back, catching another tear with her thumb as she spoke. "You're glad it was me?"

Grace nodded, pulling Adel into her and burying her face in her neck Adel's arms closed around her.

"I'm so glad it was you." Her eyes fluttered closed and her body relaxed against Adel's. When she spoke, her voice had done the same thing. "I'm glad it was us."

The moon dipped behind a cloud outside the curtain, taking the last of the pale glow of moonlight with it, just as her last word melted into the soft, dense darkness around them.

Chapter Fifteen

Adel had promised Bethany she'd meet her at the stables first thing the next morning, but it had been hard to drag herself away from Grace's warm, naked body in time to get a quick bath before she started up the hill. Bethany's texts had gotten increasingly urgent, but Adel had assured her that talking in person was the only safe way to communicate. Adel had a moment of panic that her secret might be out, eventually decided that was impossible, but the weight of hiding her true self was starting to get heavier. Adel zipped up her Carhartt jacket and ran a hand through her hair, then held it to her face for a long second before she shoved it back in her pocket, memorizing the last delicious trace of Grace's scent before it faded away.

The right thing to do was tell Grace everything and just let the damn chips fall.

"But is that the right thing to do?" Adel realized suddenly she was talking out loud to herself in the damn woods as the stables came into view. If Grace felt betrayed, she might cut off contact completely, or worse, tip off Whittier and the Brethren out of some twisted sense of duty.

Adel whipped around when she heard Bethany's golf cart come up suddenly behind her, dodging major trees and taking out the smaller ones as she headed up the hill toward her. Bethany grinned and pulled her beanie down on her head as she skidded onto the path. The back end fishtailed as she hit the brakes, stopping in a cloud of dust before it grazed the side of Adel's boots.

"Hey, stranger. Get the hell in."

"Jesus Christ."

Adel smiled as she walked around to climb in, taking a loaded paper bag off the seat and holding it in her lap as Bethany hit the gas, narrowly avoiding the scuffed side of a spruce tree that had clearly not been so lucky in the past. Adel settled into the seat and peered into the bag, noting there were three wrapped bagels and a brownie.

"So what's the big secret?"

Adel turned to look at Bethany as she spoke. She had a different energy today, almost somber, and didn't reply. Adel turned her eyes back to the road and tried to ignore the sinking feeling in her stomach.

"That bad, huh?"

Bethany narrowed her eyes as her hands tightened on the steering wheel. "Dude. You have no idea."

As they pulled up to the stables, Bethany took a long look around before heading into the tack room with Adel, and before she did, she locked the stable doors, something she'd never seen her do before unless she was locking up for the night.

The steamy scent of hazelnut java hung warm in the air as they walked through the door. Nora had just finished pouring the coffee, dumping what looked like a half bag of sugar into her mug. At least Adel hoped it was hers.

She set the coffees on the table and upended the bag, flashing Bethany a smile when she grabbed the brownie first.

Adel shook her head. "So what do I have to do to rate a brownie around here?"

"Yeah, yeah." Nora pulled a sandwich packaged in plastic wrap out of her jacket pocket and tossed it to Adel. "I didn't forget your Wham salad."

Adel bumped her shoulder to Nora's, which almost earned her a smile. She unwrapped the sandwich and bit into it, reminded again that fake meat tasted nothing at all like the real stuff. Like, not even close. But damn, it was good.

"So," she said, catching a bit of wayward crust and wedging it back into her mouth. "What's the big secret?"

Bethany glanced at Nora and sat back, hands woven behind her head. She had the look she'd had in the loft when she'd shown Adel the picture of Audrey—at once both tightly wound and exhausted. Adel waited until one of them decided to speak, and that turned out to be Nora.

"You know how when a staff member is sick or whatever, we take food down to their cabin so they don't have to come to the cafeteria, right?"

"Yeah, I've seen you guys carrying trays back and forth."

"Well, sometimes one of the Brethren will call and want lunch or dinner delivered for a few of the Priesthood Holders, so we have to take it down to the main room in the Fellowship Hall, wait for them to come out, and then pick the dishes up later."

"Hold up." Adel raised her hand and picked the second half of her sandwich up with the other. "Who the hell are the Priesthood Holders? And where are they coming from? The Fellowship Hall is just one big room downstairs, right?"

Nora nodded, blowing on the surface of her coffee. "I thought that too. Until I saw one of them coming out of a door behind the podium a few weeks ago when I came to pick up the dishes. I mean, I guess you can see it, but no one would notice unless you knew it was there because of the sanctuary cushions."

"What was his reaction?" Adel asked.

Bethany glanced at Adel and back to Nora. "Right? Because the one time I was in there, one of the Brethren came out and it was like I was being bounced from a damn club or something."

"He didn't look pleased to see me, but I don't think he realized I'd seen the door. He waited until I'd gotten the dishes from the side table by the front entrance, then locked the door behind me."

Bethany shook her head, breaking her brownie apart down the middle and pushing half over to Adel. "Anyway, this weekend they did the same thing, and when Nora went back to get the dishes, one of them had left the door ajar. The one behind the podium."

"Nora," Adel said, finishing the last of the Wham sandwich and reaching for one of the bagels. "I know you didn't do something stupid like go in there, right?"

"I certainly did." Nora sniffed, as if the mere suggestion that she pass up an opportunity like that was insulting. "It's like you don't know me at all."

Bethany glanced at Nora and set her coffee cup on the table, watching the steam rise into the air. "Long story short, the Prophet's office is back there, and it was unlocked."

Adel paused and slowly put down her bagel. "Holy shit."

"And this," Bethany got up and lifted a saddle off a chair in the corner, picked up what looked like a photo album, and plunked it down in front of Adel, "was on his desk."

It was one of those padded albums covered in floral chintz fabric found on old ladies' coffee tables with dishes of dusty potpourri. The edges looked yellowed, and someone had glued strips of white lace in the shape of a heart on the front of it.

Adel leaned back in the chair and lifted the cover slightly with her index finger. "What the hell is this?"

Bethany shook her head, her fingers gripping the edge of the table, white with tension. "Just open it, dude."

Adel opened the front cover. On the first page was a sheet of paper under the plastic with lettering done in an arch shape, carefully colored in with colored pencil. *The Joy Book*. Adel spoke without looking up, her fingertip poised at the corner of the stiff cardboard page.

"I'd ask what the hell a Joy Book is," she said, her voice low and cautious as if the book would answer. "But I'm afraid you'll tell me."

"So this was Friday that she took it, which I think may have something to do with them searching Grace's cabin. They've got to be looking for it. I didn't find out about it until after I'd called you." Bethany cleared her throat, as still as the dust motes that hung in the air around them. "Turn the page."

On the next page was an eight-by-ten photo of a young girl. She was smiling, standing stiffly in front of a wood-paneled wall and wearing a white lace blouse tucked into a long, pastel skirt. Under her picture was a small, typed label printed onto copy paper and trimmed carefully around the edges.

Rebecca Hargrove
March 14, 2007

Adel lifted her head. "If that's her date of birth, she's fourteen years old."

Nora nodded, and Adel turned the page. The next was a different girl, posing in the exact same place, hands clasped in front of her, her glossy ash-blond hair gathered at the front with a golden barrette. It seemed oddly sparse. If any other information had been written about this young girl before, like details about her intelligence or personality, it was as if only her age mattered once she reached the Joy Book. The rest had been carefully cut away and discarded.

Adel turned the pages slowly, mentally calculating the age of each girl; the last few pages looked to be the most recent additions. Adel looked up at Nora. "Do you recognize any of the girls?"

"Yeah," she said, sinking back down into her chair, her fingers tracing the silver bracelet on her left wrist. "The last three have to be from this summer, because I definitely see them coming through the line at the cafeteria."

"So…what? This is like a catalog of 'available' girls for the Brethren to look through like they're at a fucking cattle auction?" Adel shook her head and looked at the last, stiff page in her hand. "This girl, Alyssa. She was born in 2009."

"Yeah, man." Bethany looked to the ceiling to compose herself. "She's fucking twelve years old. I don't know exactly what's going on there, but it doesn't take a genius to know it's not good. I've gotta do something to stop this." She let out a long, slow breath. "I just don't know what the fuck to do."

Adel raked her hand through her hair, leaning back in her chair and glancing at the cabinet under the coffee maker.

"You got any breakfast whiskey up in here?" Adel locked her eyes on Bethany. "Because I've got something to tell you about the real reason I'm here, and you might need a shot to take it all in."

❖

Later that morning Adel skidded into her classroom at the last second, and by the time she'd gotten there, the rest of the class was already gathered around the semicircle of tables with the exception of one empty chair. Sunlight poured through the window into a luminous liquid square and spread slowly across the maple floor as Adel dropped her bag on her desk, then sank down into her chair and opened her own journal.

The girls all took a pen from the mason jars set around the table and looked up expectantly, waiting for the day's writing prompt.

Adel caught a stray lock of hair that had escaped the ponytail at her neck and tucked it behind her ear. The writing prompts she usually provided were fairly detailed and designed to get them thinking in a particular direction that she then took forward into the class, but today was different. She looked up, started to speak, but then paused until every eye was on her.

"Today we're going to write about secrets."

Adel cleared her throat as the girls looked at each other, then back at her, awaiting further instruction. When they didn't get it, they looked nervously at each other until Addison, a delicate-looking brunette who rarely spoke in class, raised her hand.

"That's all?" Addison looked down at her open journal, pen poised. "What about secrets?"

Johanna, a talented writer but also the most devout of the group, pushed her journal away from her and toward the center of the table as she closed the cover. "We can't. We're not supposed to have secrets."

The door opened noisily just then, and everyone turned as Ruth Blankenship edged through it, her bag slipping heavily from her shoulder to dangle at her elbow as she shut the door behind her and walked to her seat, eyes focused on the floor. Ruth was always perfectly put together, and if there was a popular group of girls at camp, she was the pinnacle of that—which made even more sense now that Adel knew her father was the Prophet. But, Adel realized as she watched her loop her bag over the back of her chair, today something was not quite right.

Ruth laid her journal on the table in front of her and pushed at the gold barrette that was slipping from the crown of her head to the side. Her eyes were damp and bloodshot as she tucked the crumpled wad of tissue in her fist down into her skirt pocket. The black-and-white banker's clock on the wall ticked off deafening seconds as Adel waited for Ruth to lift her head. She did not.

"Okay." Adel looked around at the group, bringing their attention back to her. "Can anyone tell Ruth what she missed?"

"It's secrets." Addison leaned over to Ruth and dropped her voice to a whisper. "We're supposed to write about our secrets."

Ruth wrote the word in tall, block letters at the top of her blank journal page, slowly darkening each letter before going on to the next.

Carla, a heavyset girl who was usually trying to make the other girls laugh, looked around and winked. "Well, it looks like Ruth has plenty of those. Every page she's written is folded over."

It was true. Ruth had never handed in a journal entry without the page folded over, which she knew meant Adel couldn't look at it. Adel looked at Ruth and noticed that the hand poised over the journal was shaking and her eyes were locked onto Carla. Carla's laugh faded and she somehow managed to duck right before Ruth's journal sailed past her head and hit the wall behind her, sinking to the floor with a hollow *thunk*.

"Ruth!" Adel jumped up and retrieved the journal, stopping to check that it hadn't actually made contact with Carla's temple.

Carla shook her head, glaring in Ruth's direction. "Geez, it was only a joke. You didn't have to try to knock my head off."

Ruth covered her face with her hands and started to cry quietly. The girls looked at each other silently as Ruth's shoulders sank and her head slid slowly down until it was resting on the table, her hands still covering her face. Adel lightened her voice, peering through the window at the green lawn below as she clicked her pen closed and dropped it back into the jar.

"It's a gorgeous day. Maybe we should take advantage of it and do our class outside today." She nodded toward the door as the girls hesitantly closed their journals, looking around at each other as if Adel had asked them to rob a bank. "Go ahead. Just pick a spot to sit and I'll be out there in a few minutes."

Chairs scraped the floor as everyone gathered their things and shuffled out the door. The silence was heavy and still as the last girl left the room, closing the door carefully behind her. Ruth's head was still in her hands, still resting on the table in front of her.

"Ruth." Adel's voice softened as she reached out to touch Ruth's shoulder. Ruth flinched at the touch and lifted her head as Adel went to get the open box of tissues she kept on her desk. She handed Ruth a handful of them and sat back down.

"I'm sorry." Ruth's eyes met hers for just a second before she turned and looked out the window. "I don't know why I did that."

"Well, that was excellent aim." Adel smiled and raised an eyebrow. "You should look into playing softball."

A sudden hint of a smile flashed across Ruth's face. She reached out for the journal Adel put on the table between them and pulled it to her. Adel looked at it, the cover warped and forced open by the folded pages stacked within it. Every journal assignment had been handed in that way. Adel had never read a single word she'd written.

"She's not wrong, you know." Adel glanced down at the lopsided journal. "Why do you fold every page over before you hand it in?" Adel looked over and waited for her to answer. She didn't. "But fair enough. That's your choice."

Ruth lifted her swollen eyes to Adel's and swiped at the last of her tears with the back of her hand. "And have you?"

"Have I what?" Adel knew what she was asking but paused anyway. "Read your journal entries?"

Ruth nodded.

"No." Adel shook her head and handed her yet another handful of tissues. "I wouldn't do that. I've never read a single page that was folded over in anyone's journal."

Ruth shook her head slightly and smiled, but the smile never reached her eyes and quickly dropped to the table with her words.

"Yeah, well, maybe you should."

After giving Adel attitude on the docks for weeks, which she'd sensed was primarily bravado, whatever had her so upset had stripped her of all her former cockiness. If Adel ever wanted to see what was in that journal, now was the time.

"Are you giving me permission to look at your pages?"

Ruth shoved more damp tissues into her pocket and looked at the ceiling, her eyes closing slowly as she nodded her head, tears rolling from the corners of her eyes down over her cheeks.

"Go ahead. She's gone. They've taken her." She turned her head to look at Adel, and it was as if someone had turned out the light behind her dove-blue eyes. "This is Blood Atonement. Nothing matters anymore."

❖

Later that evening, Hannah opened the door suddenly just as Adel was lifting her hand to knock. Dusk had just fallen, and gold interior light spilled out into the darkness that blanketed the porch as Adel stepped inside. The air was heavy with the scent of baking cheese, and Hannah had a wooden spoon in her hand, covered with what looked like a white wine sauce that was threatening to drip all over the hardwood floor. Hannah flashed a smile and closed the door behind her.

"I was just on the way to change, but Kate is in the kitchen." She untied her apron as she spoke and handed Adel the spoon with a wink. "Take this with you, but you're not authorized to use it, Rosse. Stay in your lane."

Adel laughed as she rounded the corner and found the spoon rest on the stovetop. Kate was already sitting at the table with a scotch and Adel pulled out another chair and sat beside her, slinging her bag onto the next chair. She nodded at the second tumbler of scotch.

"Is this mine or Hannah's?"

"I learned my lesson about giving her a real drink a long time ago," Kate said. "That girl can eat anyone under the table but she's a lightweight when it comes to anything in a rocks glass." She leaned in slightly and lowered her voice. "Not that that's always a bad thing."

"Hey." Adel leaned back in her chair and glanced down the hall toward the back of the house. "Where's Audrey?"

"Hannah's mom came by today." Kate clinked the solid ball of ice slowly against the edges of her glass. "She's a retired psychotherapist and runs that rescue farm for horses out at the edge of town." Kate set her glass down on the table with a slow clink. "They rehabilitate neglected horses, then use them to treat PTSD in survivors of violent crime. It's impressive, actually. The *New York Times* even did an article on her last year."

"That sounds perfect for Audrey right now." Adel rolled her scotch and watched the light from the candles at the center of the table flicker like fire at the edges. "I've seen Hannah at work, though. Can't say it surprises me all that much."

"Yeah. Runs in the family, I guess. Her mom was here five minutes and Audrey just loved her. She's going to stay with her for a few days while we try to sort this mess out."

"Well." Adel ran her hand through her hair and leaned over to her bag, her fingertips hesitating before they closed around Ruth's journal. "I have something major to tell you about that just fell in my lap, but let's start with this first."

She set the journal on the table between them, and Kate leaned down to look at it, almost as if afraid to touch it. "What the fuck is wrong with this? What is it, a book?"

Hannah came through the doorway wearing faded black jeans and an oversized white button-down shirt unbuttoned to the center of her chest. She was barefoot and her hair was wound into a wild pile on the top of her head again, this time pierced with a pen that looked like it might fall at any moment. She fired up one of the burners and glanced over her shoulder at Kate.

"What's with you? You look like that book might be armed."

Kate shot her a dubious look and sat back in her chair, lifting the cover with the tip of the pen she'd been rolling through her fingers.

"It's one of the girls' journals, from my creative writing class." Adel paused for a long second and lofted an eyebrow at Kate. "Specifically, it's Ruth Blankenship's journal, Audrey's younger sister."

Hannah picked up the spoon and lifted the foil covering a dish in the oven as the rich scent of browning cheddar instantly intensified. "Why are half the pages folded over?"

"The girls write at the beginning of every class on a topic I give them, and if they want me to read it, they leave the page the way it is. If not, they fold it over and I don't."

Kate looked up at Adel, who watched as the meaning of her words sunk in. "Tell me you have permission to open these pages."

Adel nodded. "I do. I actually haven't looked yet. I figured the more eyes we have on it, the better."

Kate opened the cover, pointing to the small, penciled writing in the top left-hand corner. *Ruth Blankenship, age 13. June 2nd, 2021.*

Hannah came over and read over Kate's shoulder. "The oldest Blankenship sister was Chelsey, right? Then Audrey is next at fifteen, and Ruth is the youngest at thirteen?" She took a deep breath and looked at Kate. "Jesus Christ."

Kate unfolded the first page and stared. It was blank. So was the next page, and the page after that. Hannah retrieved her wineglass from the kitchen island and came back to the table, her hand resting lightly at the back of Kate's neck. A vein stood out on Kate's forehead as frustration tightened her hand around on her glass.

Hannah looked closer over Kate's shoulder. "Are they all blank?"

Kate unfolded every page, smoothing it flat with the palm of her hand before she went to the next. When she came to the last blank folded page, she closed the book and slid it to the center of the table.

"I don't get it." Adel shook her head, her forehead furrowed in concentration. "Why would she tell me I could read it if there's nothing in it?"

"In official police terms, she's fucking with you." Kate stared at the book for a long moment before her eyes returned to Adel. "How did she seem when she said it?"

Adel paused, remembering the raw sadness that had clung like damp to every one of Ruth's words that day. The anger was flash fire when she'd flung the book across the room, the slow, carefully chosen words; even her voice had sharp edges.

"Don't get me wrong, she's been a pain in my ass since I got to that camp, both in class and on the water." The memory of Ruth's shaking hand as she lifted that book flashed across her mind. "But she seemed like a completely different person today. Stripped, almost. Raw."

Kate raised an eyebrow and thought for a second before she spoke, looking up to meet Adel's eyes. "You think there's something else at play here?"

"And it's big." Adel nodded, tracing the edge of the book with her fingertip. "Either that, or she's the best actress in New York."

A timer went off in the kitchen and Hannah hurried to take the dish out of the oven wearing oversized oven mitts that reached nearly to her elbows. She placed it on the cooling rack, replaced it with a long baguette stuffed with butter and fresh herbs, then closed the door tightly and set the timer again, looking back over her shoulder at Kate.

"You only looked at the folded-over pages, though, right?" She grabbed the wine bottle and returned to the table, topping up her glass and settling into the chair across from Adel. She took a long sip, then set down her glass and pulled the journal toward her. "What about the ones that are still flat?"

"We haven't gotten to those yet. We're only halfway through the summer."

Hannah thumbed through the pages again and sighed. "Maybe I watch too much television, but if she didn't write anything, I guess I'm just hoping to see a pattern of some kind, drawings, maybe a hidden code. But there's literally nothing at all on these pages." She handed the book back to Kate, who shook her head and tossed it back to the middle of the table.

"Well, would you look at that?" Kate stared at the journal like it had just burst into flames. "Looks like your Ruth gave us something better than journal entries."

Chapter Sixteen

Grace hung up the last of her pastel dresses in the closet, resisting the now daily urge to pile them back into her laundry basket with a generous sprinkle of gasoline and set them on fire. Lately, they'd started to feel more like straightjackets than *fitting attire for a godly woman*, a phrase she'd heard since she was a child.

Since she'd been back from Mystic, the Brethren seemed to be around every corner, even more frequently than usual. Elder Jameson, a short, portly man with a yellowed ring around his collar and a penetrating stare, was in the boathouse when she'd arrived that morning, rifling through the papers on the old metal desk in the corner. He didn't even pause as she came in, just slammed the drawer closed when he was finished and looked up at her. His eyes scanned her body languidly, as if it belonged to him, then settled on hers as he rolled up his shirtsleeves, slowly, first one and then the other. The heat of the day was already rising, silent and cloying, and the faint scent of stale urine followed him as he finally walked out the door of the boathouse without a word.

A sudden knock on the door of her cabin startled her out of the memory, her heart stealing her breath with the offer of panic, but she straightened her shoulders and refused. *It's not the Brethren*, she told herself, consciously letting go of the breath she was holding. *They wouldn't have knocked.*

When she opened the door, a girl she recognized as cafeteria staff was there, the one with a quick laugh and the chin-length hair that looked like it was always in motion. She was holding a mason jar.

"Hey, I'm Nora. You might have seen me in the cafeteria?" She paused to look Grace up and down and blew a stray lock of hair out of her eyes. "Do you know if this is Adel Rosse's cabin, the one next to you?"

"Yeah, that's hers." Grace nodded, her eyes dropping to the jar in her hand. "Is that…Wham salad?"

"Um, yeah." Nora laughed, her eyes sparkling like sunlit lake water. "It's a long story, but I said I'd get her some more of this. She goes through this stuff like it's chocolate or something."

"I'm pretty sure she went to town this evening." Grace leaned out far enough to glance in the direction of Adel's door. "I don't know when she'll be back."

"Great." Nora glanced back at Adel's door and snapped the pink wad of gum in her mouth. "It's still too hot to leave it outside. It's got mayonnaise in it."

Grace opened the door wider and motioned for Nora to come inside. "I probably have room for it in my fridge. I can give it to her for you if you want."

Nora stepped inside and handed Grace the mason jar, looking around as Grace stashed it in the fridge and looked back, the door still open in her hand.

"Do you want a Coke?"

"What?" Nora's eyes automatically narrowed at the offer. "Like a real Coke?"

"Yeah." Grace smiled and grabbed two cans, tossing one to Nora as she came back to the living area and sat on the couch, nodding at the chair across from it. "Like a real Coke."

Nora flashed her a smile and popped the top on the can as she sat down. "You guys aren't supposed to have these, are you?"

"Yeah, well," Grace said, taking a long swig of Coke and setting the can down on the coffee table, "I'm not supposed to do a lot of things."

"Same here." Nora smiled lovingly at the Coke in her hand. "I knew I liked you."

"You were here last summer, too, right?"

Nora nodded. "And the one before that. After a while it all starts to blur together."

"That's the truth." Grace pulled a hairband off her wrist and pulled her hair into a quick ponytail. "Although this summer may be my last."

"Really, why? How you pull all the events together is really impressive. I'm usually on the food crew, and I've never once seen you break a sweat."

Grace smiled, leaning over to clink her can to Nora's. "Then I'm also a great actress, because I'm usually stressed the hell out."

"*And* you curse?" Nora shook her head and smiled. "How have we not hung out before this?"

"Probably because we're not really supposed to speak to the staff unless it's specifically about something camp related."

"You're shitting me." The furrow popped back up on Nora's brow. "I thought you guys just didn't like us."

"We just want to keep our jobs. If they caught us hanging out with the townies, we'd be out of here in a heartbeat."

Nora nodded, twisting the tab on the can until it popped off. "So why are you leaving?"

Grace pulled her face into neutral and fought back the ridiculous tears gathering in her eyes. "I don't actually have a choice after this summer ends." She traced the rim of the can with the tip of her finger as she spoke. "Apparently, because I'm twenty-six and unmarried, I'm no longer a positive influence on the girls."

"Well, that's clearly bullshit." Nora paused, started to say something, then stopped herself.

Grace met her eyes with a weary look. "Just say it."

"Listen, I totally understand that you might not be able to answer this, but I have a reason I'm asking. Have you ever heard of something called the Joy Book?"

Grace jumped as if someone had slammed a door in her face. "How did you hear about that?"

Nora shook her head, then set her can on the coffee table and leaned forward, elbows on her knees. When she spoke, her voice was a whisper, as if she somehow knew everything was a secret.

"I can't tell you. Not yet, anyway." She hesitated, sorting through her words slowly before she chose them, one by one. "But I think something really fucked up is going on at Valley of Rubies. And I can't…just do nothing anymore."

Grace closed her eyes and dropped her head into her hands. It was one of those moments when time slowed down enough for her to touch it. To run her fingers over it like cool, smooth clay. To shape it into something else. Her past, and all the secrets in it, started to feel suddenly tangible, like something she could rip off her body, crumple in her fists, and light on fire. She felt a tear fall from the corner of her eye and swiped at it with her fingertips as she met Nora's eyes. Nora's words were as soft as the hand that settled over Grace's.

"Are you okay?"

Grace let out a slow breath and closed her eyes. Talking about this place, and what happened here, to someone else was like standing barefoot on the slick, dark edge of a boat and pulling the anchor up from the bottom of the ocean with her bare hands. It was only possible if you were willing to go down with the anchor.

"Yeah," Grace said, her gaze strong and even. "I will be."

❖

Adel stared at the slim blue plastic thumb drive for a moment before she reached for it.

"Whoa." Kate put her hand out to stop her and shook her head. "I don't know what's on that. It could just be another tease, but it could also be evidence, so don't touch it."

Hannah looked up at Kate. "Do you need some latex gloves?"

Kate nodded, still staring at the drive as she lifted the corner of it with her pen as Hannah got up and disappeared down the hall.

"God." Kate lowered her voice and looked up to wink at Adel. "I love dating a doctor."

Hannah's voice carried back to the dining room from the opposite end of the hall. "We're not dating, Detective."

Kate rolled her eyes, still focused on the drive. "Yeah, you keep telling yourself that, Dr. McDreamy."

Hannah returned with a box of latex gloves and plunked it down on the table between them just as her phone rang. She stepped out on the deck to answer it and tossed a wink over her shoulder at Kate.

Adel pulled on a pair of gloves and lifted the thumb drive to see if there was any kind of a label. Nothing.

"Wait, how are we going to play this thing?"

Kate looked around the room, her gaze settling on the end table at the far side of the couch. "Hannah's ancient laptop might be able to play it. We can hope, anyway." Kate grabbed the computer and flashed Adel a rare smile as she clicked the thumb drive into the port on the side. An icon flashed up on the screen. "Looks like we finally caught a break. It's about damn time."

As Kate navigated the computer, Adel thought about an email she'd sent to her editor the previous night. She'd assured him she was still working the story, but that it had turned out to have a much further reach than she was expecting. The truth was, she wasn't sure if she was going to write the story at all, a decision that would tank her career. If she didn't scoop this story, word would get around that she'd let it slip through her fingers. After which her next career move would be a job at the docks in Mystic, courtesy of her mother. If she was lucky.

"Okay, I think I've got it up." Kate clicked a key and took a sip of her whiskey. "And it looks like there's only one file on this drive."

Kate pulled the laptop evenly between them and pressed play. After a few seconds of static, a simply shot video started with a jerk: a single-camera view of an all-white windowless room with a concrete floor and plain wooden risers on one side. But it wasn't the room that held their attention. It was what stood in the center that turned the air between them suddenly dense and silent as it pulled them both closer to the screen. Kate stopped the video with a click, her eyes still locked onto the screen.

"What the *hell* is that?"

❖

Grace and Nora decided eventually it might be safer to talk out on one of the boats, and by the time they'd walked outside and locked the door behind them, the sun had set over the edge of the lake. The last salmon-pink brushstrokes of light sank quietly through the trees, painting the edges of the blue spruce grove fiery orange as they faded into the darkness. The scent of cooling water swept in gently from the surface of the lake and ran its fingers through Grace's hair.

"Follow me," Grace whispered, ducking into the grove of trees that separated the Fellowship Hall and the shore. "We can get to the boathouse just as easily, and it's way less obvious."

Nora followed her and lowered her voice to a whisper that was almost covered by the swish of branches against her jean jacket as they wove through the evergreens.

"You know I can't row, right?" A branch cracked under her boot as she stepped through the trees. "I'm not exactly athletic. Although Bethany might tell you otherwise."

"Yeah." Grace stared straight ahead as she walked, her eyes scanning the path ahead. "You know I'm a rowing instructor, right? We'll be fine."

Both of them slowed suddenly to a wordless stop and stared straight ahead. The Fellowship Hall loomed on the other side of the trees, and the branches on the evergreens were high enough to give them a clear view of the west side of the building. A small black car pulled up to a lighted side door and idled as three Brethren popped the back hatch and started loading boxes into the back. Each was loaded with what looked to be rows of brown padded envelopes.

"What are they doing?" Grace whispered as she peered through the darkening forest.

Nora's eyes narrowed. "I don't know, but I've seen them do it before. Doesn't make any sense. Why are they using their personal vehicles and not the camp trucks?"

One of the Brethren tapped the hood of the car with the flat of his hand, and it slowly pulled away and disappeared out of sight. The Brethren walked back into the hall, the last one pausing to scan the surroundings before closing the door behind him.

"When did you see them do this before?" Grace turned to look over her shoulder at Nora, her voice low. "Were they loading boxes?"

"Bethany and I were in the woods one night and we watched them do this same damn thing. Same three Brethren, and right about this time."

"Bethany's the horse wrangler, right?" Grace whispered. "I've seen her on the trails. She's hard to miss in that golf cart. She drives that thing like she stole it."

"Yeah." Nora leaned to the right to avoid a broken evergreen branch. "She does a lot of things like that."

They watched the back of the building as the entry light went out. A few minutes later, a small group of Brethren exited the building and headed up the hill toward the Campfire Bowl.

"Hey," Nora said, watching as the last of them disappeared up the trail. "Isn't the consecration ceremony coming up?"

"How do you know about that?"

"I can read." Nora leaned against the tree beside her and smiled. "There's a schedule on the notice board in the cafeteria." She tilted her head and dropped her voice. "Aren't you supposed to be running that thing?"

"Yeah. But Whittier sent me a notice over the weekend. I'm still teaching rowing, but my programming duties are suspended."

Both looked back to the Fellowship Hall, which was becoming harder to see as night closed in around it. Nora stood, shaking out her arms and zipping her jacket around her. "Ready?"

Grace looked at her, then shook her head. "I know you're not suggesting that we break into the Fellowship Hall after hours, right?"

"Nope." Nora started up the trail, then stopped and turned back around to look at Grace as she pulled a key ring out of her pocket. "I'm suggesting we let ourselves in and see what they're being so damn secretive about. They're acting like a bunch of amateur mobsters, and I'm going to find out what it is."

"How do you have the key to the Fellowship Hall? No one is supposed to be in there without being accompanied by an elder."

"Good God, you sound like you're reading from a rulebook." Nora swished her ponytail out of the grasp of a tree branch as she held the keys up and clinked them in the darkness. "And I don't have the Fellowship Hall keys. Technically, I have the keys to everything. I swiped the master key out of the office in case I had to get into Adel's cabin to leave the Wham salad."

Grace tilted her head to the side and peered through the darkness at Nora. "You never did tell me what's up with the Wham."

"Saddle up, Waters." Nora dangled the keys between them again and winked. "I have a feeling we're about to get into something a lot more interesting than Wham."

Five tense minutes later, Nora was tentatively leading the way through a seemingly endless pitch-black hallway. At least until she tripped over a box of hymnals and forgot to whisper when her knee hit the floor and the word *fuck* shot out of her mouth at ballpark volume.

"Lord, you're delicate for a delinquent." Grace stepped over her and continued walking, trailing her hand down the wall in the dark to keep her bearings. "Suck it up. Let's go."

"Damn, girl." Nora lowered her voice back to a whisper and followed, rubbing her knee and dropping the keys down the front of her bra. "Maybe it's you that missed your calling in the mob."

"Shhhh..." Grace stopped and listened for any footsteps overhead. "I noticed when we walked up there was a light on upstairs, but I think we might be the only ones in here."

"Yeah, I think that light is always on." Nora stepped ahead and headed toward the dark shimmer of a silver doorknob at the end of the hall. "Everyone else should be at campfire."

She slipped the master key into the lock and slowly opened the door, dropping the keys back down the front of her shirt. The door led to a long, dimly lit hall, with three evenly spaced doors to the left and one to the right.

"Where are we?" Grace turned around slowly and nodded at the single door to the right at the end of the hall. "That leads to the main

Fellowship Hall, right?" She paused and looked back at Nora. "So this must be the office? I see the Prophet come in and out sometimes when I'm setting up for events, but I've never been back here. The door is always locked."

"Yeah, there's a dead bolt on that door to the Fellowship Hall," Nora whispered as she walked toward the first door on the left and tried the knob. "What idiot dead bolts the front entrance and not the back?" She turned the key again and swung the door open quietly. "Amateurs."

"How do you know there's a dead bolt?"

Nora motioned her into the room and shut the door behind them. "You don't want to know. Trust me."

Grace flicked the switch on the wall. "It never made sense that only the second level of this building has windows, but I guess it's working in our favor at the moment."

A single fluorescent bulb flickered to life overhead and they looked around the mostly bare room, silent for a moment while they took it in. Six long tables were lined up in two rows, each with an older desktop computer in the center. Most were laden with boxes of padded envelopes, with stacks of additional boxes containing small, oblong pieces of plastic that looked like bright blue key chain fobs. Jars, all filled with huge black markers, were scattered over the surface of each.

Nora walked among the tables, stopping to see if any of the computers had been left on, but every one of them was dead to the touch. "Something tells me they're not doing arts and crafts." She held up a jar of markers and narrowed her eyes. "Only the Brethren come back here. Why would they need this stuff?"

Stacked at the end of every table were open boxes of those envelopes, only this time, they'd been sealed and addressed with typed labels. Nora picked one up and ripped it open. She peered into it, raising her head slowly and meeting Grace's eyes. "These are flash drives. Why are they sending these out?"

"Shit!" Grace slapped her hand over her mouth and jerked her head toward the door, but Nora had also heard the door outside in the hall shut, the dead bolt slide, and the footsteps that were moving closer by the second.

Nora shoved the ripped envelope to the bottom of the box and ran silently to the custodial closet at the back of the room, wedging herself in and closing the door behind Grace as she did the same. The door had just clicked shut, leaving them in cramped darkness, when they heard the door to the room open and shut. A tiny strip of light from underneath the door was just enough for Grace to see Nora put her finger to her lips and focus her eyes on the back side of the closet door.

A metal chair scraped across the floor and creaked heavily as someone sat. A computer fired up, followed by clicking keys. The air in the closet was metallic and heavily close, and the sharp outline of a broom dug into Grace's back. Even in the darkness, she sensed Nora rolling her eyes and squeezed her hand in a silent reminder to shut up.

They both jerked to attention when they heard a phone ring, then a voice pierced the stillness.

"Yeah, I'm here. Randy?"

Grace turned to look at Nora, the obvious question heavy in the air between them. Her eyes had adjusted to the low light a bit and she could just make out the outline of Nora's face as shook her head in answer.

"I thought you guys took the ones from that event last night?" A long pause followed, and Grace had to remind herself to exhale. "Well, they missed some because there's a box of them sitting right here. They left the light on and the door unlocked too."

Silence was followed by the sound of the box being picked up and dropped onto the surface of the table.

"Yeah, fine. I can do it when I leave here." Grace heard him pick up one of the markers and clink it on the side of the jar as he pulled it out. "I know the drill. I'll get it done, and then I'll double-check to make sure this room and downstairs is locked up."

The phone clicked off and Grace heard some muttering as he turned off the computer. Then there was silence again until the screech of packing tape pierced the air, then a sharp clatter as the metal folding chair was kicked back under the table. Footsteps toward the door were followed by the sound of it being pulled firmly shut and a key turning in the lock. The strip of light under the door disappeared at the same instant and Nora and Grace looked at each other through the darkness, slowly exhaling the same breath. At least until they heard the key slide back into the lock again.

❖

Adel's shoulder brushed Kate's as they both leaned closer to the laptop screen.

"What the hell is that?" Kate asked the question again but sounded like she didn't expect an answer. Which worked out, because Adel had no idea what they were looking at either.

The room that surrounded the fixed structure in the center of it was nondescript, plain white drywall with no windows or identifying details except for a single door on the far wall. The structure that stood in the center of the room looked like a cross between a table and a sculpture. The top was a flat platform, made of a single slab of luminous white marble, with intricately carved sides that tapered down to a narrower concrete base. Winding stairs leading to the top were carved into the side, and the carvings looked familiar, even biblical in nature. They'd clearly been carved by hand, then rubbed with bronzing wax to bring out the detail.

Hannah came back into the room and leaned over Kate's shoulder, staring at the screen as she reached forward to drop her phone back on the table.

"What does this look like to you?"

Kate looked back over her shoulder at Hannah, who was now squinting at the screen.

"I don't know." She stood up slowly and raised an eyebrow in Adel's direction. "Like the world's biggest cake stand?"

Adel snorted and choked on her whiskey, which made even Kate laugh.

"Yeah, I don't know what that thing is, but I can tell you it gives me the creeps." Hannah handed Adel a tissue from the box on the sofa end table. "Where is this thing supposed to be? Even the room looks weird. It's just a huge white box."

Before anyone could open their mouth to answer, the video jerked into motion and the door at the back of the room opened slowly. A line of twelve men, each carrying Bibles, filed in, dressed in church clothes. Their faces were blurred; even smaller identifying details like facial hair or the outline of their features were obscured.

"That's the Brethren."

Kate looked over at her and paused the video. "How do you know that?"

Hannah held a hand up before she could answer and asked her own question. "Who the hell are the Brethren?"

Adel looked at Kate and waited until she nodded to answer.

"They're the church elders, sometimes called Priesthood Holders, who are assigned to the camp as pastors and security. Every one of them wears a tiny gold pin on his lapel. I've seen them in the cafeteria. I don't know what it means, but only the Brethren wear them."

Kate started the video again and the men filed in and headed toward the white risers built along the far wall. They sat down stiffly, one by one, their eyes fixed on the door they'd just walked through.

"What the hell is this?" Hannah pulled up a chair and shook her head as she stared at the screen. "I'm going to need a stronger word than 'creepy.'"

The three of them waited in tense silence, staring at the screen for what seemed like forever. There was no movement except for the shuffling of hands over Bibles, nervous fingers tracing the outline of the gold-edged pages. A few silent minutes later, the screen jerked into motion. The door at the back of the room opened for the second time and a thin, older man in a white robe tied with a gold braided cord entered the room. He had a narrow face with a red, prominent nose, and his graying, oily hair was combed over the top of his shiny head.

"That's the Prophet." Kate's words were almost a whisper. "I've seen pictures at the station."

He wore a beatific expression, but his eyes shifted too quickly from the Bible in his hands back to the slight girl following meekly behind him. She was also wearing a white robe, though hers was thin, shorter, with embroidered edges, more like a dressing gown than a ceremonial robe. Her hair was pulled back in an ornate blond updo, though a few wisps brushed her cheek and she immediately tucked them behind her ear. The girl stopped at the door frame, holding it with white fingers, as if unable to move. She closed her eyes tight for a moment, and Adel watched as she forced herself to let go.

When the last finger was unanchored, they watched her draw in a sharp breath and freeze in place. The older man reached for her hand and guided her to the bottom step of the structure, indicating silently that she climb in front of him. When she got to the top, she stood stiffly and looked down at the Brethren, then quickly focused her eyes on her bare feet, splayed and stiff on the flat marble surface. Her hands held each other tight, as tense as the silence.

The man started to speak, but there was no sound.

"What the hell?"

Kate clicked the volume button until the indicator on the screen reached the maximum, but there was just silence, despite his mouth still moving. He leaned down to the risers to take something from one of the Brethren, the man's face still blurred as he handed him an open Bible.

He read a passage, following the words with his finger, then looked up at the audience.

Suddenly, the audio kicked in and the Prophet's voice filled the room. It was surprisingly rich—which was almost a shock given his frail appearance—a deep, confident baritone, as if he had never doubted one of his own words.

"Has seen fit to entrust me with this sacred duty." He paused to glance down at the girl, who did not meet his eyes. "He's called me to instruct and counsel young women on how to become a godly wife." He turned then to face the camera he seemed not to acknowledge before. "To be a comfort to a man of God is both a privilege and a duty. It is my fervent hope that by viewing this, young husbands will learn to mold their wives into the God-given path of righteous submission that is revealed to us in the Holy Bible."

Hannah leaned forward on her elbows and rubbed her temples with her fingertips as they watched the Prophet pause and turn to face the girl. He loosened the belt on his robe as her eyes flicked back to the door and lingered, the color draining from her face. Several of the elders, before as still as salt statues, shifted in their seats and slid their Bibles to cover their laps. Every eye was locked on the altar as the Prophet pushed the robe from her shoulders and watched it fall in an ivory pool around her feet.

She was naked now, her eyes shut tight as he took her hand and guided it into his robe. He looked to the sky and pulled her closer, smoothing her hair under his hand in robotic, measured strokes as he guided her movements inside his robe.

The audience leaned forward slowly, some shifting in their chairs, others shrugging off their jackets to place over their laps, but every eye was locked onto the girl's pale, trembling body as the Prophet lowered her to the surface of the altar underneath him. His robe fell away beside them as he parted her thighs with his, stopping to whisper direction in her ear. A tear slipped suddenly down her cheek as she opened her eyes, her arms stiffly at her sides and fingers splayed and tense against the altar. Every muscle in her body tensed and she cried out in pain when he entered her.

It was over quickly. She seemed frozen, then grabbed at the tangled white pool of her robe as he calmly lifted his body from hers and stood, smoothly pulling his own around his body and tying the cord as he stared out to the audience. He bent down in the tense silence, swiping his fingers through the small, dark pool of blood that had appeared when she stood and jerked her robe around her body, eyes fixed and stiff on the door, as if the sight of it was the one thing that allowed her to draw air into her lungs. Her gaze dropped to her feet, cheeks branded with sudden red splotches as the Prophet slowly held his bloodstained fingers up to the crowd.

As he opened his mouth to speak the video jerked to a stop, then started again without sound, then dissolved into a gray sea of static. Kate pressed pause and leaned back in her chair as her phone pinged on the table, the vibration making it spin slowly in a jerky circle. She opened a text, then reached for her jacket.

"The chief wants to see me, and I might as well drop the video with one of the tech guys I trust to see if he can get any more out of it." She paused, buttoning her jacket with one hand and removing the thumb drive with the other. "But we need more details. We need to know who these men are and who the hell else is watching these videos."

"What we need to know is who that girl is." Hannah leaned back in her chair and scraped both hands through her hair. "She's the one who needs us the most."

Kate nodded, dropping her phone into her jacket pocket. "Maybe they can pull something else from the video that will give us a start with that." Fine lines around her eyes deepened and she paused, her gaze still trained on the empty black screen as if it might suddenly spring to life. "And while I'm there, I'll fill the chief in on the live grenade spinning in our laps."

She slung her bag over her shoulder and headed for the door, then walked back and took Hannah's face in her hands. She kissed her slowly, then turned and left without a word, the sound of the front door closing behind her hanging in the air.

Hannah's eyes sank to the table as she reached for Kate's whiskey glass. She downed it without a flinch and leaned back in the chair, winding her hair into a knot at the nape of her neck. Adel watched, her eyes soft and light until Hannah finally stood with a glance at the stove.

"You hungry, Rosse?"

"The answer to the question is always going to be yes." Adel smiled and arched an eyebrow. "Just for future reference."

Hannah flicked the rim of Adel's whiskey glass as she walked into the kitchen.

Chapter Seventeen

Grace slapped her hand over her mouth and locked her eyes to Nora's in the semidarkness of the closet. The smell of dust and stale air crowded the cramped space between them and the door that was inches beyond their faces.

"Yeah, but I don't see it." The sound of papers rifling on the table as he went through them was deafening. "And I *would* see it. It's not exactly small."

Grace held her breath as the shuffling stopped.

"Why would he think it's even here at all?" Another long pause. "No, not really, there's just a utility closet in the back."

Carpet-muffled footsteps moved closer to the closet door, and Nora squeezed Grace's arm. Grace shut her eyes tight, every muscle in her body tense and straining.

"How did that even happen? Is he sure?" The footsteps stopped and silence filled the closet again until he spoke. "Yeah, yeah, I know. I was just asking. But I don't have to tell you that this could be really bad if it gets into the wrong hands."

His steps moved closer to the door as he spoke, and then Grace's heart stopped as they watched the doorknob move slightly with the weight of his hand.

"We've gotta find it, but this is a waste of time. The only thing in here is a broom closet, and no one ever comes in this room but the—"

His voice stopped mid-sentence and he walked away from the closet, taking their breath with him.

"I'm coming over. I want a list of everyone who has access to the Prophet's office. Everyone with a key."

The strip of light under the door switched to darkness again as

Nora and Grace exhaled, finally. Nora finally shook her head and reached for the door handle.

"Did you recognize his voice?"

"No." Grace's voice was a low whisper as she followed her out into the darkness of the main room. "But did you hear him say he was going downstairs to make sure everything was locked up?"

"Yeah, and I know for a fact this is the ground floor." Nora walked to the door and pressed her ear against it, waving Grace over to her after a minute or two. "I don't think there's anyone else in the building now, so it should be fine to sneak the way we came in, I guess."

Grace paused, then looked back at the tables. "What was he looking for, do you think? He said it'd be bad if it got into the wrong hands, and from the way he sounded, I believe him. He seemed pretty worried about it."

Nora opened the door slowly, motioning for Grace to follow as she shut the door behind them. The hall pressed into them on both sides with heavy silence as they slipped past the back door, both letting out a shaky breath as they were quickly enveloped by the dark woods. Twigs cracked beneath their feet as they walked back down toward the cabins, but Grace quickened her steps when she heard the service on the hill behind them ending.

After what seemed like forever, they reached the row of staff cabins. Grace paused, her hand on the doorknob to her cabin as she glanced over at Nora.

"Hey, do you want to come in?"

Nora looked back up toward the lodge for a long second, then nodded, slipping through the door Grace held open for her. Inside, they sank down on the sofa and turned at the same moment to look at each other. Grace drew in a deep breath and lowered her voice to a whisper.

"You know what he's looking for, don't you?"

Nora said nothing. The silence was intense as Grace went on.

"They searched my place this weekend too." She paused, pulling the tie from her hair and leaning forward as it dropped down her back like a bolt of silk. "And I don't have anything they'd be interested in, so it has to be something they're looking everywhere to find."

Nora nodded slowly and leaned back into the sofa, her brows shoved together and tense as if they alone held all the secrets. She waited, silent, then looked at Grace.

"And maybe it's a coincidence that you asked me tonight about the Joy Book..." Grace returned Nora's gaze, her words slow and controlled. "But something tells me those two things are connected."

Nora's head fell into her hands and she let out a long, hard breath.

"Yeah. I have it." Her fingertips moved in slow circles at the sides of her head. "But I didn't know what the hell it was. I didn't know what I was getting into, and now I wish I'd never picked it up." She looked up finally, her eyes awash with tears she didn't acknowledge as they fell down her cheeks. "I wish I could just forget it, but I know bad things are happening to these girls. Otherwise, the Joy Book wouldn't exist."

Grace sank back into the sofa beside her. "I know about the book. I know probably more than I should."

Nora opened her mouth to reply, then closed it. She looked up at the ceiling, and when she finally spoke her voice was as soft as air. "Do you know you're still in it?"

Grace nodded, her voice breaking slightly when she spoke. "All the girls are there until they're married, and I'm obviously not." She leaned forward and rubbed at a spot on the coffee table with her thumb. "I hate the thought of still being in there. But there's nothing I can do about it."

When Grace finally looked up, one of Nora's eyebrows was arched and a slow smile was spreading across her face.

❖

Adel opened the bottle of Malbec Hannah had chosen while she finished up with the food and set the table. Mismatched pottery plates glazed in translucent yellow and turquoise anchored wrinkled linen napkins, and the cutlery was clearly vintage silver, but not one piece matched the others. Hannah lit a taper candle in the center of the table and blew out the match, shaking it with a flick of her wrist. The table was rustic, but effortlessly beautiful.

As they sat, Adel tried not to stare at Hannah, but the white button-down shirt she wore made that difficult. It wasn't sheer, but it was unbuttoned low enough to show that she was bare underneath, and every time she moved there was a new glimpse of the soft curve of her breast.

Hannah held out her hand for Adel's plate, then dished up a generous portion of what looked like the ultimate macaroni and cheese, with crispy browned edges and the faintest trace of black truffle oil rising with the steam. She topped that with a sprinkle of savory, crisp pancetta and freshly torn parsley, then handed the plate back to Adel.

Adel tried to stifle a sudden moan of pleasure as the first bite melted in her mouth but wasn't quite successful. The contrast between the salty bite of the pancetta and sharp, creamy cheese was too much not to completely sink into. She savored the first few bites in silence, then looked up at Hannah, who was polishing off her glass of wine in record time.

"So." Adel took the wooden bowl of arugula salad tossed with fresh lemon dressing Hannah passed over the table. "Why haven't you taken the plunge with the detective?"

Hannah looked up with sudden shock before a slow smile spread across her face like sunlight. "You certainly get right to the point, don't you?"

"It's pretty obvious she adores you."

"Yeah." The smile faded as Hannah speared some arugula with her fork. "She does. That's kinda the problem."

She waited a moment for her to go on, but Hannah said nothing and finished her salad like it was her job as Adel turned her attention back to the creamy pile of mac and cheese. They slipped into other topics of conversation, and before Adel knew it, it was two hours later and Hannah had polished off the wine and reached for the bottle of whiskey Kate had left on the table. She poured three fingers of it into her glass. Adel sat back in her chair as Hannah tossed the entire glass back like it was spring water and set it back on the table, staring at the remaining amber rivulets clinging to the sides of the glass.

"Damn, girl." Adel waited, pushing her plate away and raking her fingers through her hair. "You gonna tell me what that was all about?"

Hannah didn't say no, but she didn't talk, either. Adel finally pushed back her chair, walked over to the sliding glass door that led out to the patio, and unlatched it. She glanced outside to the silky black sky then looked back to the table.

"You coming?"

Hannah finally smiled and followed her out to the patio, the darkness close and dense around them. There was a patio light—Adel had spotted it beside the door on the outside of the house—but Hannah didn't click it on, and left the door to the house partially open. The light was behind them now, but far enough from the railing not to penetrate the darkness. Hannah walked over instead to the small table that Kate had pulled the cigarettes from before she came back to the railing that looked out over the water, now an expanse of undulating mercury under the light of the full moon.

Adel looked at the soft leather pouch she'd brought and arched an eyebrow. "You don't strike me as the pot-smoking type."

"Well, you're right," Hannah said, lining up some rolling papers and a lighter on the railing. "It's just tobacco. I rarely smoke if I have to actually roll them myself, which keeps me in check. I keep the normal lazy ones in there for Kate."

"Fair enough." Adel winked at her and looked back out over the water. "Roll it loose and I'll share it with you."

Hannah touched the tip of her tongue delicately to the edge of the paper and rolled it through her fingers, twisting the ends and handing Adel the lighter. Adel flicked it into flame and held it under the end of the cigarette. A breeze shifted from water to land in that moment and sifted through Hannah's light blond hair as she put it to her lips. She inhaled and the end blazed to life, red-gold against the inky darkness.

"You feeling that whiskey yet, badass?"

Adel reached for the cigarette and smiled, looking out over the water as she drew in, letting the translucent gray smoke swirl around them like a makeshift temple as the breeze drifted out to sea.

"Gonna tell me why you sank the whiskey like that?"

Hannah ran her palm over the railing and looked over at Adel, reaching for the cigarette. "Nope."

Adel leaned on one arm, turning toward Hannah. "Did you talk to your mom?"

"Yeah."

Adel's next words weren't a question. Because there was no question. "Yeah, I figured it would be bad."

Hannah just nodded, passing the glowing cigarette back to Adel and holding the smoke in her lungs for just a second before she let it out and watched it drift into the darkness. "It's bigger than..." Her voice trailed off and she shook her head. "It's a lot."

The air was delicate, almost briny, but lightened by the freshness of the tall lakeside grasses as the wind moved through them.

"That's not all it is, though, is it?"

Hannah held Adel's eyes then gazed out to the water, flicking the spent cigarette butt into the darkness beneath the railing. She shook her head slightly, then stepped closer to Adel. So close Adel felt the warmth of Hannah's breath against her neck. When she spoke, Adel's words were barely a whisper between them.

"Hannah, what are you doing?"

Hannah stepped forward again, this time the entire length of her body warm and soft against Adel's. Adel closed her eyes, holding the railing with one hand, the other frozen in the air at Hannah's shoulder.

"Hannah." Adel's voice was a whisper, Hannah's lips still so close to her neck she could count her breaths. She laid her hand on Hannah's shoulder and gently pushed her back, creating enough space between them for her to draw a breath. "You don't want to do this. I know you don't."

"Fuck." Hannah stepped back again, her head falling into her hands. "What am I doing?"

"Well." Adel smiled, her voice lightening to an almost teasing tone. "If I had to guess, I'd go with 'you're trying to fuck things up with Kate because you're in love and it scares the shit out of you.'"

"Why would you say that?" Adel let the silence settle between them until Hannah lifted her head. "How did you know?"

"Because it's obvious." Adel zipped up her jacket and looked down enough to catch Hannah's eye and hold the gaze. "You're in love with her, right? Because she's clearly in love with you."

"You think?"

Adel nodded, pulling her into a hug and stepping back again. "Want some advice?"

"Yeah."

The air above them stirred and they both looked up. A crane the color of blown ash swooped dramatically over the water and glided out of sight. Adel smiled and turned her attention back to Hannah, who was dabbing under her eye with cold fingertips as she swept away a tear.

"Be brave. That's my advice." Adel paused. "Yeah, you might get your heart broken, but you'll break your own heart if you keep being a dumbass and lose her. She's one of the good ones."

"I'm so sorry about what happened before." Hannah's eyes filled again with tears as she nodded and gently knocked Adel's shoulder with her own. "Thanks for—"

They both turned suddenly at the sound of Kate stepping through the glass patio door, pulling it closed behind her. Hannah swiped at her eyes again with the back of her hand and muttered something about the bathroom as she passed Kate.

Kate stepped up to the railing and looked out over the water, her jaw tense and still. There was no way to know what she saw. Adel sifted through words and explanations in her mind but finally decided the story wasn't hers to tell. She glanced sideways at Kate, still gazing out on the black water that disappeared seamlessly into the night sky at the horizon.

"Hey, man." Adel leaned back from the railing, her fingers slowly loosening from the rail. "I'm going to take off." She paused. "And your girl might have something she needs to talk to you about."

Kate didn't say anything, just kept her eyes on the horizon until Adel had almost stepped into the pool of warm light spilling through the patio door. Adel felt her turn then and slowed her steps, looking back to meet Kate's gaze.

"You were a real friend just now. To both of us." Kate's face softened with emotion and she shook her head slightly, still holding Adel's eyes. "I don't forget loyalty like that."

Adel smiled and, with a single nod, stepped through the door and closed it gently behind her.

❖

Later, on the drive back to camp, Adel peered through the window at the full moon hanging low over the lake. Again, she realized it was past time to tell Grace who she really was and why she was at Valley of Rubies, but with every passing day, the secret had become more shadowed, dense, and untouchable.

She'd woken in the early hours the night before, hoping to figure out a gentle way to tell her without it sounding like a betrayal. She never came up with one, and Adel knew she never would because it wasn't possible. It was a betrayal. This thing was getting bigger by the day, and it was already too much to have kept from her. She'd never meant to lie to her, she just hadn't expected to fall in love, and by the time she had, it was too late. She raked a hand through her hair and lowered the window, grateful for the chilled evergreen air brushing her cheeks.

Adel parked her camp vehicle in the lower lot and walked along the water on the way back to her cabin. She felt as flat as the lake water enveloping her feet. The last few days had been intense, and on top of everything else, the damn article was hanging over her head. Her editor usually let her set her own timeline, but she had to get a draft, or at the very least some solid content points, across his desk in the next few days or he was going to start paying attention, and not in a good way.

As Adel neared the boathouse, the shoreline shimmered in the distance. The slick of wet sand reflecting the pewter moonlight was also illuminating the dock...and the fire blazing next to it on the surface of the water. Adel took off running toward it, trying to make sense of a fire hovering above the dark lake water. It wasn't until she was almost to the docks that she saw two hazy figures on either side of the blaze.

Adel slowed to a stop as they both turned to look back at her. It was too dark to make out who it was, but the person on the left was literally holding the fire in their hand. Both figures turned back to the blaze that had started to fade slowly and dropped it into the surface of the water. The figure on the left started walking toward the shore, the movement of the water intensifying the dying hiss of the flames as they sank solemnly into darkness. It was Nora.

"What are you doing here? Who's still out there?"

The questions tumbled over themselves as Nora put her finger to her lips, glancing over her shoulder at the water. "That's Grace out there. But it's kind of a private moment, so don't go charging—"

The rest of her words were lost in the rush of the water as Adel tossed her jacket and bag onto the sand and ran into the dark lake. When she finally reached Grace, she held her tight for a few long moments before she let her go just enough to brush the tears from her cheeks with her lips.

"Baby." Adel's voice was husky with emotion. "What happened? Did someone hurt you?"

Grace shook her head and looked into Adel's eyes. "I'm okay. Just burning a picture from the past." She hesitated, then smiled, tilting her head to the side. "You just called me 'baby.'"

"Of course I did." Adel pulled Grace tight into her chest and wrapped her arms around her, breathing in the soft floral scent of her hair.

"Grace, I'm falling in love with you." She paused, trying to control the emotion in her voice. "I thought something had happened, and I swear to God if they do anything else to you..." Adel's voice trailed off and she held Grace's face in her hands. "I'm never going to let them hurt you again."

"But..." Grace searched Adel's eyes. "They didn't..." She faltered, her voice unsteady. "It was different for me, I could've told someone." The words that followed fell from her mouth and disappeared into the dark water. "I could have stopped them."

"Grace." Adel's eyes were as soft as the water lapping around them. "You're not responsible for saving anyone but yourself."

Adel held Grace's pale blue eyes, luminous and silent as the moon, and waited. When she finally spoke, Grace's words hovered between them like warmth rising from the water. "We all need saving."

Grace's head sank slowly onto Adel's chest as the words faded. She was still for a moment, then silent sobs shook her shoulders, and it was a long few moments before her breath started to slow. Adel's arms stayed firm and constant around her, one hand cradling the back of her head. When she finally looked up, Adel tipped her face up and kissed her gently, catching the last tear on Grace's cheek with her thumb.

The sudden sound of someone clearing their throat made both of them look toward the shore. It was Nora, standing on the sand, holding Adel's jacket in one hand, the other firmly planted on her hip. She did not look amused.

"Just a thought…" Her words were an emphatic hiss, only barely audible over the lapping water. "But this might not be the best place to have this little romantic fucking moment?"

Grace broke into stifled laughter, and they walked back to the shore, holding hands until they reached the edge of the water. Adel reached for her jacket, which she put around Grace's shoulders, and slung her bag back over her own.

"I stayed so we could walk back together. Might be less obvious that way."

Nora shot them a glance and tried to look annoyed. A bird the color of dark water flew over their heads into the trees lining the other side of the shore and called, answered by dozens of identical voices in the darkness.

"Actually"—she shot Adel a look over her shoulder—"I shouldn't be hanging out with you. You look like a big ol' dyke. It's bad for my rep."

"Mm-hmm." Adel rolled her eyes, turning to Grace. "You might want to ask Miss Congeniality here why I never run out of Wham salad."

Nora smacked Adel's shoulder, then dropped her voice to a whisper, leaning closer to Grace as they walked. "You know we were just talking about Bethany, the horse wrangler?"

"Yeah." Grace smiled and nodded. "We've never actually met, but she's hard to miss. She's taller than any of the men here."

"Well, we're kind of..." She glanced over at Adel. "Dating, I guess you could say."

"So we're all..." Grace stopped in her tracks as her voice trailed off.

"*Really* fucking gay?" Nora grinned, winking at Adel. "Looks like it."

"Well." Grace pulled the band out of her hair and smiled as it fell around her shoulders like sudden sunlight. "The express train to hell suddenly sounds like a lot more fun."

❖

After a whispered promise to meet up the next day, Nora took off up the hill before they reached the instructor's cabins. Adel kept her eyes on Grace as her steps slowed and they lingered in the shadows.

"You're still freaked out about them being in your place, aren't you?"

Grace stopped, her eyes focused on the dim lamplight just visible through the front window of her cabin. The air was heavy and still around them. Too still.

"Yeah. I mean, now that I know what they were looking for, it makes more sense, but..." Her voice trailed off and she glanced suddenly at Adel, wanting to sweep up her words and take them back.

"It's okay, Grace," Adel whispered. "I already know about the book."

Grace's eyes locked with Adel's. It was a long moment before she decided not to ask whether Adel had seen her picture. It didn't matter. That person didn't exist anymore.

Adel brushed Grace's cheek with her fingertips, then slipped them lightly around the back of her neck, pulling her closer. "Do you want to come to my cabin?"

A branch broke in the darkened forest and Grace jumped, her body instantly stiff and still. Adel pulled her key chain from the outside pocket of her bag and clicked on the mini Maglite, focusing it in the direction of the noise until silence turned to scurry. Grace stifled a laugh as they watched a portly raccoon attempt to duck out of sight, obviously unaware that most of his substantial girth was still visible from both sides of the seedling tree.

Adel's whisper was low and warm against the slope of Grace's neck. "What do you say we get inside before that raccoon decides we look like a tasty midnight snack?"

Adel squeezed Grace's hand in the shadows, then ducked through the door of her cabin first, leaving the door cracked for Grace to slip in after. When she finally did, she realized she was still barefoot, her wet dress clinging heavily to her legs. Adel took one look and grabbed some jeans and a hoodie from her closet, setting them on the sink and winking as she came back into the room.

"What are the chances of a beautiful woman showing up at my cabin in a soaking wet dress…twice?"

Grace laughed, passing Adel with a kiss as she headed for the bathroom. "Excellent, apparently."

Grace slipped into the bathroom and unzipped the wet dress, watching as it clung to her shoulders, then hips, as if unwilling to leave her body. She knew at that moment, as it slowly loosened its grip and slid reluctantly over her hips and down into a lifeless pool at her feet, that she'd never wear one of their dresses again.

Every one of them was the same, cut from a single pattern in the same cloying, pastel colors. The same style, length, and palette for every woman, worn from childhood to the grave. Even their hairstyles were similar: waist-length hair, pulled up in the front and worn in a plain bun at the base of their necks. The only change in their appearance that was allowed was the addition of a plain gold wedding band, and even that was chosen by her husband.

She hung the dress over the radiator with her bra and pulled on the sweatshirt and jeans Adel had given her, fastening them slowly around her hips. She stood, her feet cold and flat against the white tile floor, listening to her breath deepen as her muscles started to relax and unfold onto her bones. She felt herself growing, past the ropes they'd weighed her down with, the ones coiled around her soul since she was too young to realize that they were a part of them, not her. She closed her eyes against the memory of that summer, the summer she'd gotten her period and started developing. The summer she'd shifted from child to currency in the space of one violet evening.

Grace wound her damp hair into a bun at the top of her head, airy wisps slipping out as if on cue to brush her neck and the tops of her shoulders. She tucked them behind her ears, then closed her eyes, pausing for just a second before she chose to fill her lungs with the first breath of her own air.

Chapter Eighteen

"Hey there." Adel looked up from the couch with a wink in Grace's direction as she heard the bathroom door open. "I thought maybe you'd made a run for it."

Grace smiled, curling up next to Adel on the couch and leaning into her shoulder. "Not yet." She paused and looked up at Adel. "Do you think I could borrow these jeans and this hoodie until I can get into town and get my own?"

Adel nodded, her eyes questioning, but she reminded herself to hold space for Grace to speak.

"I can't put one of those dresses on again. I can't explain it. I just can't." She stopped, closing her eyes at the tears that slipped silently down her cheek. "I know that means I'll have to leave camp, but I just can't. Not anymore."

"Baby, the only thing you have to do is breathe." Adel brushed the tear from her cheek and her thumb lingered on her lower lip. "We'll start on the future tomorrow." Adel pulled something from the drawer under the coffee table and handed it to Grace.

"What's this?"

"It's a cell phone. I got you one when I went into town the other day, and put my number in it. I'd just feel safer if you had a way to reach me if you…" She paused, then kissed Grace's hand and smiled. "If you need fashion advice."

"I've never had one." Grace turned it over and over in her hand, her eyes shimmering with tears when she finally looked up. "Thank you for this."

Adel smiled and looked over her shoulder at the coffee table in front of them. "Are you hungry?"

"Um…" Grace sat up immediately when she noticed the cheeses in front of them, then smiled, her head tilted in thought. "Is that one of our teakwood oars from the boathouse?"

"Well, yes." Adel shrugged, popping a crumbly slice of Sunset Bay chèvre into her mouth. "I figured my chances of finding an actual cheese board around here in Haystack Central were slim, so I improvised."

Four beautiful pieces of cheese were set out on the widest part of the paddle, surrounded by fresh sliced figs and almonds that she'd tossed in oil and rosemary, then dusted with cayenne for a little heat. A chunk of honeycomb sat beside them, the amber slick of honey flowing dangerously close to the edge of the oar.

"These," Adel said, handing her a glass of pale gold Sauvignon Blanc, "are from that little wine and cheese store downtown. You loved the gruyère in those crepes so much that night I thought I'd bring you a few more to try." Adel folded a wafer-thin slice of pale yellow muenster onto a black-pepper-dusted water cracker and handed it to Grace.

"So what have you tasted, when it comes to cheese?" Adel smiled, glancing down at the handle extending far past the end of the coffee table. "The information I'm really looking for here is, are you partial to cheeses on oars?"

"Oh, definitely. I've been waiting all my life for that." Grace reached up and kissed Adel, her fingertips lingering on her cheek as she sat back into the couch beside her. "I loved whatever you gave me before. But other than that, I guess the only cheeses I know are the basic ones at the store like cheddar and swiss."

"Okay, so, when you eat cheddar, do you like it to be sharp?" Adel paused, cutting a thin slice of a pale yellow cheese dotted with herbs and placed it on another cracker. "Or do you prefer more mild flavors? Cheeses that taste more creamy than tangy?"

"I was in a rush in the grocery store one day and mistakenly picked up extra sharp cheddar for haystacks that night at home, and everyone hated it."

"Except you?" Adel raised an eyebrow, offering her the cracker.

"Except me." Grace laughed, then stood to draw in the scent of the cheese. "I loved it so much, I piled it on saltines that night and snuck it into my room."

Grace closed her eyes and bit into it, chewing slowly and swallowing before she opened her eyes.

"I'm in *love* with this." She reached for another cracker and cut another wafer-thin slice, folding it like a wide ribbon onto the top. "It has an oniony bite that's just perfect with that sharp flavor. Is it cheddar?"

"Look at you, talking cheeses like a pro." Adel smiled and waited while she finished the last bite. "That one was double Gloucester with chives, a common English export, and this one is a cave-aged Gouda, so it's intensely flavored and rich with crystals. The jam-looking stuff on top is a sour cherry compote. You wouldn't think those flavors would work together, but they do."

"There are...crystals in it? Like rocks?"

"There's no way to describe this so it makes sense until you've tasted it." Adel smiled, sliding her hand warm and slow across Grace's thigh. "Just put it in your mouth."

Grace arched an eyebrow as she bit into the cracker. A slow look of bliss melted across her face as she leaned back into the couch and popped the rest of it into her mouth, pulling the hair tie out of her hair.

Adel watched her as she savored the new flavors, her hair falling loose and wild to her waist as she tucked her tanned, bare feet underneath her on the couch. She licked a syrupy dab of cherry compote off her fingers and leaned in to kiss Adel, the bright cherry flavor still lingering on her lips. Adel slid a hand warm around the back of her neck, her mouth soft and light against Grace's neck, then slicked her tongue gently across the edge of Grace's earlobe until she felt a slow shudder move through her body.

She wrapped an arm around her waist and slid Grace underneath her on the couch, sinking a thigh between her legs as she leaned into her neck, tracing the curve on it with her breath. She felt Grace's fingers, warm and light, on the back of her shoulders, her touch deepening as Adel eased down the zipper of her hoodie and surrounded Grace's nipple with the sudden warmth of her tongue.

"So, what do I have to do to lure you away from this cheese situation and get you into my bed?"

Adel's voice was teasing as she lowered the zipper even more, cradling the lush heaviness of one breast with her hand as she pulled the other nipple into her mouth, slicking her tongue around it until she felt Grace arch underneath her. She leaned in closer, her thigh heavy and warm between Grace's legs, savoring the moan that escaped suddenly as Adel moved against her, nipple still slick and warm under her tongue. Adel finally leaned back slightly and smiled, glancing back at the oar piled with savory cheeses and a wanton scatter of rosemary almonds.

Grace narrowed her brows and made a show of taking a moment to consider her options.

"I'm willing to part with the cheese temporarily, but only if I get to come back to it later."

Adel laughed as she picked Grace up off the couch, wrapped her legs around her waist, and carried her to the bed. A single candle in a faceted jar on the nightstand scattered gold light onto the bed as Adel came back with wineglasses in hand.

"So," Grace said, reaching for the glass of Sauvignon Blanc as Adel settled beside her onto the bed, "You know when you asked me if I'd ever…touched myself?"

Adel nodded, taking a sip of her wine and setting it on the bedside table. She pulled her fleece over her head and tossed it onto the desk chair, leaving her barefoot, wearing only faded jeans and a white T-shirt.

"So, I've been thinking I want to learn how to…" Grace's voice trailed off, her cheeks flushed suddenly as she looked into her wineglass.

"Baby." Grace bit her bottom lip as Adel brought her face gently to her own before she spoke. "I know it feels strange to talk about, but this is so natural. You want to know how to give yourself an orgasm, right?"

Grace nodded. "I mean, I explored a bit, years ago, but that wasn't remotely close to how you make me feel. I must have been doing it wrong."

Adel tucked a loose lock of hair behind Grace's ear and stroked her cheek with her thumb as she spoke. "Honestly, there's no wrong way to do it. It just takes exploring enough to get familiar with what feels good to you. Everybody just has to find what they like, so that's normal, I promise."

Grace looked into her wineglass again, started to speak, then hesitated and bit her lip, fingers tensing around the stem. Adel tipped her face up with a gentle finger until she was looking into Grace's eyes.

"Do you want me to show you?"

Grace nodded and smiled as Adel pulled her own T-shirt and sports bra over her head, leaving her naked to the waist as she settled back against the headboard. Grace unzipped the hoodie to bare the full curves of her breasts as Adel turned her around to sit between her thighs, pulling her gently back to rest against the warmth of her chest.

She traced the curve of Grace's waist with light fingertips, then slid slowly up to her dusky pink nipples, already tightening under her touch. Adel warmed the slope of Grace's neck with her breath as she brushed them again with the back of her hands, using just enough pressure to feel like a soft scrape, a contrast to the velvet softness of her fingertips.

"When you do that," Grace whispered, her voice deepening with desire, words lingering in the dark as if waiting for each other, "I feel it everywhere."

Adel flicked open the button of Grace's jeans and whispered into her ear until she slid out of them, pushing them to the end of the bed with her feet. Adel slid her hands around to surround the lush curves of Grace's breasts, fingertips gently squeezing both of her nipples at once. Grace let out a surprised breath, her head falling back onto Adel's bare shoulder.

"Remember," Adel said, her words warm against Grace's ear. "All you have to do is pay attention to what feels good to you, okay?"

Adel caressed her nipples as one hand dipped lower to warm the delicate skin of her inner thighs. Grace sank back against her, parting her thighs until they rested just inside Adel's.

Adel ran her fingers over Grace's sheer silk panties, struggling to keep herself in check as she closed her eyes and traced Grace's delicate inner lips under the fabric from memory, then circled her clit.

Grace's breath was the only sound in the darkness as she slipped off the panties, put her hand over Adel's, and pressed Adel's fingers slowly over her clit. Adel stroked her lightly, then guided Grace's fingers to her clit as she moved lower into the liquid heat of her. She stayed inside her for a few seconds, then brought her hand up and slid those fingers gently into Grace's mouth. Adel felt her body respond hard as Grace's tongue slicked over her fingers, tasting herself hesitantly, then drawing Adel's fingers deeper into her mouth. Adel took Grace's hand back gently and put it underneath hers, bringing her fingers again to the tense bud of her clit. She guided Grace's touch into long, slow strokes first, then wordlessly showed her how to part her fingers and stroke her clit using one finger on each side.

"How do you feel, baby?"

Adel whispered the words against Grace's neck, then traced them with her tongue. "Just tell me if something is too much, okay?"

Grace nodded, her breath deepening, her touch deeper and more confident now under Adel's hand.

"Can you show me what you do inside?" Grace looked up at Adel, her eyes sparkling in the candlelight. "When you're there, it's just…so intense."

Adel showed her the basics of what might feel good to her, but getting the rhythm of working both hands together, one inside and the other on her clit, proved tricky.

Adel put her hand on Grace's shoulder and whispered, "Lean up for a second, baby. I'll be right back." Adel slid out of bed and dropped her jeans on the desk chair, then opened the nightstand drawer as she climbed back in beside Grace.

"What's that?" Grace reached out a tentative finger and touched the toy Adel had pulled out of the nightstand. It was silicone, pearlescent white, and shaped subtly like the curves of a woman. "This is yours?"

"Yes. I knew I was going to be here for a few months, so I brought it with me."

"For yourself?"

Adel nodded, trying not to smile at the dubious look on Grace's face. "I love this one. I bought it on a trip to San Francisco years ago, right after college."

Grace reached out for it, still sporting the same doubtful look. She rolled it around in her hand, smiling when she realized it was shaped like a beautiful naked woman.

"Sometimes these are a bit easier than trying to work both your hands at once when you're not used to that rhythm—it takes practice. And this is a fairly small one, not much bigger than what you're familiar with already."

Grace raised an eyebrow and handed it back to Adel. "Will you show me?"

"Yes, ma'am."

Adel smiled and leaned into her, looking in her eyes for a moment before she kissed her again, slipping her arm around the small of her back and pulling Grace underneath her body as she spoke. She worked Grace's clit in slow, soft circles with her thumb until she felt her hips start to move and her thighs tense. Grace was so wet, her clit pink and beautifully visible, straining for Adel's touch.

"Here," Adel said, replacing her fingers with Grace's and guiding her into a rhythm. "I'll be gentle. Just tell me if something doesn't feel good, okay?"

Grace nodded, watching as Adel moved on her knees between Grace's thighs. Adel held her gaze as she reached down to her own clit, matching Grace's movements with her own, only stopping when she knew she'd come if she didn't. Watching Grace touch her own body, her hair wild and beautiful around her, nipples tense and thighs spread, was almost too much. Adel wanted to keep stroking her own clit, to come hard while she watched Grace go over the edge, but made herself stop. Barely.

Grace was close. Adel saw her eyes, heavy with desire, the pink flush across her chest, heard her shallow, tense breaths. She sat back between Grace's thighs and held her eyes while she slicked the toy with Grace's own wetness, pausing to work her clit with it until Grace moaned and arched her back, every muscle tensed. After a moment she started to slowly slip the toy inside her until Grace stilled and Adel stopped where she was, giving her time to adjust to the feeling. She waited, searching Grace's face for any sign of hesitation, but Grace just nodded, her fingers starting to work her own clit again as Adel slipped the rest of it gently inside her.

Grace's fingers moved in quick, heavy circles, her hips restless. Adel started a slow, gentle rhythm and held the curve of Grace's hip with her other hand.

"How do you feel?" Adel heard the husky scrape of her own voice, knew the answer before she asked, but she needed to hear it.

"Adel." Grace's eyes met hers, her voice breathless and soft. "I love it. Don't stop."

Adel angled the toy to stroke Grace's G-spot, sensitive and tense just inside her. She matched the rhythm of Grace's fingers, watching her face as her thighs started to tremble. It was only a few seconds until Adel saw the orgasm start to roll through her body in slow motion, her back arched hard and lush breasts shimmering with a fine mist of sweat, glistening in the candlelight.

Adel savored every second until the last shudder subsided, then pulled Grace into her arms, covering both of them with the duvet until Grace's breath finally slowed and she turned to face Adel, eyes shining.

"I think we need to store that in my cabin." She tried to look serious and failed instantly. "For safekeeping, of course."

Adel smiled and kissed her neck, brushing her nipples lazily with the palm of her hand.

"After that, you get anything you want, baby."

Adel watched a thought cross Grace's face like a windblown leaf, gold and crisp at the edges. Adel just waited, brushing her skin with her fingertips, light as breath. Grace was already brave, all she needed was space to be herself.

"I think I want to watch you when…" Grace's voice trailed off and she bit her lip.

Adel waited until she thought Grace might not say it at all, then stepped in. "You want to watch me come?"

Grace nodded, her cheeks instantly flushed. "When it happened before, I was so into it I didn't see your face, and I've been thinking about it since."

Adel held her eyes as she moved over Grace on her knees, straddling her hips. She was so wet, close, already intensely turned on after seeing Grace come, watching that orgasm crash through her, shake her, leave her breathless and trembling on the bed.

"You're so beautiful." Grace's voice was a hushed whisper as she wrapped her hands around the back of Adel's thighs, around her hips, and over her abs, pausing when she reached the center of her chest. Grace turned her hand over and brushed Adel's nipples gently with the back of her fingers like Adel had, until Adel caught her hand and brought it to her mouth, swirling her tongue around the middle finger then licking slowly down to her wrist.

"Can I have this hand?"

Grace nodded, watching as Adel pulled it underneath her and turned it over so the back of Grace's hand pressed against her own body, palm facing up. Grace raised her two middle fingers, and Adel closed her eyes as she sank down onto them, slow and deep, until they were inside her and her clit met the heel of Grace's hand.

"Fuck."

It was more breath than a word as Adel started working her hips slowly, her breath catching as she felt Grace inside her. She slid slowly against Grace's slick hand, spreading her thighs wider until she found the perfect pressure on her clit.

Grace watched her intently, holding her hip with one hand as Adel slid back and forth against her palm. Adel felt herself getting wetter, tighter, her hips working in a steady rhythm until she started to sink forward onto Grace's body.

"No." Grace's voice was gentle and breathless, her hand braced at the center of Adel's chest. "I want to see you."

Adel met her gaze as she raised her arms and laced her fingers behind her head. Grace looked mesmerized as she followed every move of Adel's hips as they slid back and forth over her upturned hand. Grace's eyes dropped to Adel's abs and she held her other hand in the center of them, her body absorbing the rhythm of Adel's hips, moving with her. Adel closed her eyes and tensed her arms, her hands still laced behind her head, working her hips harder across Grace's slick hand.

"Baby, I'm close." Adel's eyes were heavy, her hips working in a hard rhythm, and she pulled Grace's other hand up and held it under hers in the center of her chest. "Do you want to see me come for you?"

"Yeah." Grace's gaze locked onto hers, her voice surprisingly strong, her eyes reflecting the lust flowing between them like sudden lightning over dark water. "Come for me."

That was enough to send Adel over the edge. She gripped the back of Grace's head, fingers tangled hard in her hair, as she melted into one of the strongest orgasms of her life, her body slicking fast and hard across Grace's upturned hand. Adel heard herself moan, every muscle tight and straining as her first orgasm flowed into the second and seemed to go on forever, with Grace's fingers moving inside her, her other hand still braced at the center of Adel's chest.

As she finally caught her breath, she sank down slowly onto Grace's body, whispering warm words into her neck as she slipped behind her and wrapped Grace's body with hers. Grace shifted slightly in Adel's arms and whispered her name.

She didn't continue, and Adel listened to her breath slowly deepening, settling into the softness of her own, both of them balanced at the feathery edge of sleep.

Long after that night, she'd wonder if the words she'd heard were a whisper or a dream.

I love you too.

❖

By the time Grace woke the next day, a wide beam of sunlight had fallen across her face and Adel had already left to get to her early class. She rolled over lazily in bed, taking the covers with her, and picked up the note she knew would be on the nightstand.

Good morning, beautiful.
I had to get to class, but I'll see you down at the docks for rowing later.
Already counting the minutes...Just so you know.
Adel

She brought the note to her nose in case any trace of Adel's scent still lingered on the paper as a sudden, raw memory of Adel kneeling over her body the previous night flashed across her mind like a scene from a movie. Grace closed her eyes and tried to remember every detail of how she looked, wishing she could burn it into her memory so she could never forget. Just the thought of Adel kneeling over her, touching herself, her eyes magnetic and heavy with desire, made her instantly wet.

Last night had felt different, somehow. The panic on Adel's face when she'd thought Grace was hurt and ran into the water, the strength of her arms closing protectively around her, even the softness of her eyes later, lying in bed. Everything was suddenly deeper, more intense and meaningful. Grace sat up in bed and gathered her hair into the hair tie she found on her wrist, twisting it into a soft bun at the nape of her neck. Everything felt different because it was different. She was in love.

The familiar, furious dust storm of shame at the thought of falling in love with another woman seemed to have settled into powerless drifts in the shadowy corners of her mind as Grace sat up in bed, rubbing the sleep from her eyes. She eyed the jeans and sweatshirt she'd laid over the desk chair, then turned to look toward the bathroom, where the edge of the pale blue dress she'd taken off last night was reflected in the mirror, lying drained and powerless over the side of the radiator.

For once in her life, she had a choice. She could step into the pastel cage she'd worn every year of her life, or she could choose what reflected the person she was becoming, even if she wasn't sure what that looked like yet. What she did know was if she ever stepped into one of those dresses again, then they'd won for the final time. She'd drift quietly underwater, slowly sinking toward the pastel heap at the bottom. The power, the weight of the water undulating above her would slip silently past the point of no return, like it had for a thousand others before her.

She smiled, folded the note carefully, and reached over to set it on the nightstand. It dropped off the edge and disappeared into the open nightstand drawer, landing on a notebook, a composition book Adel used in her creative writing class. Grace knew from listening to the girls in class that they used them as a diary, a journal to hold all their secrets and innermost thoughts. Not that it would be the same for Adel; it was probably just a notebook she used to jot down class notes. Her heart pounded as she picked it up and laid it on the bed in front of her, her stomach instantly twisting into the same shape as her thoughts. Of course, she wouldn't open it. It wasn't even a question.

Then slowly, as if watching herself as a character on yet another stage, she felt the cool edges of the pages sliding under her fingers, and watched as the book fell silently open to the last entry. A single page written in Adel's neat, square handwriting.

> *At this point, I'm just fucked. If I tell Grace who I am now, she'll hate me for lying to her; but if I wait, she's going to find out anyway. What's going to happen when I go back to Manhattan and write this article, all hell breaks loose, and the camp she loves is shut down? She'll know I've been lying to her about who I am since that first day in the diner.*

Grace closed the notebook quietly, her open palm smoothing over the cold, flat cover. The next thing she felt was her stomach as it started to churn, the deafening crack of her knees hitting the cold white tile of the bathroom floor, and the acrid burn of the first twenty-six years of her life rising in her throat.

Chapter Nineteen

Adel's day was swift but uneventful until she reached the sun-warmed docks to prepare for rowing class. Almost everyone was already lounging in the sun on the outstretched wing of the silvered dock, but Ruth was noticeably absent, and the other girls seemed subdued without her presence. Adel waited as long as she could for Grace to appear before she reluctantly loaded the boats and headed out with the class, fighting off a sinking feeling of dread building around her like night swells of dark lake water.

Class seemed to drag on forever, but they finally headed back to the docks, where Adel quickly scanned the shore for Grace. It was silent in the late afternoon light and eerily deserted. The sun stung the back of her neck as she tied off the boats and the girls returned their life jackets to the boathouse, until Adel caught sight of Bethany out of the corner of her eye, galloping down the beach on horseback, ponytail flying behind her. She bent to collect the last of the jackets quickly and stepped out of the boathouse just as Bethany rode up. She tugged the reins tight, and the horse's sudden side halt sprayed sand with enough force to hear the hiss of it as it hit the sun-bleached boards of the boathouse. Adel closed the boathouse door behind her slowly and shielded her eyes from the sun.

"I'd ask what's up," she said, noting the tense lines around Bethany's mouth, "but I don't think I want to know."

"Dude." Bethany whispered the words, but her eyes were locked on Adel's. "Do you know where Grace is?"

Adel's heart shifted into long-delayed panic and pounded against her chest. "What's wrong? She missed class today, and she never does that." She searched Bethany's face. "Is she okay?"

Bethany looked down the shore toward the cabins and paused, her voice dropping an octave into an urgent whisper. "She was supposed to meet Nora this morning, but when she got to Grace's cabin, two of the Brethren were hauling out boxes of her stuff and clearing the whole place out. When she came back later, there was a padlock on the door and no sign of Grace."

"What the *fuck*?" Adel tried to quell the mounting panic making her heart vibrate against her chest. "She's got to be here somewhere. She can't just disappear."

Bethany looked out into the distance in the direction of the main lodge. When she dragged her gaze back to Adel and finally spoke again, her voice was rough, stilted. "But she can, Adel. Nora said Grace told her all about it. They call it Blood Atonement, and it means paying for your sins with your own spilled blood." Bethany shook her head, blood visibly coursing through the taut veins in her neck. Her hand wrapped tighter around the reins and she locked her gaze onto Adel's. "Basically, it's murder on the Prophet's directive. *Anyone* can just disappear."

❖

When Grace had finally pulled herself together enough to go next door to her own cabin, there was a padlock on it. She looked through the curtains, which had been pulled to each side, and there was not a single thing of hers left inside. It was as if she had never lived there, never existed. She stepped back, feeling exposed, as if she felt the burn of a red laser scope dancing between her eyes. She spun around, looking for anyone who might be watching her, but there was no one. Just a single white heron tracking her with its eyes from the shore across the lake. The sun warmed her face, the water lapping quietly onto the sand a few feet down from the cabins, but there was not a breath of another sound. Even the wind was silent as it swept across the water and disappeared into the feathery treetops. She'd pulled the sleeves of her hoodie down over her hands and turned to leave when she noticed the small, folded note tucked behind the doorknob. It was a handwritten summons to Mrs. Whittier's office. It wasn't signed. There was no need.

There was no point trying to convince herself that it might be nothing; of course they were sending her home. The delay between this visit to the office and the last was probably just Whittier getting in touch with her parents to consult about the "situation," as if she were a child. To discuss how to "return" her, the proof she was simply a defective product, rejected by the buyer.

She returned to Adel's cabin and locked the door behind her. Cold water from the kitchen tap poured through her fingers for a long moment while she stared, unable to remember why she'd turned it on. She pushed thoughts of Adel from her mind, but the truth was that she'd known all along it was too good to be true. What was she thinking, that Adel from the big city would actually have feelings for somebody who knew nothing about the world? That a stupid virgin with no experience would be able to compare with whoever she had waiting for her back in the city?

Grace splashed water onto her face, letting the icy sting of the water ground her back in the present, remind her that nothing mattered except what she needed to do next, what she needed to do to survive now.

It was her own fault. She'd started to let herself believe she had choices, that she might be able to create a life she actually wanted. Of course, now her only option was to return home and marry Edward Dooney. She closed her fists around the cool ceramic sides of the sink and shut her eyes, leaning her forehead on the cabinet. Dooney, with the uneven comb tracks in his grease-soaked hair and the dull, piercing eyes that lingered on girls too young to notice. Everyone knew there was something wrong with him, which must be why he'd finally been paired off with her. Clearly there was something wrong with her as well. The thought of just disappearing, stealing one of the camp vehicles and driving out of state, flashed across her mind, but all she'd be doing was prolonging the inevitable. This was what she deserved for letting her mind wander toward a life of her own. She twisted the tap and the sound of the water stopped, leaving the soundless swirl of silence to press into her from every side.

Grace swiped her keys off the tabletop as she left the cabin, pausing as she took a last look at the lake outside the door. Sunlight sparkled on the water that had suddenly stilled, as if it were also watching her. She started walking, but paused and took a long, slow breath when she saw the lodge at the end of the trail. The air was hovering in the shape of a still gold afternoon, but a cool breeze swept through the trees and brought her back to reality as it stirred the evergreen branches above her head. She closed her eyes and stood still on the trail, wood chips shifting under her feet, before she squared her shoulders and set her gaze on the lodge.

Distant laughter from the waterfront finally floated past as she pulled open the enormous door to the main lobby. Sunlight poured through the plate glass front windows and pooled on the floor around her. Aside from the faint sounds of cleaning from the cafeteria, the lobby was strangely quiet. Her shoes squeaked against the hardwood floor as she walked down the hall to Whittier's office, the air around her slowly becoming viscous, then stiffening like quicksand. She felt the breath being pressed from her lungs and had an insane urge to run the other direction, but where would she go? She had no one but her parents now, and she was an embarrassment to them. No, now it was worse than embarrassment. Now everyone knew.

She knocked and stepped inside Whittier's office without waiting for an answer. Whittier was standing with her back to her, facing the filing cabinet, and turned around slowly, her watery gray eyes narrowing when she saw Grace.

"Miss Waters." Whittier's voice was as terse as her gaze. "Please have a seat."

Grace closed the door behind her and leaned against it, her hands braced hard on the door behind her. "No, thank you. I'll stand."

An instant of white-hot hatred flashed across Whittier's face, and Grace felt the walls close in around her again when she remembered she'd pulled on Adel's jeans and sweatshirt that morning. She was being fired anyway, but to walk into Whittier's office in anything but a dress was a direct act of disrespect.

Whittier's next words clattered like stones and gouged the desk in front of her.

"Miss Waters, I asked you to sit. If I need to bring some of the elders in to remind you how to do that, I most certainly will."

Grace held her eyes for a long moment before she walked to the chair in front of Whittier's desk and sat down. Whittier pulled her Bible toward her and folded her hands over the creased leather cover as if it were an altar. Grace watched as the lines across her forehead deepened and a vein in her neck twitched with her heartbeat. A fly buzzed around the light fixture above her head, launching itself at the light. When she spoke, her eyes were still locked onto the Bible in front of her.

"Do you know why you're here today, Grace?"

Grace said nothing. If Whittier was going to fire her, she wasn't going to do the work for her. She finally lifted her gaze to meet Grace's eyes, but really, there was no need. There was nothing there. They were cold. Cold gray concrete.

"I've been concerned lately about your walk with the Lord." She paused. "So a few weeks ago, I had some surveillance equipment installed in your cabin."

Grace's mind spun through everything in her cabin; anything that might have given away her secret. But there was nothing. The clothes she wore today were her first outward sign of defiance. If Whittier was about to say they had proof of wrongdoing, Grace would know she was lying. Grace leveled her eyes to Whittier's.

"If you'd really done that," she said, forcing herself to hold Whittier's gaze, "you'd know you have no reason to doubt my walk with the Lord."

Whittier's eyes lifted to the two tall men with broad shoulders who entered the room quietly and stood behind Grace's chair. She knew who they were—everyone referred to them as the God Squad. They were the Prophet's security detail, usually patrolling the perimeter of the camp in blacked-out SUVs.

Whittier's face unexpectedly softened as she looked back at Grace. "You're correct. And I owe you an apology for invading your privacy."

Whittier reached behind her to the laptop sitting on the bookcase. Grace shifted and looked back at the men standing behind her chair, but they continued to stare straight ahead. They were standing so close Grace felt the radiating heat from their bodies, turning the air around her into a vacuum and slowly dragging oxygen from her lungs as she turned back around to face the desk.

Whittier turned the computer screen to face Grace and clicked the keys slowly, as if willing each click to hang in the air as long as possible. The silence was palpable as the last click faded and the screen lit up. It was the interior of Grace's cabin, but everything was silent, in place. Even her keys were still hanging on the hook by the door.

Grace felt her patience thinning as if being strung to the limit of its tenacity between her body and the door. "You're wasting your time."

"We were, yes." The vein in Whittier's neck throbbed grotesquely. "You're right."

"Then I don't know what you're—"

Grace's words scraped into the air only to fall flat with another click from Whittier. This time the camera was angled to face the bed. Adel's bed. Grace was naked, kneeling over Adel's face, her hands on the headboard, hair falling in wild undone waves down her back as Adel wrapped her hands around Grace's hips and pulled her slowly down to her mouth.

Grace lunged for the computer. The crack of her forehead hitting the desk was deafening as the elders yanked her back into the chair, then everything went dark as a needle sank silently into her neck.

❖

Bethany was already in her truck with the engine running by the time Adel changed and ran up the trail to the stables. She lowered the volume of Warrant's "Cherry Pie" to just below deafening and leaned out the window to roll her eyes at Adel.

"*Dude*, what are you doing, a nature walk? Get your ass in here."

Adel swung open the creaky door of Bethany's lime-green Chevy Silverado—although to be accurate, only the front was rust-tinted lime green. The truck bed was primer gray and loaded with coils of dusty ropes and crushed Coke cans.

She slid onto the bench seat and gripped the dashboard as Bethany gunned the engine and took off down the dirt access path at the edge of camp that led to the main road into town. Adel dug down into the seat behind her almost to her elbow and finally looked up, reaching for the handle just below the ceiling as Bethany took the corner on two wheels and skidded onto the main road, tires leaving a trail of acrid smoke behind her.

"I'm just wasting my time here asking where the seat belt is, right?"

Bethany looked over as she lifted both hands off the steering wheel and pulled the windblown blond hair whipping around her head into a ponytail.

"You've met me, right?" Bethany pulled her hair halfway through the last loop and left it, which cut down on the amount that was actively hitting Adel in the face. "I cut those out last winter and used them to haul some girl's fancy-ass car out of a snow ditch."

Adel smirked halfheartedly, then stared out the window at the evergreens whizzing past her window. The thought that Grace might be in trouble somewhere made her sick to her stomach, but when she'd returned to her cabin after rowing to change, she'd noticed that her journal was on the desk, open. Her heart sank to her stomach when she read the last entry; obviously Grace had seen it and left it there so Adel would know why she was gone. The camp wasn't the reason she'd disappeared—Adel knew now that it was her. She also knew by the brick in the pit of her gut that she'd never see her again.

"Hey, I should tell you something."

Bethany nodded and reached across Adel to the glove compartment to pull a crumpled pack of cigarettes out and fish for her lighter. Adel handed her the pack and flicked the Zippo she'd yanked out of her shorts pocket, holding it close enough for Bethany to lean into and light her cigarette.

"I didn't even know you smoked." Adel slid the lighter back into her shorts and glanced over at Bethany, who looked suddenly blissful as she inhaled the smoke deeply before the wind from her open window whipped it from her mouth.

"That's because I don't. These aren't like regular cigarettes." She held up the Marlboro Menthol package and winked. "They're green. Which obviously means they're healthy."

"Really?" Adel finally cracked a smile and shook her head. "You just keep telling yourself that."

As they wound themselves down into the town of Lockwood, the last of the afternoon sun warmed the air and café windows spilled gold light to pool onto the darkening sidewalks. It was a typical lake town, filled with working-class locals and upper-crust tourists, and at that point, Adel would have happily traded places with any of them. Grace was gone. She'd lost the woman she knew was the love of her life because she was a cowardly piece of shit, basically. Now nothing else mattered.

Bethany spun the steering wheel into a sharp right turn at the police station and skidded to a stop directly over the middle of two parking places. She nervously lit another cigarette, her outstretched arm hanging out the window. She glanced over to Adel and nodded toward the station.

"I guess I didn't even tell you where we were headed. I figured you knew."

"Yeah." Adel closed her eyes and exhaled every drop of air in her lungs, then found the door handle and swung the door open. It offered a deafening screech in protest and buried itself in the divot it had already carved into the side of the truck. Adel got out and wedged it free, then shut the door, leaning in the open window and arching an eyebrow at Bethany, whose boots were already in place on the dashboard.

"You coming?"

Bethany shook her head and flicked the rest of her cigarette out the window onto the pavement.

"Fuck no."

Adel resisted the urge to roll her eyes and waited. Bethany sighed and looked again toward the station like they might have guns already pointed at her windshield.

"I've had some past...legal transgressions." She paused and fired up the next cigarette. "Well, to put a finer point on it, they're more current legal issues, and I'm a shitty liar. Not a good combo."

"What, so they're just going to immediately pull up your record the second you walk in and ship you off to the pen?"

Bethany looked nervously into the rearview mirror and pulled the keys out of the ignition, then dropped them into the dented chrome ashtray and nodded. "Yeah. They might."

This time Adel did roll her eyes, then smiled at her friend with a backward glance at the station door. "Fine. Just do me a favor and lose the eighties hair band soundtrack. That's what they should arrest you for."

Adel smiled and shook her head as she turned toward the station, but her footsteps slowed steadily as she neared the doors. What was she going to say once she got in there? That she thought some illegal shit was going down at camp but had no actual proof of anything? That the girl she loved was suddenly "missing" hours after she found out that Adel was jerking her around? The best she'd be able to do was relay the things Bethany had told her, which at that point was nearly useless because even she knew that would be hearsay without Bethany to back it up.

She was considering retreating back to the truck when what sounded like thundering horse hooves approaching at breakneck speed made her stop and turn around. It was Bethany running toward her, bag slung haphazardly over her arm. Adel smiled as Bethany slowed, fixing her eyes on the door as she spoke.

"Fine. Fuck it." Bethany looked over at Adel and straightened her shoulders. "But when I get arrested, you've gotta get Nora to go up and feed the horses tonight."

Adel laughed and ran her hand through her hair, suddenly grateful for the company and comic relief. Which lasted until she realized Bethany wasn't laughing and splotchy patches of red were starting to creep up her neck.

"Damn, girl. You're serious." Adel nodded, the smile falling from her face. "I promise. I'll make sure they're taken care of, no matter what."

Bethany's eyes were still locked on the doors, but she matched

Adel's steps and walked into the lobby, her eyes shifting from one wall to the next and landing on the prim-looking cop in uniform manning the reception window. Adel left her where she was and stepped up to the window, awkwardly aiming her words at the silver vents in the glass between her and the cop.

"Um, I need to speak to Kate if she's here."

The cop raised an eyebrow and sat back in her chair. "Kate who?"

Shit. Adel thought. *Really? I seriously don't even remember her last name?*

The woman behind the glass waited for an answer, taking the time to look Adel up and down. "Are you speaking of Detective Kilcullen?"

Adel remembered suddenly she still had Kate's card in her wallet, but when she looked in every card slot, even the hidden one on the outside, it was nowhere to be found.

"Listen, she gave me her card. If you bring her out here, she can tell you herself that we know each other."

She looked Adel up and down, then glanced behind her at the open area of the station. "Stay here, please."

She got up, walked back toward the main open area of the station, and disappeared through a door in the back. Adel turned back toward Bethany, who was standing beside the glass door with one tense, white fist wrapped around the handle.

"Betts." Adel waited until Bethany met her eyes. "Are you okay?"

She'd just started to say something when the side door to the lobby opened and Kate strode out with a glance toward the doors where Bethany was still impersonating an ice sculpture.

"Hey, Adel." She extended her hand with a smile. "Good to see you."

"I hope it's okay that we just dropped by." Adel paused, suddenly unsure of what to say. Or if she should actually say anything at all. "I think we have some information about the Valley of Rubies case that you may need."

Kate nodded and dropped her voice. "And by 'we' you mean you and Twitchy over there?"

"Yeah, that's Bethany. She's not usually like this. I don't know what's wrong with her today," Adel whispered, angling her body away from Bethany. "Remember that picture of Audrey I showed you that night she turned up at the stables with no shirt?"

Kate nodded. "Yeah, I remember. She's the one that took it, right?" She paused, eyes still on Bethany, who was suddenly studying the ceiling tiles. "Ordinarily I would pat her down before I let her into the station, but she looks like she might bolt if we do that."

Adel nodded. "That's a certainty."

"Do you think there's any chance she has a weapon on her?"

"Nah." Adel smiled. "The only thing she's gonna have on her is a leftover brownie smashed into her pocket."

Kate attempted to stifle a laugh and nodded. "That's good enough for me. Can you get her over here?"

Adel waved her over and they both followed Kate back through the door and into the back of the station.

"You've actually got some great timing." Kate glanced back at them and swerved to avoid another officer carrying a stack of boxes crammed to the top with files. "You remember I told you this has been an ongoing case for over a year, right? Well, the FBI are actively involved now that we have an underage girl as the complaining witness, so any additional info might be exactly what we need to clinch it at this point."

They reached the back of the station and turned down a hall to a small conference room where two agents wearing FBI badges were pouring coffee into their mismatched mugs. Kate introduced them while one of the agents, an older man with a shock of white hair and a sun-lined face, smacked his handful of sugar packets against the table once and a spray of white granules exploded into the air. Kate didn't even try to conceal her laughter at what looked like a snowdrift across the table. The agent was auditioning military-grade swear words for the occasion as he dropped the packets back on the condiment tray with a look of disgust.

When they'd finally contained the mess, Kate invited Bethany and Adel to sit in the two empty chairs around the table. Adel took off her jacket and sank into one of the chairs, but it wasn't until she'd gotten settled that she noticed that Bethany was still standing rigidly by the doors.

One of her hands was behind her on the doorknob, which seemed to make one of the agents nervous, but Kate held out her hand in a subtle *stay* gesture, then spoke to Bethany.

"Hey, Bethany." She smiled. "You look a little nervous. What do you need to feel comfortable here?"

A fine mist of sweat broke out across Bethany's scarlet cheeks. She cleared her throat, and when she finally spoke, the words shot out of her mouth in rapid fire.

"I park on sidewalks."

Kate looked at Adel, then asked the obvious question. "You *what*?"

"I have that lime-green truck and I park on the sidewalks in Lockwood sometimes when I'm in a hurry. On purpose." She jammed her hands into the pockets of her jeans. "And I have four parking tickets. Four."

Kate started to smile, then visibly shifted her face into neutral.

Bethany waited for a moment, then tried again to underscore again for them the obvious severity of her crime.

"They're *unpaid*."

The older agent, sporting a neat gray beard and a bolo tie, glanced at Kate with a twinkle in his eye. "According to what you just told us, Detective Kilcullen, these two are here to possibly help us with this case?"

"Absolutely." She nodded. "They may have some more information, and what Adel has supplied us with in the past has been invaluable."

The other agent, a rounded, middle-aged woman with a sassy gray haircut, waited for a nod from Kate, then smiled warmly at Bethany. "Then that's not a problem. Just leave your name and license plate number at the front desk today on your way out and we'll make sure those get taken care of for you. Consider it a thank-you."

Bethany let go of the tension she'd been holding since the parking lot. "Really?"

Kate smiled and gestured toward the chair, which this time Bethany gratefully sank into, her bag settling onto the floor with a loud thump. "Thank you. I seriously thought I was having a heart attack for a minute."

Kate introduced them as Special Agents Martine Wingate and Harvey Portman, then turned to Adel and Bethany, the strain suddenly sinking into creases across her forehead.

"It might take a miracle to pull this together. We finally have Audrey as a complaining witness—"

"Yes, thank God." This from Agent Wingate, as she tore the tops off five sugar packets at once and dumped them into Agent Portman's cup. "And it's huge that she's one of the Prophet's daughters. But that's all we have. Valley of Rubies is locked up like it's housing military secrets, and we only have one shot here."

"It's not like the raid a few years ago at the FLDS compound in Utah." Agent Portman stirred the sugar into his coffee with the bottom of his pen. "There were babies there, women with young children, and it frankly ended up being a…"

Wingate lofted an eyebrow, her mouth set in a thin, tense line. "A shit show."

"Well." Agent Portman seemed to consider the situation. "That's the technical term, but a lot of good did come out of that raid. Their Prophet Warren Jeffs is now in prison for the rest of his life for his abuse of underage girls, thanks in no small part to Elissa Wall."

Bethany narrowed her eyebrows. "Who's that?"

"Well, she was fourteen when she was forced to marry her first cousin by Warren Jeffs, and she found the courage to be the first woman from the compound to step out and offer to be a witness for the prosecution. If she hadn't done that, the other witnesses wouldn't have come forward and he wouldn't be sitting in prison today."

"Exactly where he should be." Martine glanced at Kate. "And in some ways, this case is not as difficult. For the most part, these are children with stable families that are only at Valley of Rubies for the summer. But I think we've only begun to uncover the depth of sustained abuse in that place."

Kate nodded, spinning her pen through her fingers with slow ease as she spoke. "And the one thing we need to accomplish that—time—is the one thing we don't have. Once the girls leave camp in a few weeks, our opportunity to bust this place wide open disappears with them."

"So what is it that you need at this point?" Adel closed her eyes and rubbed her temples with the pads of her fingers, trying to ignore the headache gathering like a dark storm around her forehead. All she could think about was Grace, but she tried to push the thought from her mind and focus.

"We need proof. Something solid in writing that ties the men in power there—"

"The Brethren." Adel glanced at Bethany, who rolled her eyes.

"Exactly. The Brethren. We need something tangible to tie them specifically to the abuse of the girls. Right now we have a video, but the faces on it are blurred and the location is unrecognizable."

Bethany reached into her bag and pulled out the stained floral photo album. The solid thump as it hit the table was the only sound in the room.

"This might help."

Chapter Twenty

Grace's mind woke before her eyes. The dusty scent of the car seat pressed against her cheek, but her head was too heavy to lift. Her body felt leaden, as if it were strapped down, but as she started to move, she realized the only real restraint was the zip tie looped around her wrists, the sharp edges of which were cutting into her skin. She opened her eyes slowly and waited as they focused on the interior of the car.

It was an older sedan, with gray cloth seats that were worn at the edges. She'd been placed in the back seat on her side, and the flash of pain in her neck when she tried to move jerked her back to being in Whittier's office, lunging forward over the desk and falling back…but everything was dark after that.

Grace carefully tried to sit up, supporting her neck with hands that were tied together. There was a bit of dried blood on her palm, and her brain felt heavy and unanchored as she looked around her. The man driving the car was dressed in jeans and a black polo shirt, so that cleared up who he was at least. God Squad. He glanced up into the rearview mirror, then focused his eyes back on the road, his hands tightening around the steering wheel.

"Where are you taking me?"

He looked into the rearview again, then dropped his eyes back to the road, silent. It was hard to read his facial expressions through the thick red beard that covered the lower part of his face, but Grace was too tired to care anyway. The car finally slowed and he pulled into an ancient Exxon station, the engine sputtering as he shifted into park, dust swirling around them, settling slowly in a thousand hazy layers.

"Do you have to use the bathroom?"

This time he didn't meet her eyes in the mirror, just waited until she didn't answer, then got out of the car, slamming the door shut behind him. Grace watched him push open the greasy glass door of the convenience store with his elbow and dove for the car door handle. It was locked, so she reached over the front seats and tried those, although she knew they'd be locked as well, and the interior power lock buttons disabled. She sank back down against the seat. Theirs was the only car in the parking lot, so Grace knew it was pointless to scream. She stared out the window at an open wheat field to the right of the station as the afternoon sun settled in wavy layers of heat over the undulating tips.

The click of the door locks sliding open a few minutes later startled her, and she jerked her head toward the sound, which only deepened the sharp ache gathering at the back of her neck. He got in and locked the doors, then tossed a bottle of Sprite into the back seat. Grace watched as it hit the bench seat beside her and rolled to her feet.

"You don't have to drink it, but the stuff they gave you can make you nauseous when it wears off, so you might want it later."

Grace waited to speak, staring to the front until he looked back at her.

"Where are you taking me?"

"We're only about an hour out now. Won't be long."

The engine roared back to life and dust swirled as they pulled back onto the highway.

Grace lay down facing the back seat. She didn't know where they were going, but it didn't really matter now. Nothing did.

❖

The second her eyes closed, the car jerked to a stop again, or at least that was how it felt. Grace struggled to rub her eyes with the back of her wrists and sat up slowly. It was evening, and the last orange sliver of sun was sinking quickly behind the mountains in the distance. The driver got out and opened her door, gesturing for her to follow him. Grace watched as he got a paper bag out of the trunk, then walked up the path to a small log cabin balanced on the edge of a cliff overlooking the valley.

She managed to stand up and steady herself enough on the car to then follow him up onto a porch made of unfinished split logs. Pine needles gathered into the corners, and an old porch swing swayed gently in the wind with a rhythmic creak. The driver turned the key in the lock and held the door open for her to walk in first.

"Just have a seat on the couch while I put this stuff away."

The driver unloaded a bag of what looked like groceries into the cabinets, glancing back every few seconds to make sure Grace was still sitting on the couch.

"I'm supposed to have your ankles zip-tied." He kept his eyes focused on the cabinet in front of him as he spoke. "If you try to run, I'll slap them on you so quick it'll make your head spin." He paused, then looked back at Grace, his voice softening for the first time. "But if we have an understanding, I'll give you a break on those."

Grace nodded, taking in his bright red hair with deep waves and pale skin. She'd seen his eyes in the rearview mirror; they were the darkest brown, as if they could turn to black at any moment. He was taller than most, with broad shoulders and graceful hands. Hands that were never far from the Glock handgun strapped to his belt.

"My name is Grace."

He turned around slowly and looked her in the eyes for a long second, then seemed to snap out of it and walked to the entrance to place the empty bag by the door.

Grace picked up the Sprite bottle she'd laid on the couch and tried to open it, which proved impossible with the zip ties pulled tight around her wrists. Her skin was swollen and red around the white plastic strips, so Grace let the bottle drop back onto the couch. She felt weak, and it was an effort for her chest to rise and fall with her breath.

The driver glanced back at Grace, then walked over and took the bottle from the couch, opened it easily, and handed it back to her. She watched him sink into a chair across from the couch and pick up the remote, only to turn it over and see the empty battery slots. He closed his eyes tightly for a second, then leaned back and stared at the ceiling, his hands tight around the arms of the chair.

It was probably better to be friendly, to try to make him like her, but Grace didn't have the energy. There was a lead weight in her stomach telling her she'd regret asking the next question, but she couldn't stop the words before they tumbled out of her mouth.

"Why am I here?"

He didn't answer right away, just stared at the ceiling for a moment longer and turned slowly to look at her. There was something familiar about his face; she could have seen him around camp, although she made it a point not to speak to any of the God Squad unless absolutely necessary. His shoulders were broad, muscled, and he was young, maybe still in his twenties. Somehow it made her feel better that he was clearly not enjoying being there any more than she was. She watched as he rubbed his forehead with his fingertips, a bright wave of red hair falling onto his forehead as he spoke. It was a moment before he pushed it back with his hand and looked up at her.

"Are you hungry?"

Grace shook her head but turned to watch as he wandered back into the kitchen. He filled a pan with water and started the flame underneath, opening a package of wide pasta noodles beside it. He tossed some tiny grape tomatoes under the tap for a minute and laid them out to dry, then rinsed a fresh handful of basil leaves. When he finally spoke again, the water was almost boiling over.

"What year was your Purity Ball?"

Grace didn't know what she was expecting, but it wasn't that. She let it sink in before she looked up at him. He'd turned around and leaned back on the counter, staring at her as he dried his hands on a kitchen towel.

Grace felt a sudden, inexplicable anger rising inside her, and she fought to keep her voice even.

"Why do you even want to know that?"

A cell phone pierced the silence, and he was still looking at her when he pulled it out of his back pocket.

"Hey," he said, turning back around and adding pasta and a few pinches of salt to the pot of boiling water. "I can't talk. I'm on a transport job."

Whoever was on the other end was clearly doing the talking for both of them, because it was a long couple of minutes before Grace heard him speak again.

"I know." He paused, glancing back at Grace. "But I can't. Maybe after."

Grace sank down into the couch and covered her face with a throw pillow that smelled like dank carpet. She felt angry. Angry that she was there, angry that she didn't know what was going to happen next, and angry that beneath all that, she missed Adel. It was a deep ache, one that made her feel lonelier than before she knew her. The sudden leaden thought that she might never see Adel again pressed hot tears from her eyes that slipped past her cheeks to her temples.

"Baby. I know. I just can't."

Grace held her breath at the sudden intimacy in his whispered words.

"You don't know." She listened as he let out a ragged breath before he went on. "It's not that easy. We've talked about this."

Grace listened hard, but those were the last words she was able to make out before the audible beep of the cell phone turning off. She sat up slowly to see him dropping the phone back into his pocket and draining the steaming bowl of pasta into a colander. He put the empty pot back on the counter and leaned over the sink on the heel of his hands for a moment, then swiped at his eyes with his sleeve.

"Okay." He didn't turn around, just pulled two plates out of the cabinet and dumped the pasta into a bowl. "Time to eat."

Grace got up slowly and sank into a chair at the table, reaching for the glass of water in front of her before she realized her wrists were bound too tight to get her fingers around it.

He didn't seem to notice as he mixed the fresh tomatoes into the steaming pasta, added some chunks of creamy buffalo mozzarella, then tossed it all with a glug of olive oil, the torn basil, and crushed garlic.

He put the bowl on the table between them and dished the pasta onto both their plates.

"Look." He lowered himself into the chair across from Grace and looked her in the eyes for the first time. "If I get you out of those ties and you bolt, I'm just gonna have to go after you, and it won't be pretty."

"Yeah." Grace glanced down at the gun on his hip. "I know."

He stood, flipped a leather-encased pocketknife open and sliced through the zip ties around Grace's wrists. She rubbed the raw red rings and met his eyes over the table.

They ate in silence for the next few minutes. Grace was suddenly hungry, and also very aware that for some inexplicable reason, the God Squad meathead could cook.

"This is good." She wound the pasta around her fork and met his eyes over the table. "Which means you're not married."

He tried to suppress a smile and failed, covering it by dishing more tomatoes onto Grace's plate. He sat, then glanced down at Grace's wrists, his forehead tense.

"Just so you know, I didn't put those ties on your wrists. That was way too tight." He took a sip of water and set the glass down. It was a long few seconds before he spoke. "They did. The Squad guys. I mean, technically I guess I'm with them, but I just do transport."

Grace nodded, rubbing the angry red rings still around her wrists. "Where are you taking me?"

"Not that I should be telling you this." He paused to take a bite, then hesitated a beat more before he spoke again. "But I don't know, which is unusual. I'm supposed to get a call in the morning." He speared a forkful of pasta and looked her up and down for the first time. "I'm guessing your outfit was unacceptable to Whittier?"

"I think *I'm* just unacceptable." Grace set her fork down on her plate and sank back into her chair, smoothing her thumb over the edge of the old pine plank table. "But this time they've got something on me. Something big."

"I figured." He raised an eyebrow and shook his head as he loaded his fork with three cherry tomatoes. "Someone like you doesn't usually get relocated."

"What do you mean, relocated?" Grace sat up, searching his eyes, her fingers tightening around the edge of the table. Her head began to throb again, and she touched the painful lump on the side of her neck.

"Look, I honestly don't know where you're going, and I couldn't tell you even if I did." He twirled the last of the pasta around his fork and looked up. "You gonna finish that?"

Grace slid the plate over to him and watched as he loaded it onto his. Nothing mattered anymore, so she finally asked the question she'd never wanted to know the answer to. "Some of the girls transferred to other compounds, the ones marked for Blood Atonement…some of them never come back, right?"

The question hung in the air between them, slowly settling into something dense, opaque, yet still suspended. He started to say something, then broke their eye contact to drop his gaze to his plate.

Grace waited for him to say something, but he didn't. She slouched back into her chair and pulled the sleeves of Adel's sweatshirt over her hands.

"It was July 2007." Grace watched as he raised his eyes to hers. "My Purity Ball."

It was in that second that Grace recognized him. That they recognized each other.

Chapter Twenty-one

"Is that what I think it is?"
Special Agent Wingate pulled some latex gloves out of her jacket pocket and slowly pulled them on, her eyes fixed on the overstuffed photo album in the center of the table.

Bethany nodded as Special Agent Portman smacked his hand down on the table with a wide grin. "Well, if that's the mythical Joy Book, you can park on any damn sidewalk you want, Miss Bethany."

Kate started pulling on her own gloves and shook her head with a glance down the table at Bethany.

"This couldn't be better timing. We have our witness, but what we didn't have was proof of the actual intent to marry underage girls to adult men. This may be it."

"Yeah, well." Bethany sat back in her chair and crossed her legs, her dusty riding boots somehow perfectly at home in the room. "Don't give me the credit. It was my badass girlfriend that swiped it, but if I never see that thing again it'll be too soon. Some of those girls are twelve. *Twelve.*" She stopped, struggling to keep the emotion out of her voice. "I just can't believe I've worked there for so long and this was going on all around me. And I didn't do a damn thing to stop it."

"Bethany," Agent Portman said, sliding the book to the center of the table and opening the cover carefully to the first page, "these people are experts at dodging suspicion and hiding their abuse. It could have been any one of us in your job and we probably wouldn't have had any idea either."

Bethany nodded, picking at the edge of the table with her fingernail. "Well, something about those Purity Balls always felt weird. It wouldn't have killed me to look around me a little more."

Agent Portman spoke thoughtfully as he rolled up his sleeves. "These are the girls that are eligible for marriage, correct?"

Kate nodded, turning to the next page.

"So when they actually marry, they could be anywhere. We have no way to trace them or even prove their true ages because of the records issue."

Adel held up a hand as she kneaded the knots in the back of her neck with the other. "The what?"

"Sorry, there's a lot of background to this stuff." Agent Portman paused to take a sip of his coffee and turned back to Adel and Bethany. "A huge percentage of these girls are married so young that they can't have their babies in a hospital without raising eyebrows, so to speak. Historically they've had no choice but to have them at home, usually just with a self-taught midwife in attendance, if that, but no official birth records are ever logged. Birth certificates are hidden or nonexistent."

"So that's why this is so important," Kate said. "These are the girls' pictures with their dates of birth."

"But we still can't prove it," Agent Portman said as he cracked his knuckles. "Just because it's written in there doesn't mean it's correct."

Kate nodded. "Unless it's the girls themselves stating it as fact. That's as close as we can get here, but it's an important difference. That's the holy grail here."

"Good luck with that," Bethany said, pulling her length of blond hair out of her ponytail and sweeping it over one shoulder. "They don't talk about their ages, which I never understood before, but it's starting to make sense."

"You're right about that." Agent Wingate nodded. "That's drilled into them from a pretty young age for obvious reasons. I hate to put it like this, but unless we have both complaining witnesses and witnesses that will attest to their real ages, we don't have shit. And to be honest, as happy as I am that Audrey's come forward, we're gonna need a lot more than just her to make this stick."

Adel looked at Bethany and held her gaze for a long few seconds, until Bethany nodded toward the agents.

"There's something else we're concerned about." Adel's voice was quiet, as if by saying the words out loud she was acknowledging that Grace was in danger. "Although I'm not sure there's any way to know what really happened, and it's possible that she left of her own free will."

"What?" Bethany said, shaking her head. "That fast? Not likely. That has the God Squad goons written all over it."

One of Agent Wingate's eyebrows cocked like a hammer. "What the hell is the God Squad?"

Bethany smiled, pushing the sleeves of her shirt back up her arms as she spoke. "I can't really tell you much because they're kind of separate from everyone, but basically they're men from the church that act as security. They're always in the background at events like a Purity Ball, and sometimes just roaming the perimeter of camp for no reason, but they're always armed. If someone was forced to leave camp, they'd be the ones to clear out the cabin." She paused, pulling at a loose thread dangling from the sleeve of her T-shirt. "And more often than not, we never see her again."

A younger female officer knocked on the door, then stepped in with a tray of water and cans of cold soda, which Bethany snapped up before she'd even reached the table.

"You can always tell who they are because of the uniform: black cargo pants and a black polo. Everyone knows we're not supposed to talk to them."

"So." Kate cracked open a can of Sprite and leaned back in her chair with a sideways glance at Adel. "Who is this woman you're concerned about?"

"She's the program director, Grace Waters, and she's twenty-six, so she's not one of the girls, although she was a camper there when she was younger." Adel took a few seconds to think, unsure of how much to reveal. "I'm sure Kate filled you in that I'm on assignment at Valley of Rubies with *Vanity Fair*?"

The agents nodded and waited for her to continue.

"I'm writing an exposé, so obviously I couldn't tell anyone the real reason I was at camp, which was easy until I fell in love with the program director..." Adel realized she was close to tears and forced them back, steadying her voice before she continued. "She spent the night in my cabin last night, and when I got back after class I found my open journal and my *Vanity Fair* press pass from my wallet on my desk. There was no note, but I knew she was gone. And I knew why."

Kate's voice was soft. "Why did she leave?"

"Basically, she thinks I was just using her for insider information, which isn't true." Adel rubbed her pounding forehead hard with the tips of her fingers before she looked up again. "I did need some of the details she gave me when I started, but then I realized I was in love with her…and it was too late to tell her the truth."

The lines between Agent Portman's wiry white eyebrows deepened and he leaned forward, dropping his voice as if suddenly revealing classified information. Adel caught Agent Wingate's head dropping into her hand out of the corner of her eye, but focused her attention on whatever Portman was having such a hard time wrapping words around.

"So, this Grace Waters," he said, still leaning forward and whispering as if all five of them weren't sitting at the same damn table. "She's a woman, right?"

"All right, let me stop you here." Agent Wingate lifted her head from her hand and elbowed her colleague until he sat back in his chair. "He can be a little slow around these concepts, so I'm just going to save us all the time and clear it up."

"What?" He sputtered, a red flush creeping up his cheeks to the edge of his thick white hair. "I was just asking."

"And I'm just answering." She glanced at Adel with a wink. "If that's okay with you, of course."

"Please." Adel smiled for what felt like the first time that day and leaned forward on her elbows as she listened. "Be my guest."

She locked eyes with Portman. "I'm going to go out on a ledge here and say that Grace is a woman, and clearly, so is Adel. And the rest is…" She paused abruptly, looking around at the files stacked at the end of the table. "Wait a second, I just had it here…" She stopped, rifling through a stack of paperwork on the table in front of her for a moment before she looked up. "Oh yeah, I remember. It's none of your damn business."

Bethany let out a snort that made everyone laugh, including Portman, and the tension lifted as Bethany looked at her watch and reminded Adel she had to get home to feed and stable the horses.

"I can give Adel a ride after we get some more details on the Grace situation, if that's okay with her," Kate said.

Bethany slung her bag over her shoulder and slipped out the door, but it popped open again before it had even shut. A swath of blond hair rounded the edge of the door before Bethany's face reappeared and she flashed Agent Portman a grin.

"So I can park on any sidewalk I want now, right?"

❖

It was early evening before Adel had given all the information she had about Grace. Most of the station was empty as Kate and Adel pushed past the double glass doors and walked to Kate's car, a black Jeep 4x4 with a custom hardtop and more chrome than should ever be on an off-road vehicle.

"Okay," Kate said as she slid in and turned on the air conditioning. "I texted Hannah already and told her to expect you. Did you bring your stuff with you, or…?"

"What?" Adel turned to look at her, shaking the fog from her head. "Why?"

Kate paused, letting her meaning soak in without blurring it with words. Adel realized with the click of her seat belt that if they'd taken Grace because they knew about their relationship, she wasn't safe either at Valley of Rubies. At best they'd kick her out, and at worst… well, there was no telling what that might be with Whittier at the helm.

"I didn't bring anything." Adel sighed and leaned back against the seat. "And it's too late now." She sat straight up in her seat suddenly and looked over at Kate. "But this morning, when Grace found everything and figured out I was there to write an article, she left it all out on the desk for me to see…"

"Which means it's still there." Kate fired up the Jeep and pulled out of the parking lot on what felt like two wheels. "For anyone to find."

❖

"Oh, my God. Kellan." Grace's hand shot up to her mouth and she pushed herself back from the table, the chair legs scraping over the wood floors as the memory of that night hit her from behind and pitched her forward. "It's you."

She watched the blood drain from Kellan's face as he leaned back in his chair and raked his hand back through the unruly waves of hair. Neither one said a word, just stared, unable to take their eyes from the other, until finally Kellan shook his head and dropped his forehead into his palm.

"Fuck."

That single word hovered between them as if it had been stamped onto the silence in raised black ink.

"I can't…I need…" Grace heard herself say the words, but they seemed foreign, as if she didn't recognize her own voice. She stood up slowly and looked toward the door. "I feel sick."

Kellan nodded toward the heavy pine door just past the living room, and Grace felt herself run toward it, only to slide down the other side of it the second it closed behind her. She hadn't thought about turning on a light, and the silent darkness was almost comforting as it closed around her like a pair of black wings, pulling her into a single moment of safety.

But nothing was safe anymore. Not even her own thoughts.

She dropped her head into her hands, hot tears slipping between her fingers as her memory played like an old movie reel in her mind, starting, stopping, then gaining shaky speed as the film caught and rolled into a rhythm of whirrs and clicks.

She'd turned twelve the day before her Purity Ball, which was one of her first summers as a camper at Valley of Rubies. It was also the first time she'd ever been the sole focus of her father's attention—a heady, intoxicating experience. He'd flown to New York for the event just for her, and she'd spent hours ironing every inch of her dress and styling her hair, examining it endlessly in the mirror from every angle. Her dress had been chosen by her mother: pure white, delicate, and accented along the sleeves and neckline with airy, fluttery lace. It was one of the two times in her life she'd ever wear something other than the standard pastel dresses—the other would be her wedding day, but even then her husband would choose her dress. Her nerves were buzzing in her ears as she waited with the other girls outside the Fellowship Hall, nervously adjusting her sleeves to show off the lace and smoothing cherry ChapStick over her lips, pretending it was grown-up lipstick.

Finally, she saw her father striding up the path from the lodge, the setting sun gold and luminous behind him. He smiled and offered her his arm to walk up the steps to the Fellowship Hall. The scent of his aftershave sliced through the warm evening air with a spicy edge and Grace was giddy with excitement, but the night seemed to go by in a flash. The ceremony, in which she pledged her chastity and obedience to her father until he transferred that right to her future husband, was performed by a Covenant pastor, and everything was perfect. Even the Prophet was there, one of the only times she'd actually been in the same room with him.

As they left the reception at the end of the night, one of the Brethren called her father over to a group of elders, where they spoke in hushed tones for a few seconds. After, he'd walked her back on the trail that led to her cabin and told her how proud he was, that she was the brightest jewel in his celestial crown. He pulled her to him in a hug, then stepped back, his hands on her shoulders with a look of pride in his eyes that Grace had never seen before.

"Grace, the Prophet has chosen you to take part in a very special ceremony tonight. Only the purest and most beautiful girls are ever even considered, and this summer, he's chosen *you*."

Grace smiled and pulled her length of wavy blond hair over her shoulder to her waist, grateful yet unsure why she was chosen or what it all meant. But her father's hands were warm and heavy on her shoulders, and she smiled up at him as he asked if she remembered the words painted on the wall of the Fellowship Hall.

Grace recited them perfectly. "Modesty, submission, and denial of self."

"That's right, my beautiful girl. Let those be your guiding principles." He pulled her to his chest for a long moment before he turned to go, then glanced back at her over his shoulder. His eyes flashed pale blue under the lights lining the path as he hesitated for just a moment, looking out over the lake, then told her to be at the Fellowship Hall in one hour.

"Will you be there?"

Her father met her gaze for just a second before he shook his head. Then he turned and walked toward the lodge.

Her eyes were still shut tight against the memory when Kellan knocked on the bathroom door. She sat on the floor in the dark on the other side, pulling at the sleeves of her sweatshirt, stretching them tight over the fists that wouldn't seem to release.

"Grace. Please." His voice was tense, but softer than before. "Come out."

Grace counted seven breaths before she struggled to her feet in the dark and opened the door. He stepped back and gave her space to come back into the living room and sit down, where there was a glass of water waiting for her on the coffee table. He'd opened the windows, and a cool breeze lifted the dusty, dated curtains. A single coyote howled in the distance, and the full moon glazed the tips of the swaying pines with liquid silver. She was exhausted, and for the first time in her life she knew she didn't care if she woke up in the morning.

"Hey." Kellan's voice was soft, and he shifted in the chair across from the sofa. "Talk to me."

Grace shook her head but looked up after a moment and met his eyes. They were a warm honey color, rimmed with darkest brown. They were tired and red around the edges, and worry creased his forehead.

He smiled then, just the smallest smile that lifted one corner of his mouth as he reached out a hand, slowly, spanning the space between them.

Grace took it, the warmth of his hand melting into hers as she returned the smile. "I can't believe you saved me."

Kellen pulled a flask out of his back pocket and unscrewed the stainless steel top. "I couldn't take you down to them." He took a long swig and handed it over to Grace, who took it and locked her eyes onto his.

"But why? You were one of them."

"Hell, no, I wasn't. Not yet. Remember? I was working in the cafeteria that summer. I was just sixteen, so I wasn't a Priesthood Holder yet."

"What?" Grace's neck throbbed as she tried to recall the long-ago details. "What does that mean?"

"It means I wasn't yet officially one of them. And it turns out I never got to be. They stuck me on transport a few years later. I was a pastor's kid, so they had to put me somewhere, and I've been doing it ever since."

Grace took a sip of whatever was in the flask, the memory of reaching for the white robe that night flickering in her mind. She didn't remember much after being shown to the changing room, just ragged pieces of memories like torn photos scattered across a table. The acrid scent of mothballs in the room that intensified as the cold white satin robe slipped over her bare shoulders. Faint laughter that seemed suddenly out of place drifting in from the row of cabins at the bottom of the hill. A sudden gust of wind that scraped a tree branch against the window. And the excitement in her stomach shapeshifting into something she didn't recognize, instantly pulling every muscle in her body taut.

The knock on the door had filled her with the sudden urge to climb out the window, but she knew she couldn't do that to her father. She'd just pledged her purity to his safekeeping a few hours before, and he'd said the Prophet had a special plan for her. Of course she was safe. She took a deep breath and shook her hands at her sides, willing blood to flow back into them.

Then the door opened and her friend Kellan stood in the doorway, the blood draining slowly from his face. He was older than her by a few years, but they'd bonded that summer over their shared love of rowing. He'd taken her out after dark, in the camp's brand-new rowboat, to the island across the lake where they'd lain on the sand, trading secrets and memorizing the patterns of the stars.

"What are *you* doing here?"

They'd said it at the exact same time, but neither one of them laughed. Kellan stepped in, closing the door behind him, a fine mist of sweat shimmering on his freckled forehead. His voice was low and hard.

"You have to go, Grace. Now." He looked back at the door he'd just locked. "You have to get out of here and not come back."

"What?" Grace pulled her robe tight around her. The elder had told her to be naked underneath and she suddenly felt exposed, as if wearing nothing at all. "I'm supposed to be here. The Prophet chose me for the special ceremony." She lifted her chin and tightened the belt around her waist. "You don't know what you're talking about."

Kellan stepped up to her and wrapped his hand around her arm. Hard. "Grace, I know more than you think." His voice rose, and he pulled on her arm, reaching for the doorknob. "You've got to get the hell out of here or they're going to take you downstairs to the altar room." He paused for breath with a glance back at the door and lowered his voice. "I want you to run to the girls' bathrooms by the cabins and lock yourself in a stall. Don't come out for at least a half hour. Now, go." He opened the door and pushed her through it, pointing to an exit door at the back of the Fellowship Hall that Grace had never noticed. His eyes were wild, and he spat the last words at her so hard she felt them hit her skin. "Grace, *GO!*"

Then he shoved her, pushing her by her shoulders all the way down the hall and out the door, watching until she ran down the hill and disappeared into the woods. She turned around when she got to the bathrooms, but he was gone and the door was shut.

Grace squeezed his hand, her eyes soft.

"I thought I'd done something wrong. You looked so angry, but it worked. I ran to the bathrooms and didn't come out for hours."

"I wasn't angry at you." Kellan smiled. "You were my friend. I didn't know what they were going to do, exactly—it was the first time I'd been included in a viewing—but I knew I couldn't let it be you."

"Where did you go after that? I didn't see you for the rest of the summer."

"Yeah." Kellan lofted an eyebrow and smiled. "My dad sent me home the next day. He was the one who had invited me to the viewing and sent me downstairs to get you that night. Everyone believed me when I came back. It would have been hard not to...I'd thought of a good story. Everyone but him. He knew I was lying."

"What did you tell them?"

Kellan shook his head, laughter coloring his words. "You don't want to know."

"Kellan!" Grace laughed and smacked him with the couch pillow behind her. "You scared me to death that night! You're gonna tell me anything I want to know."

"Fine." He laughed and raked a hand through his hair. "I made myself throw up all over my shirt and the front of your robe and told them you were sick and I'd sent you to the nurse. No one but my dad even questioned it."

Grace sank back into the couch and locked eyes with her friend.

"Thank you." She felt the burn of tears behind her eyes and blinked them away before she saw the same tears reflected in Kellan's eyes. "You saved me."

Kellan reached out for the flask. Grace wiped her eyes and handed it to him with a wink. "But what the hell's in that flask?"

He unscrewed the top with a smirk. "Super manly apricot schnapps, as you might expect." He handed it back to her and they both relaxed back into their seats, Kellan swinging his boots up on the coffee table with a thunk.

Grace watched, wondering now how she hadn't recognized him before, but in fairness, that thick red beard hid half his face. "So, you're thirty now, right? And you've just been doing transport all this time?"

"Yeah. I mean, I'm a big guy at six five. It's a given that they wanted me on the God Squad, but I got the transport position and just never left. It lets me spend most of my time out of sight."

Grace handed him the flask and swung her feet up on the coffee table beside his. "I know your dad's a pastor around here, but have you ever thought about leaving? You can't tell me you're happy doing this."

"Damn, girl. Don't sugarcoat it for me." He laughed, then fell into silence, as if he didn't want to hear himself say the words. "I've thought about it for years, but I can't just leave. I'd be leaving the church, and if I do that, my family will disown me." He took a long swig from the flask. "And they're all I have."

"Yeah?" Grace waited until he looked back up at her and held his eyes. "Well, I'm calling bullshit on that."

"What the hell?" His words were slow, as if trying to sort through hers at the same time. "What do you mean?"

Grace leaned forward, her elbows on her knees, and looked him square in the eye.

"You're in love with someone. I heard you talking to her on the phone when I was on the couch."

He smiled, shaking his head. "Grace. You don't miss much, do you?"

"So what's the deal? She's not Covenant?"

"Um…" His voice trailed off and he thought for a beat before he looked back up at her. "Nah. Not by a long shot."

Grace nodded as her hand found the sore spot on her neck with hesitant fingers. "Yeah, I get it."

"That neck is going to be sore for a while." Kellan leaned forward and reached out for her hand. "Let me see your wrists."

He looked at the red raw rings the zip ties left, then dug into the bag he'd dropped by the door. He came back with a small tube of Vaseline.

"It's really for lips, but if you smooth a little over those spots before you go to bed, they should be somewhat better by morning."

Grace nodded. "And what happens in the morning?"

"Honestly, I don't know yet. I should get a call fairly early, and then we'll figure it out, okay?"

She felt her eyes closing then and realized she'd never felt so exhausted, as if she literally could not keep them open. Kellan opened the door to the bedroom and turned on a light by the bed, then walked to the dresser and opened the top drawer. Grace was almost asleep by the time he came back, her eyes fluttering open when he touched her arm.

"I put one of my T-shirts on the bed for you." He offered his hand to pull her up off the couch and nodded toward the open bedroom door. "I'll sleep out here on the couch."

Grace walked toward the bedroom but turned back to Kellan before she reached the door. "They assume you take advantage of the girls you transport, don't they?"

Kellan reached down and untied his boots, taking off one, then the other, before he answered, eyes still on the floor. "Yeah. I'm sure they do."

Grace nodded and walked through to the bedroom, pausing with her hand on the doorknob when he spoke again.

"I don't, you know." His soft brown eyes met hers and held them. "I'd never do that."

Grace nodded, then closed the door partway and folded Adel's jeans and sweatshirt on the chair by the door. The walk to the bed seemed endless, and as she fell on the bed, the last thing she remembered was him picking up the fallen clothes and the click of the lamp on the bedside table.

Chapter Twenty-two

Later that evening, Adel and Kate sank into the chairs at the table at Hannah's house. Kate reached over and popped the top off Adel's beer bottle and then her own, leaning back into her chair and scraping a hand through her hair, then rubbing her eyes hard with the heel of her hand. Hannah turned around and leaned against the stove, spatula in hand. "Is somebody going to tell me what the hell happened today, or do I have to finish these burgers before you guys will focus on anything else?"

She was wearing red chino shorts and a denim shirt, and pulled a raspberry lip balm from her pocket as she waited for an answer.

"Sorry, baby. I'm just wiped." Kate shifted slightly in her chair toward Adel. "But fortunately, Adel here just volunteered to give you all the details while I down the rest of this beer." Kate and Hannah looked at Adel expectantly, Kate lofting an eyebrow in an attempt to look serious.

"Yeah, thanks, dude." Adel shook the weariness from her head and rolled her eyes at Kate. "I'm going to give you the abbreviated version, since Kate here said she'd get me my next beer while I do it."

Hannah reached into the fridge and lofted a bottle across the room, which Kate reached out and caught with one hand, setting it in front of Adel.

"You were saying?"

Adel filled Hannah in on the day, describing the Joy Book, Bethany's near heart attack at the thought of being arrested, and Kate driving at breakneck speed across the lake so Adel could retrieve her belongings before anyone found them and figured out she was undercover.

In a sheer stroke of luck, they'd arrived during the evening worship service, and everyone was still at the Campfire Bowl. The last notes of evening camp songs hovered over the treetops as Kate pulled as close as possible to the shore and shifted the boat into a cautious idle. Adel lowered herself into the chest-deep water and waded in, then hurried to unlock the door to her cabin, which surprisingly looked like it hadn't been touched. Adel packed in less than two minutes and tossed her bags into the boat from the shore. She ducked under the water and swam until she reached the teak platform at the back, pulling herself up and into the back seat just as Kate revved the engine and pulled away. The wind whipped her wet hair around her face as she locked her eyes on the shoreline, the rolling, foamy wake framing the cabins that eventually disappeared when Kate whipped a sharp right and headed back toward Lockwood.

Hannah split the sourdough buns and settled them onto a wide grill at the back of the cooktop, brushing them with an obscene amount of butter as she winked at Kate over her shoulder. "I didn't know you could drive a boat. That's pretty hot."

"I borrowed one from Lake Patrol here in town so we stood an outside chance of getting in and out of that camp without them seeing us." She smiled. "But if I'd known that, I would have taken you out on the water way before now."

Hannah winked and held Kate's gaze until Adel cleared her throat and nodded toward the buns smoking on the grill. Hannah laughed as she buttered more buns and started again, then checked the internal temp of the burgers with a meat thermometer.

"So where did you learn to drive like that?" Adel finished the last of her first beer and cracked open the second, welcoming the slow warmth of it that was starting to ease the ache from her head.

"I have a buddy I went to the police academy with like twenty years ago and she taught me one summer. Lockwood is too small to have their own training center, so they basically just send our recruits to whatever police academy has an opening, and I got sent to Boise, Idaho. I met Sam Draper there, and we've been close ever since."

"Isn't that the wedding you went to last summer?" Hannah stopped, holding the spatula aloft as she thought. "Sam and Sara's wedding in McCall, Idaho?"

"Yep, that's it. They had it at sunset on the grounds of Sam's lake house, which is incredible. I mean, I don't often say things like this, but that was one of the most romantic weddings I've ever been to. I've never seen Sam so happy."

Hannah assembled the burgers and slid them onto a serving platter, handing it to Kate to place on the table. "And she's the one starting that new lesbian retreat center, right?"

"Yep, not far from their lake house. She owns the whole side of the lake—she inherited it from her dad when he passed away a few years ago."

Hannah turned back to collect the plates and cutlery, passing them to Adel to set the table, when Kate's phone rang. Kate looked at it, picked it up, and walked outside to the deck to take the call.

"Hannah, these burgers smell amazing. What do you *do* to them?" Adel was suddenly ravenous, and it was all she could do to not pick one of them up from the serving tray and stuff it into her mouth.

Hannah shot Adel a smile. "Officially, I can't tell you, since it's my secret recipe, but unofficially, I sauté onions in butter, fresh minced garlic, and steak sauce, then add a blend of sharp cheddar and roasted jalapeños before I stuff the mixture into the center of each of the burgers." Hannah glanced out at Kate leaning on the railing outside, phone to her ear. "I made these on our first date, actually."

Hannah got Kate a fresh beer and sat down with her glass of Chardonnay, setting a bowl of crisp green salad in the center of the table. Right on cue, Kate walked back through the sliding glass door and clicked off her phone.

"I can't believe I'm saying this, but I have to go."

Hannah squeezed her hand as she stood up. "I can pack this up for you, no worries. Is everything okay?"

"Actually," Kate glanced at Adel and dropped her phone into the back pocket, "considering who that was, probably not. I don't have a fucking clue what I'm stepping into."

Hannah nodded and took Kate's plate into the kitchen as Kate slid on her jacket, clipping her badge back onto her belt.

"You can't tell me who it is, can you?"

Kate shook her head. "I trust you, but I can't. I'm not even clearing this with my chief, which is probably not smart, but I know what he'd say, and I'm going either way."

"I get it." Adel nodded, pushing her plate away and leaning back into her chair. "But call me after, okay? You look like you have a bad feeling about this."

Kate took the Tupperware Hannah handed her when she came back into the room and kissed her on the cheek.

"Yeah. That's the understatement of the year."

❖

It was still dark when Grace woke to Kellan shaking her shoulder.

"Grace, get up. We've got to go."

Grace's eyes focused slowly. Kellan was wearing the same clothes he'd been in the night before, and his gun was clearly visible on his belt.

"But..." Grace felt as if she was wading through deep water and had to concentrate on each word to speak. "Where are we going? What time is it?"

"It's early. Real early." Kellan handed her the jeans and sweatshirt she'd taken off the night before. "And you know I can't tell you."

The sleep fog thinned as Kellan led her out of the cabin and into the back seat of the car, slamming the door shut behind her. She should ask again where they were going, but Kellan was too silent, the sharp angles of his face glinting like cut steel in the haze of dawn. She watched his jaw tense in the rearview mirror and then stared out the side window, watching the orange molten sun rise over the mountains in the distance.

They drove for about twenty minutes, then pulled into the parking lot of a tiny abandoned gas station. The wind had picked up out of nowhere, swirling dust into eddies on the ground. The only sound was a rusty metal *Open* sign still half hanging on the door of the station as the wind caught it and clanked it against the glass. Kellan rolled down his window and looked at his watch, then at his phone. Grace leaned up against the front seat and looked out the window.

"Kellan." She waited, but he didn't answer. Her stomach sank when he didn't even turn to meet her eyes. "Why are we here?"

But he just looked again at his watch, his gaze lingering, as if willing it to bend time. By the time he finally looked back at her, she'd slumped back into her seat. It didn't matter now. Whatever was going to happen had already been set in motion; she saw it on his face.

"Grace." Kellan turned back to look out the window, his eyes locked on the horizon. "After you went to bed, I stayed up all night. I wanted to find a way out of this."

"Kellan, don't." Grace's voice faded away and it was a moment before she found her words again. "I know there's no way out of this. Not at this point, anyway. They know you have me, and if you let me go, they'll—"

"They'll fucking kill me." Kellan slammed his hand down onto the steering wheel, shaking the entire dash of the car. "I know too much."

"You can't." Grace closed her eyes, the tears she hadn't noticed sliding silently down her cheeks. "Even if you wanted to do that, I wouldn't let you."

It was silent then, the dust swirling up with the wind and sliding across the dented hood of the car. Grace leaned up again, her hand warm on Kellan's shoulder. Kellan took it, and she saw the tears shimmering in his eyes as he covered it with his.

"I'll never forget you, Grace." His eyes were locked onto a black SUV as it slowed and turned into the abandoned station, coming to a stop about ten yards away. A man got out, peered across at them, then slammed the door shut and leaned back against the car. Kellan looked back at her. "Tell me you know that."

Grace nodded, the jagged edge of fear penetrating her heart for the first time. Kellan squeezed her hand one last time and turned the car off, leaving the keys in the ignition. The man started to walk toward them, his gaze locked on Kellan, who got out and walked around to open Grace's door.

"It's time."

Grace had the sudden, maniacal urge to run. But even if she got away, which she knew was impossible, where was she going to go? She had no idea where she even was, no money, and no car. The thought faded as she listened to her breath move through her body. It was the only choice she still had.

"Grace."

She nodded, stepping out of the car and leaning against it to keep her knees from buckling. Grace knew what was happening—she'd known since the second she'd recognized herself on that video, naked in Adel's bed. They weren't transferring her to another camp or compound.

This was Blood Atonement.

The man walking toward them was tall and broad shouldered, with sandy blond hair blown in both directions across his forehead. He didn't speak when he reached them, just shoved his hands into the pockets of his jeans and waited. Kellan turned toward Grace.

"Grace, I called back to camp last night, and someone finally told me why you're here. I know what they saw."

His words sucked the air from her lungs. She looked into his eyes to hold herself upright, her heart beating like a revved engine against the cage of her chest.

"I thought I was going to have to come up with a way to hide you, to rescue you…" Kellan's voice cracked and he cleared his throat, tears beginning to gather in his eyes. "To save you from them."

Grace nodded. How long it had been since she'd taken a breath?

"But this time, you saved me." Kellan reached out for the man's hand and turned back to her. "I'd like you to meet Jeremiah." He paused, holding his gaze as he continued. "My boyfriend."

Grace saw the tears well up in Jeremiah's eyes and watched as they hugged like they'd been apart for a hundred years. When they finally turned back to her, Kellan looked at his watch and then the horizon. His gaze stayed fixed for a long second, then he turned back around to her.

"Grace, this is the hard part. We can't take you with us." His voice broke and he paused. "If they find me, then they find you too, and I can't take that risk."

"But…" Grace's voice trailed off and she looked around at the abandoned station. A crow let out an ear-splitting caw and landed on the awning over the pumps, fixing his black, beady eyes on Grace.

"Grace, you know I wouldn't leave you here without a plan. You're just going to have to trust me." Jeremiah looked at his watch and nodded back toward the SUV. Kellan held her eyes as he started to walk away. "Get in that car and lock the doors. I want you to promise me you won't leave for twenty minutes."

Grace nodded, her heart sinking as Kellan turned and took Jeremiah's hand. She watched them walk away for what seemed like forever. They were almost at the SUV when Kellan turned around, his eyes trained on Grace, and they both started running toward each other at the same time. He swept her up in his arms when he reached her, burying his face in her hair as he held her tight. When they finally let go, Grace held his face in the warmth of her hands.

"Thank you, Kellan." She smiled, tears smearing the dust blowing around them like a curtain. "Thank you for saving me. Again."

Kellan smiled. "Grace, I meant it when I said you saved me. You had the courage to be yourself. I never realized I even had a choice until I saw you do it."

He let her go and squeezed her hands, then turned and ran toward

Jeremiah. They both jumped into the vehicle and Grace barely had time to blink before the hazy sunlight enveloped them at the crest of the hill. And then he was gone.

She turned slowly and walked back toward the car. The same crow eyed her warily, shifting his weight from one spindly leg to the other, and the wind jammed a cluster of leaves against one of the pumps below. The air smelled empty, the scent of dust and desolation swirling around her neck like a noose before she climbed back into the car and shut the door against it. It was then, when she slid into the driver's seat and locked all four doors around her, that she glanced down and saw it.

It was a homemade hair tie, just a scrap of nondescript floral fabric sewn around an elastic band. It was on the floor, almost under the passenger's seat, and when Grace reached down slowly and picked it up, she saw a tangle of long, blond hair wrapped around one side of it. The last girl had clearly put up a fight and lost, but Grace knew somehow she'd left it there on purpose, that she didn't want to just disappear. She tucked it into her pocket, trying not to listen to the wind scraping the windows. Grace knew how that felt. She couldn't just leave it there, like the girl had never existed.

She looked at her watch. It had only been four minutes. Two cars had whizzed past on the highway in that time; Grace had ducked, hoping the car appeared abandoned and uninteresting. She'd promised Kellan she'd stay for sixteen more minutes, but they both knew she had nowhere to go after that. She could slink back in shame to Arkansas, back to her parents' house, but she felt physically ill at the thought. Besides, they'd find her there eventually and carry out the punishment regardless.

She shifted in her seat, suddenly aware that she'd not even gone to the bathroom that morning before Kellan hustled her to the car. She shot a glance toward the service station. Maybe there was a bathroom on the side of the building. Maybe it was even unlocked. She stepped out of the car and tugged the sleeves of her hoodie down over her hands, pulling them tight into both fists. She hurried toward the building and tried the door with the rusted bathroom sign clinging to it by one screw. The peeling doorknob came off in her hand, and what she saw through the hole in the door made it clear the only choice was behind the building.

She'd just unbuttoned her jeans and sat on an abandoned red plastic milk crate when she heard a car peeling out of the parking lot.

Shit, she thought with a hot rush of panic. *I left the keys in the ignition.*

She zipped up and flattened herself to the side of the building, edging over to the corner and looking around it just enough to see that not only was Kellan's car still there, there was another one pulled up right behind it. How the hell did they find her so quickly? She knew Kellan wouldn't have set her up, and this place was just so…remote. It didn't make sense.

She looked again and saw a man get out of the car and walk up to Kellan's driver side window. He looked inside, then slammed his fist down on the hood, turning toward the empty road and yelling *FUCK* into the distance. He ran his hand through his hair as he turned around, and just at that moment, the crow took off from her perch on top of the gas pumps into the sky with a deafening caw that echoed endlessly through the empty sky. The man's head snapped up and he locked eyes with Grace, who was frozen, her head just visible around the chipped brick corner of the building.

It didn't matter now, what she did. He'd seen her. She stepped around the corner and waited, willing him to step away from the car. If she could get him far enough from the car, maybe she could run fast enough to jump in it and go before he caught her. That thought faded fast as he rounded the corner of the car and started walking toward her. Grace felt physically pushed back by every step he took and stepped back herself. He was tall, slender, and seemed surprisingly sensitive. He seemed to understand he was scaring her and stopped where he was.

"Grace." The voice carried over the drifting silence of the empty lot. "Are you Grace?"

Grace held her breath and she felt her heartbeat slow, then stop. He was a *woman*.

"Look, I drove all night to get here." She paused, seeming to choose her words one by one. "I'm here to help you."

Grace froze in her tracks but didn't respond. This was a trick. She just had to figure out how to get whoever the hell that was away from her car. She stepped away from the building, squaring her shoulders and looking directly in the woman's eyes. She'd learned a long time ago that showing fear was the quickest way to lose a standoff.

"How do you know my name?"

"Your friend Kellan called me last night. He said he found my card in the pocket of your jeans."

Grace thought back to being in Adel's cabin the previous morning and caught a dim flash of slipping the card she'd found into the pocket of her jeans. Everything after Whittier's office was running together in her memory, bleeding like watercolor paint into no shape at all. She held her face in neutral and said the only thing she was sure of.

"I don't believe you."

The woman smiled and rubbed her forehead with her fingertips. She looked tired.

"Yeah, I don't blame you. I don't know if I would either."

So they stood there, staring at each other. The awning on the front of the station building flapped in the wind, the rope clanging around the closest pole.

But she was almost starting to believe this woman. The hazy memory of that card in Adel's cabin, combined with the fact that there was no way in hell the Brethren would let a woman dressed in men's clothing anywhere near them, had started to make a slow kind of sense.

Grace started walking slowly toward her, and the woman had the good sense to stay where she was until Adel stopped about five feet away.

"My name is Kate." When she spoke, she held Grace's gaze gently and put her hands in her pockets, which strangely made Grace relax enough to take a breath. "And I'm a friend of Adel Rosse."

Chapter Twenty-three

"You're up early." Adel smiled at Hannah as she shuffled into the kitchen about five minutes after Adel had started the coffee, hair in a tangled fluff around her face, wearing one slipper and carrying the other. "Clearly you're a morning person."

"Shut it, Rosse." Hannah found the coffee cup Adel left for her by the pot and poured a steaming mugful of Starbucks Blonde Roast. "I was up half the night worrying about Kate. She finally sent me a text this morning early and said she was fine. She thinks she'll be home tonight, but, damn. I hate when I don't know where the hell she is."

"Did she say anything else?"

"No. She can't." Hannah leaned against the counter and wrapped both her hands around her coffee cup. "She's ethical to a fucking fault. But I get it. I am too, I guess."

Adel nodded in the direction of the railroad clock above the stove, smiling at Hannah's single slipper. "Aren't you supposed to be at work in, like, five minutes, Cinderella?"

"Nah. I have an obscene number of vacation days accumulated, so I'm taking the next week or so off. I thought I'd go out this morning and see how Audrey's doing at the rescue ranch with my mom."

Hannah reached into the pantry for a haphazard handful of Oreos and shuffled off toward the hall. She dropped one on the way and watched it roll toward Adel's shoe.

"We're leaving in five minutes. See if you can pull yourself together by then, Rosse." She flashed Adel a smile as she rounded the corner, dropping a shower of chocolate crumbs when she bit into the side of a cookie. "You're driving."

❖

An hour later they pulled into Hannah's mom's place at the end of a long gravel drive framed by a timber arch carved with tall, hand-charred letters: *Haven Ranch*. A massive split cedar home came into view as they rounded the bend, with wide plank porches on three sides and an outdoor kitchen built around an expansive stone fireplace.

"Damn. I'm jealous and I haven't even met your mom yet." Adel took in the view as Hannah got out of the truck and motioned for her to follow. "What's back there?"

Hannah followed her eyes and nodded toward the cluster of sprawling buildings behind the house. "Those are the stables. The majority of the acreage is taken up by her horse rescue. She takes in abandoned or mistreated animals and loves them back to health. She's done it since I was in high school."

A horse whinnied in the distance, the sound filtering through the firs and fluttering aspens surrounding the cabin as they climbed the steps to the porch.

"Mom!" Hannah called into the house as she opened the front door and led Adel through a long hall lined with her school pictures and awards, family vacation photos, and some antique prints. The hall opened at the end into a bright, airy kitchen, the back wall painted a soft yellow that brought out the warm tones of the cedar logs. A two-story bay window sparkled in the sunlight, and Adel smiled when a plump, older woman with wild silver hair giggled into her phone and held her finger to her lips.

Hannah rolled her eyes. "Oh, God, she's talking to Harry."

"Who's Harry?" Adel took the cookie Hannah passed her from the heaping tray on the counter and bit into it, instantly melting into the decadent white chocolate chunks and crunch of roasted almonds.

"Her boyfriend." Hannah shook her head and bit into her own cookie. "He lives in Hawaii, and he adores her. I've met him a couple of times. Not a bad guy, I guess, if my sixty-five-year-old mother has to have a…*boyfriend*."

Hannah gave a little shudder and folded the rest of the cookie into her mouth as her mother ended the call and pulled her into an excited hug.

"Hannah-Bug! I didn't know you were coming!"

Her mother hugged Adel next and told her to call her Carol, holding her at arm's length afterward, her eyes sparkling. "You're Adel, right? The one that finally managed to talk some sense into my baby about settling down?"

Adel nodded with a wink at Hannah, thoroughly enjoying the sudden splash of flush across her cheeks.

"Mom! Geez."

"I'm just saying, that handsome cop wasn't going to wait around forever. I've said it a thousand times." She paused, her smile softening as she looked at her daughter. "But not everyone in the world is like your ex."

Carol stacked three cookies onto a saucer and handed it to Adel with a tall glass of milk. She chattered as if she'd known Adel forever and winked at her daughter as she made another cheeky remark about Kate someday being her daughter-in-law.

"I feel like I have only half the story here." Adel smiled, turning on her barstool at the kitchen island to face Hannah, who was peeling a banana she'd found in the fruit bowl. "Do tell. Are you and Kate officially together now?"

"Yeah." A genuine smile lit up Hannah's face. "We had a heart-to-heart after that night you and I talked on the porch."

"Yeah." Adel winked at Hannah and popped the rest of her cookie into her mouth. "I thought you might."

Hannah dropped the peel in the trash at the end of the counter and lowered her voice, leaning to the side to glance down the hall.

"Hey, Mom, how's Audrey doing?"

Carol shook her head and looked out the bay window to the stables. "She's slowly starting to talk, but she spends most of her time out there with the horses. They help her more than I ever could."

Hannah nodded, her gaze meeting her mother's. Adel felt the same energy from both of them, like puzzle pieces coming together with a deep click, a mirrored understanding about what it took to go from shattered to the first glimpse of healing. And whatever that was, it was likely the same for an abused horse or a frightened teenager.

"I knew right away when you brought her here that she wasn't in a space to trust humans. Even the good ones." Carol topped up her coffee from the pot, then wrapped her hands around the steaming warmth of her mug. "She hadn't spoken a single word at the end of that first day she was here, not that I blame her, so I convinced her to walk out to the fields with me that evening." Carol smiled and nodded toward the stables. "You know Greystone, the Appaloosa mare I rescued a couple of summers ago from that abandoned farm upstate?"

Hannah nodded. "I remember the first night she was here. You thought she might not make it because she was so malnourished."

Hannah paused, as if focused on a silent reel of memories in front of her. "She's the only one of your horses that has never let me near her."

"That's her." Carol turned to gaze out the window at the sunlit grass below. "But the second we got into the field, Audrey and Greystone started walking toward each other. I just stopped and watched. It was the damndest thing, but then when I saw Audrey whispering to her, I knew somehow she was going to be okay."

Hannah smiled "So what happened after that?"

"She slept out in the stables with Greystone that night and then started talking after that." Carol took back Adel's empty saucer and stacked it with more cookies, handing it back to her with a wink before she turned back to her daughter, her voice suddenly low and soft like every word was a story. "You know the first thing she said to me?"

Hannah and Adel answered at the same time. "What?"

"We were clearing up after dinner, and she just turned to me and asked. 'Do you think there are some things, that if they happen to you… just make you worth nothing?'"

"Oh, my God." Hannah held her mother's gaze and shook her head. "What did you say?"

"I said that there are certain things"—Carol laid her hand over her daughter's on the counter and squeezed it—"that if you're strong enough to come through them…well, it's like tempering steel, isn't it? Those things make you stronger, better than you ever were before."

Hannah started to say something, then paused. "What do you know so far?"

"Well, she still hasn't said much, at least to me, but I know her heart is broken about the sister she lost. She's worried sick about the one still at that camp too."

Hannah twisted her hair into a bun at the back of her neck and speared it with a pen from the kitchen counter. "That's Ruth, right?"

Carol nodded, still looking out the window, her voice subdued when she did speak. "From what she's said, Ruth is the youngest of the three of them, and she's her father's favorite, apparently. Audrey has been trying to get her to understand what's happening there, what she thinks happened to their sister, but Ruth refuses to believe it." She glanced back to Hannah and Adel and reached for the bright aqua teakettle on the stove. "Then Ruth told her father—"

Hannah arched an eyebrow. "The Prophet?"

Carol nodded. "And he married Audrey off to a man three times her age the next week."

"Ruth loves her, though. I know she does." Adel rubbed her forehead with her fingertips, trying to ease away the headache gathering behind her eyes. "When she realized Audrey was gone, she was in tears in class—"

Hannah's eyebrow shot up and she looked at Adel. "Isn't that when she gave you the book with the thumb drive in it?"

"Exactly. She said nothing else mattered after her sister vanished. I think it had just dawned on her that Audrey might have been telling the truth and she might not ever see her again."

Hannah's mom dropped tea bags into three pottery mugs and turned to look at Adel.

"Bless her heart. So the poor girl still thinks Audrey was taken from camp…or worse?"

Adel nodded. "Unfortunately, we can't tell her otherwise at the moment. Kate said it could compromise her case, and that already has enough challenges."

The teakettle whistled and Carol poured the steaming water into the cups, tucking a gray-blond wisp of hair behind her ear. "What do they need to make some arrests and shut that place down?"

"Kate said it's almost impossible without complaining witnesses, more than just Audrey, who are willing to make a statement and possibly testify in court down the line. They have the Joy Book, but it's not enough without corroboration. We need girls to be honest about what's happening to them and that they're underage, and that's a lot to ask."

Carol handed Hannah and Adel a mug and set out the sugar and a matching glazed milk jug. "So not only are they being victimized, it's up to these young girls to find the courage to talk about what happens to them there or nothing can be done to stop it?"

Adel felt tears gathering in her eyes as she remembered Grace reliving the memory of her Purity Ball that night on the island. The silent, tangible intensity of memories around her, the way she stared at the dark crimson blood flowing down her hand as if the pain was a relief, a distraction, as if anything was better than the images in her mind.

Everything inside Adel just wanted to see her, to somehow make Grace understand how much she loved her and that she never meant to lie to her. Her stomach churned suddenly as the truth of the situation hit for the first time: There was no reason to even believe Grace was still alive.

Adel stood and set her mug of tea back down on the counter as she met Carol's eyes. "Would it be possible to use your restroom?"

"Of course, dear. Just down that hall, and it's the second door on the right."

Adel kept it together until she closed the bathroom door behind her. She didn't even bother to turn on the light, just sank down on the side of the claw-foot tub and dropped her face into her hands, the tears flowing as hot and fast as the feeling of utter powerlessness that gripped her heart like a tightening vise.

❖

A sudden dusty wind kicked up across the deserted parking lot of the gas station, sweeping a swath of leaves across the ground between Kate and Grace like an emerging line neither one would cross.

"How do you know Adel?"

Grace shaded her eyes from the sun that had ignited the headache threatening to combust at her temples. The knot from whatever the God Squad had given her was still tight, tender, and starting to feel warm under her fingertips. Too warm.

"She knows my girlfriend, Hannah. They met at Planned Parenthood in Lockwood. Adel is a volunteer interpreter."

"What language?"

Kate paused, a wide smile creeping across her face. "Portuguese."

Grace fell silent, choosing the words for the question she really wanted the answer to. The only one that mattered.

"Do you know if Adel is okay?" She paused, her hands tensing into fists around the sleeves of her sweatshirt, her words coming fast and thick. "If they find out why she's really there, they'll come after her. I left all those things out on her desk when I was there, and what if they found them? What if they already know and she's in danger, and it's my fault? You've got to tell her to—"

"Grace."

Grace stopped, her hand raising to cover the side of her neck. It was starting to feel heavy, like an anchor slung around her shoulders.

"She's safe. I'm not going to let anything happen to her."

It was silent then, as Grace's eyes went from the gold shield on Kate's belt to the gun in the leather holster on her hip.

"And why do you care about what happens to me?"

Kate held her eyes as she extended her hand to Grace.

"Adel helped me and my girlfriend Hannah once when we really needed it. No way I'm going to let something happen to the love of her life now." She paused, smiling as Grace slowly took her hand and stepped over the line between them. "Not on my watch."

❖

By the time they got back to Hannah's place, the sun had started to set, and Hannah's phone rang, spinning itself in a small circle on the coffee table.

Adel arched an eyebrow. "Aren't you going to answer that?"

"Yeah, I just…" She paused. "I just have a bad feeling."

Then Adel felt it. The taut, silent air, sharp with the fear that things were about to get worse. Way worse.

"Hannah." Adel scraped her hand through her hair. "Answer it."

Hannah reached for the phone and clicked it on, holding it to her ear as she walked toward the glass doors that led to the deck. She rubbed her eyes as she listened, then said something in a low voice about a picture.

"Who is it?" Adel's feeling of dread was growing, squeezing her torso like winding black vines. "What's wrong?"

Hannah didn't answer, just stepped out on the patio and shut the door softly behind her. Adel watched for what seemed like forever as she paced the length of the patio, her mouth set into a thin, tense line as she listened. Adel caught the words *emergency room* and was almost ready to open the door when Hannah clicked off her phone and headed back. She grabbed her jacket off the kitchen chair as soon as she walked in and slipped her phone into her pocket.

"Hannah, what the hell? What's going on?"

She turned around as she got to the hall. "Adel, I hate not being able to tell you anything, but you know I can't." She paused, her face as serious as Adel had ever seen it. Whatever was happening, it was bad. "I'll call you as soon as I can."

Adel dropped her face into her hands and sank down into one of the kitchen chairs. She already knew. She knew in her heart that it was Grace.

❖

Night was falling by the time her phone echoed through the empty house. Adel lunged at it, knocking over her water glass in the process. It was Bethany.

"Hey, buddy, what the hell?" The words tumbled over each other in a relieved rush, and Adel couldn't have answered if she wanted to. "The God Squad goons just came in and cleared out your cabin today, I saw it when I came back from dinner. Where the hell *are* you?"

"I should have told you, man, sorry." Adel dropped her head into her hand, the room slowly darkening around her. "Everything just happened at once."

"Listen, where are you? I'll come over and you can start from the beginning." She paused. "And I have beer. Cold beer."

Adel felt herself tearing up at the thought; Bethany had always had some great fucking timing. She texted the address and hung up, then walked out on the deck, leaning over the railing and staring into the still, dark lake. She'd received a terse text from Katya that morning as they were leaving the ranch. Apparently, she'd had movers come in and box up Adel's things and move them to a storage unit in Queens, which was a blinking neon sign that she was seeing someone else. Then about two hours later, an email from her editor hit her phone. He needed to see an outline, or at the least a workable collection of ideas, within a week or he was going to pull the project.

Adel stepped back from the railing and raked both hands through her hair. Her old life, including the lucrative career any New York journalist would kill for, was crumbling to dust around her feet, and she just didn't care. Adel knew Grace would never forgive her—she had no illusions about that—but nothing else mattered to her until she knew Grace was safe.

But strangely, she'd started to realize she didn't miss anything about her old life; in fact, what she'd started to miss was the camp. The cool lap of the lake water at camp as the orange-fire sun sank behind it, the shifting, shadowed silhouette of the fir trees at night, and the sudden swoop of owls as they stirred violet dusk into the inky night sky. The quiet had seeped into her blood and made her miss a place that before that summer she had never known existed. But not once had she missed Manhattan.

Eventually, Bethany's voice calling through the house sliced through her thoughts, and Adel waved her out to the patio, smiling at the familiar clack of Bethany's cowboy boots on the deck.

Bethany plunked the beer on the deck railing and shook her head.

"Damn, buddy, way to just fucking disappear. One minute you were there and the next you'd disappeared into the Covenant vortex." She popped the top on a Foster's Lager and handed it over to Adel.

"Thanks." Adel took a long swig and set her bottle down, running her thumb over the label. "I don't know for sure why they took Grace, but I'd bet the damn farm it was because someone found out about our relationship, and I didn't feel like waiting around to see what they were planning to do with me."

"Good timing. Shit's going down out there, I can feel it." She took a long swig of her own beer and leaned onto the railing. "So, whose house is this, anyway? It's beautiful."

"Remember Kate? The detective you met at the station?"

Bethany nodded.

"This is her girlfriend's house, whom I knew before I met Kate, actually."

Bethany turned to watch a black hawk cut through the last of the fading light, disappearing into the path of the rising moon. She turned around slowly and leaned back on the railing, meeting Adel's eyes "Any news on Grace?"

The automatic patio lights clicked on, and Adel fought to keep her voice even when she finally felt steady enough to speak. "No, nothing." She downed the rest of her beer and took the next open bottle Bethany handed her. "And it's killing me."

A breeze coming off the water shifted a translucent lock of Bethany's hair across her face before she tucked it behind her ear. "Yeah, Nora's going crazy. I guess those two really bonded before she disappeared."

Adel cracked a smile for the first time. "By the way, don't think I didn't notice you used the G-word when we were at the station."

Bethany threw her head back and laughed before she downed the rest of her beer. "What, you mean 'girlfriend'? Yeah, whatever, I guess she got me in the end. It was the brownies." Bethany shot her an indignant look. "Dude, she started putting *butterscotch* chips in them. What was I supposed to do?"

"How's she doing, anyway?" Adel slapped at a mosquito that landed on her wrist, sloshing her beer up and over the rim of the bottle in the process. "I know she was really upset when she figured out what the Joy Book was, and now Grace has up and disappeared. It can't be easy."

Bethany nodded, rolling up the sleeves of her shirt as she answered. "The staff got a notice today that they're wrapping PCW camp early…"

Adel raised an eyebrow, then nodded. "Principles of Christian Womanhood?"

"Exactly. Family camp starts the first of September as usual, but they're shutting this one down almost a month early. There's some sort of closing ceremony this weekend, and—get this—Nora actually volunteered to take charge of planning it."

"I'd bet she's doing it because she knows Grace would want it to still be special for the girls." Adel held her cold bottle against her throbbing temple. She was suddenly beyond tired of the constant fucking headache lurking behind her eyes every hour of the day. "That's actually sweet of her."

"Well, no one else was volunteering, and I'm pretty sure that's the only reason they're letting her do it." She paused, looking back out over the water. "I handed in my notice today, and Nora says she's out of there after the ceremony too. I'd rather be out of a job than stay there another second." She shook her head and smoothed her hand over the worn varnish of the railing as she spoke. "I can't believe I stayed so long in the first place."

Adel looked up at the sky that seemed suddenly dark, unfurled like a bolt of navy silk scattered with a tossed handful of stars. Bethany handed her another beer, and she realized she was gripping her bottle so hard her fingers were white and stiff around it. Bethany took the bottle from her and popped the top before she handed it back.

"You're worried, aren't you?"

Adel nodded. "She found out about the article and who I really am before I had a chance to tell her." She paused, trying to wrap words around the tangled intensity of the emotions twisting in her gut. "I know I fucked everything up, but I *have* to know she's okay." A tear slid down Adel's cheek before she swiped it away with the heel of her hand. "I won't be able to forgive myself if something happens to her."

Bethany pulled Adel into her arms and hugged her hard, but she didn't say anything because there was nothing to say. They both knew she might already be gone.

Chapter Twenty-four

Adel had just opened her eyes the next morning when her phone rang, vibrating against the nightstand of Hannah's guest room. Her heart sank as she reached for it—the stillness in the house told her it was still empty.

She looked at the number, hoping to see that it was Hannah, but it was a number she didn't recognize. She hesitated, then fumbled the phone on its way to her ear. It slid down her cheek before she managed to catch it and click the green answer button.

"Hello?" Her voice was still hoarse from last night's tears. "Grace? Baby, tell me this is you."

There was silence on the other end for a few long seconds, then a voice she couldn't place, although it seemed vaguely familiar.

"Adel? Is this you?"

"It is." Adel sank back into the pillows, wishing now she hadn't answered the phone. "How can I help you?"

"Adel, this is Carol, Hannah's mom."

"Oh, of course! We met yesterday." Adel sat up in bed and looked at the time on her phone. Just before seven. "What can I do for you?"

"I'm sorry to call you out of the blue, but Hannah says she's with an emergency patient, and I can't reach Kate. She did have time to text me your number, though, and hopefully you can help me." Carol paused, and when she spoke again, Adel heard the tears tightening her voice. "I just don't know what to do."

Adel softened her voice and slowed her words. "Don't worry at all, Carol. I was awake already. What's going on?"

She listened as Carol took a measured breath on the other end of the line.

"I can't find Audrey. She's gone."

"What?" Adel threw off the duvet and climbed out of bed as she spoke, scanning the room for the jeans she'd worn the night before. "What do you mean she's gone?"

"I went to get her for breakfast this morning, and all there was was this note on the desk in her room."

Adel held the phone with her shoulder as she plucked the jeans off the desk chair and stepped into them. "What does it say?"

"It was so short. It just said she had something she needed to do, and not to worry about her, but of course I'm worried. She's just fifteen, and so fragile. I don't know what to do…" Her voice trailed off and she paused, the silence dense with emotion. "I feel like I've let her down."

"Carol, don't worry. I'll be there in ten minutes, okay?" She paused, the relief on the other end of the line as audible as words. "Just get some coffee and try to relax. She can't have gone far. We'll find her."

Adel hung up the phone, scraping her hair into a ponytail as she pulled her last clean shirt from her bag. She had a sinking feeling about Audrey disappearing out of the blue, but then again, what did she not have a sinking feeling about lately? She slid into her shoes on the way out the door and dropped her phone into her jacket pocket, closing the front door behind her as she stepped into the late summer sun that seemed unnecessarily bright.

It took her five seconds to remember she no longer had a vehicle to drive, ten seconds to realize she'd just locked her keys in the house, and exactly fifteen minutes for Bethany to pull halfway onto the sidewalk in front of the house, Ashley McBryde blaring out both open windows.

Bethany leaned out the driver's side and cracked open a can of Coke, foam spilling down every side and forming a river on the sidewalk below.

"Damn, buddy. If you wanted a breakfast date, you could've just asked." Bethany grinned and nodded toward the passenger seat, errant wisps of hair blowing across her face. "I think I've got some spray cheese and saltines in the glove compartment there. Just take a look under them maps."

"Yeah, yeah, very funny." Adel slid into the passenger seat and smacked Bethany's shoulder. "Thanks for picking me up. What do you have to do today, by the way?"

Bethany slid on a pair of blue mirrored aviators and grinned at Adel as she pulled from the sidewalk onto the actual road.

"Not a goddamn thing, really. Camp classes are over, so I'm just feeding twice a day. Why, you got something going on?"

She handed Adel the open Coke and reached down into the cooler at her feet for another.

"Actually, yeah. Audrey disappeared."

"What? Isn't she supposed to be at that horse ranch?" Bethany glanced into the rearview mirror and smoothed the wisps of hair back from her face. "I've heard about that place for years. It's the best of the best."

"Well, saddle up." Adel shot a smile in her friend's direction. "Because that's exactly where we're headed."

After fifteen minutes of wishing Bethany's truck had seat belts to stave off certain death, Adel looked over at Bethany as she scanned the road for the turnoff. The pure excitement on her friend's face at the prospect of seeing Carol's ranch made it worth almost dying in a fiery crash on the side of the road.

"You'll see the sign for the ranch coming up on the left in about a quarter mile. Just turn down the—"

"Are you kidding me?" Bethany flashed her a smile and rolled her eyes. "I know where it is. I've been dying to see this place forever. Anyone that knows her way around a saddle knows the woman that owns it has been written up in magazines all over the country…Did you know she used to be some famous shrink in Manhattan before she just started that rescue ranch out of the blue?"

Adel didn't have a chance to answer before Bethany whipped the steering wheel to the left on what felt like two wheels, her hand tightening around the door handle with a grip that threatened to bend the steel.

"So anyway." Bethany glanced into her rearview mirror and then over at Adel. "How is Audrey doing? I mean, before today, I guess?"

"Better, or at least it sounded like that from what Hannah's mom said yesterday. Which is why her suddenly being gone doesn't make any sense."

As they pulled up to the expansive, honey-toned cabin, Bethany actually parked like a normal person for once beside a massive red Chevy truck with *Carol* on the license plate. The truck bed was rusted, the tailgate so dented it resembled a crumpled handful of rusting foil, and at least four dusty, coiled ropes hung from the back window.

Bethany swung her long legs out of the truck, and Adel smiled as she heard her boots hit the pavement. Bethany's mouth dropped open as if admiring a centuries-old painting in a European museum. "Damn, she even has excellent taste in trucks."

"All right, Sparky, you can swoon later." Adel winked at her and nodded toward the cabin. "We have more pressing things to focus on at the moment."

"Yeah, totally." Bethany leaned in to peer at the coils of ropes hanging from the back of the passenger's seat. "I'm just sayin'…"

"She's straight."

"Dammit." Bethany winked and fell into step with Adel as they headed to the porch. "I was afraid of that."

The door was standing open, and as they walked down the hall, the scent of frying ham and the faint percolating rhythm of fresh coffee hung in the air.

Carol turned when she heard them walk into the kitchen, ashy curls flying around her shoulders. She tucked them behind her ear as she hurried over to hug Adel.

"Adel, you're an angel. I know we don't know each other very well yet, but I didn't know who else to call. I didn't want to worry Hannah any more than she is, and I can't reach Kate."

Adel squeezed both of her cold hands in hers and smiled. "I'm so glad you called, Carol. Don't worry, we're going to find her." She nodded at Bethany. "I even brought backup. This is my buddy Bethany Willison, she's the horse wrangler at Valley of Rubies."

Carol flashed Bethany a bright smile and extended her hand. "Hi, I'm Carol Myers."

Bethany swallowed twice before she answered, then took her hand and visibly relaxed at Carol's warmth, glancing out the back window at the stables. "It's an honor, Ms. Myers. I've read about your work out here for years."

"Oh, dear, I'm not fancy. Call me Carol." She waved them over to the kitchen island and poured each of them a steaming mug of what smelled like roasted hazelnut coffee. "But no introduction is necessary. We've actually met. Well, almost, anyway."

Bethany arched an eyebrow and lifted the pitcher of cream, pouring it into her mug. "We did? I have a feeling I would have remembered you."

"Do you remember a colt that got loose on the highway out of town last summer? A little pinto?"

"Oh, yeah." Bethany smiled. "She'd somehow gotten out of the pasture there and no one could catch her, poor thing. And cars kept whizzing past and scaring the life out of her."

"Well, someone passing called me to come out and help, but by the time I got there, you were leading her off the road and back through that broken fence. I'd recognize that hair anywhere—it reminded me of mine back in the day."

Carol winked at Bethany and turned to pull a pan of biscuits out of the oven, then picked up a wide brush and slathered them with melted butter, the scent instantly hovering rich and heavy in the air. She stacked the steaming biscuits onto a platter, and Adel smiled as she caught the printing on the handle of the butter brush. Sherwin-Williams.

"Anyway, I pulled up and waited until I saw you whip out that wire from your truck and tack up that hole in the fence. I was impressed. If it wasn't for you, she'd probably gotten hurt."

Bethany smiled, a deep flush creeping up her neck and into her cheeks. "Nah, it wasn't a big deal. I think she just needed to see a friendly face."

"Bullshit." Carol winked and flashed a smile at Bethany. "She was so scared she was in a tailspin, and you got her off the road and back to safety. I know skill when I see it."

She slid the platter of biscuits between them on the island and turned to lift the cover off a pan of fluffy scrambled eggs and crisp bacon resting on the stove. "Well, I hope you girls are hungry, because when I'm nervous, I cook." Another pan held golden roast potatoes with bright peppers and tender strips of onion, and Carol didn't wait for an answer before she loaded up two plates and slid them across the island. It was hard not to laugh at Bethany's blissful expression—she suddenly looked like she might actually die of happiness overload.

Over breakfast Carol relayed the few details she had about Audrey's disappearance. She'd been out late at the stables, which Carol said was nothing unusual, so she'd gone to bed, only to find the note in her room the next morning.

"Where do you think she's gone?"

Even as Adel heard the question come out of her mouth, she knew the answer. The three of them locked eyes and Bethany pulled her phone out of the back pocket of her Levi's. She typed a quick text, and before she'd even picked up her fork again, it pinged.

Bethany held it up for Adel and Carol to read. It was from Nora. *She's fine. She's with me, and I'm not letting her out of my sight.*

Carol exhaled as if she'd been holding her breath all morning, then pulled a bright pitcher of fresh orange juice out of the fridge and poured three glasses, pushing two toward Bethany and Adel.

"I can't tell you how glad I am to hear she's okay, but who the hell is Nora?"

"Nora's my girlfriend, resident badass, and Audrey's closest friend at camp." Bethany folded a thick, peppery slice of bacon into her mouth. "I don't know why she's back, but believe me, you've got nothing to worry about."

❖

Grace's eyes fluttered open and she touched the side of her neck, the dry brush of gauze silent and telling under her fingertips. She turned her head slowly to see a pink plastic pitcher on a small rolling table beside her, condensation sliding slowly down the sides, but there was no cup. Her throat was dry, rubbed raw from the inside out. A steady series of faint beeps behind her head seemed to be connected to the clear tubes leading to the tape wrapped across the back of her hand. She tugged at them and winced as they seemed to lodge themselves deeper into her skin.

"Hey, there."

Grace jolted, twisting sharply to the side to see who else was in the room. It was the cop she'd met at the gas station. *What's her name?* Grace winced at the pain slicing hot and fast across her neck and shoulder at the sudden movement. *And why the hell is she here?*

The cop stood to come closer but stopped in her tracks when the insistent beeps coming from behind Grace's head accelerated sharply.

"Hey, relax," she said, slowly pulling the chair she'd been sitting in closer to Grace's bed. "We know each other, remember? My name is Kate."

"Yeah. I remember," Grace said, her eyelids closing into a dark, slow burn. "I remember that I can't seem to shake you."

Kate's look of surprise relaxed into kind crinkles that framed her eyes when she laughed. She was wearing the same clothes as yesterday, and her rumpled hair fought back as she raked a hand through it and sat back in her chair.

"How are you feeling?"

Grace closed her eyes again, the burn behind them slipping silent down her cheeks as she shook her head.

"That good, huh?" Kate shifted in her chair and caught Grace's eye when she finally opened them. She smiled, arching an eyebrow. "Well. I think you should just walk it off, personally. It's not like some murderous freaks kidnapped you and stabbed you in the neck with a dirty needle or something."

Grace froze, her fingertips still at her cheek. A slow smile spread across the cop's face and she winked as she handed Grace a tissue from the box by the bed. Grace smiled back despite herself and rolled her eyes.

"You're just jealous." She nodded toward the door. "I don't see a line of murderous freaks waiting to pounce on *you* out there."

Kate laughed as a nurse breezed through the door to check Grace's vitals and adjust the flow on her IV bag. She asked Grace about her pain level and promised food wouldn't be long on her way out the door.

Grace's stomach churned and she shook her head. "No, I—"

The nurse was gone before she got the words out, and Grace fell back again onto the pillows. The hazy memory of being put on a stretcher and wheeled into the emergency room flashed across her mind. She remembered voices, fluorescent lights whizzing by overhead, and the squeak of the stretcher wheels on the cold tile underneath. She'd vomited at some point and remembered the soft brown eyes of the nurse who held the basin to her face. She'd had a British accent and said everything was going to be okay, that they'd gotten her to the hospital just in time.

"So, what happened to me?" Grace said, turning toward Kate. "I mean, other than the obvious. Why did I get so sick?"

Kate leaned forward in her chair, her elbows on her knees. "The simple answer is that you got blood poisoning from the unsterilized needle that went into your neck. And by the time I realized how sick you were, you were already unconscious, so I called Hannah from the road and had her meet us here."

Grace looked around as Kate answered the obvious question.

"You're in Lockwood. We were almost home when you passed out."

"Hannah...that's your girlfriend, right?"

"She is. But lucky for you she's also a kickass doctor who saved your life last night. She said the antibiotics are working fast, though. You might actually get out of here as soon as tonight."

Grace leaned back on the pillows and closed her eyes, her hand gripping the sheet beside her and gathering it into her fist.

"She shouldn't have bothered." She listened as a long, slow breath escaped her lungs, and she wondered for a moment what would happen if she just didn't take another. "They'll just find me eventually."

Kate nodded, then leaned over and pulled a bottle of water out of the pocket of a jacket slung over the back of her chair. She raised an eyebrow in question, then handed it over after she'd twisted open the cap. Grace drank it fast, squeezing the bottle without realizing it and soaking the front of her hospital gown.

"So, tell me why."

Grace looked over at Kate, holding out the empty bottle and examining the damp front of her gown. "Why what?"

Kate took it and lobbed it into the trash can in the corner by the door. "If they want you dead, there must be a reason."

Grace nodded, pulling the sheet up around her and leaning back against the pillows. Suddenly it seemed too much to inhale and exhale. She closed her eyes against the memory of Adel's face, the stone she'd handed her to throw into the sea, falling asleep tangled into the warmth of her body. Everything.

"It was Adel. They found out we were together. But they knew there was something..." She paused, searching for the right word. "Different about me, for a while, I guess."

"Damn. They want to kill you because you have a girlfriend? That seems harsh even for them."

Grace brushed the gauze bandage across her neck with her fingertips. She never knew for certain they intended to carry out Blood Atonement. "I don't know that, actually. Kellan called you before either one of us found out for sure."

Kate leaned forward in her chair, rubbing her forehead with the tips of her fingers. Grace heard the scrape of exhaustion in her voice when she finally spoke.

"Look, this is none of my business, but Adel is worried sick about you, and Hannah and I can't tell her you're okay without your permission." She paused and looked up at Grace. "I know she lied to you about why she was at camp, and I don't blame you for being upset about that—anyone would be. But she didn't expect to fall in love, and by the time she realized, it was too late to come clean without risking losing you."

Grace sighed, too tired to talk and knowing nothing would change no matter what she said. "Kate, I appreciate what you're trying to do here, but I have no idea who she even is. I thought I did, but...she was using me for information." She shook her head, pulling up the edge of the clear, ribbed tape holding the tubes in the back of her hand. "It's as simple as that."

"No. It's not." Kate's voice was intense but soft at the edges, and she met Grace's eyes before she continued. "Adel has done nothing but fight for you, even though she thinks you'll never speak to her again, since the second she found out you were missing. No matter how it happened, that's love."

Grace nodded, suddenly too exhausted to care about the foreign plastic tubes snaking out of her body, connecting her to a world she didn't even know if she wanted to be in anymore. After a long second, she turned her head to stare at the white perforated tiles on the ceiling.

"You can tell her I'm okay." A tear escaped down her cheek, and she felt it slip into the dark gold hair at her temple before she continued. "But I don't want to see her again. How can I know what's real after she lied to me about who she was—about everything, really—since the second we met?"

Kate nodded and pulled a small black cell phone out of the inside pocket of her jacket. She placed it on the bed beside Grace and stood, slipping her bag onto her shoulder. She turned to go, then looked back at Grace and raked a hand through her hair. "I put a few numbers into that phone, including mine, and I hope you use it. But either way, I'm going to give you some advice I overheard someone tell my girlfriend."

Kate put her hand on the door handle and paused long enough that Grace wondered if she was going to go on.

"You're right, you might get your heart broken. But you'll break your own heart if you let Adel go." Kate's voice softened and Grace just caught her last words as she walked out the door. "She's one of the good ones."

Chapter Twenty-five

Adel slid into the bench at the diner, the ripped red Naugahyde covering the booth catching on the back pocket of her jeans. She picked up the menu, set it down, then picked it up again, wishing again the diner in Lockwood served beer.

She saw Hannah as she breezed through the door a few minutes later, still wearing a white lab coat, pale blue scrubs, and white leather Tretorns. She tossed her bag into the booth as she sat down, unclipping her cell phone from her waistband and sighing so hard it lofted the wisps of hair that had fallen from the French twist at the back of her head. Hannah picked up the menu and read it to herself, her lips moving as she followed the list down with her fingers.

Adel glanced at the embroidery on the front of Hannah's lab coat and smiled despite herself. "I was wondering when you were going to tell me your real name."

Hannah dragged her eyes away from the fluorescent pink Post-it note clipped to the top of the menu. It was the daily special. Adel had seen it too: chopped steak and creamed spinach.

"What?" She paused, still distracted by the menu. "What are you talking about?"

She glanced down at her jacket and immediately shrugged it off like it was on fire when she saw *Dr. Boris McKelty* embroidered on the front with dull gray thread. She wadded it up with a look of disdain and chucked it over her shoulder into the empty booth behind her.

"I must have picked his jacket up in the break room. No wonder the arms have been so long all day!" She quickly regained her awareness of what was actually important and picked her menu back up. "And that also explains why I smelled fried pickles in the car the entire way from the hospital."

Adel started to ask why Boris smelled like pickles but stopped when the waitress, Doris, arrived and Hannah instantly jumped up to hug her. She was still wearing a western shirt with pearl buttons, yellow this time, and Wrangler jeans cinched up with a belt buckle almost as wide as the tabletop. Hannah kissed her cheek with genuine affection and gave her a mock look of disdain.

"Doris, how do I ever have a hope in hell of being nominated for Lakewood Rodeo Queen this summer with you walking around looking all fine-ass like that?"

Doris winked at her and shook her head, whipping out her order pad as she answered. "Well, darlin', I've been telling your mama since she was little: blond and gorgeous ain't got nothin' on mean and quick."

Hannah laughed, sliding back into the booth and handing Doris the menus. "Adel, this is my aunt Doris, my mom's older sister."

Doris cleared her throat and gazed at her order pad, tapping it with her pen.

"Sorry." Hannah rolled her eyes and giggled. "This is Doris, Carol's better-looking sister."

Adel smiled despite herself and winked at Doris. "We've actually met. Although they always say one sister is always better looking, and I see now that it's a gospel fact."

Doris sniffed and looked like she was trying hard to suppress her delight. She took their orders and sauntered back over to the kitchen window, slamming the orders down and ringing the bell twice for emphasis. Adel watched her, thankful for something else to focus on besides the blinding ball of worry blocking out every thought for the last two days. She hated the tear that she felt slip down her cheek but there was no stopping it, and truth be told, she was way past giving a damn.

"Hannah, thanks for meeting me." She leaned back as Doris plunked two tall Cokes they didn't order in front of them. "I know you can't tell me anything, and I'm not asking you to, but I'm going crazy with worry."

Hannah reached out and gave Adel's hand a squeeze, then handed her a napkin from the chrome dispenser on the table.

"Adel, don't apologize. You know I'd feel the same way if it was Kate. Although I would've been decidedly less patient than you are." She plucked two more napkins out and pushed them over to Adel, kindness softening her eyes. "I'd have probably jumped you in the parking lot and demanded information before you even made it into the diner."

The air was heavy with the scent of mashed potatoes and kitchen steam. The bell over the door clanged hard against the glass as a group of teenage boys spilled into the diner, shoving each other in turn and laughing until Doris caught their eye and nodded toward a table in the back. She gave a deep sigh, plucked the pen out from between her hair-sprayed curls, and ambled over in their direction.

Adel traced the silver flecks in the Formica tabletop with her finger. They were endless, like an American diner version of painting of a starry night sky, complete with a dented aluminum frame.

"She's okay, Adel."

Adel's head snapped up and she sat back against the booth, staring at Hannah, afraid to speak in case Hannah might offer more details.

"I'm not saying it wasn't serious, but that girl is made of stubborn steel." She paused, peeling the paper back on her straw and balling it up. "Kate stayed with her all night at the hospital so she wouldn't be alone, and I stopped in to check on her every hour."

"Kate stayed with her?" Adel tried to keep the emotion out of her voice and failed. "Wow."

"She did. I'm actually meeting her for lunch in an hour, so I'll know more after that."

"Seriously? You're eating lunch in an hour?" Adel glanced up at Doris, who was headed toward them with two enormous patty melts and a mountain of French fries, as she arched an eyebrow at Hannah.

"What?" Hannah's cell phone rang between them. "You've met me, right?"

She picked it up and held it to her ear, her eyebrows quickly sinking into worry.

"What do you mean, 'she's gone'?" Hannah looked at her watch and leaned back hard against the booth. "I didn't sign discharge orders. She just walked out?"

Adel felt her heart speed up again and thanked Doris silently as she set the plates down on the table.

She stared at Hannah, who didn't say much more until she clicked her phone off and looked at Adel.

"Grace is gone." She paused, shaking her head, her eyes locked onto Adel's. "No one saw her leave, and now no one knows where the hell she is."

❖

Grace felt her stomach roil as she saw the sign looming at the end of the road and leaned back against the seat until she felt the car stop and heard the driver clear her throat. She'd walked up to a woman wearing scrubs in the hospital parking lot and asked if she could give her a ride. The woman hesitated, then spotted the hospital bracelet around her wrist and told her to get in.

"Okay. We're here." The woman looked over to Grace with a worried expression. "Are you sure you're gonna be okay? You know people in there?"

Grace shook the weariness from her head and thanked her, climbing out of the sedan and staring at her reflection in the tall, mirrored windows of the lodge. She closed her eyes again and melted into the sound of the lake lapping against the shore in the distance and the wind moving lazily through the tops of the trees. Despite what she might be walking into, despite all the turmoil and fear that had left a silent stain on the last few days, she'd missed this.

The sound of the glass double doors opening snapped Grace back to reality. When she opened her eyes, a girl she didn't recognize in a pastel dress was holding the door open for her. She nodded as she walked through it, but as it closed behind her, she felt as if she were moving through quicksand and had a crazy urge to run after the girl on the other side, to save her, to tell her to run and not look back. When she turned back to look at her, the girl had turned to look at her too.

It was early afternoon, not even close to dinnertime, although she heard the sounds of kitchen staff as they set up for the onslaught of campers for the evening meal. She forced herself to turn down the hall to the right, taking slow steps toward Whittier's office. Kate had given her a phone with a few numbers saved into contacts, but she hadn't called before she left the hospital. She knew enough to be afraid of what might be waiting for her if she announced her arrival.

She stopped at Whittier's office door, her fingers resting lightly on the tarnished brass doorknob. "Lead Thou Me On" played softly on the other side, and as Grace lifted her hand to knock, she heard the rustle of papers and a muffled cough through the door.

"Come in."

Grace was startled at Whittier's voice; she hadn't even realized she'd knocked. She took a deep breath, steadied herself, and walked into the office, closing the door softly behind her. She breathed in the scent of mothballs and dust as Whittier looked her up and down, the expression on her face unmoving.

Grace shifted her weight from one foot to the other as she realized she was still wearing Adel's jeans and sweatshirt from the day they'd taken her. She smoothed her hand over her hair and pulled it over one shoulder, her eyes sinking to the floor as if she'd forgotten again there was a world above it.

Whittier gestured for her to sit, and Grace forced herself to look up and meet her gaze. There was a glimmer of something, surprise maybe, behind them, and Whittier crossed her hands primly in front of her before she spoke.

"You're here." She paused as if searching for the words. "Did Kellan bring you back?"

Grace forced her face to stay neutral as her mind raced. She hadn't expected to be asked about Kellan, but it made sense. In their minds, he'd disappeared too. She shifted in her chair; they could do whatever they wanted to her, but she wasn't going to give them a crumb of information about her friend.

"I don't know where he is." She shook her head and pushed the dirty sleeves of her sweatshirt to her elbows. "He dropped me off at some gas station and took off, never said a word. I hitchhiked back to Lockwood."

Whittier's fingers brushed across the tiny gold cross at the base of her throat. "And why did you return?"

The last of Grace's energy escaped with her breath, and her fingers fluttered to the small, square Band-Aid on the side of her neck. The truthful answer to that question was that Valley of Rubies was the only thing she'd thought of since the moment she'd woken up in the hospital. She needed to be here, she needed—

"If you don't have an answer, this conversation is over."

Grace raised her eyes to Whittier and squared her shoulders almost imperceptibly. She didn't have an answer. But she had a Bible reference, and that was just as good.

"Well, I guess I'm the prodigal daughter." Her eyes dropped to the worn, black leather Bible on Whittier's desk. "I can't believe I let myself stray so far from the teachings of our Prophet, but now I've returned to camp…" Her voice faltered, the last few words barely audible. "To atone. If that's even possible."

Whittier ran her fingertips over the cover of her Bible and said nothing. Grace counted the seconds on the clock on the bookshelf behind her, dropping her eyes when Whittier turned her attention back to her. It had been almost two minutes.

"Grace, what we saw on that tape was egregious." She slowed for emphasis. "The most *disgusting* thing I have ever seen in my life." Grace listened to the raw hate creep into Whittier's voice. "And frankly, after being forced to witness that kind of blatant disrespect for our Lord and Savior, I don't trust you. How am I to know that you won't inflict that kind of unrighteous behavior on the girls at Valley of Rubies?"

Grace's body threatened to betray her, and she swallowed several times in a row to quell the rising contents of her stomach. The magnitude of hypocrisy in that statement alone swept her voice from her throat. The white robe she'd been instructed to wrap around her naked, twelve-year-old body flashed through her mind like a starting flag, and an avalanche of raw torn memories followed, dozens crowded into a single second. The worn carpet in the basement of the Fellowship Hall, the crowd of staring men she'd seen congregating upstairs as she was walked to the basement, and the look of anger on Kellan's face as he reached the room and realized which lamb he'd been sent to lead to slaughter.

"Grace!"

Whittier's hand slapped down onto her desk with a crack, and Grace whipped her neck up. The pain cut through her like hot steel, and she instinctively covered the side of it with her palm.

"The least you can do is assure me that that is not an issue I need to be concerned about." She paused, a blue vein throbbing in her neck. "That is the very least you can do."

Grace forced herself to meet Whittier's eyes. "Of course not. I have unnatural desires toward women, yes, but that is not the same as being a *pedophile*."

She spat the last word out with enough force to startle Whittier, who leaned back after a few seconds and picked up her phone. She spoke softly into it from behind her hand for a moment and stood up as she put it back in its cradle.

"When we cleared out your cabin, we saved your clothing to give to charity. It's in storage at the stables. I suggest you find that box, dress appropriately if you can remember how to do that, and return to the Prophet's office as soon as possible."

A pointed glance at the door was her dismissal.

Grace left the office and pulled the hair tie out of the length of her hair, letting it sink warm and heavy to her waist. Everything inside her wanted to run down to the docks and row to the center of the lake, to watch her oar slide into the depths of the water, moving slick and silent, forcing the lake water to part and move around it. Anything to remember the fading feeling of what it was like to have power. Any power.

She slowed her steps on the way up to the stables, the sun warming the tops of her shoulders, and leaned against a fir tree, letting her gaze melt into the sky-blue horizon. Her body sank slowly, the bark scratching at her spine until she reached the ground. She let her head fall back against the sharp bark of the tree and pictured rowing to the island again, the dark lake water flowing around her oar, shapeshifting silently into movement. The image was vivid, potent, like another movie reel jerking to life in a darkened room.

Grace heard the whisper then, in the brush of a sudden breeze that shifted the tops of the trees like gentle paintbrushes against the azure sky.

If you're going to reject their plan, you'd better have one of your own.

Her fingers closed around the phone in her pocket, and as she lifted it to her ear, the breeze dropped to nothing as suddenly as it had swelled, the echo of the words fading into the sounds of the forest as if they were never there. As if it was her idea all along.

❖

It took long, involved conversations both on the phone and in person to convince Bethany that she was physically fine, and to finally allow her to prepare for her meeting with the Prophet. Grace held her breath as the dress she'd dug out of the stable loft slid over her shoulders, dropping to her hips and twisting around her calves like vines. Her body felt small, the shape instantly swallowed by the dress the dull color of dry hay. She fashioned her hair into a braid at the back of her neck and coiled that into a bun, pinning it with the hairpins she'd always kept in the pockets of her dresses.

She caught a tear with the heel of her hand as she pushed down the urge to call Adel for the hundredth time. She knew what to expect of her life in the Covenant; women were lied to constantly, about themselves, their potential, even the basic right to make their own choices. On some level she'd always known that her life would be an endless lie. But there was a certain absence of fear in that knowledge. Not even that was comforting anymore.

Now when she closed her eyes at night, there was only the sharp crack of her heart breaking when she'd found Adel was lying to her too. And even worse, lying to get something she wanted. At least here she expected the lies—in fact, she knew them by heart. Which meant that if she just stuck to what she knew this time, she could go through the rest of her life without feeling her heart shatter around her feet again like it did that day.

It was time to go. Past time. Grace looked toward the pitched roof of the hayloft, then focused on the dust motes hanging in the wide beam of sunlight streaming from the west-facing open loft door. But Kate's words, the ones she wanted so desperately to forget, still smoldered in the back of her mind.

You'll break your own heart if you let her go. She's one of the good ones.

❖

Grace had been to the Prophet's office only once before, when her picture was taken for the Joy Book. It smelled the same this time, of dank air, stale paneling, and lemon furniture polish, and as she walked up onto the Fellowship Hall stage, she saw the door to the hall had been left open for her. She stopped at the threshold as her lungs screamed, refusing to hold more than a teaspoon of air, her heart beating out of her chest. She stood there, biting down on her bottom lip until she tasted blood. The sudden pain, the iron rush of blood she spat out at the base of the paneling, steeled her enough to walk down the hall.

A single bare bulb flickered against the stained white ceiling tiles above. Grace heard one of the Prophet's wives singing "The Old Rugged Cross" as she filed papers into a dented metal cabinet in a small office she passed on the left. Music seemed to replace words once women married. They talked to other wives and church members, but not like they did before marriage. They no longer spoke of themselves or expressed opinions in public—suddenly their words reflected only their husbands and duty. Something shifts when you're owned.

Grace didn't knock. The Prophet was facing the back bookshelf when Grace walked in, and he paused before he turned toward the door, neither surprised nor pleased to see her. He was thin in the way that only elderly men are, with yellowing gray hair and a white dress shirt with a faint sweat stain ringing the collar. He gestured for her to sit down, then stared over her head at the clock on the wall for a long moment before he spoke. Grace kept her eyes on the floor, staring at dust bunnies spinning at the corners by the floor ventilation grate.

"Sister Waters." He paused until Grace met his eyes. "I had a long conversation with Mrs. Whittier this afternoon, and I understand you have returned to the Valley of Rubies with the intention to repent."

"Yes, sir."

Grace realized she was clenching her fists in her lap and forced herself to uncurl her fingers slowly and rest them lightly on the arms of the chair.

"I think you'll agree this has been a long time coming, wouldn't you say?"

Grace nodded, and he continued.

"She told me of your journey back to us, and I have to say I am heartened by your determination to return to the fold. To your spiritual home." He pulled out the chair behind his desk and sat down, his eyes still locked onto Grace. "We weren't so lucky with Kellan. Do you have any idea where he went after he left you to fend for yourself?"

Grace shook her head, but it was clear instantly that the Prophet was fishing for information. Kellan's level of betrayal would be punishable by Blood Atonement without a doubt, if for no other reason than he knew too much. The second he'd abandoned his post and disappeared into the real world, he became a liability. A big one.

"If I can speak frankly." Grace forced herself to raise her head and look into the Prophet's limpid, red-rimmed eyes. "I'd be surprised if he's still alive."

The Prophet took his time narrowing his gaze. "Why would you say that?"

"Because all he talked about was wanting to end his life. He said he had been wanting to do it for a while, to just drive off the edge of a cliff and make everything stop."

"And what did you say in return?"

"Nothing." Grace held his gaze and paused for emphasis. "I was scared he was going to take me with him."

He nodded, then stood, walking around to the front of his desk and leaning against the edge of it, facing Grace. He was so close she could feel the heat of his body, and she inwardly recoiled at the smell of soured laundry he carried with him. A small stain on the fly of his dress slacks caught her eye, and he shifted against the desk when she started to speak.

"I want to be clear about the fact that I'm falling on your mercy by seeking to come back into the fold. I needed to be reminded of how far I'd gotten from the true word of God and his path for me." She paused and looked to the floor, searching for the right words. "I know I need to atone for my sins. And I'm ready." Her voice faltered and she felt the hot rush of tears filling her eyes. "Whatever that may be."

The Prophet nodded, his eyes sinking languidly to the clear outline of Grace's breasts underneath her dress. The binder she'd always worn was long gone somewhere off the coast of Mystic, and she'd searched for the bras Adel had given her in the boxes from her cabin, but they were nowhere to be found.

The Prophet cleared his throat, bringing his fingers together in a pyramid shape in front of him.

"Sister Waters, I viewed the video footage taken of you in our former staff member's cabin." His eyes left her breasts and sank slowly over the length of her body. "Obviously what transpired there was a grave transgression against the guidelines of our church, but also against the directives of our God."

Grace nodded, biting her lower lip.

"While the church in no way condones your behavior, I think we can redirect the urge you clearly have for unnatural sexual expression." He paused until she met his watery gaze. "And, by the grace of God, turn that sin into an asset for Covenant."

Grace thought quickly, sorting through every possibility to explain his train of thought.

"What do you mean?"

"As you know, our religion is based on strong marriages and creating wholesome family lives, and I think we both know that responsibility falls almost solely on the wives." He rolled up his shirtsleeves slowly. "And the girls who long for the chance to become a godly wife to a man of God."

Grace nodded, a feeling of unease shifting her body in her chair.

"Since you clearly have an affinity for the feminine, it follows that you can relate to these young women in a very special way. I think there might be a special place for you, a position that will draw you closer to our Lord and Savior through service."

His eyes sank again to Grace's nipples and stayed, even as he started to speak. "Do you understand what I'm saying?"

Grace had already been fighting to keep her voice even, to inhale and exhale, to not vomit onto the worn floral carpet under her feet. In the end, all she could manage was to shake her head. But she knew.

"The Brethren, under my direction, have been developing an instructional program to assist wives who'd benefit from a more practical example of God's will for their marriages."

Grace stared at white spittle starting to form in the corners of his mouth as he warmed to his subject. He rubbed his hands together thoughtfully, then laced his fingers and laid them on his lap, leaning back farther on the edge of the desk. Suddenly, it was clear to Grace that he was not quite hiding an erection.

"In the coming months, more instruction will be made available, some dealing with challenges like young women who are having difficulties performing their wifely duties in a joyful and willing manner. They will be brought to me for guidance and discipline, and I will in turn pass along this wisdom along to the men of God in our community in video form."

"I think I understand what you mean," Grace said quietly. "But you spoke about girls searching 'to become godly wives.'" She paused, twisting the material of her dress in her fingers. "What about the younger girls, the unmarried ones? Will they receive this instruction as well?"

"God has entrusted men with the authority to lead and discipline our wives so that they, too, may follow us into the Celestial Kingdom." He leaned forward, placing his hand, burning with a sickening warmth, on Grace's knee. "Over the last few months, I've come to understand that the sooner we start that process of sexual training, the sooner young girls understand what it really means to be of service to a man of God..." His voice trailed off as he started to stroke her knee. "And the more time they have to dedicate their lives to that service. The ideal age to start this training is between ten and fourteen years old."

"And you want me to search for girls and young wives..." Grace shifted her face into a thoughtful expression and met his eyes. "In need of training." She swallowed, the words refusing to move through her throat. "Then guide them to you so you can help them understand God's divine plan for their lives."

The Prophet slid his hand under the hem of her dress and slowly up her thigh until he was grazing the edge of her panties with his fingertips. He smiled, his gaze deliberate and unhurried.

"Grace, I had a feeling that your desire for redemption was genuine." Grace watched as he slicked his tongue over his lower lip. "And I'm excited to provide you with this opportunity."

Chapter Twenty-six

Adel ordered her second beer in the only dive bar in Lockwood and watched as a dude with a monster truck T-shirt tucked into cargo shorts pumped a pocketful of quarters into the jukebox. Then jammed his finger onto the same button seven times.

"My Heart Will Go On" by Celine Dion flooded the back of the bar as the dude wrenched the top off his Michelob Ultra. Adel watched as he fished the last quarter out of his pocket and dropped it in the jukebox like it was an underwater oxygen dispenser.

Seriously? I have to listen to this song for the next half hour because Mr. Closet McCloseted can't do this in his own freakin' trailer?

Adel shook her head and resisted the urge to pound it on to the table in front of her before she hazarded another glance at Mr. Dion, who by this time was clasping a pool cue to his chest and mouthing every word with his eyes closed.

Kate had asked to meet at the bar fifteen minutes ago, but as Adel checked her watch again, she caught Kate and Hannah out of the corner of her eye. She raised two fingers, and the bartender, a bleached blonde only somewhat contained by a Joan Jett T-shirt, nodded and leaned into the cooler.

"Sorry we're late." Kate slid into the booth across from Adel as Hannah shrugged off her jacket and squeezed in beside her. "But Lockwood's paragon of nutritional virtue here had to stop at the drive-in for an order of cheesy garlic fries—"

The waitress slid the beers onto the table, foam spilling over the sides, dropping the rag she had tucked into her apron over the mess as she sauntered off.

"With a side of bacon." Kate winked at Hannah as she sopped up

the river of foam with the questionable rag and pushed it to the end of the table. "I shit you not."
"That's not true at *all*." Hannah sniffed. "The bacon was only to crumble on top, so it wasn't technically a side at all."
"Typical." Adel shook her head and pretended to look her up and down. "What are you anyway, a hundred pounds soaking wet? With the freaky metabolism of a race car?"
"Also not true." Hannah flicked a beer cap at Adel from across the table. "I'm a hundred and twelve pounds, even like one fifteen on a good day."
Adel grinned, shaking her head. "Yeah, that's massive. So what you're saying is, Kate here can pick you up with one arm?"
"Correct," Kate teased and pulled Hannah closer. "In fact, that's been proven a few times."
Kate's phone buzzed, and she pulled it out of her pocket and clicked it on. She started to turn the phone to Adel but paused to look behind her in disbelief at the jukebox as Celine started up yet again.
"Anyway, it looks like the follow-up to the earlier text I got from Bethany." Kate scrolled up and held the phone out to Adel.

Hey, the closing ceremony for the girls camp is at 7:00 tonight at Valley of Rubies Fellowship Hall, and you might want to be there. If anyone asks, you can say I invited you. Bring Adel. No one will notice if you get there late and slip in the back.

"Wait, what?" Adel read it twice and arched an eyebrow. "What the hell is that all about?"
"I don't know, but I think we should be there."
Kate held up the second text for them both to read, which made Hannah laugh so hard she sprayed beer across the table.

And dude, no offense, but you don't exactly blend. If you have an Easter dress in the back of your closet, now's the time to bust it out.

Adel laughed despite herself, her heart racing at the sudden possibility that Grace might have gone back to camp after she left the hospital.

"Is Grace…" Her voice faltered. It was hard to know what she could and couldn't ask, but she had to try. "Do you know if Grace went back to camp?"

Kate glanced at Hannah and nodded. "She did. And Bethany says physically she's doing okay. Not great, but okay."

"Yeah, well, I'm still going to send some antibiotics with you guys tonight. I'll write my number on the bottle, and make sure she knows to call me if she has any issues, okay?"

Hannah raised her eyebrows until they had the good sense to answer. Together.

"Yes, ma'am."

Hannah smiled then and tilted her head to the side. "Bethany wasn't wrong, though. You're gonna stick out like a MILF on prom night."

Celine's soaring soprano, slick and dripping with emotional drama, ramped up again, and Kate's head sank slowly into her hands.

Adel glanced in Hannah's direction with a smile. "If you ask me, I think you should go the opposite direction."

Kate lifted her head as both of them studied her face, heads slowly tilting in the same direction.

Hannah smiled. "And I know just the person to help us out with that."

❖

Grace rubbed her temples to stave off the emerging headache as she walked from the Prophet's office up to the staff cabins. There was a marked difference between the waterfront cabins and the shabbier surroundings she was headed to now, but she felt infinitely more comfortable here. The air was lighter now somehow, and not a single person was watching her.

She counted the doors from the left to the right, then again, trying to remember which door it was. She'd just stepped up to one and raised her hand to knock when the door swung open, spilling gold light out onto the cracked concrete doorstep.

"Damn, girl. You look like shit."

Nora stood just inside the door frame with a smile that made Grace almost cry with relief. She hugged Grace hard, let her go after a long moment, then pulled her into the cabin and onto the threadbare sofa beside her.

Grace realized suddenly they weren't alone and recognized Ruth Blankenship, the former rowing class troublemaker, right away. She was the one sitting on the small bed across from the couch with her mouth open.

"Wow, Ms. Waters." Ruth glanced over at the thin strawberry-blond girl beside her in shock, as if she might be holding the words she needed. "I can't believe you're back."

"Don't worry," Nora said with a pointed glance at the girls. "These two were just leaving."

Ruth and Audrey got up from the bed, nodded politely, and left, closing the door softly behind them. Nora put her finger to her lips, then leaned over and slapped her palm against the glass of the window beside her. "All the way gone, girls."

Grace smiled as she heard them scurry away, then leaned slowly back into the couch as Nora stepped away to the tiny kitchenette. She was suddenly exhausted, as if she'd run a marathon she didn't remember, and had dragged herself over the finishing line.

"Here."

Nora cracked open a cold bottle of IPA and held it in front of her until Grace wordlessly raised her hand to take it. The condensation dripped down her fingers. Grace just stared into the bottle until Nora tipped it toward her with a gentle finger underneath as she sank down into the couch beside her.

"I've got to get out of this dress. Do you have anything that would fit me?"

Nora walked to the closet, pulled out a pale blue wraparound dress, and hung it above the sink in the bathroom. "It's never matched my cowboy boots anyway."

Grace hastily shed her drab Covenant-issued uniform, tossing it to the floor without ceremony. Once she donned the fresh frock, she studied herself in the mirror. Her pale blue eyes darkened like a Southern storm. She stood in the doorway until Nora looked at her.

"We've *got* to stop them."

❖

"Sit still." A long, dramatic sigh punctuated Amber's words. "Damn."

"But it tickles." Kate shifted in her chair, eyebrows narrowed and nose twitching. "And the glue makes me so sneezy."

"You're *positive* she's a cop?" Amber Davies, the Planned Parenthood receptionist Adel had met her first day in town, rolled her eyes at Hannah. "Like you have actual *proof?* Because I'd like to see that."

She turned to Adel with a sigh and gave her a detailed order for tequila shots, complete with a specific number of lime slices and pre-salted shot glasses. Adel dutifully flagged down the waitress and relayed the order.

Hannah couldn't even look at Kate without laughing, so she didn't bother trying. "I didn't know you even drank tequila, Amber."

Amber shook her head as she continued setting mustache hairs in place, one by one, on Kate's upper lip. "I don't. But it's the only thing that's going to get me through this shit show with your sensitive-as-a-daisy girlfriend." She grasped another hair with her superfine tweezers and dipped it in the glue dish beside her. Adel had to turn to hide a smile at Amber's outfit when she walked in: Disney scrubs with enormous pink Crocs and a black velvet Mickey Mouse pendant around her neck. "I do this all damn day on the weekends for the community theater, and I have yet to witness this level of—"

Kate twitched her nose uncontrollably just then and let go with a gigantic sneeze into a handful of bar napkins.

Amber rolled her eyes again and accessorized it this time with a meaningful sigh. "Dramatics."

The first heart-wrenching strains of "My Heart Will Go On" started up yet again.

This time Amber put down her tweezers, stood on her chair, and whistled at a deafening volume through her fingers. The entire bar turned in her direction, including Mr. Dion in the corner, now nursing a cosmopolitan daintily balanced between two fingers.

"All right, Randy." Amber paused long enough to snap her fingers over her head. Twice. "I know you're still upset, but your Tommy ain't ever coming back. So it looks like you're just going to have to grow a pair and get the hell over it."

Randy looked around hesitantly and pointed to himself with a delicate finger and a raised eyebrow.

"Yes." Amber's already impressive voice reached peak volume. "I'm talking to you. Now put on some Backstreet Boys and get the fuck over him like the rest of us have to do. If I hear that flipping Celine Dion song one more time, I'm coming over there to twist your testicles until you sing exactly like her."

With that she stepped down, picked up her tweezers, and turned her attention back to Kate.

"Now," she sighed, grabbing another mustache hair and holding it up to Kate for size, "let's get back to turning you into the man of my dreams."

❖

The sky was painted in fiery shades of mango, pink, and lavender as Kate and Adel drove into camp. The lake appeared as they neared the entrance, sparkling with the last of the late afternoon light.

"God, I know we were just here a couple of days ago getting your stuff, but I didn't really have a chance to look. This is beautiful," Kate said. "No wonder you miss it so much."

"Whatever." Adel gave her a sideways glance. "Who says I miss it?"

Kate grinned in her direction as the lodge loomed in the distance. "What the hell is that?" She squinted and reached for her mirrored sunglasses on the dash. "Upstate New York's version of the damn Taj Mahal?"

"Trust me, the lake is by far the best part. You don't even want to go into that place if you can help it."

Just before they actually reached the lodge, Adel nodded toward a small dirt road leading up the hill on the right.

"You want me to go up there?" Kate gazed up from under the visor. "What's up there?"

"The sane people." Adel grabbed the handle above the passenger window as Kate's Jeep rumbled up the steep incline. "Besides, it's not just you that doesn't blend. Even with all those cars parked everywhere for the event, someone would clock this Jeep before you had the keys out of the ignition. Trust me."

As they rolled up to the stables, Bethany came walking out of the tack room, drying her hands on a cloth that looked like it had evolved from a mud puddle.

Adel got out and waved to Bethany, who did a double take when she saw Kate.

"What the hell?" She smiled, reaching out cautiously to touch Kate's mustache. She paused for a moment, head tilted to the side. "Actually, that's genius. Almost perfect." She gave her a quick head-to-toe glance. "But you're missing something. Hang on."

With that she disappeared back into the tack room, reemerging with a ten-mile grin and an enormous felt cowboy hat. Kate started backing up the second she saw it, but Adel stepped behind her, blocking the path and laughing.

"Now," Bethany said. She dropped the hat on Kate's head, speaking in a perfect Texas drawl that flew out of nowhere. "Ain't *you* just the picture of handsome!"

Kate rolled her eyes, cramming the hat down on her head in resignation.

"Yeah, yeah. So tell me a little about what we're walking into here. I've got no idea what's really going to go down other than what you said in your text."

"You're not the only one. No one's telling me anything either. All I know is there are only two events all summer where families can show up on campus, and the closing ceremony is one of them. So I figured if you wanted a chance to check on Audrey and Grace, this was your chance."

Kate glanced down the hill, and just as she did, the opening hymn started, the sound carried on the wind through the trees. "Thanks, man. I appreciate everything."

Kate nodded at Bethany, and Adel thought she saw a look pass between them. She was just about to ask what that was about when Bethany pulled her phone out of her pocket. "I'm going to stay up here out of trouble, but you've got my number if you need me. The gathering should be fairly small, so try to blend. Because camp shut down early, most of the families didn't have time to make travel plans, so it's nearly all camp staff and campers."

"Hey, Bethany." Adel leaned to the right and peered over at the parking lot tucked behind the stables. "Are those the God Squad vehicles over there? They all seem nice enough to not be from around here."

"Nah, most of them are still hunting down one of their own that went AWOL the other day, so it's just the Brethren. They all park up here when there's an event. Always have."

Adel tossed Bethany the keys. "Thanks for this, dude. We need a break in this case or those girls go home tomorrow, where no one knows what's going on and we can't help them."

Bethany nodded. "I know enough from Nora that the scrub staff and even some of the campers have been talking lately, and the shit they put them through has escalated by a mile this year." She looked down, taking the rag out of her back pocket and knocking a chunk of dirt off her boot. "And we all know that doesn't get better."

"Who's down there right now as far as the Brethren? Is the Prophet there?"

"Yeah. He parks up here when he's on campus and has me drive his lazy ass down to the main camp in my golf cart. I just got back up here, so he's been there for about ten minutes."

They still heard singing as they turned to walk down the hill to the Fellowship Hall. Song service wasn't yet over, so they had a few moments yet before the actual ceremony started. The sun was shining with a perfect, golden warmth, and the view of the lake sparkling beyond the trees reminded Adel of Grace—not that she didn't think of her every minute already.

"Nervous about running into Grace?"

Adel smiled, stepping sideways to avoid a darting squirrel. "Is it that obvious?"

"Nah, I just know how you feel about her." She paused. "And if it was Hannah, well, I don't think I would have handled it as well as you have."

"I've been meaning to say thank you, by the way." Adel paused, steadying her voice. "For staying with Grace that night in the hospital."

Kate nodded, brushing a tree branch out of their path as they walked and looking out across the lake. "Remember that night I came home and you and Hannah were on the deck? I told you." She looked back at Adel with a wink. "I don't forget that kind of loyalty."

Adel smiled, and they walked the rest of the way until Kate paused, slowing her steps as they neared the bottom of the hill. The Fellowship Hall was packed—the door was open and it was obviously standing room only—but just before they reached the road, Kate's phone pinged and she stepped away to make a quiet call.

The early evening wind started to sweep past the lake and move through the treetops as Adel rolled her sleeves down and buttoned the cuffs, looking up just in time to spot Grace as she walked up from the lodge to the Fellowship Hall, illuminated by the pale golden path lights mounted in the trees on either side. She was wearing a beautiful sky-blue wrap dress that accentuated the graceful curve of her hips, and her hair fell in loose waves to her waist. She glanced at the crowd just inside the doors and stopped where she was on the path, her head sinking into her hands for just a moment before she raised her gaze to the sky. Adel watched the breeze run its fingers through her hair, then drop it down her back in a shimmering gold river. Adel didn't take another breath until Grace had slipped through the doors and disappeared.

Kate walked back to Adel and slipped her phone back into her suit jacket pocket. "Ready?"

Adel was still staring at the open door to the Fellowship Hall. "I just saw Grace. She's inside."

"Perfect timing, then." Kate slid on her sunglasses and strode toward the doors. "It's showtime."

Adel and Kate slipped in unnoticed and stood at the back with the rest of the people who had arrived too late for a seat. Adel looked around as they wedged themselves into a spot along the wall. Based on what Bethany had said, it was far more crowded than she'd expected. All of the campers were there, of course, and a few obvious Covenant families were in attendance, but single men she didn't recognize seemed to outnumber everyone. The room was eerily still, the air heavy and expectant. The only sounds were the audience fanning their faces with the folded programs and the occasional squeak of a metal folding chair as someone shifted in their seat.

Some things were the same, of course—the Prophet was sitting in a place of honor at the rear of the stage, flanked by Brethren—but there was something odd that Adel couldn't quite place. Something that seemed to press the air from her lungs.

As the last of the opening hymns came to a close, Grace walked to the podium and disengaged the microphone from the stand. She pulled her speaking notes out of her pocket, then just as quickly dropped them at her feet, her hands visibly shaking as she scooped them up and stood before the crowd. The second the microphone reached her mouth, it squealed with deafening feedback and she jumped back, startled, as one of the Brethren ran up to adjust the settings. She waited to the side, her gaze restless as it moved over the crowd until the instant she spotted Adel. The feedback stopped abruptly as he handed the microphone back to Grace, but her eyes never wavered.

Silence warmed the air between them. There were no words spoken, no apologies or explanation. It was more…a softening. Everything seemed to melt away, as if the last few days had never existed. Adel felt a wave of relief pass through her, the overwhelming weight of worry and fear she'd been carrying giving way to pride as she looked at the woman she loved.

Chapter Twenty-seven

Grace held the microphone as everyone but Adel faded into the background.

Suddenly, she understood why Adel never told her the real reason she was at camp. It was the same reason Grace was standing in front of everyone today, willing to risk losing everything she'd ever known. Because she was the only one who could do it.

She drew a deep breath and looked again at the audience as she started to speak, but she faltered, bringing the microphone to her mouth twice only for the words to get stuck in her throat both times. The silence hung in the air like an invisible spiderweb as the audience started to look nervously around, the tension thickening by the second. Grace felt her heart pounding in her temples as she looked back to Adel, her damp fingers tightening around the floral hair tie she'd found Kellan's car floorboard.

Adel held her eyes as she mouthed the words only they knew. Grace took them in, one by one, the intimacy between them deep and palpable.

Courage, my love.

Grace allowed her eyes to close for a heartbeat, then she placed her hand over her heart, put the microphone away, and stepped out from behind the podium.

Grace's smile swept across the first few rows of campers, as if they were the only ones in the room. Their expressions lightened and they sat back in their seats, hanging on every word as Grace started to speak.

Her voice was sure and strong now, as she opened with the story of Queen Esther, the Jewish orphan girl taken as queen by the king of Babylon. The king, she reminded the campers, thought Esther was Persian like him, and after they were married wrote a decree to kill all the Jews in the kingdom. Her only chance to save the lives of her family and the Jewish people was to go to the king and request that the decree be nullified. But a queen was never allowed to visit the king unbidden; it was an offense punishable by death and had never been attempted.

Grace slipped the hair tie in her pocket onto her wrist as she sat casually on the steps of the stage and continued with the story, pausing when she got to the part where Esther tearfully confided in her brother Mordecai about her predicament. She told him she didn't think she had the courage to risk her life by going to the king, and felt she was going into battle without a sword.

Grace paused then, for a long moment, her eyes sweeping the audience.

"And does anyone remember what Mordecai said to her?"

Dozens of eager hands went up, but it was Audrey who answered, in a clear, strong voice from the back of the room. Everyone turned to look at her as she spoke.

"He said, 'Who knows if you were made queen…'" Audrey paused and reached for Ruth's hand, who was standing beside her, her eyes filling with tears. "'For such a time as this?'"

The audience fell silent and the Brethren shifted in their seats at the rear of the stage. The air sank and thickened, and it seemed everyone suddenly held a collective breath. Grace stood up then as a wide beam of filtered sunlight fell to the floor in front of her through one of the upstairs windows. Her gaze was soft but strong, and focused on only the girls in front of her.

"For the last few weeks, we've been studying the meaning of courage. We've learned more about the story of Esther, and what being a queen truly means."

Grace nodded toward the back of the room. Audrey, Ruth, and Nora walked to the end of each row and handed them a small basket. Grace waited until it had been passed to every girl to continue.

"Today I'm giving each of you a sword, the one you're holding now." She paused and drew in a long breath. "And I'm going to ask whether you have the courage to use it."

Grace paused to look behind her at the row of Brethren, let her gaze settle on the Prophet, then slowly faced the front again.

"No one knows this yet, but recently our Prophet offered me a new position here at camp. It was made clear that my sole responsibility would be to recruit new girls for the Brethren to abuse and exploit the way they've exploited me, and many of you."

The Prophet jumped to his feet and licked nervously at the spittle gathering in the corners of his mouth before he spoke. The overhead lights glinted off the greasy dome of his head, and his voice spiked instantly to shrill, every word dripping with righteous indignation.

"I'm not sure why this accusation is being raised against me, but let me assure you that this is a *complete* fabrication." He looked at Grace with a stare like jagged glass. "And I am sickened by the suggestion I've put even one of you into harm's way."

Nora raised her cell phone to the audience and clicked a button into the shocked silence. The the first voice was Grace's.

"What about the younger girls, the unmarried ones? Will they receive this instruction as well?"

A short pause filled the tense silence before the next person on the tape spoke.

"God has entrusted men with the authority to lead and discipline our wives so that they, too, may follow into the Celestial Kingdom." A deep, collective gasp filled the room as the Prophet's distinctive voice resonated over the murmurs. "Over the last few months, I've come to understand that the sooner we start the process of sexual training, the sooner young girls understand what it really means to be of service to a man of God…"

His voice trailed off and Grace steeled herself against the memory of his hand moving up her thigh.

"The ideal age to start this training is between ten and fourteen years old…"

The Prophet bolted suddenly for the door, followed by a scrambling line of Brethren.

Nora stepped to the side as two men in suits darted out the door after them, one of them speaking into a wire at his wrist, followed by three others from the far end of the hall.

The girls looked around at each other, then up to Grace, who held their gaze long enough to calm them, then told them softly that there were people in the room now who knew what was happening and were there to help. She straightened her shoulders and glanced over at Nora, Audrey, and Ruth, who nodded silent encouragement.

"We've been taught all our lives not to talk about what happens here at camp, and even in some of our homes and churches. The places we should all feel the safest." Grace paused, her voice faltering with raw emotion. "But now is the time to have courage. If anyone at camp has ever touched you in a way that made you feel unsafe—or worse—now is the time to stand up and draw your sword." She raised the black marker Nora handed her and took a moment to meet the eyes of every single girl in the audience. "I promise you that everyone left in this room is safe. You're safe. And it's time to stop keeping their secrets."

Grace uncapped the marker and wrote on her palm, then turned it to face the undercover officers and social workers that Kate and the FBI had arranged for. In wide, black strokes was *26*, and when she spoke, her voice had become just as clear and powerful.

"My name is Grace Waters." Each word sliced through the silence like tangible courage. "And I am here for such a time as this."

Audrey was next, though it was clear even from the back of the room she was visibly shaking. She extended her arm completely, turned her palm outward, and spoke in a steady voice despite the tears streaming down her cheeks.

"My name is Audrey Blankenship." Her voice caught suddenly, and she lifted her chin almost imperceptibly to lock her eyes with the officers. "And I am here for such a time as this."

The number *15* was written on Audrey's palm in black marker, in the same wide swaths of ink that had stained her entire body the night she hid in Bethany's tack room. The acrid chemical smell of the markers saturated the air as one by one the girls drew their swords and wrote their ages on their palms. Then each turned to face the FBI agents and social workers and repeated the phrase from the story of Esther, many holding the hand of the girl beside her. The very bravest warriors were the youngest, the ones who stood on their chairs, held out their palms with their ages scrawled in shaky lettering, and bared their souls, even though for most of them it was too much to get the words out.

Grace knew as she watched that scene unfold that she'd never heard six more powerful words. And she never would again.

...For such a time as this.

❖

When the last girl had spoken her truth, and Kate and the officers had moved gently forward to help, Adel slipped out of the doors of the Fellowship Hall and ran toward the hill until she saw Bethany and Hannah's mom Carol casually ambling toward her.

"Hey, buddy. What's going on down here?"

Adel scanned the path ahead and kept going. "I'll tell you everything, but the Brethren are probably going to drive the hell out of camp any second." Adel stopped to suck in air like she'd been underwater for the last hour. "Right? Didn't you say those were their cars at the top of the hill?"

Bethany grinned, then motioned for her to step aside as several officers sped past them and up the hill in a Valley of Rubies camp cart. Bethany shot a wink in Carol's direction as she continued.

"I figured those creeps would want to skeet on outta here the second their covers got blown, so I called Ms. Waters to give me a hand while they were all still down at the service."

"Which has turned out to be most exciting Saturday night I've had in *forever*." Carol downed the last of the frosty Sam Adams she was carrying and let loose with an adorable burp. "I mean, don't get me wrong, yanking the starters out of all those fancy cars was hard work, but *damn* that was satisfying!"

"But…How did…?"

"Sorry, man, Kate told me I couldn't breathe a word of any of this, or I would've let you in on it." Bethany shook off her flannel shirt and tied it around her waist, pulling her own beer bottle from her back pocket. "Cops and FBI have been camped out up there for hours, so between them and cars that won't start, the chances of even one of them getting away is less than zero."

Carol gleefully high-fived Bethany and pulled a rag out of the front pocket of her overalls, swiping at the black engine grease that covered the lower half of her arms.

Bethany's gaze softened as she turned back to Adel. "So, did you see Grace?"

A sudden, intense wave of relief washed over Adel like she'd been hit from behind. She hadn't had time to process it, but she knew in her heart that everything was somehow okay, and drew her first truly full breath since she'd discovered Grace was missing.

"I did." Tears choked her voice, and she paused to gather her composure. "I don't know how, but when she looked at me, it was like she already understood."

Carol arched an eyebrow at Bethany, who, when Adel turned to her, seemed suddenly very interested in examining a bandage around her thumb.

"Betts, did you say something to her?"

"She and Kate both did," Carol offered cheerfully, giving Bethany a look of genuine affection. "If I remember correctly, it was something about not letting you lose the love of your life on their watch."

"Whatever." Bethany turned to peeling the label from her beer bottle. "Once Grace got here hell-bent on confronting the Prophet but with no plan whatsoever, I called Kate for backup. We had to convince Grace that a safety net was a good idea, and along the way we may have told her some other stuff she needed to know."

Carol looked past Adel to the Fellowship Hall doors and elbowed Bethany.

"I think it's about time to blow this pop stand and go get some pizza. What do you think?"

Bethany offered Carol her arm. "I think I've never had a prettier date."

Carol laughed and took the arm that Bethany offered her, silently mouthing *Turn around* to Adel as they walked away.

Adel spun around and swept Grace into her arms, whispering softly into her ear.

"Can you ever forgive me for not telling you who I was? I was so afraid to lose you."

Grace leaned back, covering Adel's mouth with her fingertip. "And I was afraid to love you."

Then, in the midst of the swirling groups of people surrounding them, Grace kissed Adel, as soft as breath, and melted into her arms. "Thank you for saving me."

"Baby, you were right all along." Adel held her tight, her answer soft and warm against Grace's lips. "We all need saving."

About the Author

Patricia Evans is currently writing your new favorite novel in her hand-built tiny house, nestled deep in the forest, where she's surrounded by a bevy of raccoons and a sleepy brown bear named Waddles.

She travels to Ireland and Scotland several times a year in search of the perfect whiskey and cigar combination and spends most of her time trying to ignore the characters from her books that boss her around as she writes by the fire.

Follow her adventures:
www.tomboyinkslinger.com
@tomboyinkslinger on Instagram
patricia@tomboyinkslinger.com

Books Available From Bold Strokes Books

All For Her: Forbidden Romance Novellas by Gun Brooke, J.J. Hale & Aurora Rey. Explore the angst and excitement of forbidden love few would dare in this heart-stopping novella collection. (978-1-63679-713-7)

Finding Harmony by CF Frizzell. Rock star Harper Cushing has to rearrange her grandmother's future and sell the family store out from under her, but she reassesses everything because Gram's helper, Frankie, could be offering the harmony her heart has been missing. (978-1-63679-741-0)

Gaze by Kris Bryant. Love at first sight is for dreamers, but the more time Lucky and Brianna spend together, the more they realize the chemistry of a gaze can make anything possible. (978-1-63679-711-3)

Laying of Hands by Patricia Evans. The mysterious new writing instructor at camp makes Grace Waters brave enough to wonder what would happen if she dared to write her own story. (978-1-63679-782-3)

The Naked Truth by Sandy Lowe. How far are Rowan and Genevieve willing to go and how much will they risk to make their most captivating and forbidden fantasies a reality? (978-1-63679-426-6)

The Roommate by Claire Forsythe. Jess Black's boyfriend is handsome and successful. That's why it comes as a shock when she meets a woman on the train who makes her pulse race. (978-1-63679-757-1)

Seducing the Widow by Jane Walsh. Former rival debutantes have a second chance at love after fifteen years apart when a spinster persuades her ex-lover to help save her family business. (978-1-63679-747-2)

Close to Home by Allisa Bahney. Eli Thomas has to decide if avoiding her hometown forever is worth losing the people who used to mean the most to her, especially Aracely Hernandez, the girl who got away. (978-1-63679-661-1)

Innis Harbor by Patricia Evans. When Amir Farzaneh meets and falls in love with Loch, a dark secret lurking in her past reappears, threatening the happiness she'd just started to believe could be hers. (978-1-63679-781-6)

The Blessed by Anne Shade. Layla and Suri are brought together by fate to defeat the darkness threatening to tear their world apart. What they don't expect to discover is a love that might set them free. (978-1-63679-715-1)

The Guardians by Sheri Lewis Wohl. Dogs, devotion, and determination are all that stand between darkness and light. (978-1-63679-681-9)

The Mogul Meets Her Match by Julia Underwood. When CEO Claire Beauchamp goes undercover as a customer of Abby Pita's café to help seal a deal that will solidify her career, she doesn't expect to be so drawn to her. When the truth is revealed, will she break Abby's heart? (978-1-63679-784-7)

Trial Run by Carsen Taite. When Reggie Knoll and Brooke Dawson wind up serving on a jury together, their one task—reaching a unanimous verdict—is derailed by the fiery clash of their personalities, the intensity of their attraction, and a secret that could threaten Brooke's life. (978-1-63555-865-4)

Waterlogged by Nance Sparks. When conservation warden Jordan Pearce discovers a body floating in the flowage, the serenity of the Northwoods is rocked. (978-1-63679-699-4)

Accidentally in Love by Kimberly Cooper Griffin. Nic and Lee have good reasons for keeping their distance. So why does their growing attraction seem more like a love-hate relationship? (978-1-63679-759-5)

Frosted by the Girl Next Door by Aurora Rey and Jaime Clevenger. When heartbroken Casey Stevens opens a sex shop next door to uptight cupcake baker Tara McCoy, things get a little frosty. (978-1-63679-723-6)

Ghost of the Heart by Catherine Friend. Being possessed by a ghost was not on Gwen's bucket list, but she must admit that ghosts might be real, and one is obviously trying to send her a message. (978-1-63555-112-9)

Hot Honey Love by Nan Campbell. When chef Stef Lombardozzi puts her cooking career into the hands of filmmaker Mallory Radowski—the pickiest eater alive—she doesn't anticipate how hard she'll fall for her. (978-1-63679-743-4)

London by Patricia Evans. Jaq's and Bronwyn's lives become entwined as dangerous secrets emerge and Bronwyn's seemingly perfect life starts to unravel. (978-1-63679-778-6)

This Christmas by Georgia Beers. When Sam's grandmother rigs the Christmas parade to make Sam and Keegan queen and queen, sparks fly, but they can't forget the Big Embarrassing Thing that makes romance a total nope. (978-1-63679-729-8)

Unwrapped by D. Jackson Leigh. Asia du Muir is not going to let some party-girl actress ruin her best chance to get noticed by a Broadway critic. Everyone knows you should never mix business and pleasure. (978-1-63679-667-3)

Language Lessons by Sage Donnell. Grace and Lenka never expected to fall in love. Is home really where the heart is if it means giving up your dreams? (978-1-63679-725-0)

New Horizons by Shia Woods. When Quinn Collins meets Alex Anders, Horizon Theater's enigmatic managing director, a passionate connection ignites, but amidst the complex backdrop of theater politics, their budding romance faces a formidable challenge. (978-1-63679-683-3)

Scrambled: A Tuesday Night Book Club Mystery by Jaime Maddox. Avery Hutchins makes a discovery about her father's death that will force her to face an impossible choice between doing what is right and finally finding a way to regain a part of herself she had lost. (978-1-63679-703-8)

BOLDSTROKESBOOKS.COM

Looking for your next great read?

Visit BOLDSTROKESBOOKS.COM
to browse our entire catalog of paperbacks, ebooks,
and audiobooks.

**Want the first word on what's new?
Visit our website for event info,
author interviews, and blogs.**

Subscribe to our free newsletter for sneak peeks,
new releases, plus first notice of promos
and daily bargains.

SIGN UP AT
BOLDSTROKESBOOKS.COM/signup

Bold Strokes Books
Quality and Diversity in LGBTQ Literature

*Bold Strokes Books is an award-winning publisher
committed to quality and diversity in LGBTQ fiction.*